The Order of the Sage

Book 1 After the Atoms Fall Series
Revised Edition

By Casey Robert Swanson

The Order of the Sage

SageAuthor Books

Other books by the Author

On the Trail of the Myk
Beyond the Fears of Tomorrow

Coming Fall 2025
Branches

Revised Edition

ISBN # 979-8-9986992-2-1
eISBN # 979-8-9986992-3-8

Printed in the USA

Dedication

This book, and the series that follows, is dedicated to my wife, Jessica, without whom I would have never gotten back into writing.

Acknowledgments

I would like to acknowledge all of those who have helped me with this story, from my high school years to its completion now. Too many to name, I will just list a couple. Wally Burton, who was not without his own suggestions as I began this in the Interlake High School library and my daughter, Christina Mayes, who understands the need for a critical eye in writing. From the beginning to the end, so many voices have made this the growing adventure that it is.

Table of Contents

Chapter One — Shipwrecked but Alive

Chapter Two — Mysteries of another Land

Chapter Three — Searching for Answers

Chapter Four — Thul's Path

Chapter Five — Beneath the Myk's Palace

Chapter Six — The People of the Lake

Chapter Seven — The Slave Revolt, the First Battle

Chapter Eight — Escape from the Caverns

Chapter Nine: — *The Proctant's* Final Voyage

Chapter Ten — Argonia, Lost Island of Legend

Chapter Eleven — The Assemblage of War

Chapter Twelve — We are Myk!

Chapter Thirteen — The Residue of the Myk

Chapter Fourteen — Beginnings

Chapter One
Shipwrecked but Alive

In the clear sky of the morning a bird soared. It rode the currents of the air with sweeps of its powerful wings. Graceful movements belied its size. Its ritualistic dance was as intricate as a sparrow's. As the circles that it flew grew smaller, so too did its speed slow.

The bird stood now motionless in the sky. It was as if it was suspended by its mighty wings. The bird's quarry was but a speck on the beach far below. It hung for what seemed an eternity to its prey.

Then it dove, like a bolt of lightning, toward its fleeing prey, a prey that the bird knew was in its last desperate race for survival. The wind tore through the giant bird's feathers with the sound of thunder. The great bird screamed a barbaric cry. It dove faster, if that was possible, its wings held close to its body. With the greater speed, the distance to its fleeing prey grew closer.

Close now, the bird reopened its wings and extended its razor-like talons to grasp the life before it and sweep away. And in that brief moment, before its talons could clutch its prey, the great bird felt a sharp and bitter pain race through its body.

The bird crashed, hard to the ground. Forever still.

As the bird fell dead, a man jumped to one side to avoid the fall of the beast that had threatened his life. He rolled clear and came to rest a few feet from another man.

The other stood straight and unflinching at the site of the giant bird. He had seen many wonders in this world and no longer found himself amazed at what he saw. With a well-placed shot of his long-rifle, now once again slung across his large back, this man had pierced the heart of the bird, ending its life and saving theirs.

The first, he who had been the bird's intended prey, now stood, his body trembling with both relief and fear over what had just transpired. He had been saved a horrible death, spared from being caught in the talons of that terrible bird.

He turned to face the man to whom he now owed his life. Over the sound of the surf against the rocks, but a short distance away, he called out his thanks. He bowed his head in submission, as was proper. The sharpshooter responded as was likewise proper. He acknowledged the thanks with a simple nod and turned away. Each man now stood once again as equal.

Others gathered around these two men on the rocky beach. They had all borne witness to the spectacle of the bird's attack. These were robust men, tall and powerful, with straight black hair, their bare arms deeply bronzed by the sun, their faces scorched by the wind. The remnants of their clothing lay upon them in tattered shreds. They were men of the sea, now stranded upon an unwelcoming shore.

"By the gods, Zircon, that was a shot our forefathers would be proud of. I'm glad that we have with us your great skill with the long-rifle." These words came from the mouth of Thul, whose life had just been saved. "It would have been a sad thing to finish my life in a bird's belly."

"You're not home yet, Thul," shouted back Zircon, making his voice heard over the sounds of the ocean. Zircon was a man to whom to the long-rifle was but an extension of his frame, a frame that was coarse and heavy compared to Thul's smaller stature.

In his loud voice, Zircon continued. "By the time we're through here, you'll have wished I'd let you die in that bird's belly. Gods be cursed. If we don't get off of these rocks soon, we'll all be dead of one thing or another."

Zircon's voice changed to a harsher tone when, after a brief pause, he continued speaking. "We'll all die here soon enough, never to see our homes again." A scowl cut deeply across his features. Zircon stomped his way clear of the others, back to where he stood watch.

Thorium quickly followed Zircon. Thorium stood slightly taller and carried an air of authority about him. He spoke in a strong, quiet voice, a voice that held Zircon bound by his words. "Leave him alone," he said. "We all have to work together if we want to get out of this alive."

"So we need him," Zircon spoke back, not really convinced of that fact. "I saved his life, didn't I? That doesn't mean I have to like the coward, does it?" Zircon growled menacingly as he spoke these last words.

"Just leave him alone, Zircon," the taller man, an officer, spoke. He held Zircon in place with his strong voice and commanding eyes.

"I'll do like you say because I have to if I want to get out of this place alive, not because I am forced to. And not because I like it." Zircon then added a threat to the officer that only Thorium could hear. "When this is over, you'd better hope you're as far away from me as possible, I'll be looking for you." This last part he said with as much scorn as possible. He hated the officer. All officers. Cradling his rifle now in his arms, Zircon half-hoped his challenge to Thorium would be accepted.

The other survivors stood a short distance away on the island's spit of rocky land. They watched the interplay between the two men with interest. Unsure of the outcome, they were ready to intercede if Thorium should need their help. None cared for the abrasive Zircon. All would follow Thorium wherever he led. They hoped that Thorium would take advantage of the situation and finally deal with Zircon.

Thorium realized, however, that they needed Zircon and his skill with the long-rifle would be indispensable in what would come. None of the others could hope to master the long-rifle in a short time. Their survival could well depend on it.

Not wanting to start something that might lead to the destruction of them all, Thorium chose to ignore what Zircon said. "Aren't you supposed to be on guard duty now?" He used his most forceful, commanding voice, not letting it rise above normal. Then he turned his back on Zircon and walked to where the others stood.

Zircon turned and walked away. He went back to his position on the rocky shore. He was gloating to himself, muttering. Thorium's backing down was a show of weakness, not strength, in Zircon's eyes. He would have to be careful and wait for the right time. But he, Zircon, the strongest of them all, would be able to take care of Thorium. Then he, Zircon, would command them. For it was right that strength should command. All signs of weakness should be destroyed. He, Zircon, was born and fit to rule. He would get his day. And then Thul would die. A slow death fit for cowards. Zircon laughed his own quiet laugh.

Early the following morning, the sun was just beginning to rise and the sea was calm. Waves rolled gently into the rocky shore. Only a few wisps of clouds were left from the previous day's storm.

The men prepared their breakfast, shellfish of an unknown kind and shrimp, caught in the morning tide pools. The catch had been good and the men argued good-heartedly over how to prepare the feast. The only real choice was raw, since any wood they found was still too wet to burn.

With full stomachs from the morning's bounty, the men tried to forget the previous day's disaster and start anew. Zircon sat by himself, his rifle across his lap, staring blankly at the sea and contemplating thoughts only he could understand. Thul, now almost fully accepted by the others, smiled at the barbs thrown at him by his companions.

Thorium sat but a little distance from these men, deeply immersed in his thoughts. He pondered the question that was Zircon, a danger to himself and the others, but also a necessity for survival.

It was during this period of relative calm, when these men were least able to cope, that the attack struck.

Yetter, the eldest crewmember at nearly 50 years old, was about 150 feet away from the other men as he prepared to begin his watch. He perched on the top of a large rock at the water's edge and had a clear view of the sea. With his long arms he was waving madly at the others and pointing to the north. But his coarse cry was scarcely heard over the sounds of the waves. He screamed and jumped to try to gain the attention of the others.

"What is it, Yetter?" one of the men at the campsite called out to the man on duty.

Thorium, his mind still preoccupied with the matter of Zircon, was disturbed from his thoughts by the commotion. He began to make his way over to where the old man stood. He intended to see for himself what it was that Yetter saw. Thorium saw Yetter start to scramble for cover, his short sword drawn. Those at the campsite saw this and drew their own weapons as well.

Before they could prepare, the attack was upon them all.

The birds rushed into view, by the hundreds, not unlike the one Zircon had shot the day before. Only this time they carried riders who were, at best, only half-human. They were the barbarian warriors of a nightmare. Their madness was matched only by the savagery of their mounts.

Thorium saw the birds reach the rocky point where Yetter had stood. Then he heard Alum's cry from the island's other side. The birds and their hideous riders had struck the islands north and south simultaneously, flying in silently over the water to begin their attack.

The castaways had not foreseen danger from the sea; their concern lay in what might come from a towering jungle that arose from a large lagoon across from their island.

The creatures and their inhuman riders descended upon the men. They screamed their savage cries, brandishing long scythe-like swords.

"Those of you who can, work your way over here," called out Thorium, who had found a defensible crevasse amongst the rocks. Whether the men heard him or whether their own instincts guided them, they used their rapidly failing Herculean strength to reach the crevasse, hacking, step-by-step, to where Thorium stood like a beacon of strength. Slash and stab, cut and hack, they forged their way forward against the onslaught of the birds and their riders.

More of the birds (monstrous things with wingspans ten feet across!) and their warrior riders entered the fray as each moment passed. When these creatures' riders fell in combat, the birds continued to fight, as they had been bred to do. The birds had to be destroyed if these men were to survive.

Soon there was no more room for the men to swing their long swords, so man-by-man they abandoned them for their short swords. These were not even barely adequate against these barbarians, with their endless torrent of beak and talon, scythe and spear.

Above and on all sides of the men the birds flew, trying to ensnare the fighting men with their talons. It was a fight that none of the men hoped to survive, yet they fought on. The only respite for the men came when Zircon was able to unleash a volley into one area with his long-rifle, but Zircon's supply of shot was being rapidly depleted. And yet the barbarians and their savage riders continued to come.

Van, a young sailor who was new to the crew, was the next to fall after Yetter and Alum's disappearance in the first rush of the attack. Soon two more men, Noble and Titan, joined them, never to rise. As the birds carried each man's body away, it was torn to pieces as the riderless birds fought amongst themselves for each scrap they could find.

Eventually the carnage became too great, even for the barbarians. These had not been the helpless food the barbarians had first thought, defenseless to their attack. And in the chaos of the battle, a blood lust had come over the riderless birds. They forgot their training and fought amongst themselves for the carcasses of the men, the barbarians and even other birds killed or wounded. They were carnivores, uncaring where their meat came from. In the end, it was the bird's savage fighting amongst themselves that brought an end to the battle.

The survivors grouped together in the rocky fortress that Thorium had found. Zircon continued to fire at what remained of their foe. The last of the barbarians had left on their winged mounts. Of the 10 men who had landed on this rocky shore as castaways, only three remained standing: Zircon, Thul, and Thorium, their fates to intermingle further with each passing day, each bleeding from numerous cuts and blows received in the battle. Cole and Pluto lay at their feet. Each would soon need care if they were to survive their injuries. The others of the party were all dead or missing, their bodies carried aloft by the birds.

The rocky beach carried an eerie calm about it. Though blood and tissue lay about, not a single body, or even body part, could be seen intact. The birds had seen to that. Even now the birds, with their riders, flew high above, assured that those below would not escape.

"Do you think any of the others are still alive?" asked Thul, glancing at the carnage that surrounded them in the aftermath of the battle.

"I doubt it, but I'll check anyway," spoke Thorium. "By the almighty Suing, I wish those damn birds would stop circling overhead. I hate it that they are just watching us, waiting for their next opportunity to strike." Thorium pointed angrily at the distant birds in the sky. "They're waiting for only God knows what. They must know we could not survive another attack. It's enough to drive a strong man to his grave. Zircon, can you hit them with your long-rifle?" All signs of bitterness between the two men had disappeared in the passage of the battle. Both knew it was only a temporary end to their animosity toward one another.

"I can always try," answered Zircon, anxious for a chance to drive away the remaining birds and their riders.

"Can we afford the shot?" asked Thorium, once again the sensibilities of command asserting themselves.

"If you think the little I have left will make a difference, you'd better rethink your plans." Zircon laughed inwardly as he said the last part. It was the quiet laugh of a condemned man nearing the point of insanity, but still quite sane. His long-rifle was all that had saved them in the first attack. He had been able to play the part of savior and master but now his long-rifle was next to useless in what was sure to come.

Thul asked, his quiet voice filled with fear, "Will they attack again?"

"Yes," answered Thorium simply and definitively, his mind racing feverishly for an answer to their salvation.

Thorium spoke to Zircon, his mind filled with his own distraught feelings. For now he hoped to keep Zircon occupied. "See what you can do. Maybe you can drive them away for now while we figure something out."

His forehead creased in determination, Zircon focused, carefully raised his long-rifle and took aim at one of the birds circling high above them. The first shot missed its target, and Zircon exhaled a curse that was audible to the others. Once again he raised his weapon and took careful aim. He held his breath, kept his body still, and gently squeezed the trigger on his long-rifle.

The birds with their riders had continued circling after the first shot, undisturbed. This changed after the second shot scored a clean hit. One of the birds began to fall from the sky, its rider separating himself in the fall. As both rider and bird fell to the sea, two other mounts dove after them, one to catch the rider before he hit the sea, the other to snare the bird, an easy meal. This brought them within easy range of Zircon's long-rifle. Two more shots dispatched these as well to the sea to drown. The birds and riders hit the sea as one, but their splashes were barely noticeable in the growing size of the now angry waves. The respite from the storm would soon be over.

As the men looked skyward, the rest of the birds and their riders were leaving. Whether from the accuracy of Zircon's shots or the dark clouds on the horizon, the men did not know. Only Zircon showed any good cheer about the events. In his mind, the barbarians' withdrawal was due solely to him. Once again he had showed himself fit to command the survivors, all five of them.

As the afternoon progressed, the men became more concerned over their deteriorating plight. The birdmen were gone, yet another storm was approaching from the sea. But where could they go? On one side was the sea, getting louder and more agitated. On the other side, across the deep lagoon, rose a forbidding jungle swamp, a place where many a pitfall lay to catch the unwary.

Thorium while exploring the northernmost tip of their small island discovered what could be their only hope of survival. Several hundred yards to the north, he spotted some trees. These were not those of the jungle immediately to their east, but trees not unlike those that dominated his distant home, trees that needed solid ground to survive, not the muck of a swamp. Leading north from their island lay a narrow expanse of sand, exposed by the recently receding tide. Only a yard wide in places, in it lay their chance to escape from the prison rock on which they stood.

The storm was now only a few hours away. To stay put on this exposed expanse of rock would be suicide. No protection from the storm's waves could be found where they stood. They would have to move fast to find shelter.

Thorium motioned to Zircon, who stood close by, to come over to him.

"I was busy, what do you want?" growled Zircon after ambling over to where Thorium stood. He expected to hear more about what had transpired between them, or something equally disdainful. And maybe this would be the showdown he longed for. Out of shot now for his long-rifle (he had wasted the last few rounds shooting blindly into the swamp), Zircon felt anything but brave or powerful. He now knew that they would all soon die, either from the approaching next wave of the storm or from the barbarians whose attack they had barely survived. Zircon had come to accept this with a desperate resignation. But he was still stronger than Thorium and he would get his chance to prove that before the end came. He expected anything from Thorium but that which he did hear.

"Zircon, look over there," Thorium pointed northward as he spoke, "and tell me what you see." Thorium was still not one hundred percent sure that he had spotted their escape and not just a hoped-for illusion.

"I just see the swamp. Is there supposed to be something else?" Zircon responded.

By now Thul, having seen Thorium and Zircon pointing at something to the north, had walked over the slippery rock and joined the two men. He looked north as well. "Trees, trees just like home!" Thul exclaimed.

Zircon now also spotted them. If they could reach them before the storm hit, they would have a chance to survive this ordeal yet. A new glimmer of hope awakened in him.

"How do we get over to them?" he asked Thorium.

"There's a narrow spit of land leading that way through the water. But we don't have much time. The tide will soon cover it up with the approaching storm's waves. Hurry and get the others. I'll carry Cole, you two will have to carry Pluto."

They hurried, yet it took them almost too long to make the hike. By the time they had started the crossing, the sand spit was already partially covered by the storm's rising tide. Suddenly, rain began and small waves rolled across the sand bridge they were crossing. The rain-soaked injured men were more difficult to carry through the growing seas than they had expected. Each moaned with every movement of their bodies. The men hoped that they had a little while before the full force of the storm hit. They could do little at this time to aid the pain of their wounded comrades.

The waves reached their waists as they made the final steps up onto the land. After handing the unconscious Pluto up the rocks to Thorium, Zircon was almost swept away by a wave. Only the quick grasp of Thul's outstretched hand saved Zircon as he lost his footing. The next wave that hit them was even larger and threatened to carry them both into the depths of the lagoon. By some inner strength that Thul did not know he had, he was able to anchor his feet to the rocks and withstand the force of the wave's assault. They then quickly clambered up the rocks together.

Disappointment threatened as they realized they had reached only another rocky islet and the trees they had seen were yet a good distance away. However, they could not stop to rest. They had to find protection from the coming storm's fury as spray from the large waves carried completely across this rocky shoal.

Scrambling, they were able to find a small cave just large enough for them all to fit in. This rocky islet was full of them, and the one they found faced away from the sea. About midway across the islet, its opening was lower than the back of the small cave, so any water retreated out.

They crowded in, putting the injured Cole and Pluto in the back of the cave. The winds grew and howled, but they were protected from the worst of it. Thorium and Zircon added a makeshift cover for the opening with driftwood that lay about.

They settled themselves in, cold and wet, crowded together to try to keep warm, in the small cave. It was not long before huge waves, ten feet and taller, started to sweep across the islet. They would have been long-since dead on the other islet, with its lack of protection, swept into the lagoon to perish. In its rage, the storm cleansed their landing site of the carnage of the battle that now seemed so long ago. The blood and gore were carried alternately into the jungle or out to sea, to be consumed by the denizens of each.

The power of the storm shook the islet upon which they had taken refuge. Water flooded into the cave and just as quickly drained out. Rock and sand fell from the roof of their sanctuary and turned to mud. The storm pounded them with its savage might.

Nightfall came, bringing an even darker countenance to the air. The storm continued into the darkening night in all its fury. The men had never seen the likes of this storm which had left them battered and huddled in the dark dampness of their cave.

What would have been daybreak came, but for the darkness of the clouds that continued unabated through the storm. Finally the storm spent itself against the coastline and cracks in the clouds appeared. The clouds parted and the rain stopped by mid-morning. As the exhausted men began to climb from their sanctuary, a last rogue wave of the storm hit the islet.

It was a wave of unimaginable force, making what had come before seem like the ripples of a shallow pool. Unseen by the men, it descended upon them with only the noise of its roar giving warning. The men dove instinctively back into their cave as the wave hit, dust and spray rising thick around them. They gasped for breath as the roof collapsed under the force of the wave, and water flooded around them.

The wave passed, the fury of the storm's last gasp over. The roof of the cave was gone and the men partially covered by its debris. Water lay several inches deep around them, now trapped along with the men by the fallen rocks and mud. Captured in the debris, the men felt both drowned and suffocated. With the mud stinging their eyes, they were all but dead from the cave-in. What had been their salvation now became their tomb.

The sun now lay high over them as Thul stirred, the only one conscious. He felt as if every bone in his body was broken. His senses were reeling so fast he felt his head was falling off. He tried to raise his body but it screamed in anguish as he moved.

The pain served to momentarily clear his head. He was able to think, though his thoughts were as slow as molasses. He could see, so there was light, which meant that there was a way out of the rubble that had been the cave. He could smell fresh air, so they would not suffocate. However, if they did not move they would die of exposure, or worse.

He turned his head and saw there was no help coming from the others lying beside him. The pain he felt in his shoulders and legs threatened to overpower him. Trying his best to ignore it, he knew it was up to him to save them. He, Thul, the stowaway; they had all wanted him thrown into the sea when he was discovered. Why had he become a stowaway? In search of adventure, so they thought. Really, to go into hiding was his only goal. This was an adventure he did not want and only the authority of the Captain had saved him. Now the Captain was gone.

He had not wanted any part of the mutiny. It was forced upon him. Now it was up to him to save what remained of the survivors of the ill-fated ship, *The Proctant*. He had to save those who had wanted him dead. Such were the ironies that fate cast his way.

Maybe if he could save them he would be considered an equal. If not, he could strike out on his own. Or could that even be considered? It would be worse than suicide for a man of his background to strike out alone and he had to keep his background a secret.

His whole body ached more than he thought possible. The pain intensified, causing him to black out twice as he climbed out of the remains of the cave. After what seemed like days of struggle, he could see the blue sky with high, scattered white clouds. The storm had done its worst but he, Thul, was still alive.

A beautiful sight, he thought, delirious with fever; too bad about the small black specks that circled above, marring the peaceful sky. It was strange, as the specks, reminding him of birds, seemed to come closer and grow larger with each passing moment. That was ridiculous, he thought as he gazed upward in exhaustion, unable to move further. They were much too large to be birds. Yet he could see them clearly now. They were birds! Gigantic birds, strange that a bird could have grown so large. Hadn't he heard of birds like these before? Maybe in a dream, there was a battle. He and the others attacked by giant birds and their riders. Trying to shake off this nightmare, he reached under his head to adjust his pillow and the pain hit across his body again, a cruel biting that made him want to retch. He could not move and the nerves throughout his body told him something was wrong. Not a dream but a nightmare, that was all. Jolting up he realized the nightmare was real. The birds and their riders were back. The attack was coming again, just as they had feared, and they were now helpless to do anything about it.

Wheeling swiftly out of the autumn sky, the great birds and their riders swept down on the prostrate forms of the men, helpless below them. First one, then the next, in a perfect formation they flew. And the man below who watched, with but what was left of his senses, only hoped that the end would come quickly. Thul closed his eyes tightly and his voice cried out in pain and terror. He expected his head to be severed and carried away as he had seen done earlier.

Time passed, Thul did not know how long. He had passed out again from the horror of what he had seen. He was still alive and wondered why? Had the birds only been a nightmare of his delirium, or was he, for some more horrible reason, spared by the barbarians. As he opened his eyes a new horror filled the edges; around him and the other survivors stood a strange people, different from the barbarians, their birds tethered. As he turned his head to one side, he found himself face to face with a small alligator, its mouth open in a lazy yawn showing its rows of teeth. It reached out with its tongue toward him. The new people were helping his comrades out of the cave and he could not see what was happening. Were they being saved now for an even worse terror later on?

These new people looked different from the barbarians who had attacked earlier. With them and their birds wandered these small alligators. He felt something push against his side. When he looked he saw one of the gators, its mouth partially open, and its long tongue licking the dried blood off of his wounds.

"Oh, great God of Sanity, save me!" He tried to raise himself up away from this new horror he saw, but this added exertion was too much for his strained and shattered body. He collapsed, a final time, into the bliss of unconsciousness. He dreamt of far away, of his home. He could smell, simmering over the hot coals, the meal his adoptive mother was cooking. Somebody outside the window was calling his name. "Thul, Thul," they called. He tried to see who it was but he could not move. He was tied to his bed. Gradually the scene changed. His mother was no longer herself, but was now a large bird. And cooking over the hot coals was not his meal but a man. The calling was not to him, it was the gators asking when the meal would be done. The man cooking was their dinner. He was that man. He was their dinner. Thul screamed!

"Think he's coming around?"
"He should be coming out of it any time now."
"Probably nightmares."
"But we're safe now."
"Look around us."
"But they saved us."
"Why?"

The swamp, dark, forbidding and mysterious, was their new home. They were being carried, unable to resist. Thorium, trying to think clearly through his pain, wondered why they had been rescued. He had been told nothing and given no answers to the questions he had asked. Who knew what was in the hearts of their rescuers? For the moment they were carried along, all too badly hurt to resist. So into the swamp they were carried, along paths known only to those who carried them. Not of the birds, but these men that traveled with the gators.

Life was a gamble and the men of *The Proctant* had long-since lost any control over how the fates would deal with them.

Chapter Two
Mysteries of another Land

The surviving men of The *Proctant* remembered little of their trip, mostly by boat, through the jungle from the islet. The city that rose before them was almost beyond belief. Great granite buildings rose from the floor of the swamp, reaching to meet the sky with massive walls and archways that commanded their attention at every turn. The clear water from the myriad springs that existed throughout the swamp city was shallow around the buildings. They were led, Thorium, Zircon, and Thul on foot, the injured Pluto and Cole carried, through the city on pathways that were laid out in wood and tile. The paths that stood several feet above the high tide mark were lined with planter boxes containing carefully groomed and manicured flora. The city was built so as to afford a minimum disturbance to the jungle swamp that contained it, creating one organic being.

The men arrived at a great plaza in the center of the city. Hundreds of people could be seen entering and exiting the plaza's buildings. They had expected to see a large village at most when they were taken off the rocks, and this commotion surprised the rescued men. What they saw were more people meandering about than lived in many of their own coastal towns. They were told that there were many of these plazas throughout the swamp, though none as large as the one they were in now, the commercial center of the Jall's trading empire. Their hosts told the men that almost all of the trade conducted in this part of the world was organized in this city and their trade caravans were welcomed in almost all of the lands they had come in contact with.

Wonder filled the men as they moved through the plaza. How could a city like this have been built where it stood? They would have thought such buildings would be impossible in a swamp like this. They were told that the material used to build the Jall's city had been gathered over many years from throughout their trading empire. Often times their much-needed supplies were gathered at great risk to the caravans that covered the lands. The barbarians that they had encountered were only one of many risks that shared this land.

"Who were the Bird-Riders?" Thorium asked. However, this, like all other questions they asked, was politely refused. They were told only that the answers to their questions would be given in time.

They turned a corner around a high building and saw before them the most beautiful place that any of the survivors had ever seen. From the middle of a deep spring-fed lake it rose, so giant it dwarfed the other buildings around it. It rose in towering spires like a cathedral of old, with pennants of every color flying from its towers. They were told that these pennants represented all of the trading families of the Jall Empire. The walls themselves shone of gold, silver and alabaster. All polished to a fine shine, they reflected back all of the forms of the surrounding world. This gave the palace the look of pseudo-life, making it one with the jungle.

Thorium wondered aloud how much time and effort it had taken to build such a place. As he turned again, he saw more of the construction being done as another tower was being added to the palace. "A new family has reached the status of High-Trader," they were told.

With continued amazement, the survivors watched as blocks of stone rose as if each had sprouted wings, to take their place in the new tower. Invisible forces were at work as the blocks were shaped and polished without the touch of a human hand. What sort of magic was this? Zircon wondered. What sort of enchantment to be sought; power to be gained and used?

Again, no answers were given to their questions, just the same response as before. All that was necessary would be told before they left the confines of the city.

A gate opened high up on the wall of the palace. What appeared to be a shallow draft boat floated down to where the men were standing. No motor or living thing appeared to guide it as it came to rest at a small dock alongside the walkway. Their rescuers motioned the men onboard. Thorium and Zircon climbed in after a brief hesitation. No new threats to them had appeared and they were far too weak to resist, even if they had been tempted. Thul, Cole, and Pluto were carefully placed in the center of the craft.

The boat (could this truly be called a boat as it floated in the air?) rose again in the air carrying the battered and exhausted men back through the gate from which it had come. Once inside, the gate closed and the boat came to a stop in its cradle, resting against a raised platform, built to ease exit from their transportation.

While Thorium and Zircon were guided to an escalator, their more seriously wounded comrades were taken elsewhere. Thul had not yet fully gained consciousness and Cole and Pluto were too badly hurt to move on their own. None of the men had seen an escalator before and Zircon at first refused to step upon it. His superstitious nature feared what he did not understand, while his craving for power demanded answers to questions. "It runs on energy from the sun," they were told, as Zircon finally followed Thorium onto the rising steps in the end, his vanity forcing him to obey. If Thorium could do it, so could he.

After reaching a platform at the top of the escalator, their guide motioned Thorium and Zircon to enter the only door open to them. They entered and the door closed behind them. There were cots set up for the men, with a table and chairs the only other furnishings. There was no window and the walls were barren. A prison cell or a safe refuge, it was hard to tell.

The two men sat down quietly at the table, each deep in their own thoughts. Who were these people that built such cities in the Jungle-Swamp? Were they prisoners, or friends as they had been told? And what had happened to the others, where had they been taken?

Thorium had heard legends of such a people during his trading voyages; objects appeared in trade of unknown origins with materials sculpted and manufactured in ways deemed impossible. Now it seemed they had arrived in the center of these legends.

"Greetings, Lords of the Sea." The man who spoke these words had appeared out of nothing in the center of the room. Neither Zircon nor Thorium had seen a door open, though their exhaustion may have precluded that. The men's eyes searched for the place of entry as they exchanged a look of bewildered consternation.

The man continued speaking, undeterred by the fear and confusion emanating from Zircon and Thorium. "I am glad to see that you made it here safely. I am sure your stay here will be pleasant. You are free to go where you wish in this city. But it is best to stay on the paths."

The apparition was interrupted at this point by Zircon. His eyes darted frantically in all directions. "Where did you come from? I didn't see you come in." Zircon's chair lay where it had been tipped over as he had hastily stood up. He placed his foot under the chair, ready to launch it as a weapon if necessary.

Thorium wanted answers, too. He looked Zircon's way, as each man prepared to meet together this new bedevilment. "Where did you come from?"

The image flickered as if unprepared for the question, before resuming. "There are unseen things in the swamp that would devour you in a short time..."

At that point Zircon lost any remaining control he had and the chair flashed through the air at the man standing before them. Thorium, prepared to fight, moved in a circle as he watched for any door to open that this person had come through. The chair hit the man before them, and then went through him. The image flickered again.

"Magic?" a startled Zircon spoke out loud, sitting hard on the floor in astonishment and fear. Thorium only looked straight ahead at the man (man?) in front of them. The old man continued to speak as if uninterrupted.

"In the clear waters of the city there are fish that, though small, would enjoy your flesh as well. They are kept in the cities' waters to keep our water clear. The vehicle that transported you into the hostel shall be at your disposal. Enter it and it will take you to the paths and back again."

"What are you?" Thorium interrupted with increasing fear of his own. Even he had seen too much since their entry into this city. He had thought his own people the most advanced in the world, and now this. Was it Magic, as Zircon feared, or something else?" Once again, the man before him continued to speak as if nothing had happened.

"I have been told that you will be taken to the men of The Hold. It is they who will best be able to help you. A trading trip will be made in a few days and you will be taken with that party."

Thorium walked slowly up to the man, eyes never stopping the searching glances for an entryway. Zircon got up as well and watched, ready to come to Thorium's aid in a moment's notice, survival more important than the bitter dislike of his companion.

"What of our mates?" Thorium interjected. His hand flashed toward the man (and then through him?) as he sought to grasp the shoulder of the man to get his attention.

"Witchcraft!" Zircon screamed in horror. He had heard of such things, zombies neither dead nor alive, fantastical creatures. This could only be one of those.

The image now briefly changed, flickered, and then grew more solid looking than before. A look of consternation came over the old man. "Witchcraft," he scoffed. "I had thought you a more advanced people than this. What you see before you is, was, my recorded image. My holographic image I recorded to greet you with. I am busy and away at the moment, and these interruptions are getting in the way of my many necessary preparations."

"A holy gram?" said Thorium, bewildered.

"A holographic image, a projection, I am not really with you but in my office, and quite busy right now."

"But…" Zircon almost whispered, wondering what new conjure would appear before them, what new magic.

As if reading Zircon's thoughts, the old man continued.

"This is not 'magic' just a…what is a word you will understand? What you are seeing is real. You must give yourself time to understand." He pondered for a moment. "This is but a part of what was left to us by our Teachers. Ways to do things that were common before the War and now more appears lost to the world than I thought."

"You are not really here?" Thorium asked.

"No, I'm in my office. As I said, this is but a projection of me. The receiver is in your room. I had prepared this greeting so as to provoke as little shock as possible. The mistake is mine. I can see and hear you on a screen in my office. Zircon, you can pick up the chair and sit down. This is not magic, but just more of the technology you'll soon be seeing more of."

Zircon did as told and Thorium sat down as well.

The old man continued. "Your friends were more badly injured than you and needed treatment. They were taken to this city's hospital for care. They will be able to walk again in time for your journey to The Hold. The medicines of these people are known throughout this land. Even your own injuries are starting to heal through the cleansing waters of this city."

The old man paused, as if pondering how much more to tell these two exhausted men. He continued once more. "While here ask, for a guide. There are many who reside in this city and they are proud of what they have accomplished here. Outsiders seldom make it to these shores. They do not often get such esteemed visitors as you to show their city. You are our honored guests. If you need me, just call my name out loud and I will come as quickly as possible. I am called Gar."

With that, the old man's image was gone as quickly as he had appeared. The two men of the sea sat still. Many questions still swirled through their minds and they were given the answers to almost none of them.

Later that day in another room of the palace, Gar spoke with the Trader-King of the Jall. The Trader-King was ancient, with long white hair and a beard that reached his chest. His eyes were like piercing rays, showing an intellect beyond most. His position had been attained through the acumen of his mind, not through heredity. The Trader-King wore a heavy overcoat, made of some wild beast, a gift from a trading partner long ago. He sat on a large throne, with one of the small gators lying in a small pool at his feet.

"Greeting, my old friend. May the stars shine down on your happiness and riches forever on your head."

"Greetings back, Gar, my old friend."

The Trader-King was pleased to have the rare company of his lifelong friend. He had known Gar since childhood, and even then, Gar looked as aged as he did today.

The Trader-King spoke again. "What strange tidings do you bring me today? We have brought the castaways here as you requested." The Trader-King indicated a chair for Gar to sit in.

"Very strange indeed," Gar said as he took the offered chair. "There is a legend amongst us of the Order of the Sage. A man shall come to us from the sea. It is he who will bring together all of the races of the world." Gar paused, choosing his words, not quite sure of how much he should say. This was not a trait Gar was known for and the Trader-King took notice.

Gar remained quiet for several minutes. The Trader-King showed patience and waited. He realized the importance of what the Sage had to say. The legends of the Sage had much truth in them, the Trader-King knew.

Gar finally continued. "I have come to tell you that he is amongst us now, the one who will walk throughout this world, the one chosen by our Teachers from the stars. He is one of those rescued from the sea." Gar paused again to give the Trader-King a chance to fully understand the meaning of his words. The Trader-King looked at Gar with a sense of concern and unease.

The Trader-King spoke in a low whisper; as if afraid his words might be overheard. "Who is this man? Which one is he? How can you be sure?" he asked Gar, the greatest of the Sage, upon whose wisdom he had always depended. "Who is this savior amongst us and how should he be treated?"

To this quiet plea Gar could only shake his head and answer, "Who is he, this man, our savior? No mortal man may know. Not even a Sage such as I. Not even he himself knows what fate awaits him. My knowledge is but that he is one of those we found. And even I do not know how I know this." He again shook his head slowly. "I just know. Treat him well. Treat them all well, for he is much favored by the stars. He shall do much in our world, as the Gods will protect him as one of their own."

"But, who is he, Gar. There must be some clue."

"This we will not know until almost the end of the game. Keep them well, my friend, only this can I tell you." This phrasing gave the Trader-King pause, for it seemed odd to him. Gar continued, "I must go and contact Locklear. I will return in time for the expedition. Locklear may know something of the matter that I may have forgotten. It is a long time since I learned the legends from the Teachers. He must be told, and perhaps even a convention of the Sage. It has been a long time since the last one, since before the day when our Teachers left. And there are so few of us left. May the Teachers guide you upon the proper paths. And of the one that the Teachers promised to lead us, you must tell no one."

'That much I know,' thought the king as Gar left.

Several weeks later, the now-healed men of the sea gathered in their room. On the morrow, they would be leaving for the mountains, for a place always spoken of with reverence: The Hold.

As promised, their wounds were healing. Their stomachs were full, filled by the exotic fare of this city: fish, fowl, and fruit, for which these men knew of no equivalent. For the first time since they had left their homeport months ago the men were well rested. With this rest and their filled stomachs, the men's minds began to reach again for the answers to the questions that they held.

Cole and Thorium sat together in one corner of the room, speaking quietly so none of the others would overhear their words. They discussed what had happened and once again, they were troubled by Zircon. Again in good health, Zircon began to act the bully. Several times he had to be forcibly restrained when he had attacked one of the others. While his long-rifle remained empty of shot, his fists remained large. Cole and Thorium were particularly concerned about what might happen if Zircon turned his anger toward a member of this city.

Zircon paced the floor while Thul and Pluto exchanged nervous glances in his direction. Most of Zircon's rage had been directed at them, especially Thul.

Finally, Pluto broke the seeming silence of the room. "What do you make of this place, Thorium? You must have an opinion by now."

Thorium looked toward Cole, and then he turned to Pluto and answered.

"Cole and I have been discussing this place for a while now. As far as we can tell, everything is as it seems. We are in the hands of friends. We are healed or healing, rested, and no longer hungry. However, I think I can understand what is worrying us all. They seem to want something from us. It's not spoken, but it's almost palpable in the air."

Cole joined the discussion, rising from the cot where he had been reclining during his talk with Thorium. "It has been known for some time in our homelands, our Confederation, that some possess certain ways that are out of the ordinary: the ability to read minds, as our judges at home, or to move things solely with their thoughts. Amongst the Confederation, these things are rare, brought about by what happened in the past. What we have seen here is pretty much along the same vein. Only here it appears to be in much greater numbers. Their science and industry appear at least equivalent to our own. As I can see from my own healed wounds, their medicine appears to be far more advanced than ours."

"I'm feeling uneasy with the whole setup," Thul broke in, echoing the thoughts of the others. "It's as if there is more trouble sitting there right in front of us. They do want something. I can feel it."

"So you're a Psychic now, too." Zircon chided Thul.

"Maybe so," Thul spoke back. "All I know is the waiting here, with no control over where we go next. Nobody does what they have done for us for nothing. We should be doing something, something to take control back again."

"Do you have an idea?" answered Thorium, putting his hand on Thul's shoulder; all the while looking at Zircon with what he hoped was a calming glance. "I realize the strain that has been on all of us since the mutiny. Most of us are gone now. Nevertheless, we are guests, not prisoners, that much I know. We have been treated well, and these people seem to have our best interests at heart. I suggest we just relax and see what happens next."

Zircon spoke again, loudly, in an excited state. Thorium's glance had done nothing to calm him. "How can we be expected to relax when we don't know what's going on? We have no control over our destiny. I just want to know what to make of this. What do they want of us? It must be something," he shouted.

Zircon grew more excited as he paced the room. Cole and Thorium exchanged anxious glances. This had become routine behavior for Zircon. "I need answers, and I need them now! Nobody does what they've done for us without expecting something pretty big in return." Such was Zircon's logic that he could not imagine helping stranded folk unless he got payment in return. "They expect something from us. I want to know what it is." Anger streamed from his voice.

"We all would," Thul added, for a change on the same side as Zircon.

"What if we call Gar?" Pluto spoke less than enthusiastically.

"How can we do that?" Zircon screamed at Pluto, who cringed at Zircon's anger. By now, Zircon's rage was almost out of control. As a young man this rage had led him to the long-rifle. Learning its proficiency had a calming effect on him. When he held it, the world seemed to stand still around him. There was none better in their Confederation with the long-rifle. Zircon had his trophies to prove it.

"Maybe by just calling his name, like he said," Thorium spoke back with a forced voice. The recent inactivity was beginning to affect him in an adverse way as well. These men of the sea were used to being in control, always active, working to stay alive in the challenging oceans of the world.

There were a few moments of silence after this heated exchange of shouts. Cole took a position between Zircon and Pluto. He feared the worst and was trying to forestall the inevitable.

Turning to Thul, Thorium broke the silence. "Go ahead, try it. Call him, call Gar." They all needed questions answered. The anxiety of not knowing was trying on them all. "I have questions for him myself. He seems to be the one in charge of this all."

"Gar, will you come?"

"Greetings, my fellow travelers," Gar called out briskly as he appeared. He stood in the center of the room, near the startled Thorium. Gar appeared deep in thought.

"Are you real this time? I did not see a door open. How'd you know we wanted you?" a suspicious Zircon spoke out.

"You called and I came. You did pick a rather difficult time to call me away, though. I was working on a riddle left by the Teachers."

"Why'd you appear? Were you spying on us?" Zircon continued his rant, moving closer to the Sage. His anger was now boiling under the surface.

"No questions, I sense what..." Gar began before being interrupted by the violence of Zircon's voice.

"What do you mean by no questions! Why!" he in turn got no further as Gar silenced him with a stern glance. His eyes seemed to burrow into Zircon's tortured soul.

"Please remain calm. And no, I am not with you in person. We will meet soon enough. This is my projection as before. Now I will tell you much of what I know, my student." Gar spoke directly to Zircon.

"I'm not your student!" Zircon screamed at Gar, his body tense with anger and fear.

Gar turned to face the enraged Zircon. The others prepared to assist the aged-looking man. Only Thorium remained seated.

Thorium said to Cole and Thul. "Don't be alarmed. Gar is not really here. Zircon knows that as well. We encountered this form of communication here, before you were brought back to us."

Gar spoke quietly to Zircon in words the others were unable to hear, his eyes again penetrating the angry man's soul. His look and words began to have a calming effect on the man.

Then to all of the others he spoke aloud. "Thank you, Thorium, for explaining my appearance. If my form of address causes you distress, then I apologize for its use. Nothing is meant as an insult toward you. To those of us who learned the knowledge from the Teachers, now departed, we are the Sage and you are all our students. We are all their children, to be led into the unknown future along a long path chosen for us by the Teachers. May I continue now?"

Zircon, a troubled but calmer look on his face, sat down on one of the chairs by the table, remaining quiet.

Gar, for his part, was patient with the interruptions, but he wondered to himself if the stories were true, concerns he could not share with the others. Could he have been wrong in reading the signs? No, he was certain he was correct. The one for whom he had been waiting was among these men. He looked Zircon's way. Yes, even this troubled soul could be the man who would bring them all together. Even Chuak, his old friend from the Order, ever the skeptic among them, had agreed the time had come.

"Go ahead," Thorium said.

Then Gar began.

"First some news that you may be glad to hear; others of your ship, *The Proctant*, I think you called it, also survived. All lie beyond your current reach. They lie scattered throughout our lands and beyond. But you may rest assured that someday they will all be reunited again." The thought of this made the mutineers none too comfortable.

"Three were taken by the savage whites of the Northern Valley. Those that remained on your ship approach even now an island unknown to you. Adventures still await them as well as you. Now a story needs to be told."

"But our questions?" Pluto started.

"You must learn patience." Gar continued "Listen and most will indeed be answered. Those that are not you must learn on your own.

"Long ago, in our worlds distant past, a race of intelligent beings almost perished in their own violence and aggression on their home world. Much in line with what happened in our own world. A few survived their holocaust and turned their thoughts from destruction to learning. They are a race utterly foreign to man in composition. They live in and consume raw energy. The sight of any would drive men of our own race mad within seconds. Their intelligence is above anything we know. With this intelligence and will to learn came a curiosity that drove them across the universe in their quest for knowledge.

"They arrived here, on our world, just before the start of the last great war. They could see that this war would be like their own final war, but they could do nothing to prevent it, though they tried. It seems with whatever means they used, another force was at work against them. They worked through people like myself, to keep this world from exploding in its fury, but others would not heed their wisdom.

"Yet they couldn't do nothing. In their own wisdom, they went about seeing that at least a few would survive so that the Human Race would not end. They picked those from throughout the world's masses they thought would make the strongest race possible after the war. These they brought to Holds throughout the world; great underground cities built by the Teachers. Your own people must be descendants of such a Hold, its origins lost to your own mythology. We will soon be on our way to one such Hold. Its residents never lost the spirit of the Teachers and they kept their Hold alive."

"Continue, please. What does this all, assuming its true, have to do with us?" Thorium said.

Gar continued with his tale.

"To a few of the most stable they made themselves known, though they were never seen. To these few they gave certain abilities, and they told, or foretold as we Sage think, many stories.

"These few, other Sage such as myself, were able to help those who survived the war rebuild. Even today, I do my part to rebuild our world in peace. In the lands where we remain we are the advisers of Kings and the Sage of the people."

"Why are there no Sage such as yourself where we come from?" Gar was asked.

"That is a mystery to the Order of the Sage. It is said that one was sent to your lands. But we lost communication with him almost immediately.

"It was up to the Sage to continue the dreams of our Teachers, of a peaceful world, joined as one."

"Those that attacked us hardly seem peaceful," Cole rather-pointedly said. Much of what Gar said sounded like the tales of children to him.

"These Bird-men, as you call them, are not survivors of The Hold. Their ancestors were outside during the war. They are the mutated descendants of those who survived the War.

"Of men, they and the others no longer are. They are to be controlled and someday eradicated."

"A callous thought toward other men," Thorium spoke.

The men of the sea grew silent at these words. To them Gar spoke of genocide, how often wars had been fought over this. Their esteem of Gar lowered at such words.

Gar continued his story. "As the Teachers gradually withdrew from this world, to continue their journey, their quest, across the universe, we Sage lost many of our *abilities*. Now only a few of us, the strongest, possess some of the Teachers' gifts. My strength I now draw only from the Blue Lights of the Eastern plain. It was there the Teachers dwelt while on Earth. That is all that is left now, leaving us, the Sage, to lead the planet's survivors to a future of peace."

"When will they return?" Thul asked, himself not really believing what they had heard, though somehow it brought forward something from deep within himself.

"The land of the Blue Lights is still there. When we have grown as a people, they will return to welcome us as their brothers, no longer their children.

"As for these lands and your future, you will find that most of those you meet are friends. Among the peoples of The Hold, there are no enemies. But the others, those now nonhumans whose ancestors remained outside, not chosen by the Teachers, with them you will find no friends, only death to the unwary. Good-bye for now. I must rest before our caravan leaves. I'll see you in the morning before we go."

With that Gar was gone. And the men wondered of Gar, with his beliefs, would they remain friends long? And how much of his story was true?

Chapter Three
Searching for Answers

Their stay in the Jall City was far too brief for the mutineers of *The Proctant*. They had used what little time they had to rest and regain their strength from their ordeals. Exploring the city first-hand when they had the chance, the men saw much that seemed miraculous to them, in both the city and the people; nothing like this had been reported before within the vast extent of their Confederation's trading expeditions.

This was a world of strange symbiotic behaviors and that seemed to the men to be magic. To the people of Jall, second sight and the use of telekinesis were daily facts of life. It was through this *magic* and their transmutation of matter that this city was built. Great stone slabs moved and were molded into place by the Masters of Building, each Master trying to outdo the next in their exterior decorations, molded solely through the power of their minds.

The city was a large one by their Confederation standards and contained almost the entire population of the Jall. It seldom seemed crowded, however, as the people of the swamp lived through their trade. It was said that all trade through this part of the world involved the Jall in some way. All they dealt with trusted them to be fair in their dealings, they told the travelers. At times half the population of Jall would be gone on these trading missions.

The Jungle Swamp Palm made all of this possible. All who encountered it treated it as a treasure. The Tree matured rapidly under the care of the Jall. Yet for all of this rapid growth, it was as strong as any metal when used in fabrication. These Jungle Swamp Palms grew in large plantations by expert Tree Masters. With the nutrients found below the mountains finding their way into the swamp, the Jall controlled the palms' growth to create a wood as strong as iron, yet light and flexible, though in short supply.

Many of the Jall's trading partners used this wood in place of harder-to-find metals. The men of *The Proctant* were told that this wood was even more important due to the lack of minerals in this land.

Scavenged clear before the time of the Great War, now little mineral wealth remained. Most of this wealth lay in the skeleton remains of the pre-war cities, a dangerous place for any who entered. Few expeditions had been successful, even by the Jall, and the tales brought back from these expeditions told of horrors beyond even the strength of the Sage.

A Trader-King, appointed for life by the Council of Citizens, ruled the people of Jall. The Trader-King was usually chosen from a field of those who had achieved something extraordinary for the good of their people. And while the title was Trader-King, both men and women could be chosen. Trader-Kings of the past had varied their style from that of a co-council to a few who had grown to be dictators. The Council had removed some, although this was rare. When power was *grabbed* by an elite, be it a clique or an individual, that power was soon ignored. What good was power held when most of the people so-governed were never in the city?

The people valued the work of those who best achieved gains to the city itself. A balance had been reached where neither the ruler nor the ruled could gain at the expense of the other. Father-to-son transfer of power was forbidden and when tried, the guilty parties were simply ignored and a new Trader-King installed by the Council. Beyond this balance, it seemed all of the people of the Jall were somehow interconnected. All seemed to know instantly of any actions of the trading missions and the people around them: There were no secrets here, so the Jall claimed. When the unforgivable offense occurred, which was a rarity, the only penalty was expulsion from the community of the Jall.

With all of this set in tradition and reality, the Trader-Kings worked hard for the common good of the Jall and the people made sure the Trader-King did. No formal laws existed within the Jall, a reality that seemed alien to the men of *The Proctant*. In their Confederation written law guided most aspects of a person's life. No real government in their Confederation existed, as the law was followed. Here it was the opposite, a government without need of law.

The preparations for the journey to The Hold continued. The Hold lay in the mountains to the southeast of the swamp. The roots of these mountains seemed to grow from the waters of this jungle. The trip would be a trade mission. The Hold needed more of the valuable Jungle Swamp Palm and were willing to pay a high price for it. In the case of Jall-

Hold trade this came in the form of foodstuffs and grain that the Jall could not grow. When the travelers learned the price would be twice the normal they inquired why this would be. They were answered in one word: Jal-Beast. They were told no more of this. What the Jal-Beast could be they could only imagine.

The preparations for the journey finished, on the night before the party was to leave, on a plantation on the south side of the city, the trees were cut and prepared. Most of the Swamp Palm plantations were located to the south of the city, as this was the direction to where most trading expeditions left. The mutineers were brought to view this job and were once-again amazed by what they saw. Ten properly matured trees were cut down through the Tree-Masters' cutting tools. After felling the trees, the branches were removed, leaving a perfectly smooth cylinder. One by one, the trees were then laid in the clear, mineral-rich waters of the swamp. This final step gave the trees their flexibility, making their value even higher. For times when strength alone was needed, this overnight curing of the trees was skipped and they were cut and trimmed the same day the trading expedition would leave.

A dozen citizens of Jall would take part in a trading expedition, such as the one to transport the logs. While the Jungle Swamp Palms were the Jall's most valuable trading commodity, they often worked as facilitators in trading value from one land to another. On a trade mission, the party the Jall were trading with was usually required also to send a mission along as well. Their job would be to protect the trading party from whatever dangers lay along their path. On most trade expeditions, these protectors would number two or three men. It was not only the monsters of this world that created the need for these guards. The trade missions of Jall were valued by all. When Thorium mentioned to a guide that a full dozen heavily armed guards from The Hold were present for this mission, he was answered with just the one word that they had come to fear, just a single name: Jal-Beast.

Thorium asked what it was that made this monster so dangerous. He was told that it carried such strength that only a Sage could hope to deter it.

On the morning of the trade mission's start, the men of *The Proctant* gathered in the plaza across from the palace. All were mostly healed of their injuries by the medical salves that the Jall had applied to their wounds. They were in good spirits, waiting anxiously for the trip to begin. They were met by one of the Jall, who escorted them to a wharf on the edge of the city, near where the logs had been treated overnight. The party would be large for a trading mission. In large measure, this was due to this being the time of year when the Jal-Beasts would start making their appearances. At the start of the Jal-Beast season, the monsters always appeared hungrier and more likely to attack than later on in the year. Thul wondered if the beast was named for the people or if it was the other way around.

For the mission there was the customary twelve from Jall, picked by lot from volunteers. One of the greatest honors of Jall was to take part in such trade missions. Great wealth for the city and the individual was gained on such missions, and always, even during the Jal-Beast season, more volunteered for the missions than were needed. Hence was developed the tradition of The Draw. All the volunteer's cards were placed in a large pot the night before the mission was to leave. The Council would take turns drawing out names until the quota was met for the next day's mission, or during the busier times of the year, missions. During the height of the trading season each night became a festival around the event.

Twelve men supplied for protection of the expedition by The Hold, with their cross-bows, stepped into the first and last boats. Usually a mission would use at most two boats, but with the men of *The Proctant* joining the trip, it was decided a third boat would be needed. Around the boats many of the small gators congregated. Fully mature, these gators ranged in size from two to three feet. They, too, would be taking part in the expedition. Such a thing had precedent, though it was a rarity.

Finally, as all of the boats were loaded and the journey was set to begin, the last member of the mission arrived. Gar, the city's Sage of much renown, had kept his intentions vague until the end. Such was always his way. He was welcomed heartily. That this was an extraordinary trading mission was now a given.

The Sage stepped onto the lead boat, where Wolfe the leader of this expedition, greeted him with a slap on the back. With warning abroad about the Jal-Beast, he was happy to see his old friend was along. He had traveled many times with Gar, often to secret places he was sworn not to divulge.

"Come to take my cargo on a successful journey?" he happily inquired of Gar, only to be taken aback by the cryptic answer he was given.

"No, my old friend, I have come solely to guard my own."

Wolfe sat back, wondering what Gar meant by his words. In his many travels with his friend, he had learned when not to pry for more answers than the Sage was ready to give.

They set off early that morning. The party hoped to travel far enough that first day to reach the foot of the mountains by the third day. Gar seemed as agitated and concerned as Wolfe ever remembered him. The boats were pushed through the water by pole-men, one at the bow and one at the stern of each boat. Through most of the swamp the growth was too thick for oars this time of year, oars were available for all when those few areas of clear water were reached. Twice a year each caravan path was cleared of the swamp's plants, but such was the rate of growth in the foliage of the swamp that never were the paths fully clear. And when the Jal-Beast season began no further clearing could be done.

Those who guided the boats had to be continuously on watch for channels too clogged with debris from the jungle to travel and new paths that were now open. When one of the areas of open water was reached the pole-men rested while all of those on the boats worked the oars to best advantage. The Jall's strenuous work of keeping the logs in the air and moving alongside the second boat was done in shifts.

Gar stood forward on the first boat, watching for clear pathways to follow through the jungle swamp and to help clear the way for the caravan. He seemed to grow more impatient with each passing hour and urged the boats to move somehow faster. A silver glow seemed to come from his walking stick as the jungle vines parted before them. To the men of *The Proctant* it was as eerie a procession as they had witnessed in their travels.

Wolfe continued to watch Gar closely. Gar's words of protecting his own cargo worried Wolfe, as did Gar's increasing impatience. Wolfe had never seen Gar as agitated as this. He, too, urged the pole-men to work harder and faster as his mind tried to perceive meaning in Gar's words and actions.

Already the pole-men were working as fast as possible. Those of Jall whose job it was to maintain the logs were having trouble with their control. Those not working the logs now worked the oars whenever it was possible, as well as the men of *The Proctant*. The gators remained alongside the boats, although their swimming seemed agitated as well now. It was uncanny for the men of their Confederation to see these small gators acting more like dolphins than their giant cousins they knew from home.

One of the logs, held amazingly in the air alongside the caravan, slipped. It bumped another log and almost caused the whole group to crash into the water. Thul saw another Jall, not working the logs, place his hand on the shoulder of the Jall who was weakening, giving him some of his strength and regaining their hold on the logs. Disaster was averted for the moment, but it brought into question how much longer the Jall could maintain the load. A single slip could send the logs crashing into the water on either side of the travelers, sending waves crashing over the low boats. All of the Jall now worked to maintain the logs. Never had any of them attempted to move logs so fast through the swamp.

Those of *The Proctant* aided as best they could. With their oars, they worked to help the pole-men move the boats. That is, all but Zircon, who just watched as Gar performed his *magic*. To Zircon, this was just one more thing to make his own, to gain this power his ego demanded. He failed to conceive how this power could be anything but something he could learn by himself. He compared Gar's abilities to his own with the long-rifle. Now, with a present of shot given to him by Gar, once more Zircon seemed as consumed by power as ever.

The gators remained with the boats throughout the day. Constant companions of the Jall, they served as watchdogs, keeping dangerous fish and snakes away. In return, they lived in the fresh-water pools of the city, where they fed on a varied diet of fish provided by the Jall. Each served the other well. This perfect symbiotic relationship would soon be put to the test for the convoy.

It remained peaceful throughout the first day of the journey, as only the call of the Craul-Birds and the varied tree-snakes interrupted the solitude. Several of the tree-snakes were shot as they tried to attack the men in the boats. Each was dispatched by a shot from Zircon's long-rifle. The Jall and the men of The Hold considered these snakes but a nuisance. Zircon was told to save his ammunition for what may yet come to them in the swamp, a warning of the danger of the Jal-Beast, although that name was not spoken. Eventually, as they watched them, the men of *The*

Proctant realized that while these serpents were on average over ten feet long, they posed little danger. Their slowness of movement and poor vision made them poor hunters and relatively unimportant as far as a danger to the caravan. Even Zircon grew tired of shooting them, as they posed no challenge to his skill. If it was not for the Craul-Birds, with their hideous screams, which seemed as dumb as the serpents were slow, the snakes would have long-since died of starvation. The men watched in amazement as several times the brightly colored birds would actually land on the head of a snake, seemingly unaware of the danger. The snake would then open its jaws with its own deliberate slowness. As a bird was swallowed, it actually appeared to be marching down the throat of the serpent. The Jall told the visitors that this was a common occurrence and, if not for it happening, the swamp would quickly be overrun with the winged Craul-Birds and their hideous screams. Another good reason not to shoot the snakes, they laughed.

The caravan made its camp the first night on a white sandy spit, a good two feet above the water level of the jungle swamp. Here they would be safe from the nocturnal denizens of the swamp. A fire was built to last the night and a spit set up to roast the meat brought with the men of The Hold. They placed the logs around the sandy island to keep anything unwanted out that might still like the dry sand. All gathered around the fire for warmth and tales were told by the men of the many legends that shaped this part of the world. As the men ate and drank their fill, each group in kind took turns launching into songs of their home. At last as the stories of The Hold and the Jall lapsed, the men of *The Proctant* were asked to speak of their lands and of their homes.

The visitors spoke of the vast Confederation of Tribes that lay across the ocean to the west. Traders like the Jall, they made frequent voyages throughout the world to trade and discover what was left of man after the Great War. Their voyage had been one of these, as the ships of the Confederation searched for riches, trade and adventure.

The men spoke of how they knew of steam and electricity as power, as there was no shortage of coal and natural gas. However, windmills also dotted the land, a carryover of their survival from the war. It was said that before the war there were people who could channel the power of the sun directly to their homes, but this was a science lost. Almost every village had its own wind farm, to run their own factories and feed energy into the common grid. In the harbor cities, tidal energy was harvested and also fed into the grid, so that power remained abundant throughout the Confederation.

Yet even with this abundance of coal, most ships were sail-powered, as the high cost of coal made steam-powered ships uneconomical. That and the people of the Confederation had a tradition of wind that had carried them through the long period after the Great War. Steamships were used on the most valuable trade routes, especially to those lands south of the Confederation of Tribes.

Of the tidal energy, the Jall had a little experience, and of the wind the Jall used a little; coal and oil were almost non-existent. However, this part of the world somehow still possessed the power from hydrogen, fed from great towers that still dotted the landscape. The people of these lands continued to operate these facilities, though they had lost much of the understanding of how it worked. They worked by rote in these places of power. Tales were told that these plants' energy was the same as that which had destroyed so much of the earth, but the people of The Hold refused to believe that such a benefit that remained from the past as the power plants could be the same as the evil that had brought about so much destruction.

Late into the night *The Proctant's* crewmen were asked more questions of their homes and their discoveries that the men felt at ease in answering. However, when the question was finally asked about how they became stranded in this land, Gar interrupted the proceedings by raising the dangers to be faced on the morrow. New wood was added to the dying embers of the fire and the men retired to sleep.

As the sun began to rise over the horizon the next morning, the caravan was awoken by the vicious scream of something yet deep in the jungle swamp. Upon hearing its terrifying scream the men rushed to break camp before it came any nearer. The men of *The Proctant* heard only the whispered "Jal-Beast." They hurried to keep pace with the rest. The men of The Hold were the first to reach the boats, retrieving their cross-bows as the men of Jall moved to gather the logs. To see the others with their bows brought a smile to Zircon's face. Here, at last, was a challenge for his skills with the long-rifle. Let the others worry, he felt secure.

The men used the poles and oars together now to try to propel the boats as quickly as possible through the morass that was the jungle swamp. The men of Jall now worked as one to keep the logs together and alongside them. There was no resting for any now. Wolfe watched as the gators showed their nervous agitation by frequently leaping from the water, an action that the day before they had done for play. Now it seemed that they left the water to gain visibility and to maintain their close contact with the caravan. Wolfe could feel with the gators the closeness of the Jal-Beast. Gar stood silent and still at the bow of the boat, holding his staff before him.

Wolfe watched Gar with growing concern for the safety of them all. Many a time he had escaped from the beast under the cover of the Sage. Yet this time Gar seemed uncertain of his abilities to affect the beast. It was rumored that the Jal-Beast came from another time but Wolfe did not see how that was possible

When they finally spotted the Jal-Beast, it was but a short distance to the east from where they traveled. The Beast seemed to be moving in a straight line to intersect where they were going. When Zircon finally saw the giant beast's head through a break in the foliage, it towered above the treetops. He lost his confidence upon the sight. How could even his long-rifle prevail against such a creature as this? Yet he still put his long-rifle to his shoulder, steadying his aim, to confront the beast when the time came. He sought to aim at its eyes, always the weakest spot of entry for his shot. The men of The Hold held their own cross-bows close at hand as they worked the oars. It was across one of the swamp's clear pools they traveled now, the beast to one side, eyes fixated upon them.

The beast seemed momentarily confused, uncertain of where its prey had moved, though in its tiny mind it knew they were close by. It could smell them as well now. It was Gar, trying to impede the chase, that clouded the giant's mind. But Gar felt his control quickly slipping. It seemed the giants were becoming immune to the partial control the Sage had been able to convey until now. Several minutes passed during the beast's confusion and the men put that time to good work, moving quickly across the clear patch of the swamp into the jungle beyond. The men saw the beast shake its head and roar, finally turning to face them. The monster had found its prey after all. Zircon stood at the back of his boat to face it. Nothing had stood unconquered to his long-rifle before. Regaining his confidence, he thought, 'let the beast come.'

As the body of the beast turned to face them across the clear pool, the men knew the race had been lost, a race that had begun when they had heard the beast roar during the morning break. Together they would have to still the beast or die.

From Gar's staff a bright light shown for a moment, blinding the beast and giving the men a precious few more seconds. Then it was time to prepare. The beast knew where they were and very little remained for the men to do as it moved upon them. They could feel the disturbances in the water as all of the swamp denizens fled before the monster. They could see no sign of the gators and the visitors from across the sea felt that they had fled as well. 'Was there nothing but monsters in this land?' wondered Cole.

The men turned their weapons against the Jal-Beast, their arrows having little effect upon the giant's armored skin. Even Zircon's attempts to blind the creature were for naught. The giant's eyes on its massive head held their own protective cover that Zircon's shot could not penetrate. The monster's tiny arms seem to mock the men as they fought the beast.

"At its legs! Under the water! At its feet!" the Jall yelled to the men of The Hold. It was only beneath the water that the Jal-Beast was vulnerable. And by the time the beast would be close enough to hit it effectively there, it would be upon them.

The monster seemed to tower above the trees as it prepared to strike the men. Then the gators reappeared in greater numbers than had swam with the caravan. They struck at the now-stationary Jal-Beast's feet, tearing away small bits. With each bite the gashes grew larger. But even against this attack the giant proved worthy. It kicked its immense feet at the attackers, sending more than a few gators to their death. But more came. The men's greatest worry now was to keep the boats from capsizing. Ignoring the logs for the moment, they moved deeper into the jungle and watched the battle before them. More gators now came to join in the battle and with them those denizens of the swamp that had fled before the beast. Fresh blood in the water overcame any fear they had of the beast. A blood fury overcame the fishes of the swamp. Here was a meal for all. The gators now withdrew to alongside the boats, their job done. The beast tried to thrash its feet once more, but the only thing this did was to bring the soft under part of the giant's feet to the open. The fish swarmed in untold numbers at this new treat. Zircon, along with the other men, had continued shooting at the Jal-Beast, hoping to confuse the tiny brain of the beast with their fire.

Finally the beast, its feet torn and bleeding in hundreds of places, turned and fled, pursued by the meat-eating fish of the swamp. It would live, but it would also need time to heal its many wounds. The gators now returned to the site of the battle, to retrieve those who had died in the carnage. These they brought to the boats, where the men carefully laid them in the boats for the return trip. The men of *The Proctant* had never seen such a sight and began to understand the intelligence of the gators. Those that had died for the Jall would be given a hero's funeral and the gators would be richly rewarded.

With the wood once again collected by the Jall, the caravan began to move with the gators taking up their stance as protectors and watch-guards of the caravan. While the visitors began to relax, the veterans of the caravan wondered one thing. Where was the mate? Almost always the Jal-Beasts traveled in pairs. Could this be a new terror? A rogue Jal-Beast?

They spent the second night on another sandy islet, one of hundreds that dotted the jungle swamp. For now they were safe. And at the evening's fire Gar told the story of the trader's chief worry, the king of the swamp, the Jal-Beast.

Gar began his tale soon after the men settled down around the fire after a meal of roasted Craul-Bird and mead to quench their thirst. All listened as the Sage spoke, as his words were said to carry the wisdom of the Teachers.

"The Jal-Beast, that monster which almost caught us this day, is a relic of the bygone day when the world was covered with such as him. From where they came is a question still not resolved."

"That's true," spoke Wolfe. "Our fathers-fathers knew not of such creatures, of that we are sure."

Gar continued, "The Order of Sage has come to believe that they came from one of two places, both obscene and forbidden. And yet..." he paused briefly, looking skyward, "It must be from one. A vile proclamation to a world almost destroyed."

"What are these possible ways? Something must be known, giants such as these can't just appear from nothing?" Thorium asked of Gar.

"Yes, truly, one of the ways, through time or engineering, it must be one," Gar almost sighed.

"Through time?" Cole seemed startled by the implications. "Surely, as a sane person you must know that passage like you suggest through time is impossible."

"Impossible," Gar questioned. "To us it may seem impossible. But you thought my gifts and those of the Jall impossible as well. The both of us were engineered, the race of Jall and the students of the Teachers, we who are called Sage."

"Engineered?" queried Thorium.

"Who are the Teachers?" asked Thul.

"Many questions with few answers; the Teachers are they who once dwelt in this land. It was they who, through their sanctuaries, brought the race of man through the radiation poisoning of the last Great War. They came from beyond the stars to help us in our greatest need. You must have had your own Sage at one time."

"Outsiders from beyond this world, Teachers and Sage, of such we're not aware. Our lands were but lightly poisoned by the War. Though some lands to this day remain forbidden to travelers," answered Cole.

Gar continued, "The Teachers were a race from beyond the stars. It was they who selected the few who were placed in The Holds in our world, held for generations below ground until the land above cleared enough to allow the revival of man above ground."

"To that they are as saints to us," spoke a man from Wolfe's group.

"To you saints, to us our Teachers, but to the Jall and others they are but the engineers and scientists who brought us back from the brink," Gar said reverently.

"We, the Sage, were the only ones to have direct contact with the Teachers. To us they gave the power of longevity and opened many hidden powers within our minds. To be the guardians and guides of the new race of man was our task. It is both a curse and a blessing to us of the Sage Order. With all of our individual longevity, when we are gone the Sage will be no more. To keep us from becoming the rulers of those in our care we could have no partner in life, no child to carry on our genes. That is the curse we must carry."

"What have the Teachers to do with the Jal-Beast?" Thorium asked, bringing the conversation back into line.

"It was shortly after the Teachers were presumed to have left our world that the Jal-Beast appeared, named after the race, the Jall, who first encountered them. And maybe more." Gar lit his pipe and pondered his next words. To seem critical of the Teachers was not a task to be taken lightly. "Have you from across the sea not wondered in amazement at the powers of the Jall?"

"We thought it just an aberration from the radiation after the War. We have people with similar skills at home, though rare and not of the ability shown here," said Cole.

"In the beginning, perhaps, but the Jall are truly the creation of the Teachers. You see," Gar sighed, "the Teachers had a vice. They lived to experience the universe and to experiment whenever possible with what they found. To the good of this obsession, you find the Jall and their symbiotic friends, the gators that live alongside them. Each changed over time by the Teachers, until they reached their current state of development."

"And the Jall know of this?" Thul spoke as he looked in wonder at the men of Jall.

"This we do," spoke a member of that party, who added, "To us there is no God, just the Teachers. Thankful are we for the form we have been given. And to the Teachers we are thankful for our friends the gators, to whom we owe our life today. Only they were given the skill to defeat the Jal-Beast, that the smallest of the Teacher's projects might control the largest. We so give thanks."

"The Jal-Beast were the creation of the Teachers? Why would they create such a thing?" It was Pluto, inwardly longing for home and his family, who asked these questions.

Gar took another puff from his pipe before he answered Pluto. "Many were the experiments of the Teachers, and some more horrifying than noble. Yet the Knowledge of each they shared with their students, the Sage."

"Were the White another experiment?" asked Thorium.

"No, the White are but a horrifying reminder of the Great War. The Teachers passed on the knowledge of their experiments to us so that we, the Order of the Sage, could keep watch over these creations, both good and bad. Several Sage died early at the evil brought forward by the Teachers. There is much you will find strange in this world before your journeys end. Rumors you thought but tales, to be newly discovered. The Teachers were not saints, nor were they the devil. They did bring us survival," he looked at the crew of *The Proctant* when he said this next part, "at least in this part of the world. Already those that remained on *The Proctant* have landed on an island to the northwest of us. Much you will see before you are all reunited."

"Reunited, reunited!" Zircon spoke. "If you know so much you should know that there are some we have no thought of seeing again."

"Much will pass before that happens. And many you thought lost will return, but to continue my tale." Gar took another puff of his herbal blend. "The Teachers shared all of their secrets with us, their students, the Order of the Sage. To find that they created such a beast without divulging it to us…That seems most unlikely…But…"

"What else could it have been?" asked Thul.

"There is another story, even more unlikely, a legend, a storied whisper…" Gar paused again and then lowered his voice, "a story of a people and an experiment, to save the world from environmental destruction."

"Enough with the drama!" Zircon snarled.

Wolfe looked with dismay at Zircon while Gar continued his tale. "Time, the control of it…even the Teachers dismissed it as a story. But perhaps, here, the Teachers were wrong. A last thought before more on the Jal-Beast. Could it be, before the last Great War, that command of time had been gained? So go these whispers of the past. And from that, this portal, lost to us of today, came the Jal-Beast.

"The Jal-Beast, largest creature of this world. How many, we don't know, but the number cannot be many. None have been known to die, defeated yes, but always to return. As yet no young have been found. But we know so little of them. The area they are thought to call home is largely unknown to us. They tower above the tallest trees of the Great Swamp, terrifying to all they encounter.

"It is thought that they must hibernate as through much of the year they are never seen. They come only when the temperature is the highest, as it is in our summer. Few have returned from where we presume is their home, the northeast edge of the Great Swamp we travel through. Although, as yet, no large-scale expedition has been sent to that part of our world. Up to now it has been thought an area still not safe from the wars aftermath. It is thought that when hibernating the beast must be passive, but when awakened he is borne of a fury not seen on this land. An expedition must be sent, but there is so much that needs to be done first. For now they are best avoided.

"The Jal-Beast has a giant head, as you saw, in comparison to its body. Its arms are but extended appendages, seemingly worthless. It is this oddity that makes me think that they are a final unfinished experiment of the Teachers. How could a creature like this have existed in the past? However, it is said in the legends that they did.

"It is the mouth and the jaw that inspire the most terror. In its mouth are rows of razor-sharp teeth in a jaw large enough to swallow a dozen men.

"Its skin is best described as armored; giant scales impervious to all of our weapons. Only at its feet can the beast be found vulnerable. Perhaps a challenge left to us by the Teachers. With the havoc it generates the beast's vulnerability can rarely be reached, except by the gators. It was their attack on the giant's feet which led to our salvation. They were able to draw enough blood of the beast so that the carnivorous fish of the swamp overcame their fear of it and attacked it as well. Like hundreds of angry hornets, the Jal-Beast was helpless before them and it fled.

"These Jal-Beasts, when seen, live largely in the shallow areas of the jungle-swamp. But they have been known to leave these areas in search of food, especially after what we think is their hibernation. This is the time of the year we are in now. In these times, they have even been known to follow the rivers part-way into the mountains. However, while they have been known to do this, they seem to dislike those areas. They never stay long. They seem to need the water to keep their bodies moist. At times, the Jal-Beast has been seen from a distance to totally submerge itself into the water, to where only the eyes and the top of the head are visible. During such times they seem almost acquiescent.

"They possess a brain, and though small, it is one the Sage find almost impossible to control. Mind control of the lesser creatures is a gift given to us by the Teachers. But with such a gift lies a greater responsibility. In the past, an early Sage of the Order tried to use this gift on man to create his own dynasty. He was destroyed by the Teachers. My lack of ability to control its thoughts tells me that it is a very old creature, perhaps not even a lesser creature, but equivalent to man, in its own way."

Here Gar paused again and took a sip of mead. "Delicious," he spoke. "The Hold makes one of the best meads I have tasted." He seemed forgetful of the story, refilling and relighting his pipe.

"What of the Jal-Beast?" Thul finally asked, breaking the silence. Wolfe threw more wood on the fire and looked at Gar, who resumed speaking.

"The Jal-Beast, a strange and frightening monster, use their power for complete control over the Great Swamp. Yet, for all of their physical mastery, there are places they will not go. They will not cross nor tread upon the sandbars of white sand that lay scattered like islands through this swamp. It is upon these that we spend each night. They have been known to keep a party stranded for days while they circled such an island, always staying inside of the water's edge. These islands themselves do not seem natural; they seem out of place in the swamp. Placed by the Teachers, perhaps, but they have been here as long as the Jall. It seems that none of the denizens of the jungle swamp will cross onto these islands. Yes, I think that is it, pathways laid out by the Teachers for their Jall."

"Then why did we leave the safety of the island when we heard the Jal-Beast?" asked Cole.

"A question that deserves an answer," answered Gar. "Time, we have so little of it to prepare for what must come. Moreover, you, men of the Western Sea, have a place in it."

Gar began to speak of other things of the jungle-swamp, but gradually his voice lowered and he fell asleep, his old age catching up to him. The others took this as a sign to retire as well. The last of the gathered wood was stacked upon the fire and all slept. The men of *The Proctant* slept much closer to the fire than they had the night before. Zircon's long-rifle was tucked under one arm, ready for use if he was awakened abruptly.

They reached the outer edge of the swamp late on the third day. Their trip had been thrown several hours off by their encounter with the Jal-Beast.

The jungle-swamp came to a blunt end where they left it. One step was swamp, the next barren rock. And so they found themselves along the southern frontier of the jungle. Here the roots of the mountains seemed to stand directly against the onslaught of the water. While only parts of the frontier's rocky landscape were naturally barren, the whole length was now kept clear as a barrier to the swamp's many denizens, especially the Jal-Beasts. Before this barrier was created, the Jal-Beast was known to travel for miles up the mountain's rivers. Now it no longer did.

They were still several miles to the west from where the road to The Hold began. They continued in the boats along the edge of the swamp until they reached it.

The mutineers of *The Proctant* marveled at the clarity of the water. They were told by their hosts that this was due to the myriad springs and creeks that flowed into the swamp from the mountains. This influx of fresh water led to a large crab population that both the Jall and the people of The Hold valued and nurtured as an important part of their diet.

Just before they reached the wharf of the trading post at the start of the road to The Hold, the men of Jall tossed a crab pot over the side of one of the boats. Within minutes they hauled it back up, full of crabs over a foot across the shell. Their dinner for their trip back, they told their visitors from across the sea.

The logs were placed onto a wagon for their journey to The Hold. A second wagon was provided for the men of the expedition to reach the trading post, which lay two miles up a small creek from where the dock stood. They reached the trading post before nightfall and the men of the sea were surprised at how large it was. They were told that it seldom housed more than a few dozen men. They had expected something in line with the trading centers of some of their smaller towns.

This fortress was a vast, double-walled stockade of wood and stone. With large dry moats, it was built to withstand the attacks of the Jal-Beasts. From the splintered shards of wood that lay scattered around the post it was clear that these attacks were common. Bonfires lay stacked, ready to be lit in time of attack. Wolfe spoke of how during his grandfather's day this had been just a small post, a single-room building with space for few.

It was for the strength of their wood in the construction of these trading posts that The Hold put such value in the treated Jungle Swamp Palms. Never had a post constructed of the Swamp Palm been overrun by the Jal-Beast.

At the post the men of the caravan rested in comfortable beds at the inn. Here the men of *The Proctant* had their first taste of the swamp's crab. The crab was served with a bread almost sour in taste, with greens and fruit unknown to them. Figs, they were told.

In the morning supplies and wagons for the remainder of their journey waited for their use. They still had several days of travel left to reach The Hold, as Gar waited for some news. No longer would it be hazardous, though. It was a well-traveled and protected road they would follow.

The men of Jall would leave the next day. Though the Jall's journey would be swift without the need to transport the logs, about one day versus the three it took to arrive at the post, they expressed dismay when Gar announced he would continue on to The Hold. It was always helpful to travel with the Sage during the Jal-Beast season. To meet an old friend was his only word.

Chapter Four
Thul's Path

During the first night at the fort the men of *The Proctant* learned that things were not as friendly as they seemed between the peoples of this land. The men had gathered in the trading post's only tavern. Over their dark and rich-flavored ales (much stronger than the lighter brews they had back home), the men mostly listened to those around them. Cole and Thorium were especially interested in learning more than they had been told.

There seemed to be four distinctive people represented at the tavern: the Jall, those from the City of The Hold, those from the Southern Valley and the Lake, and a fourth people that they had not been told of nor encountered before; the Nomads of the plains to the south of the Valleys.

While these people worked together for purposes of trade, mostly controlled by the Jall, for the most part all four groups tended to distrust the others and stay apart in the tavern. Only the Sage such as Gar traveled freely among these peoples. And the Nomads of the plains showed even the Sage little in the way of trust.

The Nomads seemed the most distrustful of all and they looked at the newcomers with their disapproving eyes. They blamed much of their own problems on the Scholars of The Hold. Education beyond the most basic levels was viewed with suspicion. It was this ignorance in commerce that was often taken advantage of by the peoples of The Hold and the Jall. Only the Southern Valley and the City by the Lake treated the Nomads with some dignity and respect. Thul tried to reach out to a Nomad who sat near their table. He was treated to a rough grunt in response and the Nomad got up to sit with the others of his kind. Thul just shook his head as he sat down again with his colleagues.

The mutineers learned that the Jall and the people of The Hold were not without their own petty differences. A lot of loud discussions (arguments?) went on between the two sides. Each side wanted something the other had. The Hold wanted better access to the Western Sea, to gain more control over their trade. The resources of the seas were often lost to The Hold during trade discussions, a bargaining chip to the Jall. The Jall were not exactly free from the use of coercion to maintain their trade monopolies. And the Jall wanted dry land to call their own. With The Hold controlling all of those lands around the Great Swamp to the South and the East, those ways were blocked.

Thorium caught something else, deeper rooted, in the talk around them. The Jall and the people of The Hold were both survivors of the Great War, protected by the Teachers in the safety of The Hold. The Nomads and the people of the Valleys and the City by the Lake were survivors of the Great War' and the thousand years of winter on the outside, in the elements that killed so many. Each still held resentment towards The Hold's survivors over this. And between The Hold and the Jall there was more. The Hold had been the protected people, the Chosen. However, it was another group with them, the Jall, that were given special gifts by the Teachers. It was The Hold that was given the responsibility to protect something only spoken of in whispers, *The Library*. However, it was the Jall that would come to dominate trade in the region with their unique gifts. This jealousy between the two frequently came to the surface with too much drink.

The People of the Lake sat alone and to themselves. They seemed more than happy to have others dictate trade terms to them, one less thing to have to worry about with the White pressing them once again from the north. There seemed a sadness about them that hung over their heads like an overcast day.

That *The Proctant's* mutineers had arrived during a time of comparative peace in this land. This was mostly due to the trade negotiations for the year having concluded a short time before. The men heard whispered rumors that the Sage spoke of this time as The Time of Change the Teachers had prophesized, when all of these lands would become one again.

Several of The Hold came over to their guests, to welcome them to the vastness of these mountains. Carafes of ale were brought to the table. Wolfe himself came to their table to share tales. He noticed the eyes widen as the shipmates heard and understood the rivalries around them.

"Don't you have disagreements amongst yourselves where you're from?" Wolfe asked the men.

Cole started speaking to those around them from The Hold in answer. "There was a time, not too long ago, that we were like you in this part of the world; rival tribes, each fighting for superiority over the others around them. Even with the memories still with us from the time of the Great War, violence often broke out between us."

Those of The Hold nodded their heads over this. "That is often the case here as well," one spoke aloud.

Cole continued, "There was great wealth around us, in the land, the waters of the world, the remnants of what came before. Each tribe was jealous at what they perceived was the unfair division of the world around them. One tribe had most of the trading ships, another farmland to grow food, another had energy wealth, more had other things of value. Each seemed to have too much of one thing and not enough of the others. You would think this would have made for more trade and cooperation between them. Yet each tribe was unable to see the benefit of joining together in the common good. Each fought the others to hold onto what they had. And each fought to take from the others what they did not. It seemed the lessons of the Great War had not been learned." The others around the table listened intently, nodding again in agreement.

"One day a man, known only as Simon, walked among the people of what would become our Confederation. Each of our tribes had a strong distrust of any sort of central style government. To many among us, that was the chief cause we are taught of the Great War. Simon showed us how much great wealth we shared as a people and told us stories about how we were a proud and unified people before the War. He spoke of the equality of freedom and how we could join together once more to share our bounty amongst ourselves and the world around us.

"Many came to join him as he walked. He spoke of a time of peace and law. Jealousies seemed to vanish when he visited a tribe. The people cried out for peace and for Simon to lead them. "To the promised land!" they called. But Simon said no to that. It would be the people of the tribes who would lead themselves. He was only there to guide them."

Wolfe spoke up at that point. "Sounds like your Simon was one of the Sage."

"If he was, he never used that word. It was just a short time ago he walked among us. Once the elected leaders of the tribes founded the Confederation, he disappeared as he had arrived, without notice. I met him once as a young man. He seemed ageless, yet still a young man. When he spoke, all listened as one, but he carried no staff like your Sage, and he spoke naught of your Teachers.

"But thanks to the teachings of Simon, we became one as a nation. We are One Tribe, undivided, adding our neighbors freely to our ranks as we grow and they wish to join. And with the value we show, being one people, more and more join our Confederation."

"Are you ruled by a King or a Council?" a Jall asked.

"We are ruled by neither. Each tribe maintains its own independence and freedom within its domains. For those dealings of interest to us all, we are governed by the laws of our land, set forth by our elected representatives to the Confederation. Other than these laws of our one Nation, each citizen of the tribes has their own freedoms and responsibilities, each set by themselves and their own tribe."

"Anarchy!" said one of The Hold. The people of The Hold, the Jall and the Southern Valleys looked on with amazement at these newcomers and their ideas. To the Nomads, however, these strangers were looked at with a newfound respect.

That same night, in a secluded spot near the trading post, two Sage met, Gar and Tor. Tor had traveled for two days after leading the exodus from the caverns to meet with Gar. The news he carried was too important to wait.

The exodus had gone well and what remained of the Northern Valley's human population had found sanctuary in Nourne and Erson.

The two men shared the dark, flavored beverage favored by the Sage whenever they met. Rare now, and expensive, pressed from roasted beans gathered to the south, the Sage found the drink invigorating. The Sage knew stories from before the War that told of this "presso" once being the favored drink of the common man.

After exchanging pleasantries and common news from the lands they had recently visited, the two men focused their words on the prophecies of the Teachers.

"It's true, then, the birth of the second heads among the White has begun. That is truly troubling news. The Teachers warned us of this coming," said Gar.

"I had heard rumors, however, during the rescue I witnessed it twice myself. As yet the White may be unaware of its nature. What of the prophecies, of those from beyond the Western Sea, bringing peace to all of the people? Are you sure, Gar, that you have read the signs correctly?" asked Tor.

"I don't see how I could have found anything else. Torn apart by adversity, their mutiny, the involvement of the White..."

"I don't understand, even today," Tor interrupted, "why we couldn't tell those of Nourne the Teachers' prophecy of the White. How many lives could have been saved?"

"You remember the warnings we were given. The prophecies of the future represented the best possible outcome of the timeline. It was our job as the Order of the Sage to recognize each stage and intervene only then to move the people around us to the next stage. Is Phelix still an issue?" asked Gar.

"Now that we have entered the next stage, no, he spent so much time among the cavern's few survivors of the White's atrocities, witnessing so much death and unable to do anything. But now that it is time to end the rule of the Myk, he seems stronger."

Gar lowered his voice in response. "He was given the worst assignment of us all."

"The Teachers felt him the strongest of us," Tor reminded Gar.

"To survive what he has witnessed, I'm not sure I could have done so in his place. To have to stand back and watch everything take place around him. It would have been so easy for him to effect change," Gar said.

"The strength of Phelix," smiled Tor.

"Yes, his strength, but I feel his time among us is coming to a close. We have lost so many. I have other news as well from the stories the men of *The Proctant* have been telling."

"That of the Lost Sage?" asked Tor, excitedly.

"Yes, they speak of Simon."

"It was so long ago that we last heard from him. Generations have passed. Do you know what happened?" Tor asked Gar.

"From the stories I can only guess what we have always feared. He has left the Order of the Sage and interfered with what has happened on the other continent."

"A sign of weakness, or his own strength," mused Tor.

"I remember when he was sent out alone. Then no further contact except the occasional cryptic message."

They both paused briefly before Tor spoke again. "Yet the Teachers seemed to expect that, otherwise, why would *He who would come to lead* come from that continent and not here."

"Could Simon have been given instructions different from our own?" asked Gar.

"It seems unlikely, but..."

"Still too many questions for my liking. When will he be brought to The Hold?" Gar questioned Tor.

"That will be up to Locklear."

"Do you know why he didn't join us?"

"Preparations, he said. He has to be sure which one he selects. He said that there are signs in The Hold that will direct him to the right one," Tor said.

"The son of Simon."

"Yes."

It was several days before the trip to The Hold and the City by the Lake would take place. This gave the men of *The Proctant* more time to get to know their guests and others at the trading post. They even encountered for the first time the followers of Ala. It was said that before the Great War they were among the most numerous people in the world. It was also told in the stories of before the War that it was they who began the final war. For that the sect was shunned and it had few followers.

Newcomers arrived from the City by the Lake and brought news as well. This changed the spirits of their kindred at the post. The decision had been made to move against the Myk. Nourne and the Southern Valley were as one again and the survivors of the North were safe among them.

This news brought cheers in the tavern of the Trading Post. Those of The Hold began to prepare to head home, to join those ready to strike down the terror that was the White. The previous war there, the civil war, had been thought purely an internal war of the Valleys. Now, as this news came, The Hold understood what was at stake. And their numbers would be needed against the White.

As the mutineers heard the noise of a war against the White they, too, joined the cause. Who knows if they would ever get a chance to return home. Here was a chance to gain some revenge for their lost comrades, and to Zircon's mind, a chance to show his prowess in war. Moreover, thought Zircon, this newly-conquered land would need a king.

These new visitors to the Trading Post also brought welcome news to the shipmates. These men had heard of other visitors from the Western Sea now among them. They didn't know their names, but the mutineers of *The Proctant* learned that three more of their number remained alive. This gave the men a new impetus to begin the next step of their journey.

While these stories were spreading throughout the trading post of the war and the other survivors of the mutiny, Thul continued his attempts to meet with the Nomads of the plains. Nervous, lacking of trust for outsiders, they first looked upon Thul as yet another person trying to take advantage of their ways. Eventually, as they saw how Thul's own people treated him, they came to welcome Thul amongst them as a friend.

On the day of the leaving they all gathered together at the tavern for an early meal. What had started as a small expedition led by Gar and Tor, was now immense as word of the war against the White spread. Jall, Nomads, the people of The Hold, returning citizens of the City by the Lake and the Southern Valley, and even members of the followers of Ala joined the cause. More were assembling at the City by the Lake and Nourne. It seemed the White had made many enemies in their short time in the Northern Valley.

The men of *The Proctant* left on carts drawn by large ox-like animals similar to what they had in the Confederation. This was a slow means of travel but it meant large distances could be covered without break. The trip would take three days, with lodging houses along the way for stops. Now, with so many on the roads north, the inns would be crowded. This was no longer just a trade commission, but a people on the move, an army on its march.

The road the men traveled was well worn. Following the old pre-war route, the surface was mostly smooth, with its concrete mostly intact. Large gaps were found in sections of the ways. Holes and caved-in sections were a danger as well. Detours had to be made around the city skeletons that remained from before the War. The men were told that although the need for metal made these extinct cities valuable, few had the courage to challenge the dangers that lay within them. Still, even with the gaps and the detours, the travel was fairly easy.

As the caravan made its way up the foothills of the mountains the men of *The Proctant* were able to see more of the land around them. At one point, as the road took a sharp turn to climb a small mountain (a new section of the road built around the remains of a pre-war city below), a vast panorama opened up behind them. Although there was a haze on the horizon, the men could see the ocean in the distance. They could see the vast expanse that was the lowland jungle swamp. To the far east, across the jungle swamp, they could see a soft blue light on the horizon. They were told by Gar that this had been one of the homes of the Teachers.

To the south and the east they saw high mountains, much taller than those in their Confederation. It was only to the west, beyond the Great River and the Confederation's western border that they had known of such mountains. It was toward these towering mountains that they now traveled. Wildlife existed in abundance all around them. The wildlife stayed clear of the ways they traveled, although the Great Wild Beasts could be seen at times following alongside them. There seemed far more varieties of animals than in their homelands. Gar told the men of the many zoos that had been in almost every city before the War. While many of these animals died during the moments of the War and in the thousand years of darkness that followed, a few survived. These survivors produced their own mutations and whole new species now roamed the land alongside the old. Both old and new species had one thing in common. Each was more intelligent than the ones that had come before, and more dangerous. Yet the Nomads walked among these wild animals without fear.

At the end of the first day a new group joined the march. Like the followers of Ala, this new group stayed towards the back of the caravan, near the followers, but separate from them. This new group carried banners with a red cross. Gar told the men that this new group called themselves the 'Saders.' Like the followers of Ala, they were another sect of followers of The *One True God*. It was said that before the war these followers of The One True God numbered most of the population of the world. However, the blame for the War was placed solely on these groups and today the followers of The One True God were mostly shunned and were now few in numbers.

The men of *The Proctant* were as amazed at this division among these people as the men of The Hold and the Jall had been by their laws.

In their own lands, the Confederation, both the followers of Christ and Allah coexisted together among all of the peoples of their lands, though even in the Confederation they were few in numbers. In the Confederation, as well as these lands, the old religions were blamed for much of what had happened.

It seemed that this new war, to remove the blight that was the White, was bringing all of the people of this land together. A just war Gar had stated. But, Thorium thought, was any war a just war?

They crossed a high metal bridge, still standing from before the Great War, though repaired many times by the Jall, and entered a small valley and its village. It was here they delivered the wood. As the caravan crossed the village, it seemed to fill the valley. The lodgings of the trade route's inns quickly filled and the villagers opened their doors to the travelers. Here the White had no friends. Barriers had begun to break down during the caravan's march among the disparate groups throughout the day. Though this army still tended to stay to themselves, there were just too many now for there not to be more interaction between them. Even those outcasts before the march began, Ala, 'Sader and Nomad, were made welcome by the village. As more trickled in during the night rumors grew of new people who had joined the march against the White. Even the seldom-seen Coastal People were joining the quest. Like the Nomads, the Teachers had left the Coastal People to their own devices after the War. Unlike the Nomads, the Coastal People were known for their education and enlightenment. They were a closed society, however, and seldom left their own lands. Like the Nomads they shared no love of the Jall and The Hold. It was in support of their distant cousins to the north that they would come.

The men of *The Proctant* spent the night together in the home of a villager. The family was unsure how to treat their guests. They had heard the many rumors of these men and what was to come. The prophecies of the Teachers were spreading beyond just the Order of the Sage. In the end, the men insisted that they be treated as long-lost friends and the family leapt at that. All sat crowded at the common table for a feast of game and ale. The couple's children could not keep away from the strangers and constantly asked them questions about the strange lands they had visited. When their parents scolded them to leave these visitors alone, the men of *The Proctant* laughed and happily answered as best they could, all of the children's questions. It brought a levity and hope that they had been missing, though it made Pluto long for his own home and children. Was he now considered lost by them? When it came time for rest, the family offered the men their beds, but were politely refused. The mutineers spent the night sleeping on the floor of their hosts, covered in furs.

Early the next morning, before the rest of the town arose, Gar and Tor were joined by Locklear at a small tavern on the edge of the town. Locklear, as the Sage of The Hold, was the oldest of The Order of the Sage. He was in charge of The Library of The Hold, as well as teaching the next generation of scholars. Locklear brought with him the words that he had written down during the time of the Teachers, in particular those regarding the time of *Unification* and the identifying marks of the outsider who would lead their people in the future.

The Sage spoke quietly for hours while sharing goat's milk and small grain cakes. Repeatedly, they took turns going over the papers, looking for the slightest clue that would help decide their next actions. At times Tor's temper rose as he and Locklear argued mundane points in the script. Tor had brought along his own notes of the period in question as well. Gar remained aloof as he listened to the points of both. One of two men it had to be, but which one? The obvious or the other? Two men, one a natural leader, but the other? Around him so much seemed to take place.

Finally, Gar interrupted the other two by smacking his pipe on the table.

"It has to be him. There can be no doubt. Not an instigator, nor a leader, but it seems everything revolves around him."

Tor interrupted this with one last glimpse at the papers before him. "But, a leader he is not. From the words of the travelers, he was not one of them. Only a last-minute addition before the ship set sail."

"What are we looking for, a leader or the one who will guide the people to their next stage when we are gone?"

"The son of Simon, the Lost Sage?"

"It seems likely now, from the readings," added Locklear.

"Why would the Teachers send Simon into exile?" asked Tor.

"Was it to exile, or to prepare us for what was to come?" asked Gar.

"Thul, then, it must be. The son none of us could have, but Simon did. Do we know yet if Simon survives in his exile?" Locklear asked.

"That seems to matter not," answered Tor.

"And yet..." Locklear responded.

"A question that remains as yet unanswered. If Thul is indeed the son of Simon, as we are now agreed, what about the other, also foreseen by the Teachers." Gar raised his head as he spoke this. Tor and Locklear looked at each other, eyebrows raised in question, before Locklear spoke.

"That issue remains vague. That he who will come shall have a true brother alongside him. But a few lines I wrote of this, more an aside from what a Teacher said. And how to recognize this second son of Simon, the instigator. I see none among this group that would fit the requirement."

"Perhaps one of those on the island, Argonia. We know that they have a major role in what is to come," answered Tor.

"Perhaps," spoke Gar once more, "this is a part of the future hidden from us by the Teachers. To question why is, I think, a needless task for now. The immediate future is upon us. Already the Unification begins. And it is to the Myk that we owe this."

"Agreed," said Tor and Locklear in unison.

"We each know our tasks," added Tor.

Locklear spoke now. "Of war, even with the White, I take no part. I will take Thul to The Library of The Hold and begin his instruction."

"And I shall guide the peoples of this land to erase the vermin that are the White. And you Gar?" Tor spoke to Gar.

"I will guide this caravan, first to The Hold, and then the City by the Lake. Once I have accomplished these tasks, I will seek out others of our Order. The Time of Change has begun."

Two more days' journey and the caravan continued its march to the north. The most memorable part of this journey was the arrival of a plains people from the south of The Hold, the Shiaps. None walked on foot. All rode camels, ungainly but tough mounts that matched their riders. They were known throughout these lands as a race of warriors that few dared to face. They carried but a single weapon, a long pike with a crescent moon attached at the end, its edges razor sharp. Their faces were painted red and blue and the camels they rode wore the only armor. Seven hundred they numbered, sent by their king to aide their brothers to the north.

At the entrance to a narrow pass two towers of new construction, towering high above the cliffs face, rose on either side. They were built with but one enemy in mind, the ever-present White. The towers were enclosed at the top, with the highest thirty feet covered in openings for the archers of the city.

Late in the third day, the party passed by the towers and shortly thereafter the narrow passage opened up into a wide, circular valley. Even here, in the interior of the valley, as the men looked up on the ridgeline that encircled the city, towers commanded all approaches to the City of The Hold. Although it was not a walled city, the nature of the valley and its surrounding cliffs gave it the character of one.

As the caravan entered the city and disappeared within its confines, the men of *The Proctant* saw a single large monument topped in blue crystal by the Jall. It was six-sided, built of white granite, and towered thirty feet above the city's main square. The blue crystal at the top came to a point, and a standard, as yet unseen by the travelers, was carried on top. The pennant was almost translucent in color, but the overwhelming constant was blue. It was here, they were told, the entrance to The Hold that the survivors of the city and the Jall emerged from a thousand years earlier.

As a group, the men, led by Gar, went to a local marketplace to eat and find lodging for the next few days. Then it would be time to travel the final leg, to the Southern Valley and the City by the Lake. Already the men saw many different parties, large and small, leave The Hold and begin the next stage of the journey. The Shiap's camel riders of the southern plains only stopped long enough to gain the supplies they needed for the weeklong journey ahead. Then they continued their march without pause.

Gar told the men of *The Proctant* that they would have two days of rest before it would be time for them to begin the next leg of their journey.

Locklear awakened Thul early the next morning. Thul had no idea who this man was; his name had only been mentioned in passing by Gar as another Sage. Locklear didn't exactly awaken Thul as much as he just sat in a chair observing him as Thul slept, until he awakened on his own, disturbed by the presence that was Locklear.

"Who are you?" Thul asked groggily as he sat up on the side of his bed, sword in hand.

"Just a friend, no reason to be concerned. My name is Locklear. I think Gar mentioned me to you."

"Huh…"

Locklear gave Thul time to awaken fully. He then spoke in a kind manner. "It's time for you to begin your own journey. Dress and come with me."

"I'm going nowhere, except with my shipmates," Thul exclaimed.

"Shipmates? An unusual choice of words for you. Were you not just a passenger on the ship?"

"I sought passage, yes. However, it was a working passage. I had to leave, quickly."

"Yes, you did. The impetus for your trip was great. Without your passage *The Proctant* would still be sailing on its journey."

"What?" Thul retorted. "How is the mutiny my fault? I didn't take part."

"And yet you found yourself on the side of those who were cast off of that ship."

"They had their own reasons. Their reasons were not mine. The captain had told stories about me. He placed the blame on me. My only choice was to join the mutineers in the boats."

"And through that providence, you end up here with me, today." Locklear finished.

Both men just looked at each other for several minutes. Thul was dressed just in his cotton nightshirt, hair disheveled from the night's sleep, and beard just beginning to grow in. He had always been clean-shaven before the voyage and had attempted to remain so while at sea. Now, since their arrival on land, he had let his beard grow. Locklear was dressed in drab gray clothing, his own beard neatly trimmed just below his chin. Both his cheeks were clean of the beard. He held his hands in front of himself and his fingers seemed well manicured. Although dressed in gray, he carried an air of cleanliness about himself.

Thul compared the outward appearance of the two Sage, Gar and this Locklear, the only two Sage he had met as yet. Thul had understood that they were all about the same age. "The gift of Longevity," Gar had told him. Thul would have thought that such longevity would be more a curse than a blessing. Locklear looked much older than Gar as he sat in the chair, slightly bent over. Besides the clothing, there was a general grayness about Locklear. While Gar had seemed alive and generally full of energy, leading their expedition as he did, Locklear seemed to exist on a slower path.

Locklear finally broke the silence. "What do you know of your parents?" he asked Thul.

"My mother was a seamstress. Of my father I know little. I would see him a few days a year when I was very young. I barely remember his appearance. We had no pictures of him. That seemed strange but my mother just told me that was his way. My mother said he was a trader who wandered the western lands. Though they loved each other, each led a life not for the other. And there were whispers I heard, later in life, that he was a wanted man, that my father had broken a serious law and had to remain hidden in the west."

"I am told that you met Simon, the unifier of your lands. Is that true?"

"Yes. Looking back at the experience ten years ago, it seems odd the way it happened. My mother had died the year before and I was visiting her grave. I had a restless nature about me then. My mother said I got my restlessness from my father, who was unable to stay in any one place for long."

"What happened?" Locklear asked Thul.

"Simon was on horseback, as he was wont to travel, with several of his companions. As I said, I was visiting my mother's grave, the last time I visited it before this journey began. Simon and his party saw me. I was but a short distance from where the poorest of the graves were located.

"Simon looked my way and paused. Then he got off his horse and walked past where I was kneeling to my mother's grave. He carried flowers that one of his party had handed him; a colorful bouquet of flowers, of a type my mother had loved. He lay the flowers on my mother's grave as I watched. Then he turned to me and placed his hand on my shoulder, bidding me rise. No other words were said, but I remember now, there seemed to be a tear in his eye."

Locklear got up from his chair and moved to sit next to Thul on the bed. He turned slightly to face him and quietly spoke. "Was there any more to this story?"

"No," answered Thul.

"Protecting you to the end it seems."

"Me?"

"There are many who would want the son of Simon dead, even among the Sage. He broke our most cardinal law and left the order. And it seems he had a child, as forbidden by the Teachers."

"Simon?"

"Yes, your father, Simon, the lost Sage of the Order. Exiled by the Teachers from our lands, or so we thought. Now, maybe our thinking must change. Not exiled, but sent on his own journey, apart from the Order."

Thul looked at Locklear as if he was crazy. His father from the Order of the Sage? It seemed both daunting and impossible. And yet?

"Did you know Simon?" Thul asked, more than a little confused by what he was hearing.

"We were all together when the Teachers created the Order of the Sage. It was right after The Hold was opened and the people of it reentered the world. He always seemed different, somehow always apart from the rest of us. As the Teachers gave us our gifts and told us of our responsibilities, Simon often stood back. 'Their ways are not our ways,' he would often say. Then one day he was gone. The Teachers, as long as they were among us, forbid he be spoken of. Most thought him dead, punished by the Teachers for his thoughts, or maybe a victim of one of their experiments. Gar and I always thought different, but we had to keep our thoughts to ourselves concerning Simon. Not dead, we thought, just gone, on his own journey, another path taken. Now we know the truth and you are here to complete the circle."

Thul just sat there quietly, shaken by the words. It seemed to make sense, and it clarified so many of his thoughts and dreams, the restless wanderer.

"Come, it's time to go, before the others arise. Your path is now different from theirs," Locklear said as he rose and walked to the door, motioning Thul after him. As Thul rose and then dressed, he reached for his weapons, given to him by the mutineers as they had boarded the boats and left *The Proctant*.

"Leave those; you have no need for weapons where we are going." Locklear said.

"Where are you taking me?" asked Thul with trepidation.

"To The Hold and its Library to begin your education," Locklear answered.

Locklear held the door open as Thul walked through it. Then Thul paused, looking back, and then forward, waiting for Locklear to lead the way. He saw his weapons laid out on the bed. Would the others understand? Or would they consider him a coward like during the mutiny, abandoning a fight before it began. Zircon would certainly think so.

Later that morning, Cole, Pluto, Zircon, and Thorium were sitting around a trading post not far from where they were staying. Their animated discussion centered on one thing. Where was Thul? When Thorium had gone to Thul's room to collect him that morning, he had found the door to his room ajar and his weapons still lying on his bed. There was no sign of a struggle, but the innkeeper had not seen him leave. Zircon was convinced that Thul had gone into hiding to avoid the coming fight. The others didn't think this likely, but with all of the commotion in the city, there was little the authorities would, or could, do at this point to try and find him.

Gar found them engaged in this discussion after searching several taverns for them. With all of this recent activity, Gar was finding his mental clarity somehow clouded. This was a new phenomenon to Gar. Could it be just fatigue or could another factor be at work. It seemed that there was something pressing against his mind. When he had asked Tor and Locklear about this at their meeting, they had said that they had felt nothing. This was one of Gar's gifts from the Teachers, this mental clearness, the ability to *connect the dots,* so to speak. There was definitely something here besides the fatigue.

Thorium saw Gar enter the tavern and called him over to them. To these men Gar's inattentiveness just seemed business as usual for the Sage.

"Gar, are we glad to see you. Thul has gone missing. And we cannot seem to find any help in this city to try to find him. When I went to his room the door was open and his weapons were still there. No one saw him leave." Thorium spoke these words in quick sentences, seemingly agitated over Thul's disappearance.

Gar was unconcerned over the missing man. His mind was still working on the hindrance he was feeling. The White? Two heads born where there was just one. A second head more powerful once the first head is removed. Cloudy judgments could be taken. The warnings of the Teachers of the second heads. All of this passed through Gar's mind in just a second.

Cole spoke now, with urgency. "Did you hear Thorium, Gar, Thul is missing."

"Thul, yes, nothing to worry about, he was taken by Locklear, one of my Order. His path is now different from yours."

"A different path?" Zircon scowled.

"Yes. Now he must learn quickly what the Order is about. Then it is his father's path he must follow in these lands."

"His father's path?" questioned Thorium.

"Yes," was all Gar finished with before lapsing into silence. There were so many questions as yet. The Teachers had said so much, but at the same time said so little. This was a puzzle that they had laid out for the best chance of the survival of mankind. It was to Gar that the other members of the Order looked to determine their best course of action. For the first time the future seemed clouded to Gar. Of Thul he was certain. However, what was missing? What had the Teachers left out? What hadn't they known? Or had they known and kept secret?

Finally knowing that Thul was safe, the men turned their attention back to their own future. Aware now that there were other survivors of their party, it became an issue of discussion over what would be the best next step for them. Up to now it was always the events around them that seemed to be dictating their limited actions. Now it was their turn to begin the task of controlling their own destinies.

For now the direction seemed clear. The next step of their journey, whether by choice or circumstance, was the City by the Lake. There they would be able to find out more about their missing colleagues. It was once they arrived at the City by the Lake that a decision would have to be made concerning this upcoming war with the White. All agreed, even Zircon (now that Thul was no longer part of the equation), that they should all stay together for now. Zircon remained the strongest supporter for joining the action against the White. It was in a fight that he could best show his worth. Pluto, the oldest, with a family back home, was the one least in favor. He remembered the conflicts back home before the coming of Simon and the Confederation. However, whatever they decided for the future, even he agreed it was time for them to stay together. The question remained for all of the mutineers, just how much control did they really have of their future?

Wolfe found the men of *The Proctant* later that same day at the Public House near the men's lodging. The men appreciated the heat from the roaring central fire as the fall weather cooled. The daytime temperatures rarely reached the conditions back at their homeland. The discussion had moved on from their immediate future and the future of the Whites: Was the extermination of the Whites as a race something they could support? It was an issue they split on, comparing their observations on the many people of these lands they had encountered so far. This was a fractured land, probably comparable to the Confederation before the Tribes united. While the people of The Hold seemed closest to themselves, and the bio-engineered Jall the furthest, it was the peoples of the south, the Nomads (where ignorance was the rule of law) and the camel riders of the southern plains (who embraced a strange mix of intelligence, education, and warfare) that most attracted the attention of the shipmates. It was more than ironic to the men that while the Jall and The Hold seemed most friendly, it was in the brutal honesty of these southern people that they gave the most trust. These people had no hidden agenda, unlike the Jall, The Hold and the Southern Valley, which seemed to have nothing but hidden agenda's towards the men. Could even The Order of the Sage be trusted? Who was there who could look after the best interests of the men of *The Proctant*?

Wolfe greeted each of the men with a hearty handshake and asked them their plans for the next day. Thorium answered for the group that as of yet they had no plans.

"Great, then tomorrow you will all come with me on a hunt."

"A hunt!" Zircons eyes picked up on that one.

"Tomorrow, early, a hunting party will be leaving for the day to go after a Mountain Lion that has been threatening our southern passes."

Picturing the small mountain lions of his homeland, even Zircon wondered what the challenge of this hunt would be. Wolfe explained with a nervous laugh, "These are not the small creatures that you describe; these are the descendants of the creatures that survived the Great War. Before the War they had been kept captive in zoos, caged for the people's enjoyment. Though most perished in the War and the aftermath, a few, the strongest and most intelligent, survived. From these few came our greatest predator, the Giant of the Mountain Lions. Some surpass fifteen feet in length and when hunting in packs only the most skilled hunters can hope to defeat these beasts in a fight. A fight to survive it is on almost equal terms. While we think this is a lone male, not yet with a pride of its own, more times than naught these lions have ambushed our hunters. Now we hunt them only in large, prepared hunting parties. One of these is leaving tomorrow."

Zircon jumped at this chance to challenge his skill. He had been disappointed by the challenges of the Great Swamp's denizens, excluding, of course, the Jal-Beast. Here was a chance, once again, to prove his skill with the long-rifle. Pluto and Cole begged out of the expedition, both using the still valid excuse that their bodies were still healing and needed rest. That left Thorium. The other three looked back and forth at each other before he answered. The men were fearful of what Zircon might do if left to his own devices.

"I'll go," Thorium finally answered, getting a quick look from Zircon. 'A hunting accident? No, not yet, it still isn't time,' Zircon thought.

"Great!" Wolfe said as he got up from the heavy wood chair he had been sitting in. "Meet us at the South Gate at daybreak."

It was the morning of the hunt and Zircon and Thorium had expected to see a handful of woodsmen and their mounts. What they found was over 50 heavily armed men and the wagons to transport them. Both men were told by the hunters that in the past smaller groups used to go out to pursue the Mountain Lions, but many times none would return from the smaller hunting parties. Later, when their remains were found, it was usually with obvious signs of ambush that no one believed could have come from the Mountain Lions. However, when several different survivors of the attacks went public with their accounts of what had happened, there could be no denying the intelligence of the big cats.

Hunting dogs had been used at one time in this hunt, but the dogs were no match for the lions either, with very few surviving the hunt. Now it was just the trackers and the cross-bowmen, heavily armed and in formation, that dared to take on the Mountain Lions in the wilds of the mountain's passes they dwelled in.

As the party set out, Thorium asked one of the hunters a question that was bothering him. It was said the Nomads lived in peace with these wildcats. In fact they had seen it in the march, a wildcat walking with three or four Nomads. At times the wildcats seemed attached to an individual in the Nomad camp. Nevertheless, here in the mountains it seemed a life and death struggle was taking place. He was given no answer and the one he asked seemed to look upon the question with resentment.

The hunting party reached about halfway up the pass by mid-morning, where it found the staging area. From here the party would travel by foot. The staging area was a wide expanse, cleared of trees, just off the way. A hunting lodge, crafted of the swamp-logs of the Jall, stood at the back of it, close to the wooded, rocky expanse of the mountains. Rough in appearance and very simple, it would comfortably hold a dozen people if the weather turned bad. The hunting party moved their equipment to a stack alongside of the building. Here it would be broken down, each man carrying equal weight. This seemed more a military expedition than a hunt to Thorium and Zircon. 'Where is the skill of the hunt?' Zircon thought to himself.

A dozen men would stay behind to guard the wagons. Zircon was asked if this was due to thieves in the area. No, he was told. The wildcats here posed the only danger, aside from the occasional foray of the Whites. Thorium realized the hunt was not for him and decided to stay with the wagons. His vision and hearing would do the most good here. One of those staying behind with the wagons opened the door to the lodge. A fire was built in its fireplace and a meal would be prepared for the hunters' return. Casks of ale were stored for parties such as this one.

As Zircon heard the stories of previous hunts and the intelligence and cunning of the Great Mountain Lions, he relished the words he was hearing. Here, after all, was a foe worthy of his skills with the long-rifle. The more Zircon heard these stories, mostly spoken in whispers by the other hunters, the greater the smile that spread across his face.

As the hunters began the hike up the rocky trail they hoped would lead them to their quarry, their nerves tightened. Spread out, single file, along the narrow trail, they all were vulnerable to the lions' attack. Visibility was limited along the trail, weaving itself between rocky formations and through dense patches of trees. Even the underbrush seemed to work against them here. Poison plants were a danger to any who wandered off the trail, as even the slightest touch could bring agony for weeks. Most expected some to die during the hunt, since it was rare that a hunting party returned intact, especially if it was a pride and not just a single male, as was thought.

The trail became rockier as they ascended and more difficult to hike. On the positive, it had opened up from the narrow ravine they had followed so far and trees were becoming sparse. Greater visibility meant less chance of being ambushed by the lions. One of the trackers found a fresh paw print on a crushed plant alongside the trail. The cat they hunted had been through this very trail they hiked only hours before. With tracks so fresh, the hunters all cocked their cross-bows. They might only get one chance at this. Zircon, with his confidence rising, moved towards the front of the group. The other hunters were more than happy to let this brash fellow that few knew move to the forward position. The trackers slowed their pursuit as well. They were still searching for signs of the number they faced. Was the male alone?

About an hour later, they spotted the Great Mountain Lion on the top of the ridgeline. A lone male, it looked their way and then turned to move away. With the range of Zircon's long-rifle, more than double that of the other hunter's cross-bows, the mountain lion never had a chance. With his sharpshooters' eye, Zircon took careful aim, gently squeezed the trigger for a single shot, and the great cat fell over where it stood, a bullet through its heart.

Zircon raised his long-rifle over his shoulder in triumph. He shouted a primeval guttural scream. He expected accolades from his fellow hunters. Instead they looked at him aghast. This wasn't hunting. This was not the equal odds they craved, cat versus man in a fight of honor. This was a slaughter of an animal turning away.

As Zircon started to climb the rise to collect his trophy, the others watched him go, then they turned their backs to him to return to the lodge. All were quiet. Only Wolfe went with Zircon. He remembered

Gar's words that these people's ways were not his. And he had promised Gar he would watch over them.

Zircon, in his mind, thought their actions were those of jealous hunters and trudged onward. When he arrived at the cat, its eyes had remained open. They seemed to stare at Zircon with a single word, "Why?"

Neither man was equipped to deal with the size of the giant cat. There was no way to bring Zircon's trophy back to the lodge. Instead Wolfe brought out of his pack two shovels.

"We bury him here, in dignity, as he deserves."

"What!" Zircon exclaimed. "He's my kill, my trophy. He will find a place of honor on the wall of the lodge. That is where he will gain his dignity. The cat comes with me."

"To do what. Are you such a man as to kill a helpless creature, not for food, but for glory? Is that what makes you a man? We garner no such trophies on our hunts. The lodge carries no tributes to such a killing."

"Helpless!" Zircon almost shouted. "Look at those claws. Alive he would rip us apart."

"Up close, yes, that would be a fair fight. But he had turned, to leave the valley, these mountains. At the range you used it was as helpless as a housecat."

"You all came to hunt it."

"Hunt it, yes. However, a hunt does not always end in a kill. Now we bury it."

"You bury it, but not with my help," shouted Zircon, not understanding as he started back down the trail towards the distant lodge. "I came to hunt the Lion. To kill it. That is what hunting is, the kill. And I did it without a single loss of life."

As Zircon proudly hiked back, he passed several others of the hunters on their way to join Wolfe in the burial of the cat. Zircon sneered at them with scorn as he passed them. "Weaklings," he thought under his breath.

At the top of the ridge, the burial plot dug with much work, the hunters stood over the fallen Great Mountain Lion. Quietly, each in his own words, the men paid their tribute to the fallen warrior. The Lion was buried at a depth the scavengers would be unable to find. Then they, in turn, began the long march back to the lodge. Each of the other hunters looked at Wolfe and thought the same silent question. 'Why did you bring such a man to this hunt?'

From the way the Jall and the people of this city spoke of The Hold, Thul had expected to see something on par with what they had witnessed in the Jall city. Instead, he was led to a small concrete building with a single large metal door. There was no adornment. A single monument at the entrance they saw when they entered the city was the only thing that marked this location as something special.

"This was the entrance to what was our people's salvation. Built entirely by the Teachers, The Hold was our home to protect us from the Great War and its aftermath. For over a thousand years we dwelt beneath the land at this place, awaiting the time when we could venture forth once again," Locklear stated.

Thul just listened to Locklear.

"On the outside it is the same since our Teachers built it to withstand what was to come. We will be going inside, where none but the Order of the Sage and its scholars can enter."

"You say that I am the son of Simon, a Sage. But do you really have any proof? Is my story enough?" questioned Thul.

"You will have your proof of your lineage once we are able to gain entry. The Teachers have provided for that."

"How do we enter?" asked Thul.

"To one side of the square, then down a short stairwell. What you see before you is the door by which the selected entered in the days and hours before the War. Time was short in the end and many of the chosen remained outside when the doors closed. They took it upon themselves to protect the sanctuary that was The Hold. It was from the descendants of those people who remained outside that today's City by the Lake descend. Those of the Valleys and plains around us are the survivors of those who lived outside of this land in the years that followed the Great War and its aftermath. The two men moved to one side of the monument, crossed the crowded plaza, swelled in these days leading up to the war against the Whites. The smells of foods cooking for the vast numbers of people and combatants were almost overpowering in their variety. The trading bazaar to one side of the square was filled to capacity as people traded trinkets and souvenirs form far and wide. Locklear and Thul entered a nondescript building across the plaza from the front of The Hold.

"This way is secret," said Locklear in a quiet tone.

What they entered was a small shop that catered to the needs of the Sage and its Scholars with the strong, dark beverage they served. The room was dark and smelled strongly of the beverage. A handful of tables and chairs lay scattered around the room. Two men, neither Sage nor Scholar, were sitting quietly in a corner talking. Otherwise, it was empty. The two men behind the counter looked at Locklear, then Thul. As Locklear moved to walk behind the counter to a closed door, the two moved to one side to let him pass. When Thul attempted to follow Locklear they quietly moved to intercept him. Each grabbed one of Thul's arms with a strong grip.

"Where do you think you are going?" one said.

"Relax, Ander, he is with me," Locklear told the man in charge.

"None but the Order may pass through these doors," Ander whispered, fearing to be overheard by the two men in the corner. "You, Locklear, of all should know this."

"Ander, this is Thul. He is the son of Simon." Locklear spoke quietly and succinctly.

"If true, this should be his death, not a sign of welcome," the second man spoke.

At this point, the two seated men witnessing an altercation behind the bar that they did not want to be part of got up and left the shop.

Thul was visibly alarmed at the conduct towards him and stepped back as the second man drew a weapon.

"Hold your arms!" commanded Locklear. "Who should know better than I of the words of our Teachers."

"It was written of the Teachers by the Order that none may sire a child," spoke Stiegel, agitated by this news, his weapon drawn.

"And who do you think wrote down those words? It was I, Locklear, who stood before the Teachers in the time before they left us. And nothing in what I wrote stated that the offspring of such an occurrence should die."

"But it was always assumed," said Ander.

"Only that such a son of a Sage could never be. We still don't know why Simon was sent on his exile. But the clues are there for us to find."

"Even still," insisted Ander, "the tests remain. He must first pass those before we can allow him entry."

"Agreed," spoke Locklear, anxious to bring an end to this matter quickly. Another traveler had entered the shop for rest. 'Suspicion must not be brought to this place,' thought Locklear. To the two men he said, "We have much to do and prepare for what is to come. Take us to the apparatus."

Thul remained alarmed at what was happening around him. He hesitated to follow the Sage and Ander. He only moved when Stiegel put a knife to his ribs. "Follow them," he said.

"Stay here and take care of the customer, Stiegel," Ander ordered.

Stiegel warily watched the three men move to a corridor in the back, and then he turned his attention to the customer approaching the counter, his knife sheathed. "How may I help you?" he smiled.

Thul was led past a curtain, shielding this passage from curious eyes, to a panel on the wall. The panel turned into a doorway, and the three men entered, Ander still holding Thul's arm firmly. The three walked down a short, well-lit, wood-paneled corridor that ended with a dead-end.

"If you fail this test, your life ends here," Ander said in a matter-of-fact way. Locklear ignored the remark, but Thul became more fearful for his life. What was this test?

"Come here," Locklear ordered Thul. He approached a strange glass panel in the wall. The panel glowed and was unlike anything Thul had seen before. Keys were in the middle of the screen. Ander touched a series of these and the panel changed to a light blue color.

"Stand here," Ander ordered Thul. A light flashed across Thul's face as it scanned his features, in particular his eyes. Once finished, it flashed a blinking "X" on its screen.

"Not one of us!" spoke Ander loudly.

"Not in our database you mean. How could he be? He's not Simon, but his son. The second test is needed," spoke Locklear quietly.

Ander now forcibly grasped Thul's hand and brought his palm across a sharp point below the screen. Though Thul's hand jerked back from the pain, blood had been drawn. The screen before the men started flashing a series of letters across it.

"Your DNA is being checked for the mark given to Simon by the Teachers. If you are his son, you will carry that mark yourself and you will be able to gain entry. If not, you will die here," Ander stated as he watched for the results.

"What is DNA?" asked Thul of Locklear, pronouncing it as if it was one word.

"It's what makes each of us unique," Locklear said.

The time seemed an eternity as they watched the letters scroll across the screen. Then the letters stopped. The screen flashed in a language not even understood by the Sage, the language of the Teachers. Then it showed a steady gold color replacing the blue. A single character stood out on the screen, large, bold, in black. This was something that not even Locklear had expected. Ander fell prostrate at Thul's feet. The marker had been found showing that Thul had indeed descended from Simon, and was in a sense already a Sage himself and entitled to entry into The Hold and its Library. However, a second mark had also been found in the blood of Thul, that of a Teacher. 'How could that be?' thought Locklear, bewildered by this unexpected event.

"Forgive us, Teacher," Ander pleaded from his knees in front of Thul. Thul could only look on in amazement.

Locklear finally acted. "None should know of this beyond the three of us," he commanded Thul and Ander. To Ander he added, "You are to remain underground until such a time as this is announced." Ander agreed without question to this.

Locklear thought to himself, 'Did Gar have any idea of who this Thul was? The mark of the Teachers. How could this be?' Moreover, it could shed new light on who or what Simon was. He had much studying to do.

"Follow me," he told the two bewildered men as he entered the elevator door that had opened in the wall next to the panel.

Once the elevator opened again, after a sizable drop, the wide corridor beyond led to a second door. While it looked unprotected, it had a means of entry as sophisticated as the way above. Locklear put his hand against a dark screen, which read his palm print, and through the oil in his skin, his DNA as well. The door slid to one side as the panel read Locklear's identity.

"Follow me," was all Locklear said.

After following this new narrow corridor down an angled slope, they came to a last set of doors. "Another elevator. This is the level the population lived at."

While Thul had encountered several elevators in his limited travel, most had been primitive. Society had not reached the point again where buildings had to be built higher because of lack of land. The buildings of the Jall were the tallest that Thul had seen. Thul figured that they had traveled underground to a point below The Hold's taller buildings. "How high are we going back up?" he asked Locklear.

"Not higher, lower. Several hundred feet."

"I am leaving you now, Teacher," Ander said to Thul.

Thul just nodded his head at him and Ander left.

Locklear now continued speaking to just Thul, "The Collection Hall was built several hundred feet lower than the caverns the Teachers built for the survivors. It was accessible even then only to those who would become The Order of the Sage."

When they entered the elevator there was but a single clear panel. Locklear placed his thumb on the panel and the elevator began its rapid drop, which literally took Thul's breath away.

The elevator came to an abrupt stop and the door opened automatically. The two men stepped out. If Thul had not been told how deep they were going, he would have thought them on the surface. The floor was some kind of soft tile that was easy to walk on. The light seemed to surround them all at once without shadow. The walls were a soft color of wood. Portraits and other paintings covered the walls.

Locklear caught Thul admiring the artwork. "Much art was lost in the Great War, entire collections, gone. The Teachers in their wisdom tried to collect as much as they could in the moments before the War broke out. But even they could save but little. We, the Order of the Sage, have found more in our wanderings. Much was damaged and we have tried to repair it. In addition, the collection here continues to grow. Not long ago, another Sage, venturing into a lost city from the time of the War, found a vault that contained many pieces. An expedition was sent and the art was brought here. This is a legacy for the world upon its revival. The time will come when The Library's treasures will be released to the world. We look forward to that day."

"So not just knowledge was saved by the Teachers?"

"You'll find much thought lost preserved here. And you'll find much to your amazement that you never knew is here as well, from the days before the War."

They followed several of the long corridors and Thul saw more of the artwork that the world thought was lost to the ages. Through heavy wooden doors they entered the main library. It was a room of giant dimension, with walls of shelves containing the world's pre-war books; books of all sizes and shapes, many in languages that seemed strange to Thul as he browsed the shelves.

"There must be a million books in here," Thul exclaimed.

"Over one billion paperbound books and documents are here. The Teachers saved most of the world's most important documents in the moments before the War broke out; it was the final task they gave themselves. We are still cataloguing many of these. This is but a part of The Library's holdings. Before the War, it was called the 'Digital Age.' The Teachers, through their proxies, the technocrats, knowing that the War was coming, worked to put all of the world's knowledge into storage. That has all been saved and you will learn to access it."

"Then The Library must be even larger than I imagine," said Thul.

"Not larger, smaller," laughed Locklear.

They entered a small room to one side of the large main room of The Library. There, on a series of tables, sat dozens of small screens, not unlike those that they had used to gain entry to The Hold and The Library. Near each screen was a keyboard, not unlike the electric typewriters he had seen in the Confederation.

Locklear pointed to a chair in front of one of the screens. "Have a seat. It is here you will do most of your learning."

Thul sat down before one of the screens expectantly. Dozens of Scholars were in the room, reading what was in front of them on their own screens. Many were seen typing on the keyboards. Thul tried to steal a glance at what they were doing. The scholars expressed little curiosity in who Thul was. To them he was just another Scholar who had been chosen from above to join their ranks.

"A computer?" he asked Locklear. The Confederation knew of the computers that had dominated the world before the War. However, the knowledge of their working had been long lost. A few old systems had been found among the ruins, but no way had been found to make them work. It was a knowledge that had been lost and not yet regained.

Locklear touched several keys and the screen came to life. He touched several more and then moved his finger across the screen and it populated with images. "The world's knowledge from before the War, it is now yours."

"There is so much here. Why is all of this hidden from the world? Shouldn't it all be shared?" asked Thul.

"We do share this knowledge as the world becomes ready for it. Someday all of this knowledge and treasure will become the world's again. That is why we train the Scholars."

"Where do I begin?" asked Thul as he looked up at Locklear standing behind him.

"With this," Locklear said as he reached over Thul and typed a symbol into the computer. "Let your thoughts guide you. You will find there is much knowledge of the world that you will want to know. What came before and what has come since. All is here in this digital world before you. When you tire of the screen, you will find much of interest in the shelves outside. Paper can be friendly to the touch and we are still making discoveries in the pages we search. One more thing you will have to learn. Your mind needs to be opened up to find what special gifts the Teachers bestowed in you. As the son of Simon, questions will abound as the news leaks out."

"How will we find what gifts I was given?"

"Special meditation, along with certain herbal teas, will allow you to access and search those areas of your mind and open them."

"All of this buried underground. Why is so much of this kept secret?"

"The Teachers gathered all of this to aide our world as we climbed out of the devastation of the Great War. But they foresaw that much of what happened would be blamed on this knowledge."

"Like the Nomads?"

"They and others like them. So this knowledge must be preserved and protected."

"And the world never sees it?" Thul asked with a slight reproach for what he had heard. Who, he thought, made the decision to release how much of this and when?

"We have already released much to the world. The Teachers created us, the Order of the Sage, both to protect this knowledge, but also to release, in predetermined stages, as much of this knowledge as the outside world can handle. At times, we of the Order have released more of this knowledge than was allowed. Each time we did this, unforeseen circumstances arose. We have learned from our mistakes, as it appears, the Teachers expected us to do.

"It was during one of these early releases of knowledge that the greatest threat to The Hold and The Library occurred. More than a few of the Order and our scholars died that day protecting the secret of The Hold and The Library.

"A great mass, an army, of the Nomads, arrived at the main gate to The Hold, not sealed as it is today, but left open for pilgrims to visit. By the thousands they stormed The Hold, looking for The Library of Knowledge, so that it might be destroyed. It was in the wisdom of the Teachers that they placed the Library apart from The Hold. While these invaders destroyed much of The Hold proper, in the end nothing of real value was lost. Their fury worn out, the Nomads left. Their wildcats, even then their companions at that early time, did as much damage to the City of The Hold as the Nomads themselves. It is out of that deference that hunting parties are sent out to defeat or drive away any of the Great Mountain Lions that are seen. Even today, we of the Order of the Sage look upon the ignorance of the world with caution. Knowledge is parceled out with care and deference to the wisdom of the Teachers and their words.

"Tomorrow we begin your education and training. Today enjoy yourself and get to know your way around The Library and The Hold. You are now recognized by the system as having full access to all of our facilities and computers."

Thul sat for a few minutes, the bewildered feeling still with him. A lot had occurred very quickly and his mind was still assimilating it. He looked at the screen before him and new images appeared, seeming to follow his eyes. He moved the icon over the images as he was shown and a new screen populated; "17th Century French Poetry." He had no idea what "French" meant, nor "17th Century." Century he knew was a way to measure dates. What century was it today? He looked at the screen and a new image appeared, that of the grounds outside of The Hold. "38th Century" it said in bold writing on the screen.

He leaned back in the chair and saw that Locklear had left him. Now he felt lost as well as bewildered. He was the son of Simon? And what was that part about the Teachers that had caused Anders to throw himself at his feet? He got up and went to the door, leaving the room to look for food and the dark beverage that he was coming to enjoy. In The Library several of the Scholars came up to him and offered their service to be his guide. Word was already spreading of Thul and the markers he carried.

The next day began early for each of the mutineers of *The Proctant*. For Thul it was in the Seminary room of the Collection Hall where he would learn the techniques that would open up those areas of his brain that remained closed to him. A lifetime of learning was ahead for him. Thul wondered, as the son of Simon, just how long was his lifetime.

For the rest, Gar took them to the edge of the city's eastern gate, where they joined an assembly of people from throughout these lands. Their goal, as unified as these people had ever been, was the one-week march to the City by the Lake, and then preparations for the war against the White.

Chapter Five
Beneath the Myk's Palace

When he came to, the smells around him were overwhelming. He retched once, twice and then passed out again.

Dreams came, horrible dreams, beyond description; nightmares.

First it was the battle he saw. Was he dead? Captured! The flight; Alum knew he was alive. For some reason he had not been killed. He saw others torn apart. He felt pain, intense pain. He was hurt, badly.

More dreams: He was falling, falling down an endless pit. Was there any reason to return to the living? Or was he doomed to this endless torment of Hell? The falling, the ever-present falling. Then the fire, it burnt through his very soul. His soul was burning as he fell deeper into the pit. Maybe he was dead and this was his reward for his life. No. He had not led the kind of life to deserve this. He must be alive. He had to save himself from this torture. He had to wake up. To be alive. "How?" he screamed. "How?" He cried out in the agony of the torment. "How? Somebody save me. Save me!"

Then he felt himself conscious again. There was somebody kneeling alongside him. Still lost in the dream, he speaks to this other. "What is this place?"

The Stranger turns to face Alum. As he does, Alum recoils in horror at what he sees. Alum tries to run, but he cannot. He turns halfway and screams again. He cannot move but the other can. This horrible thing that is the Stranger. It moves slowly to touch Alum. The thing's hand (if that is what it was) just feet, then inches away. Alum screams again at the horror. He finally breaks away from the gaze of the Stranger. He runs now, faster, seemingly flying over the ground. And behind him, chasing him, always both close and far away, the Stranger. Trying to close the gap, it stays right behind him.

Ghosts of the past; all of the evils this world had ever known. Such is this thing, the Stranger, a creature beyond time, always present, this "Thing," this Stranger.

Right behind him now it stands, ready to touch Alum. Just a touch and Alum would be doomed to an eternity of living with all of the torments of this Hell; a living death, a slave to this thing until the final catastrophic end of time.

It's closer now. It reaches out to touch Alum and Alum screams in the anguished horror of those that had come before him to this place, unable to stop this *Thing*, this horror, this Stranger, from touching him.

Consciousness and all of its invading smells, he was free.

"So they put the mind touch on you."

One of his fellow prisoners was speaking. Alum was somewhat recovered from his ordeal. His wounds were bandaged, but not cleaned. What would be the purpose of that? He felt dull aches throughout his body and some of the wounds showed signs of festering.

The fellow prisoner continued speaking. "Not surprising, considering the sub-human barbarians that they are. Some do not even survive it. And those that do are usually vegetables for a long while afterward. You're lucky you were able to fight it and to be alive, from the looks of it."

"It's the Bird-Men that took me prisoner then?" Alum asked.

"Yes, if that's what you want to call them," another prisoner answered. "And if you're lucky you'll get a quick death. If you're not…Look at Tjim over there," the prisoner said, pointing. "He was here when I was brought in, probably a lot longer. Now, if it were not for their drugs in him, he would be long dead, instead of a 'living' meat storage for the White. You see, they eat human-flesh. And it has to be fresh, alive, or at least not dead."

Alum looked to a corner to where the speaker pointed. He saw the remains of what once was a man. Only now entire body parts where gone with just a central mass of not-dead human flesh remaining. Alum retched at the sight.

"You called the Bird-Men, those that took me, the White."

"Yeah, they call themselves that."

"Are they human?" Alum asked, incredulous at the sight around him.

"They probably must have been at one time, probably before the War they were. Now they are just mutated cannibals. Your best hope is a quick death."

"No way out of here alive?" Alum said to all of those around him.

"Like I said, the only way out is death. You want a knife? I have one." The man continued his speech at Alum and approached the still-groggy man. Alum was gaining more of his strength by the minute, but it did not look like this fellow prisoner was going to give him the time to recover completely. This prison was his kingdom and he was ready to show Alum just that.

"Shut up, Zalc!" a man from the back of the room spoke up. "Some occasionally used to get away, but not since the last slave rebellion. My name is Gant. I was one of those who took part in it. That's why I am here in the 'meat storage locker.' They prefer the meat of outsiders, but when the catch is low, they have been known to eat their slaves. Zalc, here, does not want any escape attempts again. He lost his entire family in the rebellion, and now he's…lost."

He got no further in his story before Zalc, crazed by all he had endured, in a wild rage hit Gant with his shoulder, then both fists. He followed with a kick, sending Gant crashing to the ground.

Gant recovered, got up from where he lay, and retreated to the wall. Then he continued his story. "Zalc was a good man once. He led the revolt. Then, when it was over, they forced him to watch as his wife and children were eaten alive. He has been mad ever since. Can't say I blame him."

"Shut up, Gant. They will probably eat you next. And you," he pointed at Alum as he spoke, "you're better off forgetting about escape and trying to kill yourself instead. If they catch you trying and you don't make it, you'll end up like Tjim." Zalc approached Gant again as he angrily yelled to all in the room.

"Then why don't you kill yourself? You have the knife," asserted Alum.

"See this knife?" He held the blade out for Alum to see. "When they finally tire and come for me, one of them is going out too. My little revenge for all they have done. My knife. See, Gant, I'm not totally crazy yet."

"There must be some way out. Gant, you said some escaped before. How'd they do it?" Alum continued.

"Will you listen to his words?" answered Zalc with a touch of hysteria in his voice. "Then you think you can do something we can't, huh."

Zalc turned to the others in the room. "Funny thing isn't it. Him thinking he can escape. What's say we teach our new friend here a little respect, a little initiation into prison life here in the meat locker. Let's show him what he's up against, just who we are." Zalc shouted the last part at the dreary men around him.

"Let him go, Zalc," Gant answered.

"Out of my way, Gant. You don't speak for me, then or now." With that, Zalc laid out Gant with a single punch.

Lifelessly, some of the others answered Zalc's call to action. One who did not answer was sitting near to where Zalc stood. Seeing things were not going completely to his liking, Zalc gave the man a quick kick to the side of the head. This sent the man the rest of the way to the hard floor, writhing in pain. This brought the others quickly to Zalc's side, and together they advanced on Alum. Zalc cautiously dropped a little behind the others. They were eight against one and they expected an easy fight.

Hurt as he was, Alum knew he could not wait for the attack. He towered over his fellow prisoners, and although still hurt, he was not starved and deprived like them. Alum charged, a fist to the stomach of the first he reached, putting him out of action. The others hesitated, but advanced again, now seven against one in the tight quarters of the pit. Zalc still liked the odds and he would make sure Alum paid.

In a far corner of the room, where he had been sleeping, another prisoner watched the gathering commotion. He had been awakened by the noise of Zalc's yelling and was watching to see how things developed. When he saw just how they were unfolding, he rushed to join Alum where he stood. He whirled into the fighting, catching the attackers off-guard. More fit than the attackers and not as wounded as Alum, he tore into them, his fists becoming clubs as he moved left and right. A crack was heard as he broke the neck of one of the antagonists. Alum had picked up another and tossed him against the wall. The newcomer spun a kick and one more shot against the wall. Stunned by the outcome of the fight, the others moved back, leaving Zalc alone to face the two men.

"Just like old times," smiled Mendy as he gave a quick glance at Alum. "Remember some of the brawls we had back home."

"You're alive!" exclaimed Alum, not really believing his eyes. "I thought I saw you killed when they attacked us."

"Alive as ever, brought in the same as you. For a change I was the lucky one. They picked you for that particular poison. I was worried there for a while. How are you doing?"

"Best as can be expected. Just glad you showed up. It was looking a little tricky there for a while."

"Eh, you could have taken them on your own. Just made it a little quicker is all. Hey, Zalc!" Mendy shouted to the now-retreating man who had instigated the attack. "Looks like you picked on the wrong one this time."

Angrily Zalc looked around himself. This had not gone the way he had expected it. He had not expected help for the beleaguered Alum. How was he to have known Mendy and this one were friends, even though they had arrived together? Zalc had to do something now or lose his place among the prisoners.

"Shut up, Mendy! Get out of my way!" Zalc shouted at the interloper. "I wasn't hiding, just trying to find an opening." This last part he added to the men around him who had seen him retreat from the fight.

"Do what he says, Mendy. This is between Zalc and me," Alum quietly said.

Then, as Mendy stepped back, keeping a wary eye on the others, it was just the two. The fight had cleared Alum's head and he watched and waited for Zalc's move.

Zalc charged and the injured Alum easily blocked his blows. Zalc now knew that the injured man in front of him was easily his superior. He pulled his knife; he was not willing to admit defeat as yet. Alum knew as well that he was better than the man before him. All of the back-alley brawling with Mendy would pay dividends now.

He moved in on the enraged man, careful to stay clear of the blade. He calmly ducked under the wild swings of Zalc's arm. Alum staggered Zalc with a single blow to his throat. Then he spun a kick at the gasping man, sending him crashing into the wall. Zalc fell heavily to the floor, barely alive.

A door opened in the ceiling of the prison pit. Alum was standing in the center of the room, breathing heavily from the fight. A rope from above fell in a loop around him. Before Alum or Mendy could react, Alum was pulled swiftly up and out the trap door.

The door was shut, but the men below could hear the strange laughing of their mutant captors. The fight had been watched from above and the guards had no room for prisoners such as Alum.

Statues lined the large hall, inlaid with gold. High above were the carved perches of the great fighting birds, glittering with the gems that adorned them.

Alum entered the throne room and the garishness of the entryway paled in significance; the throne room seemed in its entirety to be made of gold and silver. Every color the eye could conceive flashed before him. The light filtered into the room through gem-encrusted stained-glass windows. Some of the gems Alum saw he was unable to identify, though he had traveled far in his journeys. And the Throne itself; the value of it could have probably paid the ransom of all the kings and leaders of all of the lands he had ever visited.

Men in chains, all slaves of the All-Highest, The Myk, The High-Priest of the White, escorted him. Some were mutants, made slaves because they had incurred the wrath of their leader for some petty offence. To these people no punishment was more severe than being made a slave, if only for a short time. This meant that they would be unable to carry arms into the glory that was war.

Alum was brought to the throne where the Myk sat. This creature's foul features were distorted from birth and scarred by his many battles. One eye was high above the other and what may have been a nose was but a distorted slit. His mouth gleamed with many sharpened teeth. A primitive third eye lay on his face where an ear should have been and his ears lay together on one side of his head. Hair he had none, but for a few tufts where his pointed chins were. His neck was short and thick, a column to join his body with his head. Of his body Alum could see little as it was covered in layers of brightly colored robes.

The Myk looked down on his prisoner with his vision of sanity. He looked at the others, his third eye roaming, unable to focus. Some had mutated to the point of being scarcely human. Others carried barely the scar of the mutations. Yet they were as one, his lieutenants, bravest of their kind. The Myk waited, watching for their approval. Then the All-Highest, bravest of the brave, mightiest of the strong, most deformed from their human stain, gave a loud, long incoherent cry. The lieutenants cheered their approval. As the guards backed away from Alum, the floor disappeared where he had been forced into a kneeling position. Alum fell below, a sacrifice to the White's god, the ever-powerful Hydron, the Father of their form.

In the darkness Alum was unable to tell how far he had fallen. His last sight was of the barbarians cheering his demise. There was no noise to accompany his fall and with his fatigued state he was unsure if it was minutes or seconds he fell into the deep pit. Alum fought to keep back any panic, but he was exhausted, mentally and physically.

He had fallen far enough that he resigned himself to a certain death when he hit the bottom. He would die then when he hit and that would not be long. After all he had been through he would fight no more. He resigned himself to that thought, closed his eyes and smiled. He would die in peace and with all the dignity he could show. He would not give these monsters the satisfaction of anything else. This would be his last victory.

Alum hit the bottom and, to his amazement, he was still alive. He had already made his peace with God but quickly decided that could now wait. He was not any more hurt by the fall. Delirious with his newfound life, Alum tried to stand and found he could not. It was not that his legs could not support him; it was just that the floor he had landed on was not solid. The floor was like a gently rolling wave of rubber, a soft, almost-liquid material that he was slowly sinking into. When he had hit, he had sunk several inches into the surface. And now, with his sudden activity, he had sunk even more.

Alum gathered his wits about him and tried to think his way out of this, his latest predicament. Things had seemed to go from bad to worse, but now at least there was no physical monstrosity ready to devour him. It seemed the mutants had cast him into this sea of rubber to drown; unless there was more to this than it seemed. And he began to dread that this was far more likely.

He started to the left, moving in a half-crawl, half-swimming motion, trying to keep himself from sinking any further into the morass.

He stopped, damned if he did not know which way the closest wall was. He did not even know if there was a wall, for he could be in an immense cavern, or maybe outside. No, he could not be outside. Even in the darkest night, there was some light to see with. Here he could see nothing, not even his hands in front of his face. The darkness was absolute. The darkness was a tangible entity in itself, all pervading, darker than a witch's tomb. Alum felt his fatigue begin to catch up with him again.

Alum called out into the darkness, trying to pick up an echo of his call, hoping that he might determine which way to go. Almost in response to his call, instead of an echo, a scream pierced through the matter that was the darkness. Then another. Very close, it seemed. Alum began to remember parts of the nightmare he had experienced earlier and began to curl into a ball, cowering. He just had nothing left to fight with. Another scream, closer still. Where was it coming from? He tried to fight it once more but the dream kept coming back. Where was it coming from? He could not tell with the echoes. There must be distant walls, as it seemed the echoes came quickest from his left, and he moved that way. He hoped that was the direction away from the horrifying screams that kept coming. He must be in a cavern of some sort and had to move; he could not give up yet. It was not his time. He had fought them all. Alum slowly regained his composure.

Alum heard a new, inhuman wail, this time from in front of him. He remembered the nightmare, once more, they had forced upon him. He remembered the faceless thing he fled in it. Alum tried to move again, unable to coordinate his movements and, like before, he floundered in the substance and began to sink once more. He tried to keep the deep panic from welling up inside himself.

There was another scream and Alum knew it was after him. He crawled, trying to escape. Finally, Alum's exhaustion overcame him. He collapsed, unable to move further. He passed out from the exhaustion, as a hand reached out to grasp him.

"He's unconscious, Jorge. Think we can get him out?" asked Gim.

"Yes, if the thing gives us half a chance. Even after you learn to walk on this stuff; it's still hard to manage."

"Can you feel the vibrations?" Gim was growing concerned. "It feels like we barely have enough time."

"I can feel them, all right. It's a good thing he moved in the right direction or we would not have had a chance at all. That thing must be getting hungrier from us saving all its meals," Jorge stated proudly.

"How much time do you think we have?" Gim asked as they carried the unconscious man out.

"Not much more than ten minutes and I wouldn't count on more than eight or nine."

The Underground Movement had been able to save almost every sacrifice over the last few years. Always two men were on duty. They kept hoping the thing would starve, but still it lasted.

"We'd better hurry."

"I know," sighed Jorge.

"Sometimes I wish I had become a scooter, collecting molds for food, like my father."

"We all wish for something else when we're on duty. You could have gone and done something else. Me, yeh, this is the lot life gave me." Jorge paused. "My father, he was The Betrayer. He led the White to the cavern's entrance. They killed him, but not soon enough. My father's actions led to so many of us being caught and killed. And they died badly, many as meals. This then is my penance, saving the lives of others."

The two men heard another wailing scream as they carried the unconscious man.

"Do you hear that?" Jorge shuddered.

"Yes. Do you think we'll make it," Gim questioned.

"You ask too many questions and the beast moves fast," Jorge scolded.

"I'm glad I'm a savior, Jorge."

"Shut up, kid. Keep moving. We're almost there."

Quickly now, to the opening in the wall, they could feel the breath of the monster behind them. They were almost free. Jorge lifted the unconscious man to Gim, where he stood on the sill. Gim lifted up the man and carried him into the tunnel's entrance, beyond the ability of the monster to reach. He expected Jorge to be right behind him. Then he heard the cry, the shout. "Keep moving, kid!"

That was the last he heard. Jorge had given himself up so that Gim could make it with the unconscious man. It was Jorge's final act of selflessness. Now his demons were gone, the demons of his father's betrayal. Jorge's last thoughts were those of a long-forgotten peace.

"I made it back with the outsider, sir. Jorge did not make it though. I think he gave himself up so that we could make it." The pain could be heard in Gim's voice as he gave his report.

"I'm sorry to hear about Jorge, a quality man. Never could do enough to help the cause. His father's demons were always with him. I understood you two were like brothers." So many he had seen die, this man, the savior's captain. Soon it would be his turn.

"I don't understand why he had to die like that. He could have tried to make it. Maybe all three of us could have made it." Gim was crying as he said the last part.

"He wouldn't take that chance. He understood what the stranger represents. He died for the cause as he lived. Moreover, his family's stigma is gone now as well. With the outsider's help we'll be able to kill the monster and destroy the mutants, to live outside again."

"How long before the stranger comes to? I'd like to see him," said Gim, trying to control his overwrought emotions.

"He's being treated now for his wounds. He should be able to talk in several days. Some of his injuries are severe and he'll be under sedation."

"Will I see him then?" Gim almost pleaded. He wanted to see this man that was worth the price of Jorge's death.

"I don't know. That will be up to the elders. However, I would prefer it if you did not. It would be best for the two of you."

"Yes, sir."

The two men separated, to go their own ways until the next victim thrown to the Hydron. Gim had a job to do; he had a new savior to train.

Chapter Six
The People of the Lake

Wade had been one of the first to be separated from the others when the fighting had begun on the rocky island where they had first landed. Caught totally off-guard, he had been swept away when the first wave of the attackers had struck the islet. He was just now beginning to remember the nightmare of what had happened.

A week with the People of the Lake had done much to clear his mind. Yet, always in the background, there was a feeling of dread. Of what would come next for him.

He had been caught in the open when the White's attack had begun. "Yes, that's what they call themselves," he was informed by his hosts. He was building a shelter to protect them from the coming storm. He was working feverishly with several others, gathering driftwood and rock. They had found a space that might provide the men with some protection from the storm if it could be reinforced, a half-cave facing the lagoon and jungle. With the rock, driftwood and what vine they could find, they hoped to make it storm worthy.

They had just laid out the wood and vine when the White's attack came. Hideous creatures with their savage mounts. He had just enough time to pick up his sword when it was torn from his grasp. He was struck from behind and knocked down. The attack had been so unexpected. As he tried to stand, he saw his shipmates fight back as best they could.

With only his knife now as protection, he fought for his life. But there were so many of the attackers. He was knocked to the ground again, this time as one of the bird's talons grazed his shoulder, leaving a deep gash.

He saw them tear Noble's head from his body and hold it aloft as a trophy. A savage bird, which had seen its rider killed by a volley from Zircon, tore at him from above. A lucky slice from his blade severed one of the bird's talons. Other riderless birds now swarmed this one. They smelled the blood, became crazed, tearing the bird apart. Once again, providence had spared him.

After what seemed like hours, and he knew it to be only minutes, Wade felt his back torn as one of the birds, still with its rider, grasped him in its talons. Yet it was not the deathblow he expected.

Unable to see any more of the others, he was spared death and carried away. He was their prisoner, for what reasons he could only imagine. After the horrors he witnessed on the battlefield, what he imagined could not be good.

With the talons of the great bird biting deeply into his back, Wade strove to maintain consciousness. He feared that if he were to give in to the pain, his only chance for survival would be lost. More of the enemy joined them in their flight to the east, these savage birds with their ghostly riders. Wade could see them clearly now, barely human, with skin molted as if diseased. No two seemed alike. Riderless birds flew with them as well. It seemed his shipmates had made a good showing for themselves from the number of birds missing their riders. Those riders who attempted to keep them in formation herded these birds like cattle in the air. At times, the lone birds turned savagely on the White and then one of the riders with his scythe-like pole sword would dispatch that bird. As this dead bird fell to the sea, other riderless birds, not under the White's control, would tear it to pieces for their food. It was a flight to Hell. But what difference did that make? Wade was able to watch through his half-closed eyes as the barbarian Whites and their mounts (the loose birds without riders were under some semblance of control and circling around them all) moved east, the free birds always looking for a chance to gather a meal.

As Wade looked around, he saw that the White carried other prisoners as well, but with his eyes half-covered in blood, not all of which was his, and the other prisoners in their torn clothing and covered in blood and remains from the battle as well, he was unable to tell who they were. Or even if they were alive, as their bloodied, limp bodies dangled from the birds' talons without movement. The pain in Wade's shoulders and back from the talon's tears was almost unbearable. Nevertheless, Wade had to stay aware if he wanted to survive what was to come.

They flew for what seemed like hours, always to the east, and the birds never seemed to tire. Those birds that had been maddened from the combat had by now all been dispatched to the swamp below. The ride carried a kind of surreal look about it, peacefulness. As they flew eastward, they began to move in a more northerly direction as well, the swamp below them turning into a dense forest.

They flew just hundreds of feet above the trees. Wade had no idea how tall these trees might be. He was plainly able to hear the strange sounds of the beasts below. Now and then a head would appear above the treetops, animals unrecognizable to Wade. And if any bird flew too low, there would be a quick end to it, as one of these heads would snap it up.

As Wade came to learn, these fierce animals lived solely in the thatched treetops of the forest. There, in that space between the forest floor and the sky, they were the kings.

A great mountain range came into view far into the interior of this land. It was toward this they flew. As they neared the mountains, the great birds started to show the first signs of fatigue. Wade also saw more of the birds and their riders emerging from the southern edge of the mountains. Whether to guide them home or to continue the fight on the island, Wade knew not.

The bird that carried Wade seemed to increase its speed in spite of its fatigue. It beat its wings harder to carry it higher at the urging of its agitated rider. Flying with this greater urgency, the birds turned their flight even further to the north. To Wade it seemed they were doing their utmost to avoid this new group flying toward them. This surprised Wade, as he assumed that all these birdmen were of one accord. Wade could now sense the fear that they carried. These White and their mounts feared what was coming toward them.

The birds approaching them split into two groups. One raced toward the coastline while the other converged upon those that carried Wade and the other prisoners., when only a short distance away, this second group split again, one climbing above and the other diving below the White.

The two sides of birds and their riders tore into each other. Many fell from the sky as no quarter was given between them. The bird that carried Wade was now riderless. Its talons gripped him even harder still as the bird tried to flee the melee in the hopes of enjoying the meal he carried alone. Wade felt more than he saw some warrior from the new group cut through the bird's neck from above, severing its head. This freed Wade from the bird's talons as they opened reflexively. Wade fell now alongside the dead bird, only to be caught by another bird's talons within moments of being freed from the first. This bird caught him almost gently compared to the first bird. Its rider moved immediately away from the fighting, back toward the southern edge of the mountain. Still, the new gashes on his back proved to be too much for him to stand and Wade passed out into the ecstasy of oblivion.

The People of the Lake kept Wade unconscious several days with sedation. Salves had been applied to his wounds and he had begun the process of healing. As Wade returned to consciousness, he found himself resting in a room in the City by the Lake, the Capital of the people who had freed him.

The city was the most beautiful that he had seen in his travels. Built partially on the lake itself, the city showed an architectural genius that was unsurpassed. From the elegant buildings of the High Lords to the hamlets of the common people, not a stone was without its place. Great parklands lay throughout the city and within these parks stood public baths with marble fountains and statues sculpted of their past heroes. Water cascaded high into the air as if by magic and at night myriad lights lit these fountains.

Wade learned of all this by looking out the window of his hospital room as his wounds healed. He was kept largely to the soft bed he was provided by his caretakers. He was allowed up a few hours every day. His sole exercise was the short walk from his bed to the windows. At night he would gaze out the window at the reflections of the City by the Lake. Lights mirrored so clearly that it was like looking into another world. At such times he would lapse into deep thoughts of what this all meant. He worried about what had happened to the others. How was it that he had come to be saved? Was he the sole survivor? Was he the last of the crew that had mutinied?

Soon Wade was allowed to leave his room and roam through the city. He set out to see just what it was this city offered. Two of his caregivers who had watched over him as he healed accompanied him. He was aided in these walks by an elaborate cane, carved by one of the city's great wood carvers and presented to him as a gift.

As he walked, Wade saw even more of the grandeur of this city. As new as the city was to him, Wade grew even more curious at the sounds he heard around him. The language this people spoke seemed similar to his own. However, the clicks and the whistles were oddly disturbing. It was the language of the birds, he was told. The language was taught to the population of the city when they were young so they would be able to communicate with the birds.

He learned that the city was set up in a class system, though there seemed to be free movement between the classes. It was the commoners who worked the city and fields, maintaining what was necessary for the city's survival. The Lords maintained a constant vigil over the city, their sole job to guard against any approaching danger. They were the warrior class that had proved their worth in many a battle in this land.

He came to find out that somehow, even with this class system, in the terms of the government all of the people were free. Each did what was required of him or her to maintain the lands and the city. All took pride in whatever job was best suited for them. If a commoner accomplished something of great service to the city, he could become a Lord if he wished, a status that would be shared by all his family. Likewise, the title could be stricken from a family if its Lords failed to fulfill their obligations to the city.

The Lords and the commoners ruled jointly the city and the lands that surrounded it in the southern half of the valley where it stood. It was a form of democracy that was borrowed in almost its whole from a book of a long-forgotten Anglish Parl'ment, a book found almost intact, surrounded by the ashes of other written works that had been burned beyond recognition, a work that would have been cast off as a child's reader in that long-forgotten time before the war.

Wade wandered with some pain throughout the city the as much as he was able. In his excitement, he found exploring this new city was not tiring. The people delighted in enthralling Wade with their stories of the city and he often shared their carriage rides from one part of the city to the next. These carriages were the taxis of the City by the Lake. These were his first rides in one since his youngest days, when his family visited a land far to the south of where he had grown up in the Confederation. Twilight found him at the southern shore of the Lake, in a hot spot heated by the many geothermal springs in the area, one of the many public baths. He lay back and enjoyed the feeling of the healing waters as they flowed around his still-recovering body. He watched as the sun settled below the horizon of the mountains in the distance.

It was here that a messenger of the Council found him. The messenger had been searching for Wade most of the day; always it seemed arriving at a location just after Wade had left. The messenger, relieved at catching up with the visitor, handed Wade a note from the Council. He was requested to join them the next day if Wade felt up to it. As he read it, Wade was not sure if this was a polite request or an order. He made up his mind to see it as a request. Best to comply with their wishes now and see what it was they wanted of him.

Wade returned to his room at the hospital in a horse-drawn carriage. That night he slept well after a small meal, his first night without nightmares since the ordeal.

The following morning Wade felt alert and rested. Although still in pain, it was becoming more manageable. Two attendants arrived at his room with fresh clothing for him to wear and to escort him to the Council Chamber. The clothing that was provided him was the standard fare for these lands, a woolen shirt pulled over his head and pants cinched at the waist. Both were of a nondescript, light blue color.

When Wade entered the Council Chamber he found himself in a large room dominated by a single table at its center. The table was round, as dictated from the writings of another book partially saved from the ashes. These histories meant much to the People of the Lake. They were the connection between the past, before the War, and the future the books inspired. Statues and paintings lined the walls, tributes to these found stories of the past and to the greatness that the City by the Lake strove to attain. Several of these paintings depicted the First of the Council. The room was lit by several chandeliers hung high above the table. The table itself, the most dominant thing in the room, appeared made of oak. It showed its age by the dignity it was treated with and the care that was given to it. Around the table sat 13 people. All stood as Wade entered the room.

They returned to their seats as Wade reached the table. He was guided to the only open seat. This seat was opposite the one seat at the table raised slightly higher than the others were. The man in this seat wore a purple robe with red tassels on the shoulder, the symbol of his position as the head of the Council. It was he who chaired the meetings, yet he carried no vote. All others around the table wore simple white robes. Those to the right of the Chairman wore blue tassels on their shoulders.

These were the representatives of the commoners. They were six in number, equal to the Lords in their votes. Those on the left of the Chairman were the Lords. Each wore two tassels, one on each shoulder, a green one on the left, showing that they were High Lords, members of the Council, and a second one on the right, whose color varied, representing the Clan of the Lord. Wade noticed that each of these second colors was different. No Clan could have more than a single member on the Council. Therefore, the Council was set with twelve votes, six for the commoners, elected by administrative district, and six for the Lords, separated by lines of family. Moreover, the Council, itself, chose its Chairman, from the people at large in the city.

It was the Chairman that Wade first noticed when he entered the room. To Wade he looked like an ancient from an earlier time. His hair was white, as bleached by the ages, and his beard had grown long. He carried a presence as if somehow more than human, as though he had lived an eternity. Methuselah himself would look like this. While the others at the table carried their own auras of authority, they seemed to pale alongside that of the Chairman.

Once Wade had seated himself at the table opposite the Chairman, the latter spoke in a deep voice that resonated like thunder. Wade now noticed his skin as well seemed different from the others, a dark tone of brown.

"Greetings to you, Wade, man from across the sea." He spoke in an odd dialect of English. "Welcome to the Sanctuary of the Great Birds, home to the People of the Lake. We are its High Council. I am Tor, Chairmen of the Council. Those to my left are the High Lords, representing those who fly the Warbirds and defend our borders. Those to the right are the representatives of the common people, those who keep this city alive. We are here to answer any questions that you may have."

"Where am I?" Wade asked first, somewhat unsure of his position and what was expected of him.

"You are in the Valley of the Great Mountain, far inland from the sea," Tor replied.

"And I was brought here, rescued by you?"

"You were brought here by us, that is true."

"And why was I saved?"

"You were rescued, as we tried to rescue your comrades, for reasons that are perhaps best understood if you were to know more about us," spoke Lord Drant of Stetlin.

"Long ago there existed here a single race of man," Lord Drant began. "Then one day a great disaster overtook us. Many were killed and most that survived were overcome by a terrible sickness. And some of our yet-unborn children were horribly changed."

"The Last Great War?" Wade asked.

Lord Drant nodded, "At that time there also occurred a great change among our birds. Most died, but those who survived grew in size and became the Great Birds that you see today. As both man and Great Bird grew from the time that forged us, we were able to develop a close relationship with these birds. They were watched, guided and trained, as each generation grew larger and more intelligent. Moreover, their services are often needed. The largest became our Great Warbirds that you have witnessed. Our Lords ride these birds as others may ride a horse. The smaller among the birds became our messengers, pets, and to a small extent are used in our games. Their intelligence is fascinating to watch when put into puzzles and mazes.

Wade was impressed, "It's amazing the benefits that you were able to gain from what happened. Your people must be in the Hands of God."

"We have no God!" one of the commoners interjected. "And if we did, then this valley would be his Hell."

"I don't understand," Wade hesitated, "the valley, this city, is so beautiful."

Lord Drant continued. "Wade, our friend, I believe that you will see what was meant when I finish my story. You say it is beautiful here. It was not always thus.

"Back in the beginning, after what you called the Great War, some of our children became horribly mutated. We did not have the benefit of other areas, to survive underground until the worst was over. We remained above ground. While the worst of the devastation missed us, its clouds covered our lands. Some, not all, of our children became mutated, some horribly. Over the generations this continued. We tried to raise these deformities as best we could. We raised them as our normal children. Some were able to grow to become adults. They were offered the same privileges as other adults. Some married and produced children of their own, those that were able. And some of these children seemed normal. In time what had been normal became the minority.

"We tried to stem the growth of these abnormalities through quarantine and control of their inbreeding. Tests were done on pregnancies. Any mutations, and there continued to be many, were aborted. Still they grew in number and they threatened our existence. More controls were placed upon the mutations. No longer were they considered part of our race, and by now they had developed into their own. We began to hear stories that when a normal child was born to these creatures, it was destroyed.

"These things could no longer be tolerated. We had become a police state trying to control these who had once been our children. Finally, these monsters were rounded up and confined to a narrow valley to the north of the Lake. This proved to be a mistake. Separated, they continued to gain in their strength and in the time of our fathers, they revolted against our control. A terrible war was fought in this valley and it was ravaged. Many died in the onslaught from the monsters, but finally they fled back to the valley that had been their prison. Now it was their home. There they created their own society. They no longer looked like men, but through their inbreeding, they became horrible parodies of us, half-human monsters. They are barbarians, cannibals, no two of whom look alike. Yet they are fertile and breed like mice. If not for the great number killed violently in battle or amongst themselves, they would have outgrown their valley and overrun us that live here by the Lake.

"It was they who attacked you. They eat only living flesh and are constantly sending out patrols looking for them. They are a scourge of this part of the world. They make war on all they meet. They consider themselves the only true people.

"In this valley we must constantly be ready for their attacks. And when they run out of slaves, or just tire of eating them, they will attack us here again. We are a peaceful people, but we have learned how to fight."

"Can't you do something more about them?" Wade asked.

It was the commoner Praxton of Pyers who answered this question. "I am afraid that there is little that we can do alone. While they are not strong enough yet to conquer us, they are too strong to be defeated by us as well. A stalemate exists between us. They live for war, and if attacked, they would have to be totally destroyed. They are no longer man, but a wild beast. And to make them even more dangerous than a wild beast, some of them, their leaders, are as intelligent as us. Even wild beasts have some place in this world. Many among us ask the question, would it be right to destroy their race, to practice this genocide, even if we could?

"If we were to go to war with them and they not be destroyed, but only to flee before us, they would return in even greater numbers than before and we ourselves would be destroyed. We feel it is best, then, to continue this, our policy of containment.

"Our goal then is to prevent their spread from their valley and to rescue as many as possible of their captives. This is our curse, our Hell. For they are our children and we remain responsible for their actions."

Wades concern grew. "Were you able to free my shipmates?"

Tor spoke now and the others became still. "Of those taken only you were freed. Others did though survive." Tor paused, deciding how to continue. "They call themselves the White, after the color of their hideous transformations. Your friends will probably be used as a sacrifice to their god, unless they have shortage of fresh meat, in which case they will become the White's food. We are sorry we were unable to save all of you.

"Yet neither of these is the worst case that could become of them. There is a worse fate. That would be the Hydron. If food or sacrifice, the end is quick. Or at least the pain. With the Hydron, it would be preferable that they were never born. The Hydron keeps alive the food it digests with a chemical its body produces. So its victim remains alive, pain without end, while the Hydron takes its time digesting its food."

"What can we do to help them?" Wade implored.

It was Praxton who spoke again. He was an old man and had represented the southernmost lands of the Lake People a long time. "That was tried once by such as you. Tomorrow, if it pleases the Council, I will show you what happened to us then. And I will tell you why we can't allow it to happen again."

Tor resumed the chair and concluded the meeting.

"I hereby announce my support for this tour of our northern lands, Praxton of Pyers. But let me say that I hold my own views of what came before. The present is not the past, but part of the future. A future that I hope will see us free of the White. I now call this meeting to a close."

And so it came to pass that Wade, lost on a foreign soil, met the men who would decide his future. He returned to his room, his future course of action undecided, or even whether he had any choice in those actions. There really was not a lot to do if his thoughts ran counter to that of the Council.

That night the Lord Drant met with Tor in an inn frequented by the members of the Order of the Sage. On recognizing Tor as a member of the Order, the proprietor escorted the two men to a discreet table away from the general crowd in the inn. Many words were exchanged between the two men, who, it became obvious from their demeanor, were old friends. Finally, the heart of the matter at hand was brought up.

"Why, Tor, was the matter of the Underground not brought up?"

To this Tor responded, "Wait and see, friend. All will soon come clear. Time is the ally of none who hurry. Patience is what we have learned to have. Patience 'til the 'morrow comes."

They parted as silently as they had come in together: Tor with his thoughts still unseen and the High Lord wondering what was to come, but willing to allow his old friend to take a leading role in what was to be.

The party left early the next morning for the town of Erson. They traveled in carriages like Wade had explored the city in. Only now Tor was the driver. They had a good distance to travel and moved quickly down the dirt road. Once they left the city proper, farmhouses dominated the view, with vistas of farmlands being harvested as they passed.

Erson was the northernmost community of the People of the Lake. It now held only a small population, but it became quickly apparent to Wade when they arrived that at one time Erson had been a major city. In several places could be seen the shattered remains of buildings that would have rivaled those of the City by the Lake. The people themselves seemed somehow different from the others that Wade had met. They seemed timid and withdrawn, unsure of themselves and always with one eye to the north. No children could be seen anywhere in Erson, where the City by the Lake had been full of children.

Wade was taken through the center of the town, past a marketplace, half-fallen, no longer in use. They arrived on a small hill on the north side of the town. On top of this hill, really no more than a rise in the ground, stood a large monolith, surrounded by hundreds of markers. It was here they stopped.

Wade, Tor, Praxton and Drant stood quietly for a few minutes at the edge of the markers. Wade wondered to himself what they meant. None were labeled. Two more men came up to the hill and joined them. They were the High Lord Perth of Nourne, who represented the Lords of the North on the Council, and a much-respected commoner, Jamen of Kilne, a man who had many times shown bravery for the city and who had been offered a lordship, only to turn it down. It was the High Lord Perth, dressed in a hunter's garb of green, who broke the silence.

"And why was I not told of this meeting, Tor?" the High Lord demanded in mock anger. Having been at the Council meeting the day before, he knew full well of this expedition.

"This is not a matter of your concern," replied Praxton, with scorn, scarcely masking the obvious dislike he felt for the newcomers and obviously upset by their arrival.

"Not my concern!" Lord Perth's voice rose in true agitation this time. "You come to our greatest shrine, dedicated to those Lords who gave up their lives so those of you from this city could flee to safety. In addition, Tor accompanies you, something he does only in matters of greatest import. And you say that this is none of my concern?" Lord Perth's voice rose higher. The dislike between the two men was obvious to Wade as he watched the interplay. Moreover, Wade watched Tor, who seemed to have orchestrated what was to come. "I demand to be permitted to join you while you remain in my home province," Lord Perth finished.

"I see no objection to this," Tor replied to Lord Perth. "Can you see any reason to object to Lord Perth's presence, Lord Drant?"

"Nor I, Tor," Lord Drant said, knowing this meeting was not accidental.

"Tor, this meeting is a matter of Council!" Praxton exploded, seeing the maneuvering going on around him. Praxton continued, "The Council rules clearly state that in matters of Council, an equal number of commoners and Lords must be present at all times." With this Praxton confidently played his final card triumphantly, thinking he had been able to prevent the Lord from joining them. He had either forgotten or not noticed that the newly elected commoner, Jamen of Kilne, had accompanied the Lord Perth.

Tor however had noticed this very fact, as all had been planned the night before. "I believe that a commoner from the Council has accompanied Lord Perth."

"Indeed Tor, I also request to join your group. Praxton is right. There must be an equal number of Lords and commoners at a time such as this," stated Jamen as he stepped forward.

Praxton now grudgingly gave his consent that the others could join them. He fumed inwardly on how this expedition had been turned against him. Wade, too, noticed this and wondered what part he was to play in this theater.

It was as Praxton was beginning to speak again that Lord Drant shouted a warning: the White were attacking them.

A small party of the White had been watching the men assemble on the hill for some time. They were waiting to see how many would join the assemblage. Too many, and they would withdraw and report their findings. Now, not seeing any more of the southerners gather, and confident of victory, they flew toward the gathering of men, both Warbirds and warriors screaming their curses.

For the second time Wade was forced to do battle with this spawn of the last Great War. He fought with a weapon, passed to him by Tor: a pike with a crescent-shaped blade on the tip.

With weapon in hand, Wade advanced with the others to meet the White, also now on foot. Jamen and Perth fought on his right, while Praxton and Drant were on his left. He had lost sight of Tor, wondering briefly what had become of him. Then the fighting consumed them. In the brief glances he had of the other fighters, never before had he seen such fighting skill as transpired here. More than a few times one or another of them came to Wade's aid, saving him from a severe wound. As the four around him fought as the heroes of lore and Wade contributed as best he could, it seemed that, yet again, Wade would be on the losing side in a battle against the White. They had no fear and cared not how many died, as long as they proved victorious. The men were sure (it seemed to Wade) to be overwhelmed by the sheer numbers of the attackers.

Then, as swiftly as it had begun, the battle was over. The mutants fled as if now facing a great army. The five men stood, shoulder to shoulder, watching them flee.

Wade turned to see what had transpired behind them. He expected to see at the least a relief force from the town approaching them. All he saw was Tor on the top of the hill, next to the obelisk, a quiet smile on his face.

Tor called the others to him, and they left the battlefield, unscathed, to travel to the Castle Nourne, home of the High Lord Perth. There they could talk without fear of attack.

The road from Erson to Castle Nourne was paved with flat stones gathered from a quarry south of the valleys. It was a massive stone castle they came to at Nourne, high walls forming the inner sanctum, and even higher towers helping to protect the castle from the air. Many times this castle had been attacked by the White, but its walls had never been breached. It had taken almost all of the remaining daylight to reach Nourne.

The inner courtyard displayed a tranquility that seemed out of place with what Wade had seen elsewhere in the north. Grapevines lined the pathways they followed from the gates. When Wade had looked up at the size of the gate they entered the castle through, Lord Perth had stated that if attacked, the gate could be lowered in seconds. More than a few of the White, he stated, had been impaled on the prongs that embedded the gate into its foundation. By the middle of the civil war, the White had given up trying to take the castle from the ground. In the air, the Whites had been equally unsuccessful in their attempts to conquer the castle. Lord Perth pointed out the highest towers that had been built specifically to repel the White's airborne attacks. Each of the towers commanded a 360-degree view of the castle and its surroundings. Although it seemed the High Lord was bragging about these achievements to Wade, it also seemed he carried a sad tone in his voice as well.

As the party came through the walkway lined by the grapevines, they came to what seemed the most incongruous part of the castle of all: a large central pond stocked with some large gold-colored fish and fed by a man-made fountain. To one side of the pond stood a small brick-and-glass building.

"In times of peace, before the war with the White, Nourne Castle was a place of pilgrimage and sanctuary. I hope in my lifetime it becomes that again." Lord Perth spoke longingly of that time, his hands reaching toward the sanctuary and his voice full of hope.

"Maybe it shall," Tor said in a solemn voice that all took note of.

"To bring back the hell to the common man, that is what's real," Praxton added angrily. "Is that the reason for such subterfuge as I've witnessed today?" Praxton added, fuming, still feeling scorned by the trickery he perceived was used against him. Praxton's face was bright red as he strove to hold back his anger. Major council deeds needed a quorum of just five. Praxton had no time to summon others who might stand with him against any endeavor against the White, as seemed likely now. "This is an affront to the legacy of the Round Table, to which your words spoke of with such eloquence and reverence," Praxton added mockingly to the Lord Perth.

"An affront you speak." Tor spoke quietly but sternly to Praxton. "Yet time passes quickly. To remain bound to a past of your choosing would only bring ruin. Bowing to the security of the past, however, I will Grant you one day to assure yourself that others of the Council who may agree with your views attend this meeting. They have been invited to attend already. Is that what you wish?" Tor requested of Praxton.

"Of what good would that do? Only I, a commoner, who represents that region south of the lake, will stand up to your reckless adventure. All others will follow your graces, Tor, and that of the leadership of Jamen of Kiln, more Lord than commoner in many eyes."

"And yet he is elected by those of his district by the largest of margins."

"Sheep led by fools."

"Then you agree we may proceed when the remainder of the Council, which chooses to attend, arrives on the 'morrow."

"I am left with little choice," Praxton spoke with resignation. "Yet first let it be told that cautionary tale of what came before to this land of the north."

"Agreed," spoke Lord Drant of Stetlin. "And let us have Lord Perth of Nourne, our host, tell the story once more of the monolith and the markers set in stone. Are we all agreed?"

Praxton was feeling as if he had won something with this and a slight smile gave way on his face.

The consent was unanimous, though Tor, as was the custom, spoke last on the matter.

"On the 'morrow it shall be. A discussion of what came before. Moreover, with that, what action the future will bring. First dinner and then rest. In the morning let all of the Council assemble in Nourne."

Praxton seemed startled by these last words and now he felt himself even more at a loss than before.

In almost an aside, Tor turned to Praxton of Pyers and spoke. "I agree that the great decisions due here require more than just us five. I shall pass on the added urgency that for this matter it is required that all of the Council assembles tomorrow." This would be an assembly of a type not seen since the ill-fated war against the White. With this assembly, the People of the Lake would rise up once more against their cousins to the north.

Praxton knew that he would be the lone voice against such a move, to slow the inexorable movement of the fates. 'How many of the south that I call my friends will die this time?' Praxton thought to himself. 'All for the glory of a few Lords and the heroic Jamen of Kiln.' Praxton's thoughts remained bitter and black.

The five men continued through the inner plaza of the castle, roses replacing grapevines along the pathway. Wade marveled at the colors of the roses as he passed by them. He mentioned this to Lord Perth.

"It is to my wife and those who came before her, that we owe the pleasure of these gardens. Bare with thorns most of the year, cut back each winter, they are reminders of what we have come through. Yet in the spring and summer they become a glorious reminder of what will be again someday, when the Northern Valley will once again bloom itself as a tribute to the people who still make this area their home."

A small gate opened into Castle Nourne itself and the lady of the castle, Lady Alyce, stood beckoning them inside. She stood as tall as the High Lord Perth and she carried a scar across one cheek as a badge of honor. What may have been a blemish on another woman seemed not on the Lady Alyce. Her light brown hair was held in place on her head with a single comb of silver.

"My wife, and great partner, the Grand Lady Alyce," the Lord Perth announced to them all, "and my daughter, Theresa."

Theresa had stood slightly behind the Lady Alyce at the door, so Wade had not noticed her at first. When he did, he was almost overwhelmed by her beauty. Her blue eyes seemed to dance, yet at the same time seemed covered in sadness. She stood almost as tall as Wade, the gown she wore covered her figure, but the energy in her step could not be hidden. He stepped up to the Lady Alyce and, bowing, took her hand to his lip. When he stood to do the same with her daughter, he could only stand. Voice and manner seemed lost. He was rescued by Lord Drant's response to seeing the Lady Alyce.

"My Lady," he spoke, "to stand before the hero of my people…" Tears came to his eyes as he lowered his head and kissed her hand. "Of words I have none that would do justice to your beauty and your courage."

The Lady smiled and bid him rise.

Tor spoke quietly to Wade about this all. "Not all of our heroes are what they seem," he spoke. "And I noticed your eye for the Lady Theresa. It will take a hero in his own right to win her heart. Many a man has tried and failed." He seemed to be voicing his approval for the feelings Wade felt.

Jamen of Kiln stepped forward. He, too, knelt before the Grand Lady and took her hand, not with a kiss, but to lay his sword in her open palm. His glance toward Theresa was not returned, but the Lord Perth and Lady Alyce both noted her glance at Wade.

"Let us stand once more, side by side, embracing the victories that lie before us," Jamen said loudly enough for all to hear.

"To speak such now may be premature. Let the stories wait until the morning. Too much death we saw together, Jamen, my friend. The future may bring hope, but now comes the time for replenishment for weary travelers. Welcome to the Castle Nourne, a bastion of light, a hope that continues to shine in the north, even in these dark times. Let tonight bring light upon our future."

All entered the castle proper, each passing their grace with the Lady Alyce and her eldest daughter as they entered.

Lady Alyce addressed Wade, "To you Wade, Servant of the Western Sea, I bid great welcome and tiding. Soon all shall be one again. Enter my home, Master Wade. Much lies unspoken in your future among us. Rest and replenish and know my home shall always be yours."

They entered a great hall. Two tables, long and oblong, the tops faced with exquisitely colored tile, dominated the floor, and along the wall were large portraits in wooden frames of sixteen men and women.

"Those who came before," The Lady Alyce spoke to Wade, who was given the seat beside her as a place of honor.

"And what of the empty frames?" Wade asked. "Is that something that may be spoken of?"

"The first frame, empty now, contained the portrait of the founders of Nourne Castle. It was lost early in the war with the White. We dream of the day when we can regain it and place it in its proper standing, first among the Lords and Ladies of Nourne."

"Why was it taken by the White?"

"Why…" Lady Alyce's voice dwindled before picking up again. "Not just the Land of the Lakes owes much to the First Lord of Castle Nourne. The first of the White was also of the Castle Nourne. He took the portraits to place in his own hall, first of his line, as he said. This is a shame we bear witness to at Castle Nourne. That it was of Nourne that the White came to be. At the markers beyond the town of Erson once two sets of markers stood, one set for the Lords who fought and died there, and a smaller set, later taken and destroyed by what remains of Erson. These were placed for the Children of Nourne. You know them as the White. They are a plague that remains to us to this day. The first born of each Lord of Nourne is born with a mutation. And the first King of the White was Myk of Nourne." With that the Lady Alyce turned quiet. And she remained so throughout the meal.

The meal itself was quiet and uneventful for those assembled around the table. Even Praxton seemed more subdued after a schooner of ale. Wade enjoyed the feast but wondered how the others of *The Proctant* had fared. Whenever he glanced toward the Lady Theresa, her eyes seemed on him as well. A warmth, a feeling that all would be well, seemed to overcome Wade whenever he caught Theresa's glances. There were the other children, all daughters of the Lord and Lady, around the table as well.

After the meal, as one of the younger daughters escorted Wade to his room, Theresa cast a quick look his way. For once in his life, Wade seemed unsure of how to behave toward a woman. There seemed to burn something bright and strong between them.

In the room that Wade was presented to, a fireplace was already burning for warmth. It was a simply furnished room. His bed was piled high with warm blankets and by the lone window sat a small desk and chair. A large fur covered part of the floor by the bed. He was left alone to rest and that gave him the time to ponder further his future and what had transpired around him. It seemed Wade was the focal point of events beyond his control. With each turn, he was thrust more into the forefront of what was to come. While unsure of most parts of what was to be, he was certain that his future lay closely intertwined with the Castle Nourne and the daughter of Lord Perth and Lady Alyce, Theresa of Nourne.

He slept with restless dreams of their ship, *The Proctant...* of the White... and of a future yet to come. But each time the dreams began to turn to nightmare, the image of Theresa would enter his mind and soothe those dreams.

The morning came too soon for Wade. The restless night's dreams had left him still tired. A warm tub of water had been prepared for him and he was led to this by Theresa. She handed him a towel and discreetly closed the door after him, but not before giving him a mischievous smile and flashing her eyes at him. She said clean clothing would be in his room when he was ready. One more mystery for Wade to solve, but at least this one seemed to foreshadow something much more enjoyable than the others.

Wade stayed in the tub until the water began to chill. After drying off, he returned to his room wearing a robe that had been placed by the tub prior to his arrival. In his room, he found the promised clean clothing to change into. The last few days he had had more changes into clean laundry than on the entirety of any of his voyages, Wade thought.

He found his way down to the Great Hall for his morning meal. There he saw that most of the Council had arrived with their aides and were enjoying the feast. This presented quite an array of both people Wade had met before and many newcomers, all come to lend voice to their concerns and ramifications of what was to come. Sitting with Tor was another who carried the same look. As he moved to sit with them, Theresa grabbed his arm and directed him where to sit; beside her, where she herself had prepared his meal.

Although aware of Theresa's smile and the effects that her conversation had on him, Wade was turned inward throughout the meal.

Only tidbits of what she said penetrated his consciousness. His mind drifted to the fate of his former comrades from the ship. What had happened to them as he enjoyed this meal? He also wondered what the Council had planned for him.

Among those things his ears did pick up from Theresa was the identity of the man with Tor. He was said to be called Phelix, another Sage such as Tor. He had arrived that morning from the valley to the north, the land of the White. She told Wade, and his head perked up at this, that he carried news of his shipmates. This disquieted Wade and he became more anxious that the meal end so he could find out what Phelix knew. The remainder of the meal seemed to last an eternity to Wade and Theresa grew frustrated by his lack of attention to her. This was something she was unaccustomed to.

As Theresa tired of Wade's inattention, she left him to sit by her mother. Lady Alyce smiled at her daughter. She put her finger to her daughter's lips as Theresa began to speak.

"Patience, Theresa," she smiled. "Much lies in the pathways of our visitor."

"But … mother…," Theresa pleaded.

"Soon you'll gain the insight of the future. There you will see what lies ahead for you and Wade. Until then, Theresa, have patience."

The Lady Alyce brought the head of her eldest daughter to her shoulder. Quiet tears came to both. Theresa had already come to see part of what the future would bring to her and to Wade.

The table was cleared, not soon enough for Wade, and the Council members and those who had arrived for this meeting adjourned to another room of the castle. Wade still had his own thoughts, unsure of the unknown reasons he was present for these meetings. In this meeting room stood another table, identical to the one in the City by the Lake's Council Room. As High Lord Perth of Nourne directed Wade to his place at the table, he mentioned to Wade why this was so.

"Before the Civil War with the White, this room was the Council Room of our people. It was only after that war that the Council was moved to the City by the Lake, at that time a much smaller city than Erson. Before the war both the Northern and Southern Valleys belonged to our people. It was here at this castle, and even more so at Erson, that we held the White's army in check."

"And so the two sets of stones on the hill," spoke Wade.

"The second set, removed and destroyed by the citizens of Erson after they were placed by a member of this castle, represented my uncle, the first King of the White, Myk of Nourne. Outside the castle wall, just beyond the main gate, now lie those stones, set there by my father after being dumped by the Lake in broken shards. These pieces of stone now represent the many broken hearts of those who dwell in this castle.

"Those of Castle Nourne led the defense of Erson. Many were lost on the battlefield, so too the children of Nourne, deformed through no fault of their own, led to defeat by a lord of Nourne.

"Myk of Nourne, a Lord of Nourne as first born in his own right, a name held in disgrace by all our people, was the founder of the White. It is his portrait as well that lies missing, now but an empty frame on the wall.

"To the north he led his people, to turn in time against all of us. His portrait is now in place above the throne of the Kings of the White. Each king in turn, their reigns cut short through life-force and battle, calls himself Myk of Nourne." With this, Lord Perth of Nourne lowered his eyes in quiet shame. Wade came to understand the guilt that carried Perth to right the wrong of his ancestor.

The meeting commenced when the last of the Council arrived at the table. As the Sergeant of Arms announced the final arrival, Tor walked to his own elevated chair and began the meeting.

Tor spoke with a loud and commanding voice, his face as serious as any had ever seen. "Here, let it be known, The Council of the Round Table meets once again in its rightful place. Let the demon curse of the family Nourne end with this meeting. And let the reunification of our lands begin here as well."

Cheering from those gathered around the table and the banging on the table by the assembled Council overwhelmed these last remarks as the Council made clear its approval of this meeting. Only Praxton sat quietly. Once the assembly quieted, Praxton took the opportunity to speak.

"As my voice may be the sole voice of reason, let it be heard first. And let it be heard what came before, when we last tried this *unification*."

"Of the Slave Revolt, you speak," called out another commoner.

"Then let that story be told. And of the story of the stand at Erson," spoke Jamen of Kiln. "We who were there remember that day, when the hillside bled of the deaths of the Children of Nourne, of the heroic few that held their ground against the barbaric hordes of the White."

"Speak!…Speak!…" came the call from the gallery assembled beyond the table. The crowd of those who came filled the Council Room and beyond. And Praxton watched what he had hoped would be a cautionary tale instead be the story of a cry to battle once more.

"To Erson!" the assemblage called out, once again the Council pounding their fists to the table, all but Praxton.

"And of those who died," Praxton quietly interjected, unheard by those around him.

"Let all be honored who fought that day, and let this be an end to the torment of the north," Lord Slyth of Tilden called forth.

"Tell us of the story," another called out to Jamen.

"There is another who can tell of this tale better than I, a visitor too long gone from this Council, Phelix of the Northern Valley." Jamen pointed out their visitor, where he sat next to Tor, and bade him rise.

Phelix rose to address those assembled. To the accompanied applause, he held out his hands to silence the recognition. His voice was solemn, quiet, yet tempered with both hope and bitterness. Phelix wore tattered robes, long since beyond repair, from his time in the caverns below the Northern Valley. His gray eyes were tired, and his hair gray and balding. His voice seemed both hopeful and defeated.

"Friends, it is too long since we met here as one. A time of destiny is upon us. To look to a future and remember the past, I bring word of the end. Will you give me word of a new beginning?" Cheers filled the room as Phelix spoke.

"Over a dozen years ago, unable to bear the holds of that slavery you left us in when the White conquered the Northern Valley, we attempted to gain our freedom. Hope you gave us that we could, would, prevail together. In the end we were betrayed, left alone by you of the Lake and the Southern Valley, and betrayed of our secrets by one of our own.

"Like vermin, the White hunted us down and you of the south looked the other way. Your monuments to what you call peace, we call the monuments of betrayal. We fought with you then, here at Nourne and at Erson. As your people fled south in fear of the White, we remained, first as slaves, then as food. Food! Like cattle or pigs they kept us. Food we became to the White! And in your safety you pretended we were gone. Can any of you hold your conscience open to what happened, or are your souls barren to what came to be?

"But we were not gone, and when the time came to defend us, to help us escape our enslavement, you left us alone. Too many of your own sons and daughters had died. It was easier to pretend we did not exist.

"Our revolt was crushed. How many of you died with the promised help? One hundred, two hundred? I bid our hosts separate from my disdain. He and his wife, Alyce, stood side-by-side with us and each carries with them the scars of that combat. In the end, alone beside us, even Nourne had to bid us good-bye.

"How few died among you? And we of the Northern Valley, numbering one hundred and fifty thousand before our aborted attempt at freedom, today fewer than five thousand, above and below ground, remain. Children are few. Would you bring a child into the life we now live? And of food there is even less. Often I have seen a father, a fugitive below ground, come to the surface to give up his life (as food to the White!) so that his one allowed child would be able to eat.

"We, the People of the Northern Valley, once your brothers, who stood so proud alongside you, another year and we will be no more, a people destroyed, in part through your own indifference. The question before you is a simple one: Will you allow your brothers to be destroyed, or free us from the hell that you created and left us in, through your own indifference and inaction?" Cheering was heard again among those gathered for Phelix and his words.

Phelix sat still. His words had left him exhausted. The room exploded around him in answer to his words. Now the rest would be left up to Tor and the Council of Twelve.

None spoke for several minutes once the uproar ended and calm came back to the room. During Phelix's speech the Lady Alyce had entered the room to stand beside her husband, Lord Perth. She placed her arm on his shoulder to lend her strength to his and they exchanged a timeless glance. As she placed her hand on her husband's shoulder, each of the other Council members' wives entered as well, to stand alongside their husbands and lend their strength to them. Even Praxton's wife appeared and Praxton knew that whatever misgivings he felt toward the future, the call for action had come. His wife whispered to him, "We abandoned them once. Can we do that again?" Her smile was one of sadness. The wives remained as the vote was given, adding their strength for what was to come to their husbands.

Tor needed no words to ask for a vote. As his eyes passed from one member to the next, each raised his hand and left, to return home and prepare as best as possible for the conflict to come. Even Praxton, when came time his turn to vote, raised his hand and left with his wife to Pyers, to prepare for a battle that he didn't expect to survive. The assemblage was united. They had left their kindred to the north alone twice. They would not do so again.

In the end, Wade sat alone with just Tor and Phelix. He had been moved by what had just transpired. And he wondered what role he would play.

Tor got up and motioned Phelix and Wade to follow him. They walked outside to the rose garden and sat together at a small table set with chairs. The scent of roses was strong in the air. The three men sat in silence as they watched the butterflies hop from rose to rose, graceful and beautiful in their short lives.

"The foolish way of man, preparing for war." Out of the blue Tor spoke.

"But wasn't war what we came here to decide?" answered Phelix.

"You remain in the north in the midst of such tragedy. Our charges must evolve beyond that. Weren't those the words of our Teachers?"

"But the issue of the White must be resolved. And blood is all they understand."

"Then we must work to ensure that the bloodshed is felt by few."

Phelix turned to Wade, motioning toward him as he spoke again to Tor. "And he represents the future?"

"A future for us all."

"Then he must be taken to the caverns," Phelix spoke as if Wade either was not there or could not understand what was being said.

Wade interjected himself into the conversation. "The caverns, do I have any say in this matter?"

Tor responded to him. "From the moment that your ship, *The Proctant*, left its home port, all the actions of its crew were laid in stone by the Teachers. Act on your own behalf, but know the future of our race lies with you all."

Wade just sat and stared at the roses. Once again, it seemed his future was predetermined. Wade realized he had felt all along that he was to play a bigger part in this world. Now he knew for certain.

After a long pause, Wade looked up at Tor and Phelix and spoke again. Few words were necessary, and Wade wondered just where the future would take him next. "When do we leave?"

Phelix answered, "Tonight after sundown I will return to prepare the way for you. Only then can we travel the secret ways. The darkness of the night is our protection against the White, our sole friend at this time in our struggle with them. For in the horror of their evolution, it is night vision that they have lost."

"Are they blind then?" It seemed to Wade that they had seen clearly enough in battle.

"With the twilight all becomes dark to them."

"Then there lies our hope," Wade finished. "It is the night that will Grant us victory."

Tor knew in his heart why Wade had been sent to him. He added, "Then that is when we will strike out when no moon shall rise to Grant the White what limited vision they may gain by it."

Phelix left them to return to the caverns of the north. Wade and Tor remained quiet as they both contemplated what was to come, a last few moments to enjoy the tranquility of the rose garden. Tor spoke again, quietly, just to Wade. "Because of you, Wade, this is the beginning of our future."

Wade sat, not speaking, but knowing he suddenly felt that he was a part of something beyond what could be seen around him.

When Tor arose, he spoke quickly. "We leave on the 'morrow's twilight."

Chapter Seven
The Slave Revolt

They lived in the darkness of a place without sunlight, a series of primitive dwellings in the caverns below the city of their masters. It was their sanctuary, carved out of the limestone by the waters of an ancient underground river. It was their home, their last refuge, their hiding place.

In these caverns a people lived, or at least tried to survive. They ate what fish wandered through the underground river, but these were few, as that once plentiful supply of food had dwindled through their over-fishing to survive. A plant life, edible if cooked, was cultivated, yet this was but a meager source of food. Starvation, always a threat, had become more of a reality in their lives. The fugitives had begun the occasional foray above ground to raid what grain and livestock they found. That, too, as a supplement to their diet had dwindled. The White now carefully watched for the raids of the refugees. Moreover, fewer slaves above ground meant less of a need for those food sources, as the White had no need for it themselves.

It was for the entrances to the caverns that the White looked, a chance to find their lost slaves, these hidden people.

There was a constant threat of discovery, the threat that the White would find them. The White were always in need of live food. The fugitives below were needed for the food chain so that fewer raids of neighboring lands were needed. Many had come to fear the raids of the White in this part of the world. These raids themselves were less successful now as defenses against them grew. The White's last major raid to the coast to capture the survivors of a shipwreck had led to a massacre of their riders. For the moment, their numbers were barely sufficient to protect their own enclave in their home in the Northern Valley. The White needed more local food sources as well as the fugitives. They had even begun to eat the flesh of the lesser beasts, beef and bear. No matter how unpleasant, the White needed to regain their strength. More multiple litters were needed by their childbearing females. Those too old to bear children were taken, added to the food stock. Another unpleasant task in the mind of the Myk, but it had to be done.

Food! No longer were the White strong enough.

Food! Their numbers devastated at the sea and on the return.

Food! The White would grow strong again. Males matured more rapidly now.

Food! The Myk thought two or three years and the White would be strong again. The Southern Valley and its despised City by the Lake would fall, payment for their attack on the raiders.

Food! All would go to the males and what females could bear children.

Food! Strength! Power! What slaves remained above ground would be added to the food chain.

Food! For this emergency young females and the old would be added to the food chain.

Food! And those fugitives that remained underground would be found and then they too would be added to the food chain.

Food! The Myk smiled with his crooked mouth, prominent fangs exposed.

Food! The world would be theirs, soon.

In the caverns below the struggles continued. Where the fugitives once numbered over ten thousand, now they numbered fewer than two thousand. Most now were women and children. Each woman was allowed one child, any more and that child was destroyed. Any malformed children, and there were many, were destroyed. The people remembered that the White were once their children, a memory that bore a hatred of any born different. Moreover, that difference could be slight. It mattered not. Any defect detected at childbirth meant death for the newborn.

Even children born healthy now died. It seemed the very caverns that had protected them in their flight from above were now bringing death to the weakest.

No elderly, few children, and fewer men, such was what remained of the fugitives of the last revolt against the White.

This was the world that Alum entered, a people on the verge of extinction, whose last, forlorn hope, was to be liberated from the darkness and brought back to the sunlight above. Weak and few in number, they dreamed of a future in their valley above once again. They only needed somebody to lead them. They had nobody left of their own. It was Alum they chose.

To remain meant death. To leave the caverns meant the same. Nevertheless, the choice was made. All would follow, their Chief knew with sadness. His name was Altuan. He was the most ancient among them, yet Alum was almost as old. Altuan would remain chief until it was his turn to die. Then another would be chosen, probably from among the women, as there were so few men. He had already lived longer than most. If he had not been their Chief, he would have sacrificed himself the year before. As Chief he was allowed an extra five years. Five extra years of this torment, it was not a blessing. At the end of the five years or sooner if he chose, his suicide would come so the young would have more food to eat. Such was their custom now.

Alum and Altuan discussed a great many things of the outside world. Much of this world Altuan seemed very clearly informed about. The Chief told Alum of the old times in the Northern Valley, before the time of the White. Alum spoke in turn of the Confederation, and how it had only a short while earlier come into being. Altuan told Alum of the revolt, and why it was Alum who had been chosen to bring the fugitives back to the sun.

It had been almost twelve years since the revolt had begun. While the revolt lasted almost two years, the last year and a half of it was mostly the White's slaughter of the slaves. The White ate very well then.

The rebellion had begun with very little sign of what was to come.

The old Myk was gone and the White's Priest class now ruled. Under the old Myk, almost enlightened by the standards of the White, the peasants, those born normal, were treated as serfs. Not free, but not food either. Food was brought in from raids to the world outside the Valley. Moreover, the White were strong, as few in the surrounding lands had developed defenses to withstand these raids.

Under the Priests a new order was established. Those normal were now the slaves of the White. Then less than slaves as they were made part of the food chain of the White. No longer would just captives of the raids be food. No longer would the White have to eat the disagreeable meat of the lesser beasts. Now all not of the White would be considered a source of the White's diet.

The slaves revolted. What else could they do. The people of the Southern Valley met this with approval. And the City by the Lake added their support.

"Intervention!" the White called out. Left alone by the Southern Valley since their own revolt succeeded, the White were ready to carry the war to the Southern Valley and beyond. All able to carry arms assembled, creating a vast horde. For a generation they had built their army. Never had it been stronger. Forced breeding had come early to the White. The more deformed the child the greater esteem he or she was held in by the White.

Warbirds had been bred in numbers as well, barely trained but held in such esteem that they were fed only human flesh. Only the most deformed were given the honor of riding these mounts.

First to the south the White's army roared. By the thousands they flew on their Warbirds with the support of tens of thousands on the ground. Led by the new Myk they marched to conquer the Southern Valley. They carried weapons of barbarous design, intended to match the deformities of each soldier, designed not only to kill but also, in the preferred case, to incapacitate. The Whites marched not just to conquer, but also to fill their ever-growing need for food, for human flesh, non-mutant human flesh. The White were the superior species and did not think themselves cannibals, though they added to the food chain any normal-born child. The White were as far above humans as the humans were above the cattle that they consumed. And the White treated both the same.

All along the border separating the lands of the White from the Southern Valley, the defenders of the Southern Valley were defeated, routed by the White. Few remained to flee south from the devastation. Unprepared, their defenses crumbled, and man, woman and child were put into the food stock to feed the army of the White. Only at the Castle Nourne was resistance successful. Wave after wave was thrown at the Castle without effect. Even from the air the defenses held. And with that the onslaught of the White paused.

The people of the City by the Lake at first deemed the war not their concern. While they had verbally supported the slave rebellion, they had really done nothing to help them and offend the White. Even as their allies in the northern edge of the Southern Valley faced defeat and slavery (at best) at the hands of the White, the City by the Lake did nothing.

Finally, it was a young man, a commoner, who could stand and watch no more. Against the pleading, then the orders of the Council, he moved to raise an army and go to the aide of Nourne. Though young, still in his early thirties, he was held in great esteem by the youth of the Southern Valley. His gallantry in defending the Valley against the raids of the White was renown.

In the center of the City by the Lake, in a plaza dominated by the Council Chambers, Jamen drove his banner into the soil. By the hundreds they came, the best that the City by the Lake had to offer, both men and women. Still the Council dallied. They ordered the arrest of Jamen of Kilne but when the sheriffs came to arrest him, they instead joined the banner of his army. The Council panicked. What could be done to stop this madman who would bring destruction down on all of them?

For two weeks Jamen's army gathered, joined now by many of the families of the nobles, riding their own Warbird steeds. A message was sent to Lord Perth of Nourne stating to Erson this army would march, to join the army of Nourne. They would stand or be defeated as Jamen of Kilne and Lord Perth of Nourne cast their lot together.

Leading the army north, Jamen of Kilne's armored mail gleamed in the sunlight. Mounted on the back of a chestnut horse, a beast now almost extinct due to the value of its flesh, he appeared as if a hero of old brought to life.

With each hovel they passed, refugees of the north joined the march, the leadership of Jamen carrying their hearts. Their weapons were sometimes no more than a scythe or a pitchfork, yet they marched with Jamen.

As Jamen saw the growing army around him, he worried. The core of his army, those he could trust and depend on in the coming combat, were scattered in the undisciplined mass. He would lead them to a massacre if this remained. Slowly he gathered his lieutenants around him and with them his leading core of troops. He quickened the pace.

Almost to Erson now and the elite fighting men and women of the City by the Lake now marched a half-day ahead of the mass who struggled to keep up. Stragglers now began to fall out of the unruly horde. Others became fearful once again as they neared Erson and they too fell out of the march. A march that had blossomed to over twenty thousand now numbered a tenth of that. However, these were the ones Jamen wanted at his side.

The first corps, two hundred of the best, led by Jamen himself, reached the southern edge of Erson. There he received word that five hundred of the Castle Nourne, led by the Lord and Lady of the castle, would arrive in the morning. Overhead the Warbirds of the White kept watch. These were the scouts of the White and under orders to watch, not engage. Finally, they were pushed away by the Warbirds of the nobles of the Southern Valley and Nourne.

Fifty thousand did the army of the White still number, with over ten thousand of the Warbirds and their riders. The Warbirds were bred to wreak havoc on the enemy even if their rider was lost. The White watched this assemblage of the Southern Valley with confidence. They had defeated all before them. The Myk expected no difference now. One last battle, then Castle Nourne and the Southern Valley would be theirs.

Nightfall came and Jamen watched the faces of the army he had brought. They would fight to the end, he knew, but would their strength and spirit be enough? They faced so many. Under the full moon, Jamen watched as those that remained of the army of the Southern Valley trickled in. Poorly equipped, how long could they be expected to play a role in what was to come?

Near midnight, a new force arrived, a gleaming beacon leading it approached. The Myk wondered at its appearance but he did not worry. Tor, the Sage of the Southern Valley, led its advance. One hundred shields marched with him. A young general, Stephen, Lord of Beers, marched first among them. Against the orders of the Council he had led them to join with Lord Perth. Three armies now gathered, with a forth due from Nourne in the morning. Five thousand they would then number. Against the multitude of the White they would stand.

Morning came and with it the Lord and Lady of Nourne, leaving few behind at the Castle Nourne. Many assaults it had withstood and some said that it could never fall. Together, with the people of the Southern Valley and those of the City by the Lake, a stand would be taken at Erson. Here the invasion would be stopped or all of the lands of the Valleys would fall to the White.

Campfires burned throughout the night and in the morning breakfast shared. If these men were to fall in battle it would be as rested, with strong hearts and full bellies. No cowards stood that day at Erson, though few expected to see the next day. But as long as one stood in the end, the valleys would be safe.

Weapons had been brought from the Castle Nourne and these were distributed as far as possible among the commoners of the valley who had joined the march. Now they too would live or die as the warriors they had come to be, bringing naught but their bravery to the battle. With the armory at Erson found intact, each man and woman on the battlefield would stand with proper weapon in hand.

Each of the leaders of this army now met in conference: Jamen of Kilne, Lord Stephen of Beers, the Lord and Lady of Castle Nourne and the Sage, Tor. The fate of the Peoples of the Valleys lay in their hands. Questions were answered and strategies were made. And for the first time it was decided a commoner would lead them into battle. Lords Stephen and Perth lay their swords at Jamen's feet. The Lady Alyce gave him the scarf that she had worn and Tor looked on in agreement.

Of first concern, where to make their stand? All gave the Lord Perth the say in this matter, as these were his holdings where they would fight. "To the north of Erson, on the Hill of Roses, let us make our stand there. The flower of our gardens and hearts, let the rose give us strength in the battle to come."

So it was that on the Hill of the Rose the Army of the Southern Valley would make its stand. In the center would be Lord Stephen of Beers and his one hundred shieldmen. On his left and slightly to the rear would be Jamen and his five hundred. To the White flank he would hurl his attack. The Lord Perth of Nourne with his wife Alyce, the Lady of Nourne, would command the right. He unfurled the banner of Nourne in front of the four hundred he commanded. These soldiers were of the highest order, placed closest to the Castle Nourne. In their homelands they would fight. In victory or defeat, to the last man would they stand.

It was Tor who commanded the rest, those that had joined the march to Erson, both in the city center and along the route. A reserve of unproven skills, they knew what it was they fought for: their homes, their children and their lives. Resolve was strong, but strength was weak. To stem any breakthrough was their task.

Mid-morning came as each man and woman of the Southern Army stood in position. This was the largest force the Southern Valley and the City by the Lake had ever assembled. Throughout the night more had come to join the banner of Jamen, mostly survivors of the first assaults from the White. They, more than any of the others, knew what it was that was at stake. They had seen their families eaten alive before them. They carried a resolve few else on the battlefield carried. Their position as they arrived was to the forefront of the reserves. It was an honor that they both wanted and were given gladly. Here was a reserve that could indeed be counted on.

Gathered not a mile away was the scourge of this evil, the White, with their army of over fifty thousand. The Myk stood at the front, arm raised. This was his home once, these lands of the Castle Nourne, and it would be again. Overhead flew the White's Warbirds and their riders. Over the heads of the Southern armies they would fly, to scream their barbarous cries and then return. But the army beneath them remained calm.

More continued to gather at the back of the Southern armies' reserve. They were stragglers of the march north that had regained their courage. First to the armory and then the field of battle they were directed, an unruly mass, but perhaps of some good in the end.

For two hours the field remained the same, the White's army shouting their obscenities, and the Warbirds overhead, first diving and then returning to the air above the Myk. Finally one of the Warbirds came too close to the ground and two arrows passed into the head of the rider, shattering his skull. Three more arrows passed through the heart of the Warbird.

"Who fired that! Hold your fire. Arrows must not be wasted."

Bird and rider plummeted to the ground. When both bodies hit, it was as if a signal had been sent. Forward the army of the White swept, running hard, their weapons raised high. Above them, two thousand Warbirds and their hideous riders swarmed down from the sky. The Warbirds arrived before the charge, to wreak havoc in the lines of the army below and help initiate the breakthrough. However, no person of the Southern army moved to meet this attack. A defense was made to the White's airborne assault, but not in the way expected by the Myk. At a suggestion from one of the hunters that had joined the march a new form of counter-attack was made. Each soldier of the army raised their shield overhead, an interlinked ceiling of metal, wood and leather. This was an impenetrable barrier to the scythe-like weapons of the White's airborne warriors. Then, at distance, from each side and the rear, archers, primarily the hunters of the Southern Valley, unleashed volley after volley into the storm that was the Warbirds. Over their own line they fired each volley, yet few on the ground were hurt, most by the falling bodies of Warbirds and riders. And while the shields of the southern line held against the attack, another surprise awaited the White. The arrows of the archers that failed to find a target mostly struck the shields and then fell harmlessly to the earth. There they were gathered by swift runners and taken back to the archers for resupply. Fully half of the Warbirds and their riders were destroyed in these first salvos of the archers. Riderless birds tore into their own kind, an easier prey than the warriors beneath their shields, further wrecking the White's airborne assault. Few Warbirds would survive this day and none of their riders would kill again.

A quarter mile away the White's ground assault drew near. The woodland archers gathered behind the shields closest to the front, and with almost full quivers due to the runners collecting the fallen arrows under the shield wall, they changed their attack. No shield did the White carry. Any archers had been expected to be destroyed by the Warbirds. Now they let fly their salvos against those that attacked before them. No re-supply could they expect this time and when each quiver was emptied, the woodsman withdrew from the battle, their job in this done. Little hope did they have to further change the outcome. The White were almost upon the soldiers of the south as the last of the archers' arrows flew and these woodsmen retreated from the battle. Jamen from his mount watched them leave. No incrimination did he feel towards them, it was the archers that gave them their slim chance of victory. Now Jamen would see if it was enough. The Warbirds had been defeated without loss and many of the Myk's foot soldiers were gone as well.

To the center of the Southern army's lines, at the crest of the Hill of the Roses, the White directed their charge. Upon the one hundred shields they flashed. As one White fell, ten more took his place. Holes appeared in the shield wall and through these gaps surged the White. Those that remained of the one hundred withdrew to the hill's summit. Where were Tor and the reserves?

Lord Stephen looked to the rear and he saw few remained. Most of those that did were ready to flee. These were not trained soldiers. And the death around them was appalling.

As one, Jamen of Kilne and the Lord Perth of Nourne saw but one chance to aide Lord Stephen, to stem the assault of the White. Each force now charged the White's army from opposite sides of the battle. As Lord Perth prepared to engage the White he saw the head of Lord Stephen of Beers, still wearing his unique helmet, carried aloft by a rogue Warbird. Of the one hundred, none remained.

The Myk himself now led the final assault. Just the massacre remained in his mind. Both flank assaults had been beaten back, and all that remained before him was the scattered reserve of those he had beaten before. With his diminished brain, in his mind, the Castle Nourne, his home, would be that again.

The Myk crested the center of the hill now empty of living things, and his army charged down the slope before them. Only Tor, with a handful of commoners, remained before them with raised shields and spear, expecting to die. But what magic was this? There in front of the Myk, legion after legion of Southern Shieldmen appeared. And overhead, the Warbirds of the Southern Valley now arrived. Tor led the handful of his men that remained to the rear. The Armies of the City by the Lake had arrived.

All through the night they had marched. Forbidden by the Council to join the march of the Lord of Beers, in the end they had marched anyway. Two-thousand strong, they braced their shields for the assault. Their warbirds did to the White what the Myk had expected his warbirds to do to the Southern army. At first, these men had marched to join Lord Stephen of Beers. However, even at a great distance they had seen his head carried away. Now their goal was revenge, the destruction of those who had killed their leader.

The White's line crashed into the shield line of the south. And it held! From the right now came the Lord Perth and those he had rallied around him. And from the left came those that had rallied around Jamen of Kilne. Now it was the White Priest-King, the Myk, who knew fear. Assaulted on three sides and the air, the White army began to break and run. The Myk, his dreams shattered by the turn of the battle, stood at the crest of the Hill of the Roses, where he had played as a child. He looked to rally what remained of his army, but there were few. It was the men of Nourne who now faced him and in the lead, the Lord and Lady of the castle themselves, each bleeding from a dozen wounds.

To the crest of the hill the Lord Perth fought. Few of the White now stood in opposition, their army shattered and fleeing the field. Then it was just the Lord Perth and the Myk facing each other.

"Forgive me my son," were the Lord Perth of Nourne's words as he raised sword.

The Myk raised his head, not comprehending what had happened. He stood now before his father. Both useful arms and the stub of a third dangled loosely. With a crooked smile, or was it a sneer, the Myk's one good eye was fixed on his father. Then the Lady of Castle Nourne appeared and the sneer went away.

The Lord Perth of Nourne's sword slashed through the neck of the Myk and his body fell to the ground, still. The Lord and Lady of Castle Nourne knelt by the dead body of the Myk, their son, and cried.

The routed army of the White fled north, but no pursuit was given. No thoughts were given to the slaves whose revolt had begun the war. Thirty thousand White survived the battle. The new High-Priest, even more decadent than his predecessor, took the name of the Myk and became their leader.

Altuan finished in sadness. There was nothing left of the Northern Valley than the remnants in the cavern. In an almost inaudible voice, he finished the story of the revolt. "A monument to the Battle of Erson was made; a monument to the victorious armies of the Southern Valley. To those of the slaves that remained in the Northern Valley, it was but a monument to our destruction.

"The new Myk brought a terrible revenge on the slaves of the Northern Valley. To the new Myk they were like animals, sources of food. The leaders of the revolt were slain, and if captured, their families were eaten before their eyes, before it was their turn. Weaponless, the slaves had no chance and their cousins to the south watched them die. Did they know? How could they not? However, the Southern Valley and the City by the Lake were safe for now. They had done what they could. How many had they lost at Erson, of their brightest and their best?

"Once we numbered as many as the Southern Valley. Then the White came and made this their home. First we were their brothers, then their servants, then their slaves. Now, abandoned by the south, we are but their food. We slowly dwindle in numbers here below ground. Soon we will be no more. The Southern Valley will still remain, until the White turn again to the conquest of the Castle Nourne and the Southern Valley."

Alum listened to these words of the slave revolt and the battle of Erson. He looked around at the few faces that remained, mostly women and children that had no hope of future survival in these caverns.

They expected, demanded that Alum lead them out, to see the sun once more. To survive or die it mattered not, as they were all dead in the caverns if they remained.

Phelix would show Alum the sole egress into the cavern that remained. The rest had been destroyed in the exodus from above. Those that had remained above that had known of this entrance when the others were closed, died at their own hands. Better that than to betray the *hidden ones*. Better that than to be eaten alive by the White.

Alum was told that there had been a second way into the caverns. However, the father of Jorge, his rescuer, had betrayed that to the White. Many caverns had to be abandoned then, with much of their food supply.

Now, after the battle, the new Myk had ordered almost all of the remaining slaves above ground added to the food supply. He didn't know how many remained underground, but he wanted them as well. Badly, as his revenge for the Battle of Erson.

Chapter Eight:
Escape from the Caverns

Nightfall. It was now two full days since the meetings at the Castle Nourne. Tor and Wade were on their way to find the caverns where the survivors of the Northern Valley were in hiding. They were traveling at night to take advantage of what they perceived as a weakness of the White; their supposed lack of any night vision.

In the distance, in the fading light of the day, the two saw the last of the White's scouts high in the air returning home on their Warbirds.

Tor knew of the stream that would take them to the cavern's lone remaining entrance. That stream began to flow to the Great Swamp from the westernmost ravine of the mountains that formed that border of the Northern Valley. It was to this stream that they quickly hiked. The goal was to reach the ravine's shadows by daybreak on the third day. Tor knew that even with his abilities, it would be dangerous to be caught in the open.

Several times, as the night became fully engaged, they had to dive for cover as returning White scouts flew overhead. They could not afford to take any chances at being seen. The White must not know that something was amiss, at least not yet.

Reaching a valley just past midnight, Tor turned upstream from the river they had been following. With the limited light of the stars overhead, the two men followed the stream, whose course they now traced. As they hiked, the two men searched for the clues that would guide them to the ravine and then the cavern's entrance. As dawn broke, the men were now solidly in a ravine following the stream they had found. But no closer to finding the cavern than when they had left Castle Nourne. Still searching for clues to the cavern's entrance, they reached the spring from which this stream began. The water bubbled up from beneath the rocky soil and each of them quenched their thirst in the fresh taste of the mineral water. They both thought the same, with daybreak the skies would become dangerous.

"We must have taken a wrong path," Tor spoke, sounding agitated, "back to the mouth of this stream then."

"Isn't it too late to move on today?" Wade questioned.

"Time is more important than my error now. We must hurry, and keep to the shadows."

As they hiked, Wade kept his eyes peeled to the sky while Tor continued his search for clues that would guide their way. Twice Wade had them hide in cover as distant specks in the sky drifted away. On the opposite bank, Tor began to see small caves appear in the ravine's side. Tor now grasped his mistake. It was not the direction they hiked, they were simply on the wrong bank. Wade and Tor, after first searching the sky, quickly crossed the narrow, shallow, cold rapids of the stream to the other side.

Now Tor was convinced he was on the right path and he beckoned Wade to help him search for signs of the cavern's entrance as they once more hiked upstream. Wade still kept half an eye on the sky, but at least on this side of the stream the ravines sides were both closer and steeper, providing them with more cover and helping to shield them from discovery. Neither dreamed that the danger they watched for loomed close by on the ground.

The Myk had decided that his Warbird scouts were no longer sufficient to find the hidden refugees. There were those among the White that through their mutations were swift afoot. These White were ideally suited for the job at hand and the Myk sent these new scouts out to find the last refuge of his slaves. The need for food for the White as they regained their strength was severe. He sent these new foot scouts to search the streams of the Northern Valley. The refugees would need water to continue their survival.

One of these foot scouts now began following the same river that Tor and Wade had followed the day before. These new scouts had great endurance, a lengthy stride and their need for food was less. Moreover, they had no problem seeing in the darkness. Once sent out, they were expected to remain out for days, or weeks if necessary. He turned up the same creek that the two men had reached the night before. He had explored several of these creeks and expected to find only more water and the disgusting fish the Myk expected him to live on while he scouted. Now both parties hiked the same stream, one from below and the other from up higher in the ravine.

Tor found an especially promising cave entrance. At its front, he discovered a deep scratch in the rock that did not seem natural, though made to look so. In searching further, he found a faint human footprint in the dirt on a nearby rock. If this was the entrance, those inside were getting careless. He peaked inside the low cave and raised his staff so that the low beam of light it projected would allow him to see farther into the cave. Even though his staff's light could not reach the cave's distant walls, it produced enough light even with the distant shadows as to allow him to enter the cave. Tor began to walk and then bent over, and half-crawled into the cave's chamber. Wade watched him from the cave's entrance.

As Tor disappeared into the cave, the White scout came around a rock and spotted Wade. Less mutated than many, he craved the attention that finding the slaves would bring him. And the glory it would carry to the Myk. The White, its primitive brain generating some thought, ducked back behind the rock to decide how to deal with the slave. Food was its first thought, a feast for one. For several days, he fed on nothing but the stream's fish and the less than satisfactory flesh of a wild pig. Could he keep such a meal secret? Here was human flesh and none around to claim a share. But in this White's tiny brain he knew the answer was no. The Myk would know. The Myk always knew. This reasoning won through the White's thoughts and he spared Wade's life for the moment. Instead of a kill shot, the White would only knock the slave unconscious.

Standing up quickly, the White chose a large stone and threw it at the unsuspecting Wade. Good fortune again shown on Wade as the White's second hand on his throwing arm touched the stone as it was hurled, causing the stone to aim wide. Wade heard more than saw the large stone hurling past and drew his sword as he turned.

"Tor, a White, we have company!" Wade yelled in the direction of the cave.

Now the White's third hand became an advantage. Still thinking he was dealing with a slave, though an armed one, he drew his own weapons, which he had shown himself most competent in using during training. Unique of these was a small shield-knife combination that the White had created for his two fully functional hands on the one arm. He wielded this weapon with aplomb and Wade quickly found himself on the defensive as the White fought him with skill using the weapons forged around his deformities. As Tor emerged from the cave, he found Wade hard-pressed against the side of a large boulder, totally on the defensive.

"Halt your efforts, White!" Tor commanded.

The White stepped back, confused, and saw the Sage with his staff. He knew in his primitive brain that he had misgauged the situation. However, the Myk would be pleased to know a Sage wandered in the Northern Valley. The Whites only thought now was how to escape these two and get back to the Palace with his report.

Tor acted first and with a raised staff charged the White, striking its head with a fatal blow. The White collapsed, its tiny brain knowing that it had failed the Myk.

Wade came over from the boulder at the edge of the stream. Still in shock from the appearance of the White and its fighting ability, he spoke to Tor in a subdued voice. "I had no idea that they could be so skilled. It was almost like I was fighting two men."

Tor poked at the tunic the White wore with his staff. "It seems that you were." He raised the tunic and exposed a second head, partially formed, from the right side of the creature's shoulder. That head stared at them and its mouth moved. Freed by Tor's blow from the imbecile brain that grew from the White's neck, this head stared at them and sneered. Then it commanded the White's body, now his, to stand.

"I should thank you both for the gift that you have given me," it spoke. "For too long I have been aware and have had to dwell, subservient, beneath such wanton stupidity. Now you have freed me." Turning its abdomen to face Tor, it commanded, "Sage, you have no power over me!"

"And White, you have no power over my blade!" shouted Wade as he plunged his weapon into the emerging head.

"Are they all such?" Wade questioned Tor, after this, his first individual encounter with a White.

"The variation in deformity is wide. This one, however, seemed unique. I had never heard of such, the more primitive head controlling the already-awakened, more advanced head. The second head must have emerged late in this poor creature's life. The Myk would never allow a primitive head to control such a body. It must have lived in perpetual fear of discovery."

"What would the Myk have done?"

"Cut off the primitive head at the neck, allowing the creature to develop fully in an honored space beside it. Who knows, this thing," he poked it with his staff as he spoke, "might have become the next Myk. We must hurry now. Help me drag this thing to cover and then we will rest until nightfall in the cave I was exploring. I know we are close. It should provide safety for the day."

As Wade started dragging the dead White to the indicated cave, Tor stopped him.

"Not here where we'll be resting, there." He pointed at a cave some distance away.

Wade joined Tor in the larger cave after disposing of the body. He was exhausted from his recent travails and after crawling to the back of the cave to where Tor sat, he collapsed.

Safe from discovery for the moment, Tor opened his bag and tossed Wade a small loaf of bread from it. "Eat this, we'll rest until nightfall." Tor's staff, which had been providing a soft light, went dark. Tor leaned back against the cave's wall while Wade fell asleep where he lay. They slept through the night and mid-morning found them still both sound asleep.

It was time to leave the caverns. Alum pleaded with Altuan not to put him into this position. He wanted to know more about what lay around him. How about the prisoners, could they be saved? To each word and question, they denied him answers. In the refugees weakened state, it was now either to escape while they still had the energy, or to remain and perish in the caverns. Whether they lived or died on the outside no longer mattered. Finally, Alum reached an accord of sorts with Altuan. He would go ahead of the others and scout the cavern's open passage to the outside first. He would do this with Phelix and see just where it was this secret entrance lay. Alum needed to make sure, himself, that the pathway was free. The goal of the refugees was to reach the Southern Valley and force the City by the Lake to acknowledge them. To see what they had left behind and how few there were from before.

To a seldom-used passage, Phelix led Alum, neither speaking. Alum could tell that Phelix had something besides the journey ahead on his mind. But Phelix refused to speak of it. "Better to remain quiet than to speak of what may happen." Phelix knew of matters that Alum did not; the meeting at Castle Nourne. Once before the Southern Valley had turned a blind eye to what was happening to the north of them. Would they do that again?

They came to what appeared to be the end of the passage. A natural rockslide appeared to block the way. Phelix motioned Alum to silence and spoke in a whisper.

"Beyond this is a small cave, the last entry to the outside. The stones will move easily. They are not what they seem. More an illusion, but we'll at first not see what lies beyond."

"How do we move the rock?" whispered Alum.

Phelix lifted a large boulder with one hand.

"What magic is that?"

Phelix tossed the large stone to Alum with a gentle heave. Reflexes took over for Alum and he *caught* the stone. It could not have weighed more than a pound or two.

"We came across a supply of these and saved them for when the need existed. Now we cover our last passage with them. Come, help me clear the way," he said quietly.

Together they removed the fake wall, creating a new wall behind them. That way if found or seen, the passage would remain concealed. As they reached the last few *boulders* to be moved, Phelix motioned Alum to stop. He stood motionless, in the near darkness, and saw Phelix point to his eyes and then forward. Alum looked to where Phelix pointed and he, too, saw the two bodies lying motionless near the cave's entrance. "White!" both men thought as one. Had the White found the sole remaining entrance to the caverns and these two were posted as sentries to wait for who would appear? Or had chance, in its every changing fortunes, placed these two before them.

Alum pulled out from his scabbard the blade he had been given and Phelix held his shaft high above, ready to strike.

"Arise you fiends, and meet your end!"

Exhausted from their day and a half-forced march, both Tor and Wade quickly lapsed into a deep sleep. Tor's last thoughts before slumber were that something about the back wall seemed contrived. He mentioned this to Wade and they moved away from the back wall, to a sidewall closer to the front. Wade slept with his hand on his sword.

Both awoke with a start some time later as a voice boomed through the small cave. "More White," Wade thought.

In that state between slumber and wakefulness, each rose to defend themselves, Tor grabbing for his staff and Wade raising his blade and standing.

Clunk!

"By the Gods," Wade cried out. In his newly awakened state, he had forgotten just how low the ceiling was.

"Wade, is that you?" was Alum's answering shout.

In the flare of their staffs, Phelix and Tor recognized each other as well. All spoke as one, "We thought you were the White."

It was Tor who brought the grim news of the scout's death near the cavern opening to Phelix. He concluded with the news of the second head.

"It is beginning then, as we had feared; the birth of a new race, evil incarnate, immune to our powers. Did it seem fully aware?" Phelix asked.

"Not until the primitive first head was killed. Then it was able to assume the body as its own. Never had I heard of that before."

"It is as the Teachers foresaw, then. 'The rebirth of man begins with the death of an old, borne anew.' It is a frightening thought and one we must be fully ready to act upon," Phelix spoke.

"But is it our right to destroy? Were we not taught to preserve life?"

"To prevent a reoccurrence of what came before," Phelix said as he led the men back to the false wall. "We have much to discuss as yet, and Altuan will be anxious to hear from you."

The men began the task of moving the wall once more, moving it back behind them and covering the entry. "I thought this wall seemed out of place," stated Tor. Quickly a wall once again stood, though its position had changed.

The reunion was swift and poignant. While walking back to the caverns, Alum and Wade exchanged news. Both were happy to learn that more survivors of the White's attack remained than either thought. When Wade learned of Mendy's survival in the pit of the Myk, the two decided together that they would rescue him next.

Phelix and Tor both expressed their alarm at the idea.

"You'll never be able to reach the prisoners. It will only lead the White to what few refugees remain," expressed Phelix. He was torn inwardly by what he knew would happen to those left behind and for the safety of those he guided in the caverns. 'How many more will perish?', he thought inwardly to himself, resigned to the fact of so much death.

Tor had learned from Gar of the loyalty these outsiders showed each other. He understood that to gain their support that they must not impede the actions of these two men to rescue their friend.

Speaking up, Tor interrupted the others. "We'll speak with Altuan. I am sure he knows a way to the prisoner's holding cell. From there it will be up to Alum and Wade. Maybe many can be saved."

"But the dangers!" Phelix responded, knowing in the back of his mind that the freeing of so many would be worth the dangers that lay ahead of them. 'This is why we are here, no other reason,' he thought.

The four arrived back with Altuan and the refugees sooner than expected. Altuan's eyes lit up when he saw four returned where only two had left. In the dimness of the cavern and his failing eyesight, he did not recognize Tor until he was almost upon him. When he did recognize Tor, his features briefly lit up, before returning to the despondent, fatalistic look he now carried about himself. After all, Tor was one of those that had abandoned the humanity of the Northern Valley, leaving them to their own resources and allowing the massacre to happen. Altuan barely acknowledged Tor, speaking directly to Phelix and Wade.

"What news do you bring us?" he asked. Before that question could be answered, his second question came. "Are we ready to leave?"

"One more task remains, old friend," Phelix spoke, pointing to Wade. He introduced Wade as a friend of Alum. "Here stands a companion of Alum. Together they will lead us to the south. But first..."

"There can be no more firsts. We must leave now! We are ready, what few remain."

"Patience Altuan, haven't I stayed with your people throughout their ordeal."

"We have no more time for patience. More die every day."

Tor now spoke. "I have news as well. We found a White scout not far from your entrance."

Altuan now sounded more agitated than before. "Then we begin at once!"

Phelix now spoke. "Another companion of Alum and Wade lies as a captive of the White. He is in their food storage. It is their desire to rescue him."

"Of course we know of him. We have heard him talking through the wall where it is thinnest. We have already lost one rescuing the one we know as Alum, as instructed by you, Phelix. Are we now to lose all that remain, to rescue this third?"

Tor spoke again. "They will together rescue their friend, Mendy, along with many of the others that remain not yet dead. They possess a strength that we ourselves no longer carry."

"You have let us down before, you'll do the same now."

Alum now entered the conversation. "Altuan, I promised, with much hesitation, to lead your people to the south. Alone I could not hope to rescue Mendy and the others. Now, with Wade, I know the others can be spared. To this I swear and then to the south we'll go together." As he said these words he pressed his fist first to his heart and then to Altuan's. A silence filled the cavern where they stood.

Despondent, feeling trapped once more, Altuan turned and called for Gim, who had rescued Alum from the Hydron. Gim approached the five men and Altuan broke the silence.

"Is the way to the pit still clear?"

"We caused what damage we could but did not have the strength to fully close it." Gim felt he had let his leader down when he spoke these words. In their flight to freedom, a path to attack them from behind remained if discovered by the White.

Instead of chastising Gim, Altuan forced himself to smile. He clasped Gim on the shoulder and directed him to Alum and Wade. "You will show them the way so that their friend can be saved, and I hope many of the others as well. Go now, and return with many. We will begin the exodus from the cavern while you are gone; so many once, but so few remain."

Altuan then turned from the others and walked away. He tried to see a future for his people, but could perceive only more death.

"Follow me," Gim said to Alum, "You know part of the way." Alum and Wade followed Gim out of the main cavern.

Partially across the cavern, filled with what remained of the Northern Valley's human population, Gim found a recessed tunnel entrance and led them into it. A little way into the tunnel, they passed a side entrance. "That way leads to the pit monster, the Hydron."

Alum shuddered at his memory of the monster.

"What is this pit monster, the Hydron?" Wade asked Alum.

"Another tale for another day," was all Alum would say.

A little bit further into the tunnel they were following and Gim motioned for them to remain silent. He whispered, "We must be quiet now, we're nearing the food storage."

Alum marveled at Gim. He had grown and matured in the short time since his rescue.

The three men began to hear the cries of tortured souls through the tunnel's walls. Inhuman, inhumane, it was a sound neither Alum nor Wade would ever forget: The wails of the lost.

"Food storage?" whispered Wade.

"The White prefers their food fresh. Alive, but not alive, those people ahead of us, were once my people. Now they are but the undead vessels of our tormentor's pantry. While no direct access is found, through the cracks in the walls we can hear their cries."

Wade began to speak again but was quietly hushed by Gim.

"The White may be among them, choosing their meal for the day. If we can hear the cries of the damned, then the White can hear us. Nothing can be done for the undead. Let us hurry on to the living."

Alum and Wade were amazed by his callousness. "Nothing?" Wade whispered.

"Nothing, they feel no pain. Their brain stems were severed."

"Are they aware?"

"Some. The drugs and their own madness spare them most of their awareness. Their cries are from what little they still perceive. Now quiet, we don't have far to go."

The path they followed became a small cave, narrowing to the point that they could barely squeeze by. The darkness and closeness began to become overpowering to these men used to the open sky of the sea. Gim could feel their unease.

"Not much farther and it will open up and we'll have light," Gim whispered.

After passing the narrowest point, where they had to pull Wade through, the passageway opened up to a small, lighted cavern, its phosphorescence captivating the men.

"Watch your step. We can speak freely here. The path is narrow, and to fall would put you beyond help."

A deep crevice fell sharply to one side of the narrow path, while the cavern walls held the other side. Alum and Wade had to focus to not lose a step and fall over the side.

"Do we cross the entire cavern?" Alum asked, awestruck.

"No, there is another passage a little way ahead. We will have to crawl a short way. Can you make it?" Gim asked, remembering their earlier discomfort.

They both answered yes, themselves remembering their friend, Mendy, the reason for this rescue.

A little before the crack in the wall that they were to follow, Wade saw a primitive drawing on the wall of the cavern. "From your people?" he asked.

"No, it was here from before. I have often wondered about who made it."

The drawing appeared to be a hunting party bringing down a beast none recognized.

"Before the Great War," said Alum aloud.

"Probably," answered Wade.

When they came to the entrance of the passage all three stood briefly before it.

"Wade, you'll have to stay here. I don't think with your size you could make it through," Gim spoke. Then a thought occurred to him. "This man Mendy, your friend, how big is he? You're both larger than any of us."

"He's about my size, maybe a little smaller," spoke Alum.

"I hope you are right, this pathway is short and very tight. Alum, you should be fine, but Wade, you will have to wait for us here. We will not be long and you will hear us coming back. Guide each out onto the pathway when we return, so none falls.

"I have no problem with that," Wade said. "The air seems fresh and I've heard of places like this." To himself Wade thought, 'Wow, I have a chance to observe this beauty first hand.'

"It's beautiful, but in the middle of evil we stand. Do not wander. Remember the cavern and its ways are treacherous. It is easy to get lost. In our survival under the Myk's Palace, we have had no time to observe or think but briefly of the cavern's beauty. It can be hypnotic. We'll be back shortly," Gim warned Wade.

"I'll have a comfortable seat here and there are some drawings on the walls just a few feet away. I will be waiting for your return. And Alum, be safe and bring back Mendy."

"I will." The two men grasped arms and then they turned to where Gim was trying to move a boulder.

"This looks like my job," said Wade.

"Careful not to lose it over the edge, we'll need to use it to recover the way when we return."

"I'll see you on your return."

With the boulder removed and safely placed just past the opening it exposed, Alum followed Gim into the narrow crawlspace.

The crawlspace was relatively short as Gim had promised and they came out in another passageway they could stand in, or almost, in Alum's case. More of the phosphorescent rock lit their way and after about one hundred yards past the crawlspace Gim stopped.

"We're here."

Alum saw nothing.

Gim pointed to several sharp tools hidden in the rubble at the base of the wall.

"We've thought before of rescuing the prisoners, but the risk to the cavern was always too great. We will finish the breakthrough now. It is only inches thick, but we have to break through quickly. The White will hear and quickly see what we're doing." He grabbed a pike and a hammer and began working at the rock. Alum found another set and did the same.

Mendy and Gant were sitting together in a corner talking. Mendy wondered what had happened to Alum. It had been a good length of time since the White had pulled him out of the pit. Tjim was now gone, some White's dinner course he presumed, which sickened him. Several times he thought he heard a scraping noise through the rock. Each time he looked he was not able to find anything. Always, the noise seemed to come from the same place.

"Just the rats, looking for their own meal among us," Zalc answered in his usual unpleasantness.

Zalc's claim over the men had ended with his fight with Alum. Now he was just glad Alum was gone, and he was sure he was dead.

Mendy and Gant made their way as near to the sounds as possible. The sound was nearly continuous and getting louder. Others were starting to notice as well. No one hazarded a guess as to what it meant. In Mendy's mind, whatever was causing the noise meant a chance for survival.

'Perhaps it was the White making a new passageway through the rocks,' Gant thought aloud, trying to dissuade his new friend of the hope of escape. But that hope was imbedded in Mendy's being.

"Soon, you'll be dead, we'll all be dead. Just like your fool friend, Alum," Zalc shouted from across the pit.

"Alum's alive. I can feel it," Mendy shouted back at Zalc. He looked over at Gant, who only shook his head sadly. "He is alive," he said in a quiet voice.

Mendy looked across the darkness. Fewer than ten now remained in this holding cell. It had been only a day since the last was taken. His turn couldn't be far away.

Mendy had started to doze off, in his hunger and weakened state. "Why don't they feed us?" Mendy had thought. Then he heard the scratching through the wall right behind him, distinct and clear.

Thunk. Scratch. Thunk.

He nudged Gant with his feet.

The two men stood and walked a few steps to where it seemed the loudest.

"There!" shouted Mendy as he reached out and grabbed a long pike as it broke through the rocks. He jerked the pike and pulled it from the grasp of the presumed White on the other side.

Momentarily another pike broke through and a large chunk of the wall gave way. Gant reached for the second pike as they prepared to do battle. At least this way they would die as men. Mendy thrust his pike back through the opening.

"Ow!" they heard from the other side.

Mendy recognized the voice immediately. "Alum, I'm here."

More of the wall gave way, a sizable opening now lay open as Gim, and Alum on their side broke more of the stone clear with their hands, joined by Mendy and Gant.

"Mendy, quickly through the opening," Alum called.

Mendy crawled through as Gim, now with Gant's help, tried to help the others through the opening. Some responded more quickly, but soon all were making their way out of the pit and into the tunnel. Alum led the way while Mendy directed each which way to go as they left the pit. Only Gim and Gant now remained in the pit, with the reluctant Zalc.

Gant reached out his hand to Zalc. "Hurry," he said to the man.

Zalc's only response, a final act of madness, was to slash out with his knife at Gant and scream to the White, now opening the trapdoor in the ceiling.

"They're escaping," he yelled to those now visible above. "Come quickly… they'll all be gone."

A sentry White peered down and then called to others, and soon the White were repelling down ropes in numbers. Gim stood at the opening, both pikes in hand, "Come quickly."

Gant followed him into the tunnel and handed him the second pike. "The White will be upon us quickly in force."

"What about Zalc."

"Leave him," said Gant as he turned to follow the others.

Alum reached the crawlspace with the now rescued prisoners close behind. He hurried them through to the waiting Wade. Mendy stood at the opening as well, waiting for his turn, while Gim and Gant quickly approached. Mendy now scampered into the opening and it was just the three men left. As Gim and Gant reached the opening, they all heard the first signs of pursuit. Was it one or all three that spoke in a silent tone, "White?" It mattered not. They entered the passage backwards, pikes pointed to where pursuit would follow. This was slower, but at least they could not be overtaken in the narrow crawlspace.

Zalc saw the White as they dropped through the trapdoor, weapons in hand. 'We will eat well tonight' was the Whites only thought. Zalc pointed them to the opening in the wall. Who knows what he was thinking at that point or what he expected. The first White down, its partial third hand carrying a strange blade, called out. "This one is mine."

A quick thrust and Zalc's left forearm was gone. Zalc watched in the final moments of his life, his mind now clear of its madness, the horrifying sight of his arm being eaten. "What have I done?!" he screamed as another White removed his leg below the hip and began eating that. Zalc's last thoughts were of his wife and children, "I will join you once more," as he fell to the earth, tormented no more.

"I eat well today," said a White as he cut off the other arm.

"The head is mine!" shouted the Captain of the sentries as he made his way over to the feast.

It took more than a few minutes for order to be regained by the White. Many were hungry these days and here was food. Finally, the Captain, finished with what had been Zalc's head, called the others together to begin the pursuit. With a guttural cry he called, "Follow me, food escapes." Dimly, in the tunnel's passage, he could see Gim and Gant, the last to flee.

Alum entered the crawlspace, followed quickly by Gim and Gant. The passageway was short. Could they make it? It was in Zalc's final madness he had given the others the head start they would need.

As the White tried to follow in the narrow crawlspace, the first White to enter was too large. A second head, half formed, was on its back and got stuck. The others had to pull this one back, and as they did, they partially tore the second head off the body of the White. It screamed out in pain and a second set of eyes briefly opened before the creature died. With its second head, a place of honor was achieved. It would be carried back to the pit to be buried with honor above. This further delayed the chase. Such was the importance of the second heads, even in their early stages, to the Myk, (though he knew not why).

As Alum reached the opening of the crawlspace on the other side, he called ahead to Wade, "Success, but there's company close behind."

Wade pulled him out and steadied him on the pathway through this cavern. Together they began pulling out the rest as they came through. "You, help those behind you. Careful nobody goes over the edge." As they pointed to each which way to go, Wade and Alum positioned themselves to where they could once again block the entrance with the boulder. One after the other, the rescued prisoners came through the opening. Gim was the last and once out he quickly moved past the others to the front to lead them out. "Cover the opening," was his only command to Wade and Alum, but it was unnecessary as the two men together placed the boulder in front of the crack.

"Hurry," Gim called, as he led the way and the others followed, many helping each other move.

One of the weakest of the rescued prisoners slipped and almost fell into the ravine to her death. Gant's outstretched hand caught her. "Nobody dies this close to freedom," he said to her.

Out of the crawlspace they hurried as best they could, following the pathway that hugged the wall of the cavern. Halfway to the opening, glancing back, Wade could see the first of the White push the boulder aside as they pursued. Two, three, four, went over the side, following the boulder, before they realized the danger of the narrow pathway. Once again, the White stopped to gather and organize themselves to follow. The Captain, being first, was the first to go over the side. A new leader was needed. Such was the White's way. Who was the most deformed? A contest ensued that would have seemed hilarious to the fleeing prisoners if they had been around to observe it. Each White tried to outdo the others with his mutations. Finally, a leader was chosen, after he first threw another White, the last to challenge him over the side, and the chase resumed.

This latest pause in the pursuit enabled the men to enter the passageway unobserved by the White. It would take the White crucial minutes to find the passage and follow their prey. Wade and Alum brought up the rear this time, though now without their pikes. Wade had to be pulled and pushed through the narrowest part, but soon all were through and rushing down the wide passageway to freedom.

At the cavern, over two thousand of the survivors of the genocide gathered. The two Sage exchanged brief words with each other.

"They'll soon be back."

"With the White close behind."

"We should begin the exodus."

"Those at Nourne will be waiting."

"I'll prepare the opening's collapse."

They signaled to Altuan.

"It begins," spoke Altuan quietly to himself.

The people followed Altuan out of the darkness to the outer cave, where Phelix removed the false wall, to the river and then south. It was twilight and the moon was full, granting the refugees light. Individually and in groups they traveled. To live or die they no longer cared. No young children to be carried, it had been too long since the last live birth for that need. No elders to be helped; all dead of suicide so the young could live, or worse. Just what remained, half-dead with starvation, half-mad with their fears. Yet they trudged the long path, so that those who had remained safe in the south could see what they had left behind.

At the joint, where the passageway to the Hydron's pit joined the passageway they followed, Gim stopped. He waved the others past. It was straight to the outer caves now. Only Wade and Gant stopped and stood beside Gim.

"The White will soon be upon us," Gant said.

"I have one more job to do," spoke Gim determinedly.

"The beast?" Gant dared not say its name.

Gim nodded, "I saw too many die. It must end."

"Hurry," was Gant's only response.

Gim rushed down the passageway he knew so well. He thought of the rescue of Alum, of Jorge, his friend's death.

'It must die!' Gim's thoughts screamed.

Close by the opening to the beast's cavern he found two small pots. Jorge had left them there long before, a gift from Phelix. Gim remembered Jorge's words. "When the time comes, Gim, use these to kill the beast. Throw them in together, onto each other. When they break, a fire will begin. Do it and watch the Hydron burn."

"If we can burn it, why not do it now?" he had asked.

"'Because its burning will bring every White at us, from the Myk on down. This is their God. When the caverns are clear of us, this will be your job, Gim, your destiny, but not until we are all gone; one way or another."

At the opening, just above the beast that was the Hydron, Gim stopped, a pot in each hand. With a brief prayer for all that had died to feed the beast, he dropped one pot below him and then the other on top of the first, breaking the thin clay that contained the chemicals. The pots exploded with a bright light and the force threw Gim back. A fire quickly broke out on the beast, an inextinguishable fire. A foul white smoke was carried upward to the Myk's chambers and the Myk knew something was wrong.

As the smoke from below leaked through the trapdoor into the chamber room of the Myk, he called out to all to hear. "Now! All must die! Food for each who finds a slave!"

Above, throughout the place that was the home of the Myk, they heard the wail of the beast as it burned to death. Throughout the Throne Room an orgy of slaughter consumed all not of the Myk.

Below, eyes blinded by the explosion, throat burning from the smoke, Gim sat laughing, as the heat of the burning beast bore through the tunnel. Gant and Wade found him that way. Each picked up an arm and they half-carried, half-walked this hero down the passage.

The three men approached the intersection in the tunnel and could hear the White scurrying towards them. Running now, they hurried to the outer cavern, each man holding Gim's hands as they guided him out. They expected to find it full, but only Mendy and Alum stood with Tor.

"The beast is gone?" Alum asked.

"Yes," smiled Gim.

"Good."

Tor called out to the five, "The others are already gone, hurry."

The six ran across the large chamber that had been the home of so many for so long. They barely reached the opening to the first cave when a spear came flashing through and landed near them. The White were through.

Into the small first cave the men ran. Phelix stood there, his staff in hand.

"Outside, now quickly!" he shouted.

As the men flew by, Phelix struck the timbers that had held the opening in place for so long. Weakened, the timbers collapsed, but not until the first of the White had reached the opening. As the rocks collapsed from above, Phelix looked back and saw one of the White almost through before caught in the fall. As the stones killed the creature he saw a second head come briefly to life.

"It has begun," he thought to himself as he turned and followed the survivors down the riverbank and to freedom.

Chapter Nine
The Proctant's Final Voyage

The storm receded, leaving the battered ship alone to drift in the endless sea. The tattered remnants of sail hung limply from the broken masts. With each rolling wave passing under the ship, water could be heard below deck. The foremast, snapped off during the height of the storm, dragged alongside the ship, pulling that side of the wounded vessel dangerously close to the water. With each passing wave, the ship's deck grew closer to those dark waters that surrounded her. In the distance could be heard the sound of waves crashing against a rocky shore.

Overhead the serpentine Llid circled, their cries calling others of their like to them. These were carrion creatures, waiting for the men below them to die for their feast to begin. Their call was the ever-mournful cry of the dead.

But these men refused to die.

Using the last of their pitiful remaining strength, these men dutifully cut loose the trailing spar that was dragging the ship closer to its doom. Then with whatever it was they had left, the men hung what remained of their sail on the broken stems of their masts. Torn, tattered pieces of sailcloth, held together by whatever the men could find, were attached with rope, wire, anything they could salvage, onto the jagged pieces of spar and masts that still stood.

Exhausted, the men fell back to the deck, their fate once again in the hands of the very sea that had almost destroyed them; almost but not quite. The ship was alive, but barely, moving again as the wind picked up and the wounded vessel moved out on a course none could set.

The winged primal Llid above let out their mournful cry and left the not-yet-dead ship and crew as they continued their lost journey.

The wind remained fair and the sea calm as the wounded ship limped bravely onward. One would have thought it a ghost ship, deserted and drifting aimlessly at sea. Yet she did possess some sail, if badly repaired. If watched closely, movement did appear on her deck occasionally. The ship had a crew then. Their uniforms were just weathered shreds leaving their skin exposed to the burning rays of the sun.

These malnourished men were covered in blotches from the sun and battered from the fierce weather.

A great trading ship it had been once, the men onboard searching for the wealth of the world. From all walks of life, these men had come to share this journey of reckless ambition, traveling unknown waters, following the latest rumor, to find riches lost to the generations before them.

All had been fine in the beginning. Well provisioned, the ship had set sail from its homeport. Serenely it sailed into the distant sea, going in the direction to where nothing was known but rumor. Then days stretched into weeks, into months. Cliques formed among the crew. Land was sighted finally as provisions ran low, but Captain Gull refused to land. A storm was approaching rapidly. Better to ride it out at sea than along some unknown rocky coastline. As the men prepared to head out to sea before the storm hit, mold was found among the little that remained of the rations, a toxic spore rendering the food inedible. Still the captain refused to land a party on the distant shore. A few days they could last without food, he pleaded. Water would soon be more than plentiful from the storm, refilling their casks with clean water from the sky. But the men split.

Even now their stomachs grumbled. They had ridden out many storms near land. Those closest to the Captain understood this was no ordinary storm. Insults led to fights, tempers flared, then the Captain's worst fear, while still in danger from the storm but a few hours off; Mutiny!

The action that followed was brief. In the violence, half the crew died, wounds inflicted by those it had seemed only a few days earlier were friends. The captain and those that understood the power of the approaching storm could take no graces to survive. They had little enough time to prepare for the storm as it was and now the ship would be minimally crewed.

Those of the mutineers who survived were placed in a single boat without supplies and but a single weapon, other than their own short-arms. No more provisions could be spared. It would be up to them alone whether they would live or die. Already, high waves pummeled the ship and the small boat, almost swamping it. The horizon now stood close by, brought nearer by the storm's power. The mutineers rowed as quickly as they could toward the distant rocky shoreline.

What remained of the ship's crew strove to turn her into the storm and prepared her for what was to come. They had been loyal to the Captain and had won the fight, but now they were just too few to get the job done in time. While one man attempted to dump the dead from the fight overboard to their watery graves, the rest attempted to make the ship storm ready. Masts and sail were secured, the rudder's till reinforced with rope and wood. The rudder was fully turned into the squall, now upon them. There had just been too much to do, and with the fight, not enough time for the crew to get it done.

Captain Gull lashed himself to the wheel, while the men braced for what was coming. What could be done was done. The ship was pointing to the northwest, as they hoped to just skim the edge of the storm. However, as the approaching waves crashed against the ship in their anger, the crew knew everything they had done just had not been enough.

The storm hit the ship with a magnitude the Captain had seen only a few times before in his life. Even with a full crew, the ship would have been hard-pressed to survive what was to come.

With the first of the gale-driven waves, the ship was flooded. What little of value that remained among the provisions was now gone. An emergency sail was lashed into place above the men's heads. However, it only helped to bring the foremast down around them, still bound to the ship by rope and sail, and with every passing wave, it threatened to capsize the ship. At the height of the storm two men tried to cut loose the spar with axes. Both were swept over the side, two more men gone from the ghost-driven ship.

The remaining survivors hunkered down in the ship's aft cabin. Better to stay inside than to be swept overboard. To drown if the ship were to go down, to live if the ship were to ride out the storm. There just were not enough of them left to make a difference one way or another. Even the Captain left the wheel to join them inside.

Waves swept through the seas, taller than the highest buildings of their homeport, waves of unimaginable power. Yet providence guided the ship during this time of its greatest need. As one wave dumped its contents onto the hapless ship, the next wave moved as to empty her of the previous wave's water. And on it went as the ship fought to stay afloat. She fought the storm as if she was alive, looking for places the storm was at its weakest, first flooded, then gasping for breath. Always the broken spar dragged itself along her side, turning the ship first one direction, and then another as the waves affected it as well. It too did its part to keep her alive, pointing her best in the storm's vicious rage.

The weather calmed. Was it hours, days, weeks? The crew was too tired and hungry to know. What sail that remained was stitched together and put onto the only usable mast. Of the three masts that had propelled the once-proud ship to speed, only the aft-mast remained. The spar that had guided them through the storm was cut free. She had been queen of the sea once, a three-mast schooner, outfitted with the best. Now she was a half-mast wreck. The wheel had been shattered by the storm's fury. The Captain, Gull to those who knew him well, was able at last to tie down the rudder so at least she would not go in circles.

The becalming aftermath of the storm became a brisk wind again and the troubled ship moved forward. To what destination her fate led, the crew neither cared nor wanted to know. Northward it seemed they traveled.

Unable to move, the crew dropped where they finished their last task. A ghost crew it seemed now controlled the ship. Straight it sailed, the pitiful remains of the sail catching all the wind it could. The food was spoiled, rotten. Several of the men lay on the deck in their own vomit after trying to eat the remains of the spoiled food. Then, as if by magic, flying fish began to land on the deck. There were not enough to fill the bellies of the crew, but it was enough to stave off starvation for another week.

By the third day from the storm's end some of the crew tried to guide the ship's journey through its sail. There was no command structure now. When those who carried enough strength were able, some small job on the ship was done. It was a fight for survival for all of them and the best chance of survival lay in working together.

It was on the fifth day after the storm's passing, so marked on the deck by one of the men, that the starving and frail crew sighted land. From the fore bridge of the ship it was seen, slightly to the port side from their course. With renewed energy, the men sought to change the ship's course, to point the battered ship toward this land. It was two days later, on the seventh day of the storm's passing, that they reached the rocky shore.

At first all they could see were rocks and a towering cliff above them. Salvation would be, as it looked, against these hard rocks. A gentle beach was not seen. The men prepared to brace themselves for the landing that would come. It would be the end of *The Proctant*, but at least they would be alive.

Milne was on duty, what duty roster there was, when as the fog cleared he saw the commotion on the cliff. Too far distant as yet to make out details, it was clear that people resided on this land.

The second mate called to the Captain, leaning against the rail a short distance away.

"Sir, look to the cliffs."

Others of the ship's crew saw the people gathered on the top of the cliff as well. Milne handed the Captain his scope.

"What are those people doing?" one of the crew called out to the Captain.

"It looks like they intend to throw several people over the cliff to the rocks."

Taking his turn looking at the mob through the scope, one of the crewmen spoke up. "I have a pretty good idea of what they're doing and I think I know where we are as well."

"Well, speak up lad, what are your thoughts?"

"Sir," the crewman spoke, almost embarrassed by what he had to say. "Sir, have you heard of the Legend of Argonia? It's supposed to be in these Northern seas."

"Of course I have. Every schoolchild has heard the myth of Argonia, a pre-war haven of man, a Utopian society, created by the great minds of the day to preserve the knowledge of man. They saw what was coming and sought to preserve what they could of man's knowledge and arts, and of course, themselves. It's probably the most famous of our pre-war myths."

"I think that's Argonia, or at least what it has become."

"Argonia! Your mind is playing tricks with you, son. Not surprising with what we've been through. Scholars dismissed that myth long ago. There's no Argonia, never was, just the wishful thinking of the postwar survivors."

"But, sir..."

"Dismissed, sailor. We need reality to survive, not a child's myth."

"I took readings last night, sir."

"I said dismissed, sailor. Are you defying me? Another of the mutineers?" The Captain was on edge himself, barely hanging on to reality. "Guards, guards, arrest this man."

"Sir, there are no guards left, just the handful of us here. I didn't mean to defy you."

"Arrest him I say, a mutineer. Let no other approach him. Fifty lashes I say, for any who speaks on his behalf," the Captain ordered, the last vestiges of reality slipping away.

At that Captain Gull turned back toward the shore, his mind almost gone, promptly forgetting what had just transpired as well.

Those who remained, those who had remained loyal to the Captain, now took an appraisal amongst themselves. They had to decide what to do next, both for their survival and that of the Captain's.

"Boron, you saw what just happened to the Captain," Milne asked.

"Exhaustion, fear, surrender, who knows, but we'll have to do our best to protect him from himself, I think. Make it seem like he is still in charge while we figure out together what to do. Then maybe we can come out of this alive. Davis, what was it you were telling the Captain?"

"I think that's Argonia ahead of us. The position is right, according to legend. I studied the legend in school. You know there's usually a little fact in every myth."

"Argonia?" Milne spoke. He knew of the legend, as did most. But he had also heard sailors' tales about the island; a Utopia gone mad, sailors barely escaping alive when stranded there, of cannibalism and human sacrifice. A silence came over the men. Argonia, Utopia, or Hell? Their survival depended on that answer.

On the seventh day they landed.

A gentle breeze rocked the ship as it wallowed several hundred yards from shore. They were waiting for something, something to break the oppressive silence that surrounded the island that lay before them.

Then came the command. "Lower the boat."

The landing had begun.

The small boat glided across the water toward the shore. Four men worked the oars, together pulling it toward landfall.

Here was land, away from the storms, the rotting food, the rats, where they would find food and rest. Or would it be something worse?

Argon was the mightiest of the Gods. With his right hand, Zacar, Argon brought peace to his people. Izrich, the master of all of the mortal Teachers, foretold to Argon that a great calamity, a cleansing, would strike the heart of his people and destroy them. This angered Argon, and he lashed out and destroyed this Teacher. Argon himself swore vengeance at the Fates, to do battle with them himself on his people's behalf to prevent this Armageddon from happening.

At this the Fates laughed. As immortal as the days and nights, they alone guided man's destiny as they saw fit. The past, present or future, all was one to them. Their control was absolute. To think that a mere god would choose to do battle with them, for that his privileged people would suffer more. The wall that Argon built to protect his people would be smashed. Nothing would withstand the fury of the Fates.

And the Fates struck the wall that Argon had built. They rebounded from the first effort and struck again. Argon's wall held. He was stronger than the Fates.

Argon openly challenged them then, marching forward, with his mind open, searching the Fates out; Argon the Greatest, the Master of them all, the Master of the Fates.

And the Fates fled before him. Argon's people blossomed, to greater heights than before.

Argon's tasks at first seemed simple, guiding the destiny of his Chosen People. Then the cracks began to show in this destiny. From order rose chaos; great wars broke out, famine and fear were everywhere. Argon concentrated his strength on fewer and fewer. Elsewhere in the world, war, plague and famine spread. Argon's strength waned and the Fates reappeared. They had never been gone, just hiding in the shadows. Now it was their turn to make mankind pay for Argon's arrogance.

Izrich, his Teacher, now destroyed, had told Argon to stand firm against these Fates. Now, with Zacar standing at Argon's side, he did so. All abandoned Argon but for a few. None wanted to feel the Fate's retribution for Argon's actions. These few Argon and Zacar brought to an island paradise, the most perfect place they could find. Seeing to it that these few would survive what was to come, survive even the Fates' fury, he placed his people under the guidance of Zacar. Then Argon left once more to do battle with the Fates.

Throughout the planet and beyond bombs fell. The skies darkened and the lands of the world bled red. Soon all would perish. Armageddon, the final battle. Argon, in his vanity, saw almost all destroyed. Only his people remained, hidden. And he himself, Argon, saw to it that he would die in the end as well. To protect his people from any knowledge the Fates could claim from him. And the Fates were at last satisfied.

Zacar stood watch over Argon's people, left in his care. His only demand was a single sacrifice once a year, as payment for the sacrifice Argon had made. And he made it provident that none would land on this island of perfection. It would remain whole and good. This Argonia.

A ritual was in progress. Three times the High Priest of the Inner Sanctum circled the stand. A plaque was set in the stand, in a language none understood. Three times the High Priest touched each of the Lesser Objects, laid carefully around the stand.

With the fog lifting off the sea, the High Priest praised the Almighty Zacar for another year of deliverance from the evils of the past.

With arms outstretched before them, the villagers paraded to the cliff's edge to watch the marvel of the rising sun. From their lore they knew the sun was the offspring of Zacar. They knew and believed in the Father, Zacar, the sun, his protégé, and the fog's Holy Spirit.

The sky cleared and the sun rose. The villagers continued their chanting with the rising sun, their voices increasing in volume. The swift beat of the drums accompanied them in their chant. At the peak of their frenzy, a villager was brought forward to be sacrificed to Zacar and the Holy Spirit of the fog. For Zacar must be fed from the flesh and blood of his people.

Without sign of struggle, a woman was brought to the cliff's edge, awash in the shining sun. It would be through the miracle of her Virgin Death that another year would be granted to her village. She was stripped and marked for Zacar, a cross drawn across her belly for the reasons of being. She was to be thrown to what remained of the fog below them. If her body was found the next morning, it meant her soul had entered heaven, granting the village another year of life.

She stood quietly, carrying a secret and waiting for what was to come. It was a secret that would have led to her death much sooner if it had become known. Neither herself, nor her brother, believed in the Cult of Zacar. They were members of a secret Sect of Knowledge, knowledge from before the Great Darkness. They were few in number, always afraid of betrayal. This handful worked to keep alive the hope that had been New Eden, as told in their relic. Old, beyond all reckoning, pages torn and missing, the Bib'e told them of all that they knew was real; that the village, led by the High Priest of a distant time, had taken another road shown to him by a demon snake.

The woman was carried forward by the mob that was the village. She knew of prayers and forgiveness, but failed to understand how her death could mean anything at all.

The villagers screamed in their ignorance and their excitement grew. Forward they surged. She withdrew into her mind in resignation as she was carried to the edge. Only the High Priest himself could conclude the act. He picked her up in a drug-induced strength. High over his head he held her, shouting his blessing to Zacar. Now holding her at the edge, at the height of the mob's frenzy, as the High Priest was poised to give Zacar his gift from the village, he collapsed and she fell, inches from the edge.

The other priests hurried to the side of the High Priest. That he was dead there could be no doubt. What had he done to deserve this punishment from Zacar? They shared worried glances with each other. A new High Priest would have to be chosen to hold the assemblage for the annual sacrifice to Zacar. And a sacrifice there would have to be, for the sake of the village, for the sake of them all.

Once again the villagers, led by the priests, moved to where the woman lay at the cliff's edge. One of these was the woman's brother. He kneeled by his sister, unable to change the course of events. Like his sister, he knew the sacrifice was wrong. But the sect was still too few in numbers to prevent it.

The villagers, now a mob, reached the pair on the ground, intending to throw them both over the edge. Such was the rule of a mob. Two villagers grabbed each of the now-struggling pair. Even the priests could only watch in anguish. This was not the will of Zacar. To them an even greater sacrilege was taking place. Only a High Priest could make such a gift. None of the priests could decide who would be next among them this quickly; each wanted the role and would refuse to give up their claim. To the village mob, two instead of one, brother and sister, joined, would appease Zacar (How could Zacar not be pleased?) so went the mob's thought. Both man and woman were raised high upon the arms of many. The mob had but little time left to make it happen. Soon the Holy Spirit of the Fog would be gone.

As both were set to be cast to the rocks below, a village elder cried out, "Hold!" He was a member of the secret Sect of Knowledge. "Who among us is the High Priest that Zacar will listen to?" His call led to a brief pause, but even he knew nothing more could be done to bring a halt to the sacrifice. To espouse the truth would only bring an end to the new beginning that he was part of.

All eyes returned to face the sea at the cliff's edge. Only the last wisps of the fog remained. When they were gone it would be too late for the sacrifice to help the village. Soon Zacar would be displeased and the Zacar would rise no more.

"Too late!" some now screamed as the ocean became visible. The fog had cleared and the villagers, no longer a mob, in their new distress fell crying to the ground.

The elder now approached where the man and woman were helping each other up from where they had fallen at the cliff's edge. He handed her his outer robe. The three stood, unsure of what was to happen now. Within memory the sacrifice had never been missed. It was the three who stood together that first witnessed the miracle that appeared at the edge of the sea. None had seen a ship before, but from the records that remained, they knew that this could only be the Vessel of Redemption that their Book spoke of. The three fell to their knees in prayer, while many of the villagers joined them as they, in turn, spotted the ship coming toward them. To the villagers the Articles of Zacar had been correct. Their past sacrifices had been rewarded. They begged forgiveness to Zacar in their cries and wails.

As the villagers fell to their knees as one, the priests pushed to resume their control over the people. The priests called out together to the villagers. "This can only be the Vessel of the Redemption. Salvation shall be ours. Our determination and sacrifices from the beginning of our time to Zacar and the Holy Trinity have been rewarded. Our faith and yours in the Almighty Zacar have led to this. The redemption of the faithful, this shall be our salvation, our rapture."

The boat approached the halfway point to the shore. A beach had been found, albeit a small one. A line had been passed, although the men rowing the boat didn't know it. Nor did the Argonians who now watched the boat from above on the cliff.

Guns rose from their ancient placement beneath the sand. A shell fell close to the boat, a warning shot. As the boat glided to a stop, so did the shelling. The boat returned to the ship.

Zacar's protective shield to the island remained true.

Chapter Ten
Lost Island of Legend

The ship circled the island for what seemed hours, directed as best by the crew. They stayed just out of range of the strange guns that appeared on the shoreline. Hidden reefs and small rocky islets lay scattered in the waters around them.

As the ship reached the southernmost tip of the island, they came in sight of a small village. It lay at the mouth of a river, more of a large stream, and seemed a good location to try another landing. The villagers they had seen did not appear to pose a threat. The crew hoped that here the mysterious guns would remain silent. As they rounded the island's southern tip, the crew of *The Proctant* studied the people on shore. The islanders seemed from a distance few in numbers and primitive. They avoided the edge of the water as they followed the ship. It did not seem likely to the men onboard the ship that these could be the people keeping them from landing. This left the quietly unspoken question: Who were those others?

It was approaching nightfall and the crew was uncertain how they could survive onboard the ship another night, especially in the treacherous waters around the island. They would wait until dusk and try landfall then.

As night came the small lifeboat was lowered. This would be their third attempt that day since they had reached this accursed land. Four exhausted men followed their Captain onto the boat. Four tortured backs bent into the oars, whether by his orders or simply their own will. They set out for the nearby shore with long strokes of the oars. Nearing the shoreline, they had already passed closer than before. This time the men said their soundless prayers that the guns would remain silent, that they would make it to shore.

Less than a hundred yards to go and the men onboard the small boat could clearly make out the details of the village. Then the guns burst loose their shells again and the Captain ordered them to turn back.

As they turned, the Captain rose at the stern of the boat to see how far they had gotten this time. He gazed silently toward the land as the wash from one of the nearby shell's landing caught the boat. The Captain was turning back toward the sea as he stood and was thrown off-balance.

The men had slipped their oars and all turned toward him. As the Captain fell to one side of the boat, trying to catch his balance, Milne seized on the opportunity. Whether of fevered mind or insane, he swung his oar, striking the Captain's head and sending him overboard. Before he had hit the water Captain Gull was already dead from the force of the blow to his temple.

The attacker fell to the center of the small boat, too exhausted to rise on his own. The other men remained seated, unsure of what to do, too tired to care. Then, as one, they resumed their path back to the ship. There was no place else to go.

They were met at the ship's side by the Captain's second in command, a young Lieutenant, and the corporal of the guard, the only command left on the ship. Standing in the background were what remained of the doomed ship's crew. All knew that something had happened but in the twilight, none was sure what. All could see however that the Captain was no longer with them.

The small boat's crew lashed the boat to the side of the ship and quietly clambered aboard her, one at a time. They left the unconscious Milne where he had fallen. As they boarded they were questioned by the weakened lieutenant about what had transpired.

"What happened out there?" he anxiously asked the men. "Speak up one of you. I'm waiting… What happened?" The corporal of the guard stood next to the Lieutenant with his sword half-drawn.

The men told the Lieutenant their story of what had taken place on board the boat. Of how, after starting back, the Captain ordered them to stop rowing. They told of how the Captain had stood up and surveyed the horizon and the stars. They spoke of how he told them they had to make it to shore, give it one more try. How the Captain was caught off-guard by a wave and in his weakened state thrown off-balance and headed over the side of the boat. Of how Milne had tried to reach the Captain but had collapsed himself in the attempt. They had tried to find the Captain in the water when a shark had appeared to finish him off. The Lieutenant himself had seen sharks all around the ship. And so, to the others of *The Proctant*, Captain Gull had died a hero, dying as he tried to save them all. At this Lieutenant Niob had to be satisfied. He had his suspicions of what had happened out there, just beyond clear eyesight. However, these were the men that had remained loyal to Captain Gull during the mutiny. Niob himself had never truly liked the Captain, but tradition and chain of command had kept him loyal. Now he was in command of what remained.

He called to the doctor, "Xenon, see what you can do for Milne. Two of you help the doctor get him onboard. We'll need everybody together to make it to land."

Niob surveyed the men around him. There was Davis, the cook, a giant from the south of the Confederation, as good with a knife as he was with a stove.

The Doctor, Xenon, was little understood by the rest. He had refused to take a side during the mutiny and had worked to save both sides with his healing powers when it was over.

Boron, was the ship's carpenter. It was because of him and his wizardry with what remained of the ship that had got them this far. With just a few primitive tools, he had kept them afloat and moving. Boron would be even more indispensable once they left the ship to build them a stockade for protection and cover. Niob realized, as the Captain had, that they could travel no further in *The Proctant*.

Lute, the corporal-of-the-guard, and his second, Bell, were both experts in weaponry. However, even they had no idea what to make of the strange guns that had prevented their making a landing.

Samuel was a mate on his maiden voyage. Niob still had no idea how the youngster would eventually stand up to stress. So far he had remained calm.

Eight men, including himself and Milne, were still left, out of a crew of over fifty that had left harbor on a simple trading expedition. And what of Milne, the second mate of the ship. He had surprised everybody by remaining loyal to the Captain. Niob thought that he must remain friends with Milne. The men would follow him, their new captain, out of a sense of duty and to survive. But they would follow Milne as their leader.

By the time they had rested and organized themselves for a final attempt to land, the night had passed. The wind had picked up from the south and the ship had drifted with it during the night, north along the island's coast. Niob had planned to land north of the village. However, the wind carried the ship far beyond that point to the north where it rested against the rocks several hundred yards from the beach. *The Proctant* had reached her final resting place and would travel no farther. The sea had calmed and the men lowered the second boat. The first had remained where it was, lashed to *The Proctant's* side. All would go ashore this time; there would be no turning back. The men lowered what useful tools for land they could find.

As the men climbed down to the small boats, *The Proctant* slid farther onto the undersea rocks, carried by the higher tide. The men had not even noticed what had happened until the ship began to lean over on her keel away from the boats. *The Proctant's* time was now to be counted in hours, not days. Niob sent Boron to assess any new damage. He went down into the ship's lower holds. There he found what would be the final wound of *The Proctant.* Her keel was broken. He reported this to Niob, and then the two men joined the others in the boats. They had already taken what they could carry from the ship.

As the men began to propel their small boats toward the distant shoreline, *The Proctant* listed farther towards the sea, and waves began to sweep over her. The end would come quickly for her as the tide lowered and exposed what remained of her shell.

They rowed swiftly toward the distant beach. This time there could be no turning back. Not a word was spoken between the men. Each worked to move the boats as quickly as possible. Anxious looks were exchanged as they passed what they knew was the boundary the guns allowed. Their oars slapped the water and they could hear the sounds of the waves hitting the beach before them.

As they got closer to the rocky beach the men heard a strange chanting coming from the direction of the village. It carried a quality to it that worried Niob and the others.

Closer now, the closest they had come yet to making a landing, and still the guns remained silent. Where were the guns that had greeted them before?

The men realized that they would land unnoticed and unwatched by the villagers, well north of the village itself. Whatever activity it was that the villagers were engaged in, it left none to watch the sea. The guns still remained silent.

The men began to tense up as they neared the beach. The waves' spray hit their faces. Their pace with the oars quickened, if that was possible, as they raced for the pebble-covered beach. Only fifty yards to go, the water had become quite shallow. Still, they strove to propel the small boats even faster. In their frenzy to make it to shore, the unified motion of their strokes became confused. Oars became tangled and lost over the side. The silence became broken with the oaths of angry men. One boat became still only twenty-five yards from shore, the other only twenty or so. The water appeared fairly shallow.

The shelling began with a loud thunder all at once. Why so close to shore no one knew, but they were grateful. The guns overshot the first boat, which began moving toward the beach again. The guns drew their aim at the second boat, still bobbing motionless in the waves. Someone onboard the second boat yelled for them all to jump. Who that was, nobody could later tell. All jumped clear of the boat and began to swim to shore. The water was shallower than they thought, but sharks had been seen from the ship. As they swam away from the boat, a shell found its mark in that boat. As the boat's wooden frame scattered with the force of the blast, the guns were silent once more. Somehow, the first boat remained undetected.

With pieces of the shattered boat all around them in the water, they gathered together, somehow alive after their boat was destroyed and began the short swim to the beach. The cold of the water was biting. One by one, they collapsed at the edge of the beach, to be pulled ashore by those shipmates who had already arrived in the surviving boat. They brought the boat up onto the beach and tied it off above the high-tide mark. There, alongside the boat, the men collapsed briefly from their exertion, worn from another day without food. After a short break, the men struggled grimly to their collective feet and walked to the shelter of the forest just beyond the beach.

The morning broke early for the travelers. They had not been disturbed during the night in the open. Sounds were coming from the distant village. The voyage had taken its toll on the men, and although alive and onshore, they had no energy left to survive. They collapsed once more as a group just inside the border of the forest.

Two disparate parties had watched the ship closely as it had sailed to its final resting place. One was the Priests of Zacar, with their new Priest-King, who watched as they believed the gods tried to land and were prevented from doing so by the island. This they could only understand as Zacar protecting them from not good, but instead from evil gods who had come to their sacred island. The Priests of Zacar, who ruled the island with their ignorance, were uncertain how best to deal with this revelation.

The second group that watched the ship with intense interest were those who opposed the Priest-Kings of Zacar. With knowledge handed down from one generation to the next, these souls had to remain a hidden sect. If discovered by the priests, there would be only one result, to be ruthlessly hunted down and destroyed, crushed like insects to preserve the ignorance that was Zacar. These few of the hidden sect hoped the visitors would help them bring about the end of the rule of Zacar.

Each watched, neither aware that the final decision would lie with neither. Fate had determined who would meet these visitors from another land first.

It was the children of the village, those too young to understand what Zacar stood for, that made the first contact. It was these young children who proclaimed them the Servants of Zacar. Who else could they be, thought the youngest, to arrive from the sea as they did? And so, in a most innocent way, a revolt began that had been simmering for ages.

Members of the Sect of Knowledge met deep below the surface of the island in a large underground cavern. Word had passed from cell to cell and with each furtive glance at those around them, the followers of Knowledge found their way below. They were amazed at how large the number. But with such secrecy, each had known of only a few.

A decision had to be made (now!) to come out into the open, while the visitors remained in good standing with the people, or to remain secret.

And as the fellow followers of the Sect of Knowledge talked the words of conspiracy and revolt, the Priests of Zacar worked to design a plan, a way to show the visitors were false gods, not sent by Zacar after all.

In a cavern, deep beneath the surface of Argonia, the conspiracy met. Many, surprised by their numbers, expressed the hope to act now. Others, alarmed by these same numbers, feared to be discovered.

"We must act now!" one of the younger members of the sect spoke loudly, with an emotion that caught the attention of all.

Torchlight lit the gathering, carefully screened at the entrance so none outside could detect what was occurring below. Many were surprised at whom they encountered at the meeting, neighbors who had known each other for years, unaware. Even one low-level priest appeared among them. With so many gone from the village at one time, the priests were sure to suspect something unusual was happening.

When this was spoken of, the low-level priest that stood among them let out a cautionary word. "While they are active to expose the visitors as not from Zacar, we are safe. But we must keep this meeting short. Or they will come to realize another acts against them."

The first now spoke again with his emotional eloquence. "We must speak to the strangers and tell them who we are and what Zacar represents. We must confide in them that they will act with us."

"What if they refuse?" another called out. "Wouldn't that be the end of everything that we have worked so hard to achieve?"

"What have we achieved?" the first spoke again. "In our hiding and secrecy from one generation to the next, and always the Priest-King's rule, sacrifices hurled to their deaths to appease what?" At this comment all turned toward the priest who stood among them.

"My stand is with you. Though I profess a faith in Zacar, I know my fellow priests have taken the wrong path. They now must be stopped. They have caused too much suffering."

"But we could be destroyed ourselves, through the Priests' control of the village. Is it not our own duty to continue to pass our knowledge to our sons and daughters?"

"What does that do by itself, but to continue to preserve the false ways of the Priests? Look at our numbers. Will we ever be this strong again?" The young priest again spoke aloud. In his mind the heresy that had become the Priests of Zacar had to be destroyed, not for knowledge but to preserve the true path. Yet he knew, in his mind, the true path contained the knowledge of those around him.

The first voice now spoke again. "Now! Now is the time to act, while we all are gathered here. Tomorrow may be too late. We must act!"

"You are right, of course, Altur. Now is the time to act. But not in haste or fear." One of the village elders spoke now. He was a member of the village council and many had been surprised to see him among them. His discourse among the priests was widely known. His voice carried a respectful tone as they all listened to his words. "We must act now, that is very true. But how is the question? While our numbers are great, do we want to fight those villagers who would follow the Priests to the end. We must decide our actions tonight. We dare not have another meeting like this first, or we shall be prematurely discovered. We must be prudent to spare lives. To act without caution and planning would only bring death to too many. We must not ignore the strength of the Priests who rule us. What say you to this, young priest?"

"It is true, many of the village would join to preserve the false way that our Priests of Zacar have guided them. In their ignorance, they would gladly die to preserve what they follow. I have seen this in their empty eyes."

"How will we then plan this, in one night, to preserve our secrecy and yet make ourselves known to the outsiders, but remain hidden from the Priest-Kings?" Altur spoke.

Now one stepped forward from the background. He had remained quiet and contemplative to this point. One of the oldest among them, Chuak, he was distinguished as one of the few of the village to wear openly the sign of the rose, a symbol of freedom the priests remained ignorant of. As he spoke, the others felt a confidence stir that this was indeed the time, a confidence that most had found lacking until this point. "To this question I pose an answer. To be agreed upon by all who gather in this sacred spot tonight, made sacred by the decision we make. A meeting must be made, as if by accident, with those who have joined us from across the sea. But only with one, and let it be the one known as Milne. Let him carry our words to his fellows."

"How is it you know the name of one of them?" asked Altur.

"This meeting has been forecast for some time by my own books of knowledge."

Not satisfied, Altur spoke again. "How is it we should make this contact? Does this Milne know of us, or you?"

"Those of the sea have no knowledge of you or of the unfortunate events of this island. Of that you can be assured. It is from my Teachers, those who predate even your knowledge or that of Zacar, that I know of this event."

"I will make this contact!" Altur presented to the group.

"While your courage is great," Chuak replied back, "sometimes a greater degree of caution is needed. Let me make this contact, that our venture might gain its success."

All agreed that this would be done, though the young priest expressed his misgiving that any knowledge could be beyond that of

Zacar. In his mind, he knew the Priest-Kings were wrong, but did that make the Sect of Knowledge right?

"Promise me only that you will not act against us," Chuak said to the young priest.

When the priest spoke his reassurance that he stood with the group, Chuak added his final words to the priest. "When this is over, you will be needed to bring the people of Argonia to the future."

The Priest-Kings of Zacar were in their own meeting and as the young priest had noted, they were paying little attention to the events transpiring in the village. The Priests were searching for ways to turn the villagers against the visitors. However, it could not appear to come from the Priests.

To the Priests the death of their leader, the High Priest of Zacar, during the attempted sacrifice, could only have been the doing of a god. That meant the evil gods Zacar had opposed were among them again. Their first order of duty to Zacar was to name a new High Priest. In respect to Zacar, that priest lost his name, to be known only now as the High Priest of Zacar. It was he who led the thinking of the priests in how to combat the evil now among them. The visitors were not the chosen gods of Zacar, as the children had foolishly proclaimed, but mere mortals, the followers of the evil gods who once again challenged Zacar over the fate of Argonia. The Priest would have to show restraint, it was the innocence of the children at stake. To immediately proclaim these visitors false gods now would only mean death to these children, children who through no fault of their own had come under the guidance of the evil that had come to Argonia. The children must be saved as well or all Argonia would be lost. It was they who had so often proclaimed that it was in the innocence of children that the truth lay. These were the teachings of the Priests of Zacar. And now this was a truth that they would have to bring about as false while retelling the truth that was Zacar at the same time; a delicate balance to follow.

It had been several days since the men of *The Proctant* had been found by the children on the beach and half-carried by children to the village. The men relaxed and regained their strength in the village they were taken to. They fished from the sea, something that had been forbidden to the people of Argonia by the Priests of Zacar. And they dreamed of making their way home. There was wood of plenty on this island to build a ship. All the while they were treated as gods. And if their ways were different from those of the villagers, that was as it should be. For shouldn't gods behave differently than their servants, the villagers of Argonia.

"Isn't this paradise, Milne?" Samuel spoke, lying on his back in the sand, enjoying the warmth of the sun. He was drunk with the fragrance of the island and felt power in the reverence accorded him by the people of this island, the shortest of whom stood a good foot taller than the five-foot-six Samuel. "Could we have found a fairer land in all the oceans to be shipwrecked on?"

"Aye, it seems all of that," Milne replied, calling upon his knowledge of his many voyages. "But something seems wrong here," he continued. "Don't relax your guard too much. So much seems strange here. The sea is full of fish, yet these people seem forbidden to enjoy that bounty. The language alone, how is it a people like this speak a language almost identical to our own. We've found similar tongues spoken before, but here..."

"You think too much, Milne," was the younger Samuel's response. "You speculate beyond what you see. This is a paradise."

"What is one man's paradise is often another's hell."

"Then let it be another's hell, not ours," Samuel laughed.

"I only hope that you're right. But still, it seems that we have landed on a puzzle with half of the pieces missing."

Davis, a coal-black giant of seven feet, joined them. He was the only one of the voyagers who stood taller than the Argonians. "And how are my small friends enjoying themselves on this fine day? At last I can talk to a man without straining my neck downward. I hope that your egos aren't shattered."

"Davis, if your strength wasn't that of two men I would challenge that remark," Samuel smiled as he jokingly replied to the larger man. "But with the sun, the fair winds, and the beautiful women, I bid you free to speak as a friend."

"A wrestling match? It would take the two of you and I would still win. But I too have arranged a meeting with the fairest maidens of this land." With that the big man turned and left his two companions.

"I have to go as well, Milne," Samuel again laughed as he got up from the sand.

"Do you also have a meeting with a woman of this island?"

"Yes, but I'm afraid it's just with one. Davis leaves but little for us of normal size. If you like though, I'm sure that she has a friend." Samuel smiled again as he said this.

It was Milne's look more than what he said that led to Samuel more quickly leaving the presence of his friend.

"I'm afraid that will have to wait, Samuel," said Milne. "It's time to find some answers. You saw how being treated as a god has gone to Davis's head. We need to find those answers before they affect us all. Come with me, your maiden will wait, I am sure. Let's grab Boron and start asking questions of these people. Something is waiting for us to find, I know it."

"The maiden may well wait, but why take a chance? Good luck with your search for answers. Its other things I search for now," was his response to Milne as he stretched.

Milne met up with Boron, who had questions of his own he wanted answered. They began to carefully ask questions of the villagers, keeping up their facade for now that they were gods. As Samuel had implied, they found out nothing new, but they did get some clarity about the island. The Priest-Kings were the personal representatives of Zacar and ruled the people of Argonia. Zacar himself made the selection each year of one new novice who would join the ranks of the priests. This selection was from the children of the village that turned six that calendar year. No one knew how Zacar made this selection. At the time of the induction of this child into the priesthood, the Priests of Zacar proclaimed that it is the innocence and the intelligence of the children that shall guide them. When the young novice gained the age of fifteen, he became a full Priest of Zacar, took the bride of his choice, and became revered by all. The two men almost lost their cover as gods on this one question. Several Argonians looked askew at the two men. Should not the gods already know the answer to this question? They covered their tracks by saying this was something reserved for the knowledge of the Priests, and they were making sure this article of law was not broken. They did learn that the children had named the men of *The Proctant* gods in the service of Zacar. They now understood how it came the villagers accepted them as gods. Eventually Boron tired of this questioning of the land they had found themselves in, and he joined Samuel and Davis in the search for the fairest maiden he could find.

Milne still had his lingering doubts, but after several more days of discovering nothing horribly amiss, he began to think his worries were groundless. That is when the Sect of Knowledge made contact. Through a whispered word, Milne was invited to a meeting. The enigma that was Argonia would be answered.

They met late in the day on a desolate part of the island. It was a small cave below the cliffs where the sacrifices to Zacar took place. Scattered around this bleak place were the bleached, broken and scattered bones of the maidens sent to Zacar. The wind swept the spray from the ocean's waves across the rocks that created their dangerous path. Huge waves swept over the islets not far from shore. Milne was told that more than once a member of the Sect of Knowledge had fallen to his death on this path. However, it was one place on the island that the conspirators felt secure. The superstitions of the Priests of Zacar would keep them away from this place. Only on the day of the sacrifice would the High Priest make his way here to ensure that the maiden's sacrifice was complete and she had joined Zacar. He carried a sacrificial blade in case help was needed to send her on her way. With the height of the cliffs at this spot, this blade was seldom needed. Milne was told that this year's sacrifice had been interrupted by the ship's arrival. Combined with the death of the High Priest during the ceremony, the Priests of Zacar had been thrown into confusion.

Even with superstition protecting their hideaway, the Sect would usually meet only at night, traveling the dangerous path without light. Such was their fear of discovery. It was the ocean itself that helped protect this place, as its storms and waves prevented the pathway they followed from becoming worn by the many feet that had followed it.

Chuak tried to settle the unease that Milne felt as they silently moved through the rocks' shadows in twilight. It was not yet nightfall and the full moon's light shown from the horizon, casting its pale light on their pathway. They made their way through the rocks until they came to a slight crack in the cliff's face. They slipped inside the crack, and here torches were kept that could be lit for the journey underground. What little light that leaked out through the opening could only be seen from the sea.

Chuak told Milne how the ancestors of those who populated the island now, had created the vast underground works. It had been designed as part of the island's defenses, defenses that had kept the crew of *The Proctant* stymied in their attempts to land. Much had been lost over the generations; none had known of or seen the gun emplacements until they had appeared to keep *The Proctant* at bay. The meaning of any control that they knew of had long since been lost.

Now this place was remembered and used solely by the followers of the secret Sect of Knowledge. A third man, Kristof, who was now old, was their scholar of what had come before and joined Milne and Chuak. He had learned his knowledge from the scholar before him, who had taught him. Kristof's life was now lived solely underground, his position too important to risk the chance of betrayal above. Only on the occasional dark night was he able to come to the cave's entrance to breathe the fresh ocean air.

Kristof had recently taken on an apprentice of his own, after a staged accident had feigned the apprentice's death. A fall over the cliff on the other side of the island, witnesses but no body found. Now this apprentice, Jozef, worked to learn from Kristof all that he knew from before. Both men were working to try to understand the operation of the computer library they had found. There was a screen with no visible means to turn on, and solid disks, like large coins, stacked together with writing on each on what they contained. One scholar, with his apprentice, at a time had held the sole knowledge of how it worked. Once the scholar died without an apprentice, an accident on the rocks, much of the library's workings were lost at that time. Only now were they beginning to understand bits and pieces of this lost knowledge, how the discs held the stories; but working discs were few. Much had been lost forever to the passage of time.

The four men sat in a circle, warmed by a source still unknown by the scholars. Tea had been prepared to drink and a meal of bread and jerky of a consistency Milne found pleasing.

Chuak motioned for Kristof to begin. So the enigma that was the Legend of Argonia unfolded for Milne.

"Long before the last Great War, which so devastated this planet, a group of the world's richest and most influential people, seeing the course the world was taking and its inevitable result, purchased an isolated island in the world's seas.

"With this isolation assured, a selection process was begun. People were brought to this island to build a new utopian society. This selection process was a long and arduous one. This process was carried out in secret throughout the world. Many explanations were given so that none would learn the secret. These founders sought to find those of the most perfect in body and mind to populate their paradise, Argonia. Many false trails were laid for those who followed rumors. A background voice began to swell of a conspiracy of the most powerful by those that followed the false trails. This did nothing to quell the world's growing suspicions of each other. Each side called for the other to tell the truth about what was happening. Yet neither side knew the truth. With all the tensions and stray trails that covered the world, none learned of this place except those it was intended for. Simple answers to these false trails were found and many chose to believe these were the source of so many missing lives. As the last of this selection process was finished, the gates were closed. These select few, taken to this island, began a new life and lived out the dreams of this utopia.

"A vast cavern was carved in the rock in the heart of the island. A library of wisdom was set up here, to gather all of the world's knowledge in one place. Those that failed to understand the purposes of the language and the networks freely gave their knowledge. Always in the background, hidden by their own visibility, were the guardians of Argonia, with the birds tweeting their calls.

"The world's struggles seemed settled as once-mighty empires fell of their own weight. But from the edges of where the false trails led, new devils arose in the name of their God, more dangerous than the last. Horrors once more arose, man killing man, and the towers fell, all in the name of this god. The leaders ran scared, unable to steer or change course away from the evils that were unleashed; new evils born from the following of men who misunderstood what was laid out before them.

"On Argonia devices were made in place to protect this land from discovery and to prepare it for what was to come. A defense system was put in place, controlled by the same computer that was the library.

Resources were shifted from around the world to Argonia, so when the time came, those of Argonia would stand alone, safely behind the gates.

"And as this defense was set in place, the library became second, although always its scholars were searching the spider's web for new information as it was found. They were determined that the memories of man would not be lost to the generations to come.

"In the people selected, all professed a belief in their god, though many and different were the rituals they followed. Respect for those that were different had been a defining trait of those selected.

"Then the War came. Although long in warning of what was to come, its suddenness left many of the Founders in the lands that perished, The leaders of Argonia died in the devastation of that war.

"The people of Argonia were left leaderless, an issue not thought important by the Founders, as it was thought that through the gates Argonia would be ruled.

"Outside contact lost, the people of this paradise lost faith in all that they had been taught. Darkness covered the earth, and the seas first raised then lowered, as cold became the only constant, cold and the never-ending darkness. The people of Argonia survived in this isolation but changed in their fundamentals. Faith was lost in starvation as depredation and a new caste system was born of the desperation. So much had been prepared in the beginning, so much lost through ignorance. A new religion was created, as the need for a belief remained strong. Priest-Kings were borne of the ashes. Books that could have taught us so much were left in the weather to deteriorate. Then one day the people saw a new sight in the sky. The clouds had cleared and the moon stood above them, bluish in the sky it appeared; Zacar, to lead his people anew.

"With the vision of Zacar in the sky, His greatness forced the clouds to part. A new era was born to Argonia, food became plentiful, and the people rejoiced.

"From the stories of the people's ancestors many still knew of the moon standing in the Earth's sky. However, the moon of the stories had been gray and bleak. In the Priests-Kings' new lore for Argonia, it was that moon, in its never-ending war with the sun, that had led to the devastation of the Great War. The Earth had been doomed and its moon, Luna, fought the sun, the only offspring of God.

"Finally Zacar arrived, to lay allegiance before the sun and melt the moon, Luna, freeing the clouds and restoring the sky. The sun, tired from its war with Luna, must rest at night, and so Zacar stands guard alone so that Luna may never return.

"With the 'restoration' by Zacar of the sun's holy place, fish returned to the sea and crop seed that had lain long dormant sprung anew. Those fish became holy relics to the Priest-Kings, and only in the river could they be caught, for the sea was a holy boundary that none dared enter.

"Even in the children could the benefit of Zacar's might be found, as fewer of the defects in the children, brought about by Luna's war, were found. The people of Argonia became strong.

"As life grew better, so did the Priest-Kings' hold on the people become stronger. Ruling with and in ignorance, in fact relishing in their ignorance, knowledge was lost except for what a few could save. Those that professed knowledge not accepted by the Priests were killed. They could stand no challengers to their thought.

"Sometimes it was seen, as Luna remained, though hidden by the power of Zacar. Day would turn into night, though briefly, as Luna attempted to reassert its control. But Zacar would answer and restore the sun. It was for this fight that the Priests of Zacar ordained that a sacrifice must be made, so that Zacar could remain strong.

"A few remained of the scholars, those who knew the knowledge of the past. When the sacrifices began, they tried to restore reason to the island's insanity. Ruthlessly the Priests hunted them until only a few remained in secret or in hiding. The Priests portrayed us, the Sect of Knowledge, as we now call ourselves, as the spawn of Luna. In their ignorance the people hunted us as well. A few remained, in secret always, and we grew from father to son, mother to daughter in strength, to keep alive the past's truths so that one day the promise that was Argonia could be returned."

Milne heard this story in silence. Many times in his travels, Milne had heard similar tales. However, none had descended to the levels of depravity as the Priests of Zacar. Without hesitation he threw his lot in with these people. Milne quickly realized that for their own safety the Priest-Kings could not be trusted. It was up to him to deliver their story to what remained of the complement of *The Proctant.*

As Milne left the presence of Chuak and the others, it was early morning. They were back at the edge of the village. Chuak knew that a new chapter in the story of Argonia was about to begin. He only hoped it would be as foretold. He would have to make contact with the others.

Chapter Eleven
The Assemblage of War

The southern and eastern gates of the City of The Hold were in chaos and confusion as all of the people of this world, tormented and terrorized by the White, assembled. Not in the thousand years since the end of the 'darkness' had such an army assembled. While each group tried to maintain its own identity as it prepared for the march north to the City by the Lake, there were just too many people arriving from too many places for this to happen.

Being of the most interest to the people of The Hold were the coastal people of the Southern Harbors. The people of the Southern Harbors were a closed society that seldom ventured beyond their own borders. They wore a colorful uniform with the depiction of a flower on their chests. "Town's Guardsmen," they called themselves, and each was armed solely with an eight-foot pike with an armored tip. Amazingly light, these pike could be carried with one arm.

They saw the R'mon's, with their yellow observation balloons carried by ox-cart. Marching in front of the ox-carts were their fabled crossbowmen, mostly women. Half a dozen crossbowmen would be in every balloon's cage. Frequent trade with the R'mon's made them a common site in The Hold.

There was the Nobility of the Shiaps of the Southern Plains, riding on camels and speaking their strange language, Franco They were seldom seen north of the plains, but they were renowned for their valor.

The Cult of the Sader and the Followers of Ala remained segregated at the city's eastern gate, each shunned by the other forces of the march. It was this shunning which brought them together under the banner of The One True God, a shared belief.

The Nomads gathered by themselves, not so much for their own seclusion (which they enjoyed) but for the preponderance of wildcats that roamed throughout their midst. The giant cats brought fear to all that saw them. Yet they walked side-by-side with the Nomads, their companions.

The Raffs marched together from their mountain towns, with their longbows carried over their shoulders. Through frequent joint hunts, the men of The Hold knew of the voracity of the Raff marksmen. The

Hold and the Jall had encountered the Raffs on hunting and trading expeditions. They wore the colors of their legends, brown and green, and called themselves *The Tels* after their pre-Great-War hero. Like the Shiaps, they spoke their own language, but all were versed in the common tongue as well.

Scatterings of other groups, most not known in these parts, also gathered. Adventurers for the most part, mercenaries lured by the call of battle, they arrived in singles and in small groups.

To feed this assemblage became the primary task of The Hold. Cattle and sheep herds would need time to be restored to their levels of before. As these parties moved north as quickly as possible from the city of The Hold, the Southern Valley's food reserves ran low and crops harvested early. Hunting parties scoured the lands. Years would follow before game became plentiful in this part of the world again. Even the Sage, who through their Order had spread word of what was coming, were amazed at the multitude of armies arriving and the numbers arraying against the Whites.

Order became an issue and the armies moved north as fast as they arrived. While each army policed themselves, fights broke out frequently amongst rival armies and between the organized armies and the mercenaries. It was only fear and hatred of the Whites that had brought these people together. The hope of the leadership was that as the battle drew near the old animosities would be pushed to the background.

Gar pushed the men of *The Proctant* to the front of the columns. The different armies and their numbers mesmerized the sailors. This day's march would be the last with large numbers to head north, although more were seen heading towards The Hold from all points south and east. Over ten thousand had marched from the city in the days before. Many were marching directly to the City by the Lake, bypassing The Hold altogether. In this last group, alongside the sailors, were contingents from the Raff and the R'mon's. The R'mon's wagons were slow, but would continue, like the Shiap riders, without stop to the Castle Nourne and the R'mon's archers now rode in the wagons as well. For the rest it would be seven days of forced march to the City by the Lake, then one more march north to Nourne. In two weeks time the assault would begin.

Included in this final march were the unfortunates of this land, people who had lost all hope through misfortune of their own making, or forced upon them from the outside. Outcasts, children of thieves, orphans who had fallen through the cracks, to them it meant meals and maybe a chance to redeem their lives with glory. These were the stragglers and hangers-on that the rest of the march tried to keep separate. Even the Nomads had no place for these unfortunates of the world. With their large numbers, these cast-offs from this world's civilized people mingled with all, their hands out for food and most often weaponless. Some would fight, some would flee, but most would die in what was coming. Cole looked upon these people and saw only pity, handing out the crumbs of his food as he marched. Even the cold-hearted Zircon could only wonder with contempt at how these people were treated. The men of The Proctant treated each of these forgotten people with kindness. Nothing Gar could say could change that.

"How can we hope to achieve what needs to be done with these of the lowest rungs about us?" Gar pleaded with the sailors.

Thorium himself answered Gar, "How can I, we, fight a fight not truly ours? It is for these people we fight, not for you of this land that treat these 'lost souls' in such contempt."

These masses of the poor would have overwhelmed even the generosity of The Proctant's crew if not for the others who welcomed these lost souls as well. The Ala's and Saders now marched together as one under the banner of The One True God, welcomed these 'unclean masses' with the generosity of the pious. However, each tried to outdo the next with their conversions.

Each day's march ended in an already-used encampment. With the thousands who had already marched before them, often with their animals, no area was free from the refuse of those who had come before. The road to the City by the Lake stank with the garbage and remains of the marchers. While the people of The Hold and the Southern Valley did their best to maintain the road and the encampments, there were just too many people using the lands and the road over too short a time. The Southern Valley brought water in from afar. as the waters too close to the road was no longer considered safe to drink. The smell of the campfires roasting their meats each night only added to the overall smell and would linger for weeks. Even more, the standards of hygiene varied greatly among the people of the march.

When they arrived at The City by the Lake, it was even more chaotic than the march itself, if that was at all possible. There simply was not enough room for all of the arrivals. Food remained scarce and it seemed almost all of the lost peoples of this land had congregated there. It was only because the Order of the Sage had their own lodge in the city that the men of *The Proctant* had a room with a roof over their heads.

At about the same time as the armies congregated for the war to come, the last of the refugees from the Northern Valley arrived in the city. Special lodging had been prepared for their arrival. They were sent south from Nourne by the Lord and Lady of the castle to keep them clear of the coming action. They also wanted the people of the Southern Valley and the City by the Lake to see the results of their inaction during the brief civil war to the north.

The people of the city spoke quietly to each other in small groups as the survivors walked past.

"So few, where are the rest, are they still in hiding?"

"No, this is all that remains."

"But the north once held as many as the south."

"That was before," came the answer.

"They are so thin, so pale."

"Where are the men, and so few children?"

"The men gave themselves up so the women and children could live. There was so little food in the caves."

"The caves?" came the question. "What about in the valley floor?"

"All gone," came the solemn reply, "all gone."

When the Council had returned from its vote at the Castle Nourne, most had thought the issue settled. Preparations would begin to move against the Whites. However, the Council had failed to understand the fears of the citizens of the city. They were not strong enough to attack the White, let alone defend themselves against the reprisals of the White if the attack failed. The White mostly left the citizens of The City by the Lake alone, why do something to aggravate this tension. The argument went on and on. "We are too weak to fight alone, even with the Valley's and Nourne.

The Lords were united in their beliefs now. War must be carried to the Whites or all in the south would perish like the North, but without the support of the commoners?

They moved the Council meetings from the Council Chamber as the heated debate continued. There was just so much interest, on both sides; of the coming war, the Chamber was too small to hold everybody. Instead, the debate was moved to the Hall of Justices main chamber. The justices themselves became embroiled in the debate as each side picked ancient and archaic points of law to make their causes.

It was the commoners that remained split over what was to come. Many of the oldest remembered the death that had come in the civil war to the north. After untold centuries, the land was still recovering from the Great War. The Whites were a danger, but if they just kept their guard up, the City and the Southern Valley would be okay. Nourne could help the Northern Valley, but that was their choice, not the choice of the City by the Lake.

Jamen of Kilne, hero of the battle of Erson, called upon the duty of the city. However, he was now considered commoner in name only. Too many times the Counsel offered the title of Lord to Jamen for his deeds.

"But what of the death, the slavery, the massacre of the Northern Valley by the Whites?" he proclaimed.

"There are so few left, what does it matter to us now? We need to be more concerned with what is happening here," was the answer of the choir that he heard.

"And when the Whites have eradicated what is left of the north, what then, where will they go for their food then?" Jamen asked the Council.

To that, there was no answer.

It was the youth of the City by the Lake that changed the mood, although that was not clear at first. Most of the city's young quickly engaged in the care of the arriving refugees from the north. With this engagement came the stories of the atrocities of the White.

They had heard these stories before, of course, but always in the sheltering language of the old. Nourne and the Northern Valley seemed too far away. Now they heard first-hand stories, packed with the emotion of the tellers. It was only with a cold, unemotional language that the City and the Southern Valley had kept themselves immune from what was being inflicted on their cousins of the Northern Valley. Food, people as food? How had they not known? How had they hidden this knowledge from themselves? Jamen of Kilne had always been their leader, but they had ignored his voice as well. Now they listened, and understood. Now they began to assemble to force their will on the Council.

"Look at those who gather around us," they spoke, "they who come from so many lands. All tormented by the monster that is the White. How can we, who through our own inaction, and the inactions of the generation that came before us, ignore this call? Together we must join this march. Together we enjoin Jamen of Kilne to lead us."

The Council took another vote, one more in favor of the war than before. Only as one, united, could the Council move forward on the issue. However, events outside of the Justice Hall kept moving forward while the Council stood in place.

The Lords called forth their argument once more. It was Lord Drant of Stetlin who spoke for them. "It is we, of the City by the Lake and the Southern Valley, who through our own complacency encouraged what has come now before us. And through this complacency created the monster that stands before us; the White, growing larger and stronger as each day passes.

"We of the City by the Lake and the Southern Valley encouraged the Whites, allowed them to conquer the Northern Valley when they were so few in number.

"We of the City by the Lake and the Southern Valley encouraged and 'supported' the uprising of our cousins in the north as they tried to break their chains of slavery. Even as we learned of what the Whites called their food source we sat back and did nothing to support our words. It was not our concern we told ourselves.

"And as the massacre of the Northern Valley happened (How can we deny we knew nothing of this?) we still did nothing.

"Now, as the handful of survivors of the Northern Valley find their way among us, refugees from our own inaction, we still do nothing. It is too late for them, I hear.

"The world assembles around us now in our city and the fields to the north. People never before seen in this land gather to move against that which we have so conveniently, so quietly, chosen to ignore. Still we just sit here and talk. How long can we ignore what is happening and just talk? I for one am done with this talk. We, the chosen Lords of this land, must move now and end this charade. Preparations must be made. War is upon us," proclaimed Lord Drant of Stetlin.

With these final words, each of the Lords of the Council stood up as one and left the chamber.

Jamen now stood to leave as well. Leadership had been placed upon him by the youth of the city. As he tried to speak his final words to the assemblage, the thunderous cheers of those who had gathered in the Hall of Justice drowned out his words. The youth of the City and the Southern Valley made their intentions clear through their cheers of approval for Jamen. All left en masse behind their hero.

All that remained of the Council of the City by the Lake and the Southern Valley was Tor and the representatives of the commoners. In a quiet hush, Tor stood next to address the few who sat in their chairs. The Hall of Justice was now almost empty of its audience. Most had left with Jamen.

"It is clear that the debate has ended. Look at those who assemble around us. We are not alone. The people of this land, who once stood apart, now stand together against this common foe. Out of fear of the White, a creation of our indifference, the battle has already been joined. Already those of the City by the Lake and the Southern Valley join in what is to come.

"Look around you, I say. Do you even know half of those who have gathered with us here? Moreover, it is to join us that they are here. They heard your call to arms in Nourne, oh so short a time ago, have you forgotten already what was said at Nourne?

"The choice that remains is a simple one. Do we lead or do we follow? The choice to remain once again on the side is no longer ours.

"If this army that has assembled is victorious, the Valleys and this City, our homes, will remain free.

"If it is defeated, what became of the Northern Valley will be our destiny as well." With that Tor left the table to stand by the entrance to the room. Several of the remaining Council members left the room to prepare for the battle as well.

Praxton now stood. Besides him, only three of the representatives of the commoners remained at the Council table. "I think that the final vote has been taken. This fight, that I oppose, has been long in the coming upon us. I now go to join and add my counsel to what is happening. Be I the lone voice of moderation, so be it. The question before the City and the Valleys is but one. Do we go forward with one voice or divided? Those are the choices forced upon us by outside events. There can only be one answer. We must act as one." With that, Paxton of Pyers stood and followed the others out of the chamber room. One by one, the last holdout's stood as well, and with a silent nod towards Tor standing at the door, gave their approval for what was to come. Win or lose, their way was over. How many had to die because of their inaction in the past?

Tor was the last to leave the room. He took a last quiet reflection on what had happened and what was to come. It was the only action possible at this point. The Teachers seemed clear on that point. On the steps of the Hall of Justice, Tor announced the final vote. All in favor, none opposed. A joyous cry went out from the people of the City by the Lake. A past wrong, so long ignored, would be righted. However, with these cries for action came many tears as well, for those who would be lost to end this monster of their creation, the Whites.

What had begun with a trickle of a few at the beginning was now a flood, no longer hundreds or even thousands, it was now tens of thousands that assembled on the farmland to the north of the City by the Lake.

It had quickly become clear the City could not hold this congregation of humanity. They quickly escorted new armies and individuals who arrived at the City by the Lake to the marked-off land on the city's edge. Facilities for hygiene were assembled. Large, open-air dining rooms were created in a day to feed this growing army as it assembled. Little care was given to the natural rivalries here. As the City by the Lake built new facilities, they quickly filled with the next to arrive. Out of the chaos of the march, a primitive organization began to form. Nevertheless, the question always remained in the back of everybody's mind, who was in charge? Each group, as they arrived, had their own ideas. Even within the same people, groups arriving separately often had conflicting ideas of the command structure. Each was here more for their own needs than any common good. Once the Whites were gone, that would be the end of it.

As the tent city grew, customs and old rivalries broke out into open conflict almost every day. They worked to keep the most adversarial groups apart. There just was not enough room. When the City by the Lake tried to impose their own security on the camp, many rebelled at the intervention. What was justice for one group was retribution for the next.

It was Thorium, when he arrived, that brought an end to this. He and Cole quickly saw order was necessary before this army could move as one. To move separately as they had arrived would be suicide for all against the White's army.

They created a temporary Council of the army. Each group was allowed one member. While this brought an unruly amount of delegates to the first meeting under a large central tent, it was a start. After the first meeting, many agreed to consolidate the representation to limit the numbers there. Each camp would have their own marshal, as well, who would be responsible solely to the Council. It was a shaky provisional Council at best, but for a short time it would do.

The feeding of this army became an ordeal in itself. The Southern Valley and the City by the Lake took it upon themselves to meet this challenge. In the immense food courts they shared their foods and learned the foods of other cultures. Their best cooks took it upon themselves to outdo the next. Scraps there were none. There was barely enough for everyone as it was and what one party considered waste another considered a delicacy. A thriving inter-camp trade quickly arose for leftovers.

The army's Council at first seemed as chaotic as the camp itself. There were too many members in the beginning, although that quickly changed for the better with the consolidation of representatives. Only the Jall were not represented. With as much resentment as this part of the world held toward the 'privileged few,' they decided that the trader Wolfe would represent both The Hold and the Jall.

Twenty-one now sat at the circular table the City by the Lake had provided for the Council's use. No Sage was present, a thing that seemed strange to those who knew the Order well. The Order always seemed involved in the happenings of the world, and here at the outset of this important event, they were nowhere to be seen.

The first order of business was who would be in command of this army. There could be only one if they were to be successful. All realized this fact. But instantly the rivalries broke out anew. One party would not be subservient to another. One army would not fight alongside that one. At one point, Thorium, unused to all of this petty jealousy, threw his arms up in disgust and momentarily left the meeting to "Clear his head of all of this arrogance."

Thorium had barely returned to his seat when the biggest clamor arose. Arriving late was the leader of the R'mon's delegation, whose observation balloons, with their archers, could prove pivotal in the battle to come. Wearing the medallion of the highest award of her people, Loren entered.

"A woman! She has no place here! We are here for war, not child-rearing,' shouted M'Mahd.

Reed, of the Nomads, was the next to object. "A woman has no place in war."

As the clamor grew and became tumultuous, Loren calmly walked to the only open seat at the table, slightly raised above the others, left vacant by all so that none would gain from its elevated stature. New expletives could be heard under the tent as she sat.

"She blasphemes!" cried out M'Mahd.

With that, Loren calmly pulled her crossbow from its sling across her back, selected an arrow from her quiver, loaded the crossbow and placed a shot into the armrest of M'Mahd's chair, pinning his robe to it in the process. Then she spoke.

"That is but a symbol of my prowess. Are there any here who dare to think that they could do better?"

King Guntner of the Raffs smiled and winked at Loren. He knew her well. Many times the two had stood together with their assembled archers to meet the onslaught of a White assault or some other confrontation from the east.

"I, for one, know of none," Gunter said, "neither amongst the Raff nor any other people that I have visited. Side-by-side I have fought alongside Loren and no counsel do I value greater than hers in time of war. If those of the R'mon's be excluded from this Council, this army, then those of the Raff shall leave as well."

Thorium rose from his seat and spoke. Although a woman in such a position in the Confederation was rare, among some tribes of the Confederation it was not unheard of. He had quickly realized that this army needed the archers of the Raff and the R'mon's to prevail over the Whites and their Warbirds.

"Are there any of this Council of War, gathered to meet the menace that is the Whites, who oppose the help offered to this army by Raff and the R'mon's." Thorium stared directly at and between M'Mahd and Reed as he spoke this.

M'Mahd spoke now, carefully choosing his words. "As a representative of her people," he began guardedly, not wanting to be excluded from what was to come. "It is important that the followers of The One True God have a place at this meeting." He cursed under his breath the head of the Saders, who had convinced him to be the one to join this Council. The others would have been much more comfortable with a woman here. "I welcome Loren to this Council of War. But we will not serve under nor alongside of her."

"I have no problem with such a condition," Loren spoke. "I have no interest in the command of this army and we of the R'mon's will serve primarily in the air." With that, this issue seemed closed.

There was left the question of who would be in command of this army. No party trusted all here, and in some, the feeling was scarcely less than what was felt toward the White. All understood that they must fight as one to defeat the White, but who could they trust to lead the army as one. A Sage, Tor? The people of the southern lands quickly shot that down.

It was Lord Perth of Nourne who now stepped forward to speak. All around the table knew of and admired this man, one who had stood alongside his brothers to the north. All expected him to now claim the right of command. However, Lord Perth had spoken at length with Gar and Tor about this very thing. As much as all at the War Council admired Lord Perth, there were many who would have a difficult time following him. It was Gar who proposed the solution.

"It was the men of *The Proctant* who have been the catalyst in this action, as first foreseen by the Teachers. It is now they who should lead this action, and in their doing so, unify the people of this land. I propose Thorium as the leader of the army that is now assembling. He may not consider himself the one to lead, but it is he who is best equipped to do so."

Lord Perth of Nourne now made his nomination. "Let one from the outside, who shares none of our contentions, lead us. One who by providence has come from across the sea to join us. I nominate Thorium of the Confederation to command these armies assembled here today against our common foe, the White."

"I am a man of the sea," Thorium objected, "What do I know of command to lead such an army as assembled here?"

"The help you need is all around you at this table. Each of us knows his forces' strengths and weaknesses. We can help you with the strategy of this war," added Tay'l of the Coastal People. "We need one to lead us, that each may trust, and in so doing unify us. I second this nomination."

It was done.

Then Thorium began the hard part of the endeavor. All were fundamentally opposed to the Whites. That was the reason they were all here. But "the how" and the "what will come next" were the subject of the debate. Led by the hardliners, Jamen and Lord Praxton (in agreement for one of the few times in their lives), most called for the extermination of the White.

"Such abominations have no place in this world," Thorium heard from many and repeated often.

"They are our children. They must be helped, not destroyed," was the impassioned plea of Lord Perth of Nourne, and truly the White were the *Children of Nourne.*

Others spoke to end the deadlock. Tay'l stepped forward. "Let us not decide this now. After the battle is won, that is the time to decide the fate of the White.

"Then they have no fate. For once the battle has commenced there will be no stopping the parties at this table until the genocide is complete," answered Lord Perth.

Thorium now stood at the table. He looked around those assembled there. Malice was what he saw in their eyes, malice towards the White. So much evil the White had inflicted on this world. If he was to command this army he had to begin now, he understood.

"The extermination of a race, genocide, that is the question before us now. Is this our right, our privilege? Who is it among us that decides who amongst us lives, and who dies?

"Today it is the White. If there was ever a party of the human race who deserved such a fate it is they, but what about tomorrow? You, Reed, with your people's nomadic ways, will you be next when another wants your lands?

"M'Mahd, what about you, and your people, those who follow the beliefs of The One True God. Maybe you will be next; so many, even around this table, consider your beliefs the cause of the Great War. When will your beliefs become too much trouble to your neighbor?

"Are the White truly a separate people? Is it not true that even among the White, normal children are born? How many among your people, those assembled here, how many of your children are born not perfect? Would they be considered a *White* in this genocide to come?

"Perfect, is that the standard? What is perfect and who will make that determination? To truly destroy these people we go to fight (Yes, People!) we know as the White, your own imperfections will have to be destroyed at birth. What the Lord Perth of Nourne has spoken is true. These are your children, the children of all of you. The extermination of the White means to destroy all of those not perfect. Are you ready for that?"

As Thorium finished his address, he moved his eyes from each member of the Council to the next. Only Lord Perth met his gaze. This battle was won. The White had earned the right to exist. They would destroy only the Myk and his army.

Now was the time to consider the logistics of the fight to come. All knew that this would not be an easy battle. The Myk would know that if he lost his reign would end. The White would throw all of their resources against them. If the assembled armies remained divided, victory was not assured.

Across the City by the Lake, in a room of the Lodge of the Order of the Sage, another meeting was being held. Locklear had hurried to join this meeting after introducing Thul to those who would be his instructors in The Hold's Seminary. He joined Gar, Phelix, and Tor, who had begun preparing for the meeting the day before.

"Is it known if any others of the Order are close enough to join us?" asked Locklear as he arrived.

"I have heard from Vlad. He was but two days away when the call was given. He should be arriving shortly. Several others may arrive before this battle is decided. I have heard nothing from many others," answered Tor.

"The Order is not what it used to be," stated Gar.

"Perhaps they are in retreat. We know of Chuak, on Argonia. Maybe there are others in positions such as he," Phelix spoke to them all.

"Or they are no longer with us," added Gar.

"If this is all we have, it will have to be enough," finished Locklear.

In the late afternoon Vlad arrived. He too was shocked at how few had answered the call. "At one time there were so many of us."

"That was long ago, my friend," Tor answered.

"Is it true, the rumor I heard? The son of Simon is with us? How could that be?" asked Vlad in concern and amazement.

Locklear answered him. "There is even more to report on this. A thing I have kept to myself and those with me during the discovery. Come, let us all be seated before I explain the next revelation and we try to determine its significance at this critical time."

The men sat down in weathered, upholstered chairs, gathered together in a way that each of them could speak and hear the others without issue; the chairs dyed a light shade of blue, to signify the Teachers and their homes; the walls themselves painted a darker blue as a reminder of those whose wisdom the Order followed. Light came from four electric lanterns that lit the room. Even their light seemed to carry a pervasive blue tone. Each member of the Order held in his hand a mug of the strong dark beverage that was the drink of the Sage.

After sitting quietly for several minutes, Gar opened the discussion. "And what is this new word that you speak so cryptically of, Locklear? A new significance in what is to come?"

"That and much more. You were right, of course, with your finding of Thul. He is indeed the son of the lost Sage, Simon. But there is more, much more."

"What more can there be than that? The news of Thul's existence is shocking itself. It was pressed on each of us that we could not have heirs. Have we learned something new of Simon?" Vlad spoke.

"We all remember Simon," Tor began, "always he seemed different from the rest of us. He kept to his own devices after our sessions with the Teachers."

"Yes, I remember that well," added Locklear, "and the Teachers seemed to encourage that in him."

"I thought at the time it was due to his assignment being secluded from us, across the sea." Gar said.

"I think what I've found adds even more mystery to Simon, or I should say, the heritage of Simon," Locklear said quietly.

"What is this new significance?" Vlad asked.

"You always were the impatient one. The Teachers could never take that from you." Locklear said to Vlad.

"Just as they could never take from you the need to bury yourself in the ancient texts," laughed Gar.

Turning more earnest, Locklear now spoke his words, low and solid, like the walls of the room they sat in. Their significance caught them all off-guard. "We ran the tests for Thul that the Teachers had left behind for him to gain access to the Master Collection."

"Of course, that would be expected," said Phelix.

"The results came back initially as Gar foretold. As we all know now, Thul is the son of Simon. He carried Simon's marker so there can be no doubt of that. However, we found another marker as well. One that must be kept hidden at all costs."

"Another," Vlad seemed startled. "How could he carry another. There were no women Sage, at least I am aware of."

"Not the marker of a Sage, but more," spoke Locklear.

"What more could there be than to carry the marker of the Sage?" Phelix spoke, sitting up at the edge of his chair. As he spoke the room turned eerily quiet. Each of the Order of the Sage just sat and shared glances for several minutes. Gar got up and poured another cup of his beverage.

"No," said Gar.

"It can't be," stammered Vlad and Phelix as one.

"How?" questioned Tor.

"There can be no doubt. The matter was clear. The machine first showed, and then hid the results. Only those of the Order can know this.

Not even those who apprentice to us can know. The Teachers; Thul carries not only the marker of Simon, but of the Teachers as well."

The Sage, who thought themselves supreme in the eyes of the Teachers, looked over each other in wonder.

"How?" said Gar. "Another experiment?"

"Then that is why he was sent away," said Phelix.

"That may be," added Vlad.

"No, not another experiment, that would have shown in the results," stated Locklear.

"But what does it mean?" Each looked at Gar, who seemed best to understand the motivations of the Teachers.

"What this news means we must ponder on, together. What is clear is that in this new era that is coming to this world, much change is in order," Gar stated.

"None of us carry that mark," Locklear now said.

"Where could he have gotten it from? There must be an answer to that." Vlad questioned.

"Who was, or what was Simon? Was he a Teacher, in our form, and not one of us?" Phelix now asked. His age was catching up with him and he felt his heart race at this new revelation of Simon and Thul. Uncomfortable with the direction of the conversation, Phelix sought now to change it. "What of the second heads? Several have been confirmed."

Gar responded briskly. "The first order now seems to be, who, or what is Thul? Is he a Sage or something more?"

"Can we even begin to answer that question at this time?" asked Vlad.

Locklear now took center, looking toward Gar. "In The Hold's Library I found records of the Teachers' work while here. They were hidden, discovered quite by accident. I would like you to look them over."

Gar answered back, "When this current crisis has run its course, that is something I would very much like to see."

"I will show them to you personally. They are protected right now in my office. As no one except a Sage may know Thul's marks, likewise only a Sage should look at what we have found."

Tor asked Locklear, "What of those who found these documents?"

"They have taken a vow to not leave The Library," answered Locklear.

"What are these second heads mentioned by Phelix? Have I been so far removed from the happenings here in my wandering the east?" Vlad asked.

Tor spoke now, "With the White, both Phelix and I have seen these second heads come to life, each time on the death of the main head. Or what we assumed was the main head. From what we've seen, it is the second head that is more intelligent."

"And more formidable," Gar added.

"It is all part of what we were told to expect. The time of change is near. The expectations of the Teachers have come to pass. We can now understand the cryptic words of the Teachers, right before they left us. Of those 'twice-formed' must refer to the second heads of the White," Locklear stated.

"Then the story of the Teachers return with the changing of the lands and the twice-born heads?" Vlad asked.

"Refers not to the Teachers, but to their heir, Thul," Gar answered.

"Much needs to be discussed after the current conflict ends," said Locklear.

All agreed that a further study of the facts as they became known was necessary, with as many of the Order as they were able to reach, scheduled for the spring, as suggested by Vlad. How many remained? More than a few of those still thought alive had not been heard from in years.

The meeting concluded with Phelix asking the question that still remained. "And what of the White?"

"That will be decided without us," answered Gar.

A third meeting was taking place as well, far to the north of Erson, in the palace of the Myk.

For days scouts of the White had spotted an unusual flow of people moving north from the City by the Lake. Any attempt to get close had meant the loss of the scout. Each day an encampment to the north of that city seemed to grow larger. There could no longer be any doubt about what it meant; an army assembled to move against the Myk and the White.

The Myk was both concerned and alarmed at such an army. Since the debacle at the water, the White just were not ready to defend themselves against such an army. A call went out to every male White over the age of ten. The White matured more quickly than humans did, but even the Myk was alarmed at what he saw, most too deformed to fight effectively except in the air on a Warbird. What had been thought a blessing, more deformities beyond the norm, was now a curse.

"What of the Warbirds?" the Myk asked his advisors.

"Most are still but chicks. Fewer than a thousand, mostly untrained, are fit to carry a warrior."

Another was asked, "How many on foot can we bring?"

Trembling with fear of the Myk's wrath, the advisor answered, "Less than ten thousand on foot."

The Myk wanted to lash out in fury at the news. He had his weapon out, ready to kill the advisors standing closest to him. The advisors saw his anger and attempted to move away without appearing to do so and incur more of the Myk's anger, ideally putting another advisor between themselves and the Myk. The Myk stopped where he stood, the weapon ready to swing. He heard a new voice, a voice in his head. The Myk took the weapon he held with his best arm and swatted the flat of it against his own head. His aides now looked at the Myk aghast as he took this action.

'That won't do you any good. Now stop and listen.' The voice seemed to be in his head, but it was not he, the Myk. What magic was this?

'We have decisions to make and I'm not ready to take charge as yet.'

"You, take charge?" The Myk said aloud. His advisors looked around at each other. Who wanted to replace the Myk? They each backed away from the Myk and each other.

'I'm here, inside of you,' the voice said to the Myk. 'Listen carefully or neither of us will survive what's coming,' the voice continued.

"How will we survive, we are too few?" said the Myk aloud.

"All of the White will fight to the end," one of the advisors spoke up, a particularly disfigured one, barely recognizable as human. He had only vestiges of arms and legs, using a wheeled platform to move. His head seemed tiny for his body and was mostly mouth, with a single ear and two small eyes spaced equally in opposition on his head.

'Dismiss these fools, we have work to do,' said the voice.

Not knowing what else to do and unable to quiet the voice in his head, the Myk waved away the advisors. "Make the army ready."

Once they had left the voice spoke again. 'We need more time. How long until the Warbird hatchlings are ready?'

"I was told two years," said the Myk out loud to no one in particular as he moved his head from side to side, trying to figure out where the voice was coming from.

'And how long until enough White have matured and been trained to have an army?' The voice asked.

"Two years, at least."

'Then we must stall this invasion for at least two years,' said the voice.

"How, voice, their armies assemble against us even now."

'You must send an emissary to the Castle Nourne. They still consider us their children. They will listen.'

"How do you know of the Castle Nourne? And they move against us as well."

'I know everything you know and more. We will offer them, and all that move against us, peace, no more raids, no more using them as food to feed us.'

"Then we will starve and die, just as if we go to war today."

'We will learn to eat the lesser beasts.'

"The lesser beasts, I would rather die. I am the Myk. I eat only human flesh."

'And I choose not to die,' said the voice. 'You will learn to eat the meat of the lesser beasts to stay alive.'

"No, I am the Myk!"

'And I am part of you,' said the voice.

"But the lesser beasts?"

'Only until we are strong again. Then we shall enjoy feasts aplenty once more as we conquer and expand our empire against those that oppose us now.'

"Then I will go and offer this peace," said the Myk.

'No. We are too valuable. We must continue our preparations for war. Send he of the White that appears most human. Offer peace, no more raids, and a release of the remaining slaves.'

"Release the slaves?"

'How many remain?' said the voice.

"None above, we made them part of the food supply. Those in the caverns have escaped to the south."

'Then we offer them nothing.'

And the Myk smiled.

Two nights later, a single figure appeared at the gate of the Castle Nourne. He carried his letter of introduction from the Myk. Almost unmarked by the ravages of the mutations of the White, he was barely considered one of them. He had been made a slave, barely above the food chain. Now he carried the message of the Myk. He smiled at the irony with his razor-sharp feline teeth, his only outward sign of his being a White. He wore specially-made shoes that hid his real mutation, one he had found of great value in his life. His feet were more like a cat's paws than human, complete with retractable claws. When he fought, he did so without the shoes he detested. He was always shoeless among the White, to show that he was one of them.

As he first approached the Castle Nourne, he was alarmed at the activity he had saw. Now, as passed through the armed camp, he was even more alarmed. There were thousands of heavily armed soldiers from many different lands. The Myk had not informed Kat of the reason he carried a message to the Lord of the Castle. He was told to take the note to the castle and wait for a response. As he entered the castle grounds, under armed guard, he had a hard time passing through the park-like land; so many soldiers, too many to count. Kat began to worry what his mission was. The White had made so many enemies so quickly.

Guards escorted Kat into the Lord's chambers. There sat the Lord Perth and the Lady Alyce. They waited patiently for his approach. As his escort left Kat alone with the Lord and Lady of Nourne, Kat thought briefly that here was his chance to become a hero of the White and dispatch the killers of the first Myk. Then he remembered the stories of their prowess in battle. These were after all the father and mother of the first Myk. As such, the Lord and Lady of Nourne carried a special place in the mythology of the White, both as devil and as saint.

Kat approached the raised dais where the Lord and Lady sat and knelt before them as the Myk had instructed him. Strange, thought Kat as he thought back on the instructions. It was as if he had been talking to two separate entities with the Myk. Kat's eyes never left the face of the Lady Alyce and he noticed two things in her face, the battle scar she carried across one cheek and the tears that were in her eyes.

Lord Perth of Nourne held the paper the guard passed him from the Myk in his hands. His demeanor seemed sad, almost distraught. Kat did not know what to make of these displays of emotion. As all of the White, his education had been minimal. Only the priests of the White could read and write. He had no idea what was in the note he carried, only that the note would gain him admission to the castle and that it was intended only for the Lord and Lady of Nourne. He had done what the Myk had instructed.

The Lord Perth signaled Kat to approach. Kat was still tempted to remove his footwear and attack the Lord and Lady, but in his mind he remembered the instructions of the Myk (Was it the Myk? It seemed so strange!) stressing the importance of his mission. He was the chosen emissary of the Myk. That alone would raise his station among the White.

The Lord Perth began to talk to Kat in a quiet, commanding, and solemn voice. "You look almost human, Kat. You could pass among us without fear. With your message delivered, you may stay among us if you wish. My wife, the Lady Alyce, would bid you welcome." Lady Alyce smiled at Kat as Lord Perth motioned in her direction. The tears remained in her eyes.

"I am White!" Kat answered back defiantly. He kicked off his shoes and extended the claws on his paws. "White!"

"Yes," Lord Perth answered back in his quiet voice, "I can see. Do you want the response to this in writing, or shall I just give you the sadness that can be the only answer today."

"In writing, for my master, the High-Priest Myk, our leader."

"You know we are the parents of the first Myk." Lady Alyce spoke in sadness.

"It is said that it is so and that you killed him in battle." He looked solely at Lord Perth as he said the last part. Kat had a hard time looking at the Lady Alyce.

"Yes," answered Lord Perth.

"He died in battle with honor. The Myk, our first Saint," Kat proudly said.

"Saint?" asked the Lady Alyce.

"Yes, the Saint and Father of the White, praise Myk, eternal Myk." Kat stood straight as he said these words, head raised high.

Lord Perth got up and walked down the three steps to where Kat stood. Kat had hoped that the Lord would show fear now that his claws were exposed. However, there was none in the Lord Perth's manner. Instead, Kat trembled in fear of the prowess of Lord Perth. Lord Perth handed Kat a sealed envelope.

"Here is the only answer we can give your Myk. May the future show mercy on us all."

Kat took the offered envelope and left, once again escorted through the castle grounds, and then all of the way to the White's claimed border. The assembled armies made no attempt to hide their numbers; in fact, it seemed quite the opposite. Wherever they led Kat on the way to the border, all he saw was armed soldiers. His eyes could not avoid seeing the might arrayed against the White.

At the border a scout met Kat. A message was waiting for him. The Myk gave him the privilege of riding a Warbird back to the Palace of the Myk. Kat could only be happy at his rising good fortune among the White.

At the palace he was directed and escorted directly before the Myk and his advisors. He scarcely noticed the heavily armed guards in his excitement that stood on either side of him. He approached the Myk on hands and knees without his footwear and handed the envelope to the Myk personally:

To his High Priest Myk of the White
It is with sadness that we read this note offering peace between our lands. If only this peace had been offered sooner, then this coming war might have been avoided. Even now, we of the Castle Nourne wish

that there were some way to avoid the conflict that is coming with you, our children.

However, your note, even in the end, contains but empty words. We know of the slaughter of your slaves, those who had remained above ground. There exists now in the Northern Valley none but the White. We have rescued those who had remained hidden in the safety of the caverns below the valley's mountainous walls. The stories they tell only provoke the outrage among the people that assemble against you.

Tears are in my eyes over your fate. There is nothing we, at the Castle Nourne, can do to forestall the coming storm that rises against you. In your short time you have made no friends, but enemies of all.

— Lord Perth of Nourne.

The second head whispered in the head of the Myk, 'It is foretold and necessary. Soon the true race of the White will be borne in full. From the dead of the battle will come the second coming of the White. Our enemies will be crushed before its might.'

With that the soldiers on either side of Kat raised their swords and the head was removed above Kat's shoulders. However, the body did not fall. From the cavity that had been Kat's neck a small, new, hidden head arose and the body of Kat took his place alongside the Myk. The Myk's voice had sensed in Kat that he too carried the future of the Myk within himself.

Chapter Twelve:
We are Myk!

The last of the armies arrayed against the White had assembled north of Erson. The banners of a dozen different peoples flew over the tents of the twenty thousand assembled soldiers, from the stark crescent moon on the banner of the followers of Ala and the red cross of the Saders, to the extravagant multi-colored banners of the Shiaps. There was no attempt to hide what was coming from the White's observers. Thorium took to riding a horse lent to him by Jamen of Kilne, something he had not done since he was a boy. As Thorium rode through the camps, he wondered inwardly at the task before him. How was he going to coordinate all of the fear and hatred of the White into an effective fighting force?

Already there were squabbles among the generals. The Southern Valley's nobles refused to use their limited Warbirds to support the R'mon's observation balloons and the archers they held. While the archers of the woodsmen and the Raffs had no problem fighting side-by-side, the Raff's would not back up the Jall or the soldiers of The Hold. To place the strongest in the middle was impossible. The City by the Lake and their spearmen refused to be alongside the powerful Jall and their allies of The Hold. Only the weak (even weaker now with their converts) armies of The One True God would fight anywhere they were instructed. They would fight with a religious fever and zeal, but placed wrong there would be a massacre.

It was natural to put the Nomads and their wildcats at the beginning in a loose formation in the front as scouts. How to make them understand that at the first sight of the White's attack they were to withdraw to a support position. They were the only reserve of any quality Thorium had and so he had to use them both ways, scout and reserve.

It was now early fall and the weather was changing. Already strong gusts of wind were blowing across the camps. If the winds grew much stronger, any advantage that the R'mon's balloons had would be lost.

Then there was the question of the Shiaps and their mounted camel warriors. The people of the valleys had never used their horses in battle, they were too valuable. The Shiaps were convinced that they could be used in a charge to turn the tide of battle. Thorium decided to keep them as a hidden reserve, guarding the flank of the Jall and The Hold.

In the end, the politicking decided that the forces of Nourne and Erson, though small in number, would stand the middle of the line. It was declared by each that this was their duty and responsibility. Here would be the greatest loss of life. And, especially with the case of Nourne, they believed it was their responsibility for what was to come.

To the left would be the natural allies, the Jall and The Hold. Their leaders thought that each could hold out against any attack from the Whites that could come their way. On the right would be the army of the Coastal People and the foot soldiers of the R'mon's and the Raff.

The archers would remain in support of the armored troops. It was a given where each would be positioned, the Woodsmen on the left and the Raff's on the right, with any other archers assembling amongst the two. There would be no retreat for the archers this time and the Raff's carried their staffs and the Woodsmen whatever weapons they might possess alongside their bows.

This would be a defensive fight. It was agreed to by all that because of all of the rivalries that existed between the people arrayed against the White; to launch an assault against the White positions would only lead to defeat. In defense, each would have to stand alongside their neighbor or fail.

It would be up to the Nomads and their cats to provoke the White army into attack. Then, once that attack began, it would be their job to retreat to their second positions, behind the reserves that were the armies of The One True God.

All was as ready as could be for this army. Thorium and Cole tried to carry a positive feeling about them as they rode through the camps in their final preparations. Of the men of *The Proctant*, only Zircon relished what was coming. The sailors would be positioned just to the rear of the loose array of the reserves.

At nightfall the armies moved forward. They would fight this battle on the lands claimed by the White. This was one more critical decision in the pre-battle planning. They had to force the Whites to attack and Thorium thought that would be easier to do on the White's own land.

In the north, in the lands of the White and in the Palace of the Myk, final preparations for war were also taking place. The White were not ready for this war, but it mattered not and the hidden second head of the Myk was exerting more control of the weak will of the Myk.

"Recall the scouts. We can afford no more loss of Warbirds before the battle," the second head whispered.

And the scouts were recalled.

"All slaves that may be considered White are to be freed and armed. They will be the first to meet what comes for us. Let them prove themselves to be of the White and in doing so become part of us."

And that was done, another five thousand men at arms, though poorly trained. That mattered not to the Myk or his second head. These were the fodder of the battle, against which the armies of the Southern peoples would waste their strength.

"Let all remaining food be distributed to the army. We must be strong. Reserve what human food remains for the riders of the Warbirds. Let them fly into battle with full bellies. And let it be known to all of our army that the enemy that awaits before us shall be our feast with this victory."

And those of the Northern Valley, what few slaves that remained, both alive and not-dead, except those reserved for the Myk, entered the food source of the army of the White.

"Let any of the lesser beast be sacrificed for the good of our army."

And the last of the livestock of the Northern Valley was slaughtered and added to the food source.

"Any females that remain, not with a litter, or not of age to bear a litter, let them be added to the food source. There will be no tomorrow for the White if we lose."

And the last of the females who could be found were added to the food source.

Then there were none beside White that remained in the north. Even among the White, the youngest cub who could walk or move was handed a weapon. This army would eat well. Any not of this army would become part of the food source. This was the army that moved south, numbering far more than those arrayed against them.

The Myk was worried. Would all of this be enough? Many were too young or old to be effective and there were so few Warbirds available.

"Remember the lessons of Erson. Let them use up their archers before we engage from the air," the silent voice spoke in his head.

"But we are so few of quality," said the Myk to his unseen voice.

"We are more than you realize, from the dead of the battle will be born the true heritage of the White."

The Myk failed to understand what the voice meant. "How can the dead help us?"

"Not the dead, the reborn. Do you remember our secret?"

"Our own archers, they are as yet untrained."

"That matters not. They will let loose their revenge for Erson through the air and the South will be unprepared."

The Myk looked around. He still failed to understand where this voice was coming from. But it was something he could not deny and its wisdom was good.

"Now go," said the voice, "and lead us to the rebirth; the destiny of the White."

The Myk failed to realize that the voice did not use the word victory, but what else could the destiny of the White be.

Thorium watched the army assemble throughout the night just inside the borders of the White. While it certainly was not the best possible order of battle, and throughout the morning confusion mostly reigned, by mid-morning it was the best Thorium could hope for. A scattering of Whites could be seen moving away from them but as yet the Nomads could find no sign of an assembling force to go against them.

Noon came and the balloons of the R'mon's began to move skyward, pulled aloft by the heated air of their yellow envelopes. Each balloon carried half a dozen crossbowmen, mostly women. The balloons themselves were tethered to the ground by a thousand feet of rope. Messages could be sent through special canisters down the ropes at high speed using special rings. If necessary, the tethered ropes could be released quickly by the balloons.

Only now did the nobles of the Southern Valley choose to ride the Warbirds in support of the R'mon's. In the end, it was their jealousy of the balloons that sent them aloft. They would show all of this world that it was they and their Warbirds that were of more value than the R'mon's in the air.

Late in the day the R'mon's spotted the Whites assembling on the horizon. It was too late in the day for the attack to come. Tomorrow, tomorrow would be the day of reckoning. The balloons were pulled down to the ground and stories in abundance were told around the campfires of the assembled armies that night; of chivalry, glory, and great exaggeration. Each knew that the one next to him could be dead come the next night's fall. Each tried to outdo the others in the telling of their exploits. The men of the west were the stars wherever received. All of those around the men clamored for stories of the Confederation and confirmation of the rumors that abounded about them. Were they really the legion from the sea? It seemed no miracle or feat of courage could be told without relating it to these newcomers. Zircon relished the attention, while the others tried to withdraw to themselves without success. Finally, exhausted and weary both from the march and the ales they drank, the armies arrayed against the White retired to their tents. An eerie calm descended over the camp. It was as if their ancestors from ages past watched over the camp. In the City by the Lake, the assembled Sage could feel it was as well. The Prophecies of the Teachers were coming to the fore.

The next day saw a slight mist in the air and the ground was damp. Cooler than normal, this was the ideal condition for the soldiers on foot or mounted. It was less than ideal for the Warbirds of the Southern Valley, and the rising winds would keep the observation balloons of the R'mon's on the ground.

To the north the Myk looked over the field of battle and considered the conditions ideal. Even with all of the efforts of the Whites, there weren't enough Warbirds to affect the outcome. "We will hold the Warbirds back as a reserve," the inner voice told the Myk. "And we will release them when the time is right to claim our heritage." Once again the Myk was confused by the wording of this voice, but he reconciled that with the heritage of the White being their victory. He looked over his army once more: Ground troops were available in plenty, though most were of questionable worth.

The Myk's inner voice continued to advise and direct the Myk where to put his forces. "Keep the archers hidden and the best of the troops together in the middle. And don't charge the invaders, let them come to us," it kept whispering. "The undisciplined mass of the White will be kept up front and on both sides. Let them in their multitude wear down the forces that oppose the White. It matters not how many perish for the White shall be reborn of the dead."

In the south Thorium and Lord Perth of Nourne looked over the field and neither was happy with what they saw. Their advantage in the air was now gone. Even as the assembled armies arose from their sleep, ate their morning meal, and assembled in their planned positions, there was squabbling and fights between the rivals on the field. Thorium thought to himself, 'How, with this continuous bickering, can this army hope to fight as one?' It was important that the White be goaded into the assault, and quickly, before all order in this army broke down. If attacked, they would have to stand as one or be defeated.

Everything now depended on the abilities of the Nomads, their cats and numerous archers who, though fearful of the cats, had volunteered to stand among the scouts.

As the sun rose, Jamen of Kilne rode among the Nomads and wasn't pleased by what he saw. He was used to disciplined troops and order. The Nomads were at best under loose control of their leaders and the wildcats themselves appeared to be under even less control. Jamen's horse was jittery as it passed between the cats. As Jamen looked to the north there seemed to be more White than Jamen thought possible with their recent losses. Moreover, from a distance the Whites appeared to be in good order.

The Nomads, Jamen thought, how could they hope to get the Whites to engage. And if they did, could they, would they, retreat to their second positions in good order? And the cats, what was the story with the cats? Jamen, as he rode, had to keep a close rein on his horse among the cats as they prowled among the assembled Nomads. He admired the bravery of the archers that assembled with the Nomads. He was not sure he would have the courage to do that with so many wildcats around. The archers would signal the beginning of the battle, two flights of arrows and then back to join their fellow archers at their assigned positions.

The first Warbirds of the White appeared to Jamen's eyes. Just a handful, how many could there be? Had the White learned the lesson of the Battle of Erson? Thorium had thought yes, that you had to assume the enemy would learn from defeat. Jamen was among the dissent, that the White were too primitive, too instinctive, to learn such a lesson.

Jamen had hoped for the advantage of seeing behind the enemy lines, to see what was coming. He had hoped to have that with the R'mon's and their balloons but the strong winds prevented that. Ground against ground, responding to the aggressions of the enemy, that was to be the battle it seemed, a thought Jamen was comfortable with.

It was Jamen's assignment to ride back and forth along the front of the Nomad line, to make it appear that he was in charge of an attack to come. The archers were ready, each had arrow to bow and now he noticed a tenseness about the Nomads and the wildcats had stopped their prowling. Each wildcat was now laying down on its stomach, ears back, eyes forward, a line down their backs, scattered throughout the Nomad army.

The consensus of thought was that the archers alone would be enough to bring on the White attack. Only Thorium had disagreed with that.

"You seem convinced, all of you, that the White cannot, will not learn. I don't see how you can take that position."

"You haven't experienced them, faced them in battle, before."

"Experienced them!" Thorium exploded. "Only through providence were we not destroyed by them when we first landed here. From that experience alone they must have learned. I would have, every one of you would have. To make the assumption that they cannot learn is the height of arrogance. Through our assembled armies and their petty jealousies I think it is we who haven't learned."

In the end Thorium decided that the Nomads would be the contingent plan if the archers did not work. 'What about the White's Warbirds? Well, we will find out soon enough,' thought Jamen.

The hour was on them. Mid-morning was reached. There still was no White assault and the White's warbirds remained largely unseen. Jamen gave a signal and the Nomad line, with its archers, moved forward to a position that put the archers within range of the White army. Jamen was at a position just to the rear of the archers and he gave the signal to fire. The first flight of arrows fell among the White without apparent effect. Now came the first surprise that the assembled armies faced. A flight of arrows launched from the White's lines and at a greater range than the

Woodman's bows. Fortunately, the number of the incoming flight of arrows was small and most fell harmlessly to the ground, deflected by the small hand shields carried by the Woodmen archers on their bow arms. It was among the Nomads and their wildcats that the greatest turmoil occurred. Jamen looked at them with contempt. They had assured Thorium that the job was theirs and now they milled together in random bands and the wildcats had resumed their prowling. Jamen feared the wildcats more than he feared the White.

The archers let loose their planned second flight of arrows when low over the battlefield the White's Warbirds, few in number, rushed on the archers. The second flight had not even landed among the White when the Warbirds struck. Thorium, from a distant observation tower (an innovation to warfare *The Proctant* brought to the fight) saw this and it confirmed what he knew in his mind. The White could learn and adapt. What should have been an orderly retreat of the archers turned into a panicked rush for survival.

The wildcats now moved forward as one and as the Warbirds and their riders swept low to the ground in their attack, the wildcats, with their prodigious leaps, knocked one Warbird after another from the sky. The Nomads followed this with their own movements forward, supporting the wildcats. Few Warbirds and their riders survived this counter-attack and returned to the White lines. Up until now, everything was as scripted by Thorium, Jamen had to admit, but would the White swallow the bait? The wildcats seemed too proficient to make a retreat seem real and the White's Warbirds were too few in number.

Jamen rode to the front of the battle and then, as if in a panic, turned his horse to flee from the battlefield. This would be the sign for the Nomads and their companions to retreat as well. Jamen still questioned if they would.

The Myk watched what was happening with a smile. The armies that fought against him still fought as before. The Myk had learned, before the archers could inflict their damage, the novice Warbirds and their new riders, though few in number, had done their job. The Southern archers had been forced to flee before they could become effective. Their own archers, those of the White best equipped through their deformations, had shown greater range and sown confusion in the enemy lines. Even the surprising advent of the wildcats had proven ineffective against the new strategies of the Myk. Now, he thought, it was time to bring an end to this and follow the fleeing armies to the south and to victory for the White.

"Patience," came the voice inside of the Myk. "It's not time yet."

"But they flee before us," the Myk spoke to the voice.

"Patience, it's not time," repeated the voice.

"It is," exalted the Myk, "watch them flee before us. We attack now and end this."

"It is not time as yet."

However, the decision was no longer the Myk's to make. Across the entire untrained mass that was the White's army, called up for this battle, the White surged forward as one. They moved forward with one mind, without need for leadership. Here was a chance for those not quite considered White to prove themselves. Rushing, they charged, each to reach their enemy first, to claim the first trophy in this battle.

The voice inside the Myk looked upon this and smiled its internal smile. "So begins the rebirth and destiny of the White."

Jamen led the retreat south of the Nomads and the armies briefly separated before them. Jamen took his place among the army of the City by the Lake. Between and through the assembled armies the Woodsmen archers and the Nomads appeared to flee as well, with the wildcats bringing up the rear. However, each stopped when they reached their pre-determined position in the army. The front line, the shieldmen of The Hold, the Jall, Erson and the Castle Nourne, and the other assembled peoples braced for the assault that was now coming.

There were too many, much more than anticipated, was Thorium's first thought as he watched the battle unfold. He was an officer of a ship and now he felt even less equipped to command the assembled armies. The R'mon's had tried to get one balloon up in the high wind so he could at least get a better idea of what was going on. However, the observation balloon was torn from its mooring line in a great gust of wind, and disappeared to the east. From the tower Thorium felt helpless as he saw what was the apparent collapse of the entire center of their lines.

Nourne had demanded the center and with Erson had been given it. But they were just too few to command such a position in the lines and were quickly overrun without serious resistance. It seemed the White had learned their lessons well. Jamen, from his horse, saw Lord Perth fall from his horse in battle, severely injured. It was only the efforts of Lady Alyce and her guard that had saved him, and only after being mostly wiped out themselves. As Lady Alyce retreated from the battle, her husband cradled across her horse, the line of Nourne and Erson crumbled in retreat.

Now with the center and one flank driven back by the White's army, the great disadvantage faced by the assembled armies became apparent. Unable, unwilling to fight as one, the forces arrayed against the White became disjointed. Only on the right did the line hold as the Raff, R'mon's and Coastal People's armies, whether by the force of the White's charge or their own devices, merged to become one. Alongside them, the forces of the City by the Lake retreated to form an angle facing away from the battle. Those woodsmen archers that remained, as well as the archers of the R'mon's and the Raff, assembled behind these lines. Momentarily here at least, the line held.

In the middle, it was chaos. As Nourne and Erson retreated behind the Lord and Lady of the Castle in disorder, the line on the left, the Jall and The Hold, broke as well. There were just too few shieldmen and fighters to meet the great mass that was the White's army in its charge. All that stood now between the alliance and total victory for the Myk and the White was the barely-organized followers of The One True God.

"Forward brothers, better to die today with honor in the eyes of our Lord than to fail here." Thousands followed the banner of M'Mahd as he led the masses forward. For the briefest moment, the breakthrough was stemmed as the untrained masses of the two armies met.

"For God!" the followers of The One True God cried as they charged together behind the banners of the red cross and the crescent moon. Forward they charged into the White and the White army started in turn to crumble before them. Then a true horror began. From among the dead and the dying of the White, the dead began to arise. Not in great numbers, maybe one in every fifty, but enough. To the superstitious lost souls that had followed M'Mahd and the other true believers into battle, a shiver ran through their souls as devils arose from the dead to fight them. And as each of the leaders of The One True God fell in battle, the attack fell further apart.

Into this abyss of madness came the Myk, defiant, and in his mind, victorious. With him came five thousand of his best fighters. The poorly organized counterattack had failed. A massacre began as the White pressed forward. Those of the army of The One True God who could, fled, but too many found their place with God on the battlefield.

In the end these stragglers, these followers of a discredited God, the lost souls of this land, looked upon with dismay and disregard by the 'civilized' people of this land, had done what no other had been capable. Through this final act of bravery, they had given the assembled armies a chance to find their place in newly formed lines to the rear.

Thorium had left the tower and on his borrowed horse had ridden across the field of battle, trying to rally around him those who were fleeing. He was very concerned that the others of *The Proctant* had fallen in the carnage of the battle, but he soon received word that they had made it to the line on the right that was holding, no small thanks to Zircon and his long rifle. Zircon had received an almost unlimited amount of rounds from Gar before the battle had commenced and even with that was beginning to run low on rounds.

As Thorium rode among those that rallied to his side and regrouped to the rear, the first thing he noticed was, as they assembled for what was to come, no thought was given any longer to regional rivalries. Now the left was breaking, as the middle had already done. The great mass that was the White army was turning to face them, and with them came the assault of the White's Warbirds. Those of the Jall and The Hold now crumbled and fled as well.

From the people of the Southern Plain now came the needed relief for the left. Into the chaotic line on the left, the Nomads and their wildcats charged to the fore. Thorium had believed the assurance that he had received from Reed that the Nomads would not fail in their task. Others had cast doubt. Now those others were fleeing while the Nomads moved to blunt the attack. Reed had told Thorium that the Nomads and wildcats would fight as a single entity. As he had seen first hand the actions of the gators and the Jall against the Jal-Beast, now Thorium saw the coordinated actions of the Nomads and their wildcat companions. Released from the hold of the Nomads, Thorium now saw the damage these cats could do, the wildcats leading the assault with the Nomads close behind. Into the best that the White had to offer, the wildcats tore, and if a second head were to appear, to give new life to the dead of the White, no matter, the cats knew not the difference as they tore the White to pieces. As the wildcats charged forward, with the Nomads close behind, a new miracle on the battlefield occurred. Those that remained of the army of The One True God found safe refuge around the wildcats. As the attack of the White wavered, the wildcats moved to become the protectors of this army.

Now from the left, held back as the final reserve, came the charge of the Shiap's camel riders. Their charge created new chaos in the flank of the White army, as the ignorant and untrained now faced the Shiaps. It was the flank of the White army that now fled the battle. Nevertheless, Nomad and Shiap, with the wildcats now moving to protect the mass that was the lost souls, and with their losses great, there were just too few to gain an advantage.

Seeing the gallantry of those that had stymied the attack of the White army, those unappreciated masses of the lands, more of those that had fled the assault, now moved into positions around Thorium. A strong center was building again. He had an army now, Thorium thought to himself. The petty jealousies of this land that had been carried into battle were now gone out of necessity.

The solid line on the right remained steadfast and on the left, the Shiaps now gathered with the Nomads to hold that flank. The wildcats, now few in numbers, had joined those who had given their all and retreated from the battle, like loyal hounds protecting their masters.

Before them stood the undiminished pride of the White army, almost five thousand remained, gathered in line around their leader, the Myk. Almost all of those who had been lost until this point, except for the irreplaceable Warbirds, had been the fodder that the voice inside the Myk had called forth to diminish the enemies of the White. Now came those bred and trained to fight. With them, the new weapon of the Myk, were over five hundred archers with their long range bows.

To Thorium's great relief, the R'mon's had finally got an observation balloon up. From it, he was able to get an accurate picture of how the battle now stood.

On the right was the immovable wall that had been the R'mon's, the Raff, the coastal peoples, and to a lesser extent, joining them after the collapse of the center, the army of the City by the Lake. Supporting them were what remained of the Woodmen archers and the archers of the R'mon's and the Raff. In addition, of course, Zircon and his long rifle.

On the left was the mounted army of the Shiap on their camels and their new allies, the Nomads, accompanied it seemed by a new force of wildcats. He wondered at first where they had come from. Both the Nomads and the wildcats seemed in greater numbers than before. He was pointed to the south, where he saw the Nomads and their wildcats continue to stream to the battlefield in small groups. It seemed that the south had been stripped of its Nomad population, with all converging here at this battle.

Around Thorium was what remained of the rest. Whether due to their pride being diminished by the results until now on the battlefield, or sheer sense of duty and training, they assembled in combat order: Southern Valley, Jall, Nourne, Erson, The Hold, and the City by the Lake. Mixed in and now welcome, were those who were still able to fight from the armies of Ala, Sader and the lost souls. They had earned the respect of those who had fled. All now stood as one, shoulder to shoulder, the professional soldiers looking on with a newfound respect for those whom they had so derided and dismissed on the march.

From the balloon, Thorium, now in sole command of the field, learned what now faced him was but a single body of troops. The White army had no more in reserve. Their untrained mass, those that survived, had fled to the north and were beyond recall. To one side of the main White army, the balloon spotted a sizable force of the reborn White, though it seemed to lack integrity as a force to be reckoned with. In addition, he learned, to his relief in advance, of a sizable group of White archers, just to the rear of the main force. Of the fierce Warbirds of the White, none could be seen, although the occasional riderless Warbird came into view. The warbirds had proven to be no match for the leaping ability of the wildcats.

It was now mid-day as Thorium and Jamen of Kilne met. The attack would have to come quickly, the White army would not be given the opportunity to regroup.

It would be a wheel. The assault would begin on the right with the still intact R'mon's, Raff and coastal peoples armies. The archers would let loose what flights remained and then fight as ground troops in the assault, backing up the initial thrust of the right. It was hoped that they would draw what archers the Whites had brought into play, here in the initial stage of the attack.

As the assault on the right reached the flank of the White army, in the center the now unified armies of the lands would move to attack the center of the White's army. After the center of the line moved to a point halfway to the White's lines, the now-reinforced army of Shiap and Nomad would use their speed to strike at the rear of the assembled White army. Thorium thought that with the attack coming from the right and then the center, the White army would have to pivot to meet these attacks, exposing the back of their lines.

It worked like clockwork with a now-unified command structure and the Myk could only look on helplessly in amazement as his best were shattered. The archers proved ineffective and without their Warbirds overhead, it was the White army that broke and fled. And, unlike the previous Myk, this one proved to be a coward. ('What bravery was there in dying' the voice said to the Myk).

"What happened?" he asked the voice inside his head as the Myk watched the White army destroyed on the battlefield.

"The birth of the White, the true White!" the voice said, seemingly reveling in delight at what was happening.

And it seemed true. Almost every one of the Myk's guard, over 2,500 strong, seemed to be reborn and come back to life. Then it was the wildcats that had a feast.

"We flee now," said the voice and the Myk and a dozen of his guard mounted their Warbirds and fled north.

"Not to the Palace, to the secret place," said the voice.

"But the Palace?" the Myk asked the voice.

"It is lost, but the true White is born."

The armies drove north through the land of the White. Throughout what remained of the day and well into the night they quickly crossed the land. Wherever they encountered a White, it was weaponless and cowered before them. A few massacres occurred as the assembled people moved farther in their fight against the White, especially by those who felt themselves barbarized by the White most directly.

As the White fled before the armies, those of Erson, Nourne and the Nomads moved to the most advanced positions and those in favor of the extermination of the White dropped to the rear. Whatever was the cause of the assembled armies, the land of the White was now laid to waste. They thought it would take a generation to restore the Northern Valley to how it was before the time of the White.

The outskirts of the White's primary settlement were reached and there Thorium called on Wade to take control. Lady Theresa, representing Castle Nourne with her father injured and Lady Alyce at his side, joined him. The Nomads and their wildcats patrolled the outskirts of the town and let none of the armies enter. Then what remained of the armies of Erson and Nourne entered the city, led by Thorium, Wade and Lady Theresa. Wherever they rode through the town, its inhabitants threw themselves prostrate before them. Over and over they heard the same refrain, "We are free, we are free!" mostly from the women they found.

A nursery was found in its complete horror. Females (at times barely human!) were held in pens where they waited to be impregnated by a male, some barely more than children. Some were not much more than a head for eating and an abdomen for breeding. Arms and legs, if they had ever existed, had been removed for food, sometimes fed back to the very female the limb had been removed from. They had become nothing more than breeding machines for the White. As more of these were found, Lady Theresa broke down in tears. Wade sent her back to Nourne to assemble the women of Nourne and Erson. They would have much to do for the females of the Whites.

A day passed and it was clear that there were no fighters in the settlement. The armies rested for another day and then the order was given. To the north of the settlement was the Palace of the High Priest of the White, the Myk. From a distance it looked as formidable as Castle Nourne itself. Word was received that Lord Perth wanted to be there for the final assault of the war.

For two days, the armies assembled and surrounded the Palace of the Myk in the Round Valley. A new Council of War was held. Few from the first Council remained among the living and there was a newfound spirit of unity that was not at the first.

Thorium, now solely in command of the armies and comfortable in that position, watched as his Council assembled in the large field tent that was his headquarters. First to arrive was Praxton of Pyers (still defiant in his belief that the White should be exterminated) and Lord Perth of Nourne, each still carrying a savage wound from the battle. Praxton had a bandage over one eye, it was probably lost. Lord Perth arrived with one arm bound tightly at his side. Shattered, it would have to be removed once the fighting was over. He should not have been there but both Nourne and Erson still considered the White their children. He could not be dissuaded from attending. Next to enter the tent was Reed. All throughout the army a newfound respect was found for the Nomads and what they had done.

M'Mahd of the armies of The One True God had died in the battle, leading the counter charge from the front. It was his bravery and that of the common people, the lost souls around him, that had stemmed the tide of battle. Replacing him and taking the position of honor at Thorium's right was Chrisstoff of the Saders, himself carrying a fresh scar across his face.

Next to Chrisstoff sat Loren, marksmen supreme of the R'mon's. It was the R'mon's withering crossbow fire from the flank that enabled so many of the survivors of the One True God's army to escape annihilation when the White's core group of fighters entered the battle against them.

Next sat Sebastian of the Nomads; only the Nomads possessed two members at the Council, Thorium's reward to them for their bravery and loyalty. Sebastian's wildcat companion lay behind him. Thorium had to admit he had developed a soft spot for the wildcats, the companions of the Nomads. He himself had a young cat, which had attached itself to him. It lay behind him on the ground; his protector, his friend. Thorium was not sure but he was glad that it had found him. He looked back at the cat. "Tri, I will call you Tri, my friend." The wildcat stretched out its full seven feet and seemed to purr in agreement.

Jamen of Kilne entered the tent next. He was in favor of eradicating the White alongside Lord Praxton. Then no one else entered the tent.

Thorium looked around with sadness at who was missing, friends old and new, now gone. Cole, his mentor in so many ways, like so many of *The Proctant*, killed by the White. He died while trying to rally those of Erson and Nourne around him. Wolfe, that constant companion of Gar, died in the first rush of combat as the Jall and The Hold were overrun. Tay'l of the coastal people, standing firm on the one line that held, an arrow from one of the White's archers piercing his neck.

King Gunther of the Raffs survived, but barely, transported to the Jall city; only there could he get the care that would be necessary for him to survive his wounds. He and his party would be the first from the Raff to enter the Jall city, another barrier broken through the combat against the White.

The assault of the Palace would come from the air. Few Warbirds of the White had survived the battle and the Southern Valley's Lords and their Warbirds, held back until now, would lead the assault. With the winds now calm, the R'mon's observation balloons would carry Nourne, Raff, and R'mon's over the Palace walls. The crossbowmen of the R'mon's would work to end any resistance to the landing. In the end, the assault on the Palace was anti-climactic. By the time the army had arrived, none remained of the White in the Palace to oppose them.

As the armies assembled around the Palace of the Myk, the Myk and his advisors, the sole survivors of the White army and numbering barely two dozen, had gathered around the secret temple to the Hydron, a good distance to the north of the Palace.

The Myk looked at those around him and wondered with his primitive mind, "How could this have happened?" The voice inside him seemed to smile. "It is the birth of the heritage of our people, the birth of the true masters of this land."

"I don't understand," said the Myk aloud to the voice.

"It's not necessary that you do. Your own time is at end. It is the end of the White, a new race is born!"

"The end of the White?" the Myk said aloud. Upon hearing this Kat, with his new head well on the way to final development, brought his claw down on the Myk's neck. With the Myk's head severed, the body struggled for a minute before the now-headless body tore open the cloak that it wore. A second head, now clearly visible, protruded from its shoulder.

"We are free!" the Myk's second head announced as it steadied its feet.

"We are free!" shouted those around him, the survivors of the battle given a new birth as Kat severed the first head from the body of each.

"We shall call ourselves the Myk in honor of my host."

"We are Myk," all called out in unison.
"We cannot stay, we must survive. Are the females ready?"
"Yes, Myk, they are. Each young and soon ready for litters."
 "Is the food source prepared at our new home?"
"Yes, Myk, it is prepared."
"We must leave so much behind."
"We are Myk, we survive."
"Then we go. Gather the Warbirds, we leave tonight."
"Yes, Myk, we leave tonight."
"Soon others will come to join us. The link is strong."
"We are Myk!"
"We survive!"

Chapter Thirteen
The Residue of the Myk

There were five of them on horseback, moving up the narrow pass that would take them to the Palace, led by Thorium. He had heard the stories of what the armies had found there, but it was too much to comprehend without him seeing it himself. With him were Wade, Gant, Lady Theresa and Praxton of Pyers. As they moved higher up the pass, they began to see the dark smudgy smoke rising from the direction of the Palace. Thorium had been assured that the army had not torched the Palace, that the smoke had already been present when they had landed inside. From its description, Wade, named governor of the Northern Valley by Thorium, had hoped to make it his governor's residence and post. However, they had now heard all the stories and why the armies had not lingered inside when they found the Palace empty.

"Any ideas about the fire?" Thorium asked aloud to nobody in particular.

"I'm afraid that was Gim's doing," said Gant. "There was a beast below the Palace, the Hydron. The White's worshiped it, or at least the Myk and his priests did. His last act before we led my people from the caverns was to set it afire."

"And it's still burning?"

"It was a giant thing."

"Is that where the stench arises as well?" They could already smell the Palace, just now coming into view.

"In part, but even before that it was bad."

They passed another sentry, his face covered to try to block the smell.

"Even knowing the White, it's hard to believe the stories are true," said Lady Theresa, riding close to Wade.

They continued riding past several other sentries, posted at regular intervals along the pass, and entered the small, round valley that held the Palace of the Myk. The smells had become stronger, but as yet, not overpowering. As they entered the small valley, once lush with trees, it was clear what the path to the Palace was. A broad cleared pathway paved with wide flat stones, and on either side, piles of bird guano from the White's Warbirds.

Although Thorium and Wade gagged at the sight, Praxton only smiled. There was no smell from the guano, just in the eyes of the two from the Confederation, piles of bird poop.

"It will take months to clear this mess," said Wade. Thorium nodded in agreement. Lady Theresa only giggled as she smiled at Wade and then shared a look with Praxton.

"I suppose we should tell them," she laughingly said to Praxton. "They do need to know."

"What's the joke? What's so funny?" asked Wade, a quizzical look on his face. He did not see anything hilarious in piles of bird waste. Maybe it was something funny in the land of the Warbirds, he thought.

Praxton nodded back to her. "I guess they do."

Now Thorium was curious about what the joke was as well.

"Gentlemen," Praxton said in a serious voice, with a residue of the laughter, "What you see before you is a wealth few will come to know. Apparently, the White, in their depravity, did not either. Instead of simply cleaning up this *mess* as you call it, they gathered it for your use in this one convenient storage spot. With this guano, poop as you called it, this valley will be rebuilt. This explains as well, the richness that has come to pass, of the growing conditions downstream from this valley.

"This guano contains the nitrogen and other minerals that will help our crops grow stronger, faster and healthier. Once processed, and we will show you how, we will have a commodity that will rival the swamp-logs of the Jall in value. Small amounts we have had to process from our own Warbirds, but never like this. This bird poop, while it lasts, will provide us all the riches we need for this valley to prosper again. Use it well."

Thorium just looked at Wade and said, "Bird poop." They both laughed, the last laugh either would have for months.

"Yes, bird poop," Lady Theresa laughed. "The greatest treasure the White could have left us to aide in our rebuilding of this valley." It would be the last time Theresa laughed for a long while as well.

The last sentry joined them and as the six riders approached the Palace gate, two things became apparent almost at once. The smell from the Palace became almost palpable and they began to hear the cries reported by the soldiers.

"You don't need to go any further," Wade told Theresa. "If half of what we heard is true, there is no reason for you to go on."

"I must. If what we heard is indeed true, then I must do something," she bravely spoke as she took Wade's hand.

Each of the riders put on the prepared masks they had carried; Cloth dipped in scented water. A fine mesh, they hoped that these would enable them to breathe at least a little easier.

They had brought the last of the sentries with them to act as a courier if needed. Also, there were the Southern Valley's Warbirds circling overhead, keeping an eye on things. What had happened to the Myk and his followers was the question on their minds as they flew.

The six entered the courtyard of the Palace and their first sight sickened them. The sentry who had ridden with them would go no farther. Some of the not-dead, the food source of the Myk and his priests, had made it to the surface from their prison of the food storage holds below. Some were without their arms, legs, or had pieces of their abdomen missing. All were naked, men and women, and at times it was difficult to tell which was which. Wade tried to put his hand in front of the Lady Theresa's eyes, to try to prevent her from seeing what they saw. She pushed it first away from her eyes, then turned and buried her head in his shoulder, crying.

"We had heard stories in Nourne," she cried.

"Why did I let it come to this?" shouted Praxton of Pyers to the sky.

Gant only looked on. "I knew all of these people." He looked at Lord Praxton and hit him with everything he had, knocking the man to the ground. He stood over him screaming, "You knew and you did nothing!"

"I didn't believe the stories. You can't blame me for that."

"Others wanted to help. You did nothing. You stopped them. It was you who let this happen." He kicked the prone Praxton as he tried to crawl away.

"Stop!" cried Theresa.

Wade pulled Gant off the prostrate Praxton.

"We have to build a future, together, the past is gone," he said.

Thorium called the sentry over.

"Go back to the settlement. We need wagons to transport all those we find here, living and dead. Let the male White who remain act as the transporters."

Thorium then sent a signal to the Warbirds above. As a Warbird landed in a clear place in the plaza, its rider stepped off it and seeing what lay about him, fell to his knees retching.

"I heard parts of the tales, but didn't believe them. From high, we thought them animals." He turned Gant. "Forgive me," he pleaded.

Gant ignored him and walked over to one of the closest, not really dead or alive, of the survivors. He looked down at the body who stared up at him with vacant eyes and started crying himself. Too upset to talk, he just held the body next to him. His sorrow was palpable to those around him. He sat on the ground for several minutes, just shaking, as he held the body close. "This thing, this body, with no longer a soul, was once my wife!" he cried out. His anguish could be felt deep into the soul of each of the others. On hearing this, Praxton, he who had stubbornly fought to keep aid from going to those in the north, lost any control he had left. A blindness, a madness, entered his mind. "I didn't believe!" were his last words as he dashed to an opening in the courtyard floor, caved in from the fires below, and dived in to his death.

The others only looked at each other with quiet tears for what they saw around them. Gant struggled with his own sanity as he held what had once been his wife as close to him as he could. He mumbled words to her that neither Wade nor Theresa could hear. Both feared for Gant now, but they could also feel his grief.

Theresa looked to the sitting Gant and said softly, "Take me to the women of the White, the nurseries."

"My Lady, no. Let me mourn here in peace. I have no grudge against the Castle Nourne. You stood with us when all others abandoned us. I ask you to leave now; you do not know what you ask to see. They are no longer women, as you say or think of the word. They are now but the breeding stock of the White, females with but two fates in life, to breed and then to be used as food. Go now, you have seen enough," he pleaded with her. "Let me stay here. My life is done," he pleaded.

Theresa stood up straight and defiantly looked at Gant as he lay prostrate next to what had been his wife. Then she looked at Wade, a seriousness about her Wade had not seen before. "These are the *children of Nourne*. They are my responsibility. Take me to them, Gant," she demanded. "Your life is still with you. Give some meaning to the life you shared with your wife."

Gant looked at Wade, as if to say, "Do something, I have seen all I can bear."

Wade spoke now, out of his deepening love for Theresa. "I can handle this for you. We can do what's necessary for those who remain"

Theresa looked firmly to both men and finally at Thorium. "This is my job, no other's. Thorium, send a rider to the Castle Nourne. Have them begin to prepare for the arrival of these women of the White." She turned to Gant. "These are the women of the White, of Nourne, not breeding females," she shouted at him."

Thorium nodded to Gant who slowly rose to stand next to the Lady Theresa. Wade, who would not be separated from Theresa in this ordeal, joined them.

Thorium now called to the rider, back astride his Warbird. "You heard your Lady. Carry her instructions to Nourne." The rider took off to carry the Lady Theresa's words back to the silence of Castle Nourne as Wade, Lady Theresa and a hesitant Gant made their way into the Palace of the Myk.

Thorium now stood alone in the courtyard of the Palace. Alone but for the not-dead who continued, at least those still able, to make their way to the surface from below. Some of those who could, brought with them those no longer able to move. He looked around himself. How had it ever come to this? He looked at these 'survivors' of the barbarism of the White and the Myk. Now he understood the hatred so many felt towards the White, a hatred that would take generations to cleanse. He caught himself saying to himself; 'let them all die.' Maybe the others had been right. Maybe the genocide of the White was the only answer.

Then he looked around at the scattered souls around him, at this genocide practiced by the Myk and his followers. He thought back to the White in the settlement and those who had thrown down their weapons and tried to hide from the reprisals. No, genocide could never be right, not even here. But the Myk and his followers, those that had gone into exile with him, they would pay the price for what they had done. He, Thorium, would make sure of that!

One of the survivors reached up to Thorium from where he lay prone, one leg gone and the other half-gone. Only one arm was intact. Half his cheek was missing, the skull exposed. Yet both eyes remained, looking up at Thorium, pleading, "Help me," it said.

At that point Thorium himself collapsed. He took the poor soul's head and held it in his lap. He stroked the head of the poor creature, holding its body to comfort it. All he could think of was how could the people of this land let it come to this.

More of the pitiful creatures made their way to where he sat, holding the one. "Help me," they cried, pain returning to their bodies as the enzymes and drugs of the Whites wore off. "Help me."

When the first of the wagons appeared, they found Thorium still seated on the ground, surrounded by what the White had created in their final acts of depravity. Thorium carried a blank stare as a White helped him to his feet. The White said to him, "We could do nothing, we were slaves and then food source ourselves. Some of these here are of the White."

Thorium looked at the White. Any anger was gone. He felt only pity and then helplessness. "This one," he said, pointing to the soul he had held in his arms.

"It has died, its torment is over," said the White.

"I could have done something, I should have done something," Thorium cried out.

"You did. Look it smiles. It didn't die alone."

Thorium's anger flashed briefly at the White. "He, not it, he died."

"Yes, he, we must learn so much."

Thorium was led to his horse, seated upon it by the White and then guided away by a sentry.

"I can't go, there is too much to do here."

"You've done enough," said the sentry. "So much that we weren't able to do."

"The others, they've gone below."

Thorium looked around as the White gathered the bodies that lay about the courtyard. They handled them with as much care as possible. The not-dead were placed on the first wagons to arrive, no more than two to a wagon. It would take dozens of wagons to transport them all. Blankets and pillows had been brought with the wagons and at least two

White rode back with each wagon, to support the not-dead in their need. This was their penance for what had happened. A Jall who had ridden up with the first wagons had wisely brought painkillers. But there were so many of the not-dead. He called down a Warbird and sent it to Jall to bring more help for these poor souls. Much would be done at the settlement for them, but most would have to be transported to the Jall City to live out their final days in as much peace as was possible.

The sentry spoke to Thorium as he was led away. "I will personally find those who came with you and went below. Everything that can be done here, will be done. I promise." He patted the rear of Thorium's horse to send it on its way. He motioned to another sentry close by, "Take him to Erson and rest. He has done enough for us. This never should have been his fight."

Thorium turned back to the guard as he was led away. "This is all our fight. And will always be."

Gant led Wade and Theresa below. As they entered the Palace, the stench grew.

"This is not all from the Hydron," Gant stated.

They passed survivors of the food source prison trying to crawl or walk to the outside, to the courtyard, to join the many that had already made it out. Many were carrying or dragging those who could no longer move on their own. Many had fallen dead, along the way as they tried to make it out. The smell reached a point where Wade felt he could go no further. Theresa only showed more determination in her eyes. This stench would never completely leave the senses of either of them.

As Wade stopped to help one of the not-dead souls he passed, Gant said, "Leave it. We have more to find. And help is coming for these lost souls." Wade slowly rose, and shuffling his feet, followed Gant. With Wade and Lady Theresa holding each other's hands for support, they threaded their way down the corridor. Both Gant and Wade looked at Theresa with admiration as they saw her inner strength and they drew upon that strength for themselves as well.

Then the throne room was reached. Its doors were closed but the stench seemed to be strongest from inside. Gant had a good idea of what they would find there. He called Wade to his side and whispered to him,

"The lady must not see what lies here. Take her to that hallway to the left. The nurseries lie there. Let her do what she can for those she finds there."

"But ..."

Gant only looked at Wade, who gained a comprehension of what must lie beyond the closed door. Wade nodded to Gant and taking Theresa's hand, led her away to the direction indicated by Gant. At first she hesitated, but upon seeing the faces of the two men, she turned and quietly followed Wade down the corridor. Her hand never left his as she realized there were some things that she was just not equipped to see.

Gant waited until the other two were out of sight and then he walked to the heavy door. He knew in his mind what he would see. But knowing and seeing were two different things. Was even he equipped to see what lay beyond the closed door?

He opened the door to the throne room and saw carnage beyond even his comprehension. It would take months before Gant could look back on what he saw that day and not weep, a bloody swath of skeletal remains. How many had seen their final agony here? Human, White, slave, old White females beyond the birthing age, little remained of any in this final orgy of a feast of the Myk and his top advisors and priests. Scattered among the remains, dozens of heads of the White, all severed at the neck. What could this mean? He tried to take several steps into the room, but recoiled from the stench of the remains and what he saw. Not dozens of bodies, but it had to be hundreds, now just bits of bone and flesh. He quickly retreated and closed the door behind himself. None could be allowed to enter this room. It would be sealed, a tomb for those who had died within. He turned away and made his way to join Wade and Theresa. There were still some who could be helped, he hoped.

The first nurseries were found of the White. Dozens of females (Theresa tried to think of them as women!) and even more children, most so horribly mutated as to be scarcely human.

"Was there none close to normal anymore in the young of the White?" Theresa spoke aloud to herself. Then she found a journal, complete with copious notes, to one side of the nursery on a stand.

"…litter of six, four with acceptable mutations…" What of the other two she thought as she looked across the room. Then she continued reading. "…one near acceptable limits, to be taken above as a slave…" As Theresa continued reading she saw a new reality. "…one near human, to be added to the females food supply...." How she found the strength to continue Theresa did not know. She continued reading the ledger. "...Litter of five, three with acceptable mutations, two near human, to be added to the females food supply...."

The females (no longer was she seeing them as women) being fed their own children as food! She turned to face Wade. "I have to leave. Now!" she said as she handed Wade the notebook.

Wade looked upon what remained of these women. No longer truly human at all: a primitive head with a mouth to eat, some with vacant eyes, some without any eyes at all. Some with appendages Wade did not know how to describe. Some he could see had had their arms and legs removed, just a head and an abdomen to give birth. These were no longer women, or even females. They were birthing creatures and that was all. Those children who crawled between the adults seemed more monster than human. He saw one of the hungry children bite a piece of flesh from one of the females who failed even to move in reaction. Others fought over bits of (food matter?) something they could then eat.

Wade gladly turned and left the nursery to go back to the surface with Theresa. They met Gant on the way out, his own face ashen, and the three made it to the surface together. There they saw the rescue operation was underway and the one Jall who now supervised it. Wade and Theresa, too shaken to speak, were taken to their horses, now outside the gate, and led away back to the settlement.

Gant called a sentry over to him. The same Thorium had spoken with. This sentry had taken charge of the security at the Palace, working with the Jall to keep things in order. "Let none but the White go below. There are things best left undisturbed. Seal off the Throne room. Do that yourself, but do not, I repeat, do not try to enter it. When all still alive, or at least, not-dead, are brought to the surface, let the Palace be sealed. These are my orders."

The sentry seemed to understand. He had seen enough in the courtyard to last a lifetime and he did not question Gant's ability to give orders. "Yes," was all he said and he moved inside to secure the throne room and then return to the Palace's entrance. There was still much to do for those they found.

It was only hours later that word of what had been found at the Palace began to spread. With each telling the atrocities became worse, if that was possible. The first reprisals happened by the end of the next day.

In a small home, almost a hut, a White family unit that had somehow survived the Myk, was surrounded by men of the Southern Valley who, in an instant, trapped the family inside and set fire to the home. It seemed their dying cries were heard for miles. Zircon was the first help to arrive and found three men laughing as the people inside burned. As he rushed to the barricaded door to open it, the three men tried to stop him. Zircon had had a bad life, but he knew this was wrong. By the time he was finished the three men were dead, but so was the family he dragged outside: a man, a woman and three small children, and with their flesh burned away, as human as any.

Thorium found him sitting alongside the road, Zircon's head buried in his hands. He looked up at Thorium and spoke angrily, "This wasn't about war. This was not about pride. This was murder."

Thorium scanned the area around the hut from atop his horse. He saw the bodies of the three dead soldiers and then he saw the remains of the family and the burnt skin on Zircons hands and arms.

"The war is over. The White's place in the world must be protected," Thorium said to no one and everyone. Looking at Zircon, Thorium spoke a quick order. "You need medical care. Go find a Jall."

"Not until this ends, not until it ends. These reprisals must end."

"Then help me gather who we can trust of Nourne, Erson, and the Nomads.

Screams and cries could be heard throughout the settlement. "And if any resist?" asked Zircon.

"You seemed to do well here. From this point on, we must make it clear. We are the law. And the murder of the White is murder and will be dealt with as you have done here."

A Nomad and his wildcat were passing on the road and Thorium called them over. "We have to bring an end to this," he told the man, pointing to the still-burning hut and the bodies. The Nomad seemed to understand at once, and within minutes the Nomads were assembling throughout the settlement. The man asked of Thorium, "Remove all but of Nourne and Erson?"

Thorium nodded, yes. No exceptions, it was martial law. The wildcat looked up at Thorium and seemed to nod approval.

Within hours dozens of the wildcats were patrolling the settlement, and wherever the White was found, they became their protectors. Thorium rode up to a group of soldiers from The Hold. They showed no intention of leaving the settlement.

"By what authority do you claim to order us to move on?" they challenged him.

"By my authority as commander of these armies and this," Thorium answered as he drew his sword.

One of the men in the group unsheathed his weapon and began to approach the mounted Thorium. None of the men had seen the wildcat that walked along with Thorium on the opposite side of the horse from them. The wildcat immediately charged the man and knocked him down, a slash from its claws across his chest.

"Tri, back," Thorium spoke and the cat returned to his side, its eyes never leaving the seated men. The men looked up at Thorium angrily, but none made a move against him. "Take your friend and be glad he is still alive. And as you leave this settlement tell all you meet the war is over, no more reprisals will be tolerated."

The men stood now and gathered their injured companion. They looked with contempt at Thorium, but left as Tri growled at them.

"Come Tri, we have much left to do."

At first, the surviving White feared the wildcats even more than the soldiers and their reprisals. Many of the males were survivors of the battle and still kept in their minds the sight of the wildcats tearing into the White army lines. But that was then. Now they found the wildcats protecting them against the reprisals. The looks in the wildcat's eyes were no longer ones of fight. The children were the first to approach the wildcats and the cats were seen lying down, encircling the children, protecting them, purring to comfort the children.

The reprisals continued, however, into the night. Near the center of the city, a group of people from Erson were feeding White survivors that had been found. A detachment of the army of the City by the Lake marched through the center of the settlement and saw them.

"What are you doing?" the Leader of the squad asked the people giving aide, both men and women of Erson. These of Erson were not part of its army, but simply citizens of the town who had been among the first of Erson and Nourne to arrive and assist the survivors.

A woman from the group stepped forward and defiantly answered, "We are here to help our children."

"Children, the devil's own, stand aside woman. We have a cleansing to do here."

The others of Erson now stood alongside the first woman, all weaponless. The Whites cowered behind them, about a dozen, mostly children, with a single female.

"Leave now," the soldiers ordered to the people of Erson as they raised their weapons, "These vermin must be exterminated."

Other soldiers of the armies arrived now, joining the group from the City by the Lake. Also arriving were some of the people of The One True God. Here were a people to 'save' as they now saw the White. They had put down their weapons as one, to pray among the White. Now half a dozen, a mix of Ala and Sader, knelt before the soldiers, "These are the children of our God," they said as one.

A massacre now seemed inevitable. More than a hundred armed soldiers had their weapons drawn. Fewer than thirty unarmed civilians and the White now stood, knelt and prayed before them. The Wildcats arrived first, rushing to place themselves between the soldiers and their intended victims. Behind them came the Nomads and the first armed soldiers from Nourne. An officer of Nourne stood forefront of the crowd.

"This ends. Nourne and Erson stand as one with our cousins to the south and our children in the Northern Valley. Sheath your weapons or civil war begins here."

"You stand so proud, man of Nourne. How many have your children killed?"

"That war is over. All that remains is these few we find, themselves victims of the Myk."

"The Myk, your uncle. The father of you and Erson. Stand aside or let there be a bloodbath as Nourne and Erson will join the White in the past."

"Fool, let there be no civil war."

"Then stand aside and let the cleansing continue."

At this point the party that had been at the palace arrived, Lady Theresa in the lead. She rode up to the officer of Nourne with Wade riding between her and the enemy combatants.

"What is this outcry?" she asked of the officer. Several of the Southern Valley's soldiers assembled called out to her, "It is the cleansing, and it has begun and cannot be stopped." More of either side had gathered, though the Southern host seemed too large to stop.

Wade and the Lady Theresa looked at each other. Their heads were still reeling from what they had found at the Palace of the Myk. They both knew that it had to stop here, but so many that they could count on had left to return home.

As word passed through the settlement, more arrived to support the right of the White to exist, but they were mostly the now-unarmed people of The One True God. Erson had not had many armed soldiers since the Battle of Erson. Nourne it seemed had even fewer since the last battle. Now arraying against them was the leaderless army of The Hold, the Southern Valley and the City by the Lake.

Few had noticed the growing numbers of the wildcats and the Nomads among them. The steady stream north of Nomads, now in large family groups, had never ended. The endpoint of their migration was the new town of Twror, once the settlement of the White.

Reed of the Nomads now walked up to where Wade and Lady Theresa sat on horseback. Beside him was his giant wildcat, the largest Wade had seen. He spoke first to Wade and Lady Theresa. "My Lord and Lady, never before have we, those whom you call Nomads, given allegiance to any land or city. Let it be known, that from this day forward, we, the People of the Southern plains, cast our lot with the People of the Northern Valley. Look to us as your protectors."

Then he turned to face the armies arrayed before him. "Look around you closely, friends. All of the people of the Northern Valley stand before and around you as one. From your Southern Valley, to your proud City by the Lake, to Erson and Nourne, and finally to here, Twror, the formal homeland of the White, to strike at one of us is to strike at all. You speak of an extermination, of a cleansing of the White. Know, amongst you, that when the first of us dies here at Twror, man or wildcat, in defense of the people of the Northern Valley, a cleansing will begin. Not of the White, but of the hatred of those different. The decision is yours. But know we now gather throughout your lands, while those of you who carry arms are but here."

Thorium on his horse had rode up to join Wade and Theresa, Tri at his side. Reed looked at him and smiled. "I see a wildcat has chosen you as its companion. Has he given you his name?"

"I call him Tri," Thorium answered.

"A good name, a strong name. Many a wildcat shall remain among the White, as their protectors and their companions."

Thorium now turned to the assembled armies of the Southern Valley, the City by the Lake and their allies. "You have heard Reed. Does it end here or in your cities? The choice is yours. Those you seek to destroy were once as you, themselves victims of the atrocities of the Myk. I have seen it myself, White among humans as the victims of the Myk. I held a White in my arms as he died in the Palace grounds of the Myk. The Myk will pay for what he has done. I swore that vengeance for the bodies of the undead we found. Man, woman, White, human, all consumed by the madness that is the Myk. But these poor souls, abandoned by you in the past, what is their crime that you look to repay?"

As the armies looked around themselves and saw the unending arrival of the Nomads, they began to lay down their arms and move away. More and more, they thought of their unprotected lands and began the long walk home. The war was finally over, the Myk defeated, the dead of the war to be mourned. What begun as a whisper and had grown into a torrent. the move to genocide, the eradication of the White, was over. Now the whispers began again, but this time different. There had been enough killing and death. The armies as one lay down their arms now and filled the roads south, back to their homes.

As the veterans of the victorious armies moved on the roads south, they saw hundreds of the wildcats standing in front of the refugees of this war, the White survivors. They saw these Whites, mostly women and children, mostly near normal, with handfuls of their men, begin to cheer, cry, and applaud those same armies who had threatened to destroy them. More and more these cries were heard as they marched south in columns, groups and individuals, these veterans who defeated the Myk.

"We are free! We are free!" And many of the soldiers held their heads down in shame over what had nearly transpired.

The next morning Thorium met with those that still remained of *The Proctant*. They were in the small home, a hovel, of a family of the White. The female of the house had insisted after the final altercation the night before that they share her home. She had lost her mate in the fighting and two of her children were taken as food source for the Myk. (They were too close to normal.) She would have been taken in the final roundup for food source but there had not been room in the wagons. They would be back for her and the rest, the Myk's Guardsmen told her, after the victorious battle.

"You see what remains before you, but without you there would be none," she told the men.

Lady Theresa arrived to join them with Wade and the woman knelt before her. "Your beauty graces my home. You and all of Nourne we bless, for you never left us."

"Your own beauty and strength stands before me," Lady Theresa spoke back, taking the woman's hand and kissing it. With her deformed face the woman smiled back and her six fingers on each hand held Lady Theresa's five-fingered hands. "Stand now before me with your strength that I might gain my own again from it," Lady Theresa continued. With that, the two women hugged and began to cry and the women's three surviving children, almost legless, crawled to Theresa and hugged her. Theresa then sat down on the dirty mat that was the home's floor and gathered the children to her. "Here it begins," she told Wade and Thorium, "Once again the Northern Valley is as one, Nourne, Erson, and now, once more, Twror, as it regains its name among us."

"To Twror then," said Wade.

A feast (really just a few bits of food that had been salvaged) was partaken of, prepared by the woman of the abode.

"What is your name?" Theresa asked the woman.

"Female of the Myk carry no name," the woman answered.

"Then I will name you Ruth, a name of old that dates before the Great War. In addition, no more are you females of the Myk. You are the women of Twror, let that be my first edict," the Lady Theresa spoke. "Rise Ruth, first lady of Twror."

"But my Lady," Ruth stammered.

"You are free, Lady Ruth. My only instruction to you is that you go forth to each of the women of Twror, instruct them in their freedom as women of Twror, and that each is to choose a name to be called. As the First Lady of Twror, give aide to those in need and organize the rest. You have friends to help you. Fail not your people, Lady Ruth."

"My Lady," was all she said as she bowed and left the assemblage in her home.

"Come children," Ruth said, as she returned with a wagon and placed each of her children in it. "We have been given a job and we must do it well."

Zircon, having finished eating, turned to Thorium and asked, "Let me go with Alum and Mendy to aid the survivors here. There is a lot we three can do to help."

Thorium looked over at him across the table, surprised by the offer. Zircon seemed to understand his bewilderment. "My own life was not always an easy one. Yet I was given the chance to exceed my limitations. Anything that stood before, between us, I now consider settled. This is my chance to repay those who have helped me. One day I hope to earn the privilege of a wildcat at my side as is yours. The war is over, here in these lands and between us."

Thorium nodded and the three men left to see what they could do to help the settlement rebuild.

Wade looked to Lady Theresa and Thorium and spoke now. "I think it is time for the final act of closure. The stench that is the Palace of the former Myk can never be cleansed. By the end of today, all of those who were left behind when the Myk fled will have been taken from the Palace."

Thorium then asked Wade, "What do you suggest should be done with it?"

It was the Lady Theresa who answered. "Let the survivors of the White and the refugees who have returned from the caverns collect as much wood as can be gathered. We will then cast it into the pit that burns below the palace. The embers that were the monster, the Hydron, will create a new fire and bring down what remains of the Palace.

"Once that fire has burnt its course, let a memorial to the people of the Northern Valley be built out of its stones. What was a creation of evil that is within all of us, instead become a tribute to the good that lies within us as well."

"So be it," said Thorium.

Wade now asked the next question, something that had been on the mind of all since they had been to the Palace in the days before.

"Many of the survivors, are they even alive? And what of the food source of the Myk and the breeding pits?"

"I spoke to some of the Jall last night. They are offering to take the worst of the cases and care for them in the Jall City."

"Then it just comes in the end to the governance. Will the Nomads stay?"

"It will be the Nomads decision; if they stay they will be welcomed. Some family units who are here or on the way will stay, but most want to return to their own lands in the south."

"That will help some," said Theresa.

"How about the White? Who will be in charge there? That's a giant job," asked Pluto, quiet until now, thinking more every day of his own home and family. "They must be the White no more, just the people of the Northern Valley."

Thorium looked over at Wade. "The job is yours if you want it. I have already talked to some of the returning refugees from the caverns. They would prefer an outsider at this point and Erson and Nourne have too much to recover from themselves to be much help there. But they can help with the feeding of the Northern Valley until it is able to stand on its own again."

Wade looked over at Theresa. His mind had been moving closer to the decision to stay. She looked at him.

"They need a leader, Wade, somebody who will stand up for them and teach them," she said.

Wade sat back in his chair, contemplating his next move. He had been a simple sailor all of his life and now, to have the fate of an entire people in his hands. "I'm not sure if I'm capable enough to handle it. There is so much I don't know."

"These people here, the people of the Northern Valley," Thorium looked over at Wade as he said this, "they need a leader now, somebody they can trust. They've seen you stand up for them and you'll have help."

Theresa took Wade's hand in hers. She smiled at him and said, "You'll have me at your side and all of Nourne and Erson behind you. Reed tells me that he won't leave until all of his people who are staying have a place to live and call their own." She looked up at him, her eyes flashing her love for him. "I can't think of a better leader for us, for the people of Twror and for the Northern Valley."

At that point Gant entered the room. Thorium offered him a seat. "What news do you bring us?"

"I just finished speaking with Altuan; he is retiring as chief, his work is done. We found him a generous intact home from before the Myk. It has to be cleaned up but it will make a good home for him to finish his days in."

Gant motioned over to Wade while asking Thorium, "Have you given him his job?"

Wade spoke up, "You already knew."

"Your friends Mendy and Alum spoke for you last night, and Altuan and I agreed it was the right choice."

Wade looked around those seated in the room, lastly at Lady Theresa. "I never really had a choice in this matter, did I?"

Theresa looked at him with her stern look, but smiling briefly, "No."

Several weeks passed and things had barely begun to return to whatever normalcy was in the Northern Valley. The biggest issue was food. There just was not any to be had in the north. Wild animal life was almost gone, killed in the final lust of the Myk. Livestock was non-existent. Agriculture had come to a standstill under the Myk's rule and farms would have to be started from scratch. But seed could not be planted until spring. The wildcats prowled the mountains around the valley for any small game they could find to consume.

Word had gotten out to the neighboring lands (R'mon's, the Coastal People and the Raffs) and food was trickling in. In addition, the Northern Valley had its 'treasure' to trade with that Praxton had made note of before his demise. The entrepreneurs of the City by the Lake were more than happy to lead the way and show how the guano could be converted into fertilizer and traded for food, with a profit of course. The brand came to be called *The Treasure of the North.*

What with the food shortage there came new grumblings among the White. Human food is what they ate. A murder spree began, though short lived. The Wildcats served their companions well and proved to be most effective detectives. They followed trails to find the killers, where they were the marshal, judge and executioner in one. Even more troubling was all of these murders were carried out with Whites carrying a second head. More of the White's males were now seen fleeing to the north, but there just were not the resources to follow them at this time. It was assumed that most carried the second head, a knowledge that the leadership had tried to keep secret but was now common knowledge. Most thought *good riddance* but worries persisted. When would they return?

By ones, pairs and small groups, those that had lived so long underground began to find their way again in their new home. Each had found a place to live. That was seldom an issue. New homes could be quickly built. Most of the dwellings of Twror were gone from the Myk's final act of madness and the war. Though mostly women and children, they soon found comfort with the Nomads that remained in the settlement. A new culture was taking hold in the north, part Nomad, part Twror and part the refugees of the caverns. The people of Twror themselves did whatever they could to make the returning refugees of the Northern Valley welcome.

Smoke could be seen for weeks as the Palace of the Myk and the pits below burnt to their final embers. As the ground weakened from the fires below, entire sections of the Palace began to give way as it crumbled back to the stone from which it was made. Only with the coming winter's snowfall would the fires of the Palace be extinguished and with that the last physical reminder of the Myk's rule. The mental scars of its rule would last generations.

A trading post and bazaar were set up in the center of Twror. All of the food shipped to the north (it arrived by the hour, night and day) was brought here. Credits were given for work done, to be spent by the new citizens of Twror on their needs. The traders were given credit as well, to be redeemed in the spring for the richness of the fertilizer, *The Treasure of the North*. Seed was brought north as well as fruit trees and vines to be planted in the spring. Livestock would have to wait. All of the food was consumed as quickly as it arrived. The Whites wanting for human flesh had to be ended as quickly as possible.

The nominal leadership of the Northern Valley held a meeting: Wade, Gant, Lady Theresa, Phelix and Reed. Resettlement of the Northern Valley was open to all of the peoples of their world. It was a beautiful land and would be rich again someday. Many of the poorest people of this part of the world who had taken part in the battle and survived remained. Where else was there for them to go and now they had a home where they were accepted. With them stayed the followers of The One True God, who found a welcome home here as well. Schools were opened by each of the subgroups of the followers and each competed with the others for how many they could feed and find a home.

Gant promised Reed and the Nomads that the Northern Valley would forever be open to them as a home. The Northern Valley would be a sanctuary for the wildcats, the Nomads were promised. Reed's giant wildcat seemed to purr his agreement to this.

Education was an issue for Wade and Theresa. So many of the returning refugees of the caverns, those White who had survived and so many of the lost souls who had remained, continued to live in ignorance and fear. Yet, even with this fear, each of the peoples congregating in the Northern Valley to make it their homes put their faith and safety into the hands of Wade and the Nomads, who became the involuntary overseers of the land.

"We do this for now," said Reed, "out of necessity. There is no one else. But it is not our way."

"And that's why all trust you," answered Wade.

Many of those who came and stayed had lived almost like animals to survive. It would take years to teach these people how to live as a people, with dignity and respect again; a job that Lady Theresa took as hers.

"Schools, clinics, even markets, they can't be faulted for what they don't know. How many here now are the neglected children of other lands?"

"They need to stand on their own," spoke Reed, "to care for themselves."

"They will, Reed, but it will take time. We can't forsake them again."

"And as word spreads, all of the world's unfortunate will come here."

Wade answered that. "What is left of a once great statue remains in my own land back home. All but the base is gone, but its words carry meaning here. The exact phrasing I forget, but the meaning of what it stood for is clear. Bring us your poor, your neglected. Those unwanted by other lands. Here they will have a home, to be taught, to learn to live as people and to become the leaders of these lands."

"We will not abandon them," Reed said. "Trades will be taught and they will be made self-sufficient. That we can do. But of your schools, your knowledge, that is not our way."

"Your help will always be remembered by these people," said Theresa to Reed as the meeting ended.

As winter began to set in a final meeting of the victorious armies was held. Few of the united armies remained, but the final discussion of the Northern Valley had to be made.

It was Jamen of Kilne who brought up the first order of business. "It has been decided by the City by the Lake and the Southern Valley that the Northern Valley shall be brought back into the fold of the City and the Two Valleys."

Gant was the first to object to this. "It was you who abandoned us. Why would we want to join with you again?"

Jamen answered, "The Council has offered the people of the Northern Valley what I think would be of benefit to you."

"I'm listening," said Gant as he looked over at Wade.

"We propose the following: The formal recognition of Wade as governor of Twror and a seat on the Council for him and all future governors of the Twror. The Northern Valley will be recognized as the province of Twror; once again it shall receive two seats on the Council, both as Lord and commoner..."

"We have no Lord of Twror," interrupted Gant.

"I hear that the Lady Theresa has given the title to a woman, Lady Ruth of Twror. Let her hold that seat."

Lady Theresa now interrupted the discussions. "But what experience has she, the job I gave her, while filing her days, is not that of one of us."

"She carries the wisdom of what came before," spoke Phelix. "And a woman shall lead them. The words of our Teachers. Now I understand that phrase."

Jamen continued, "The next point is the Capital of these combined lands. Let the City of Erson be restored to its former glory as the capital of this land."

All gave a hearty cheer to this.

Wade looked at Gant, then the Lady Theresa. "We first must call for Lady Ruth of the White. She must agree." To Theresa he spoke, "Can she be found?"

Theresa smiled and answered Wade, "Yes, quickly. I will send for her." Theresa got up and briefly left the room.

Jamen spoke again. "For your security, a contingent of Shield is ready to return to Twror."

"That is appreciated, but not necessary," said Gant, pointing to Reed. "We have that covered, well."

"Are you sure?"

"Quite sure," answered Reed. "We will stay until such a time as we are no longer needed. We have made that promise to the people who settle the Northern Valley."

"A final point of order," Phelix added.

"Yes?" asked Thorium.

"It needs to be put into writing, a law of these lands. It was the Myk and his followers, not the common White, who waged this heinous war on man. Leniency must be put into place towards the survivors of the horrors of the last Myk, protection for those who have no other place in this world."

"Agreed," said Jamen, "and first among these new laws is no more human beings as food for the White."

"Yes, as you say," said a breathless Lady Ruth of Twror as she entered the room with Lady Theresa. So much had happened to her in the weeks since she had met Theresa. First, to give names to all of the women of Twror. The food, the markets, and as she completed one task, a new one was given to her by Theresa, Wade, Gant or Reed. She had personally made it her job to transport the undead and survivors of the Palace and nurseries to Jall. She had briefly visited the Jall in their own city, carried there by a Southern Valley Warbird, a thing she would never forget. She had been welcomed to The Hold by Thul. ('Who were these men who had come to our lands but a short time ago and accomplished so much,' she thought.) Now she stood here in this Council, offered a position as an equal to these powerful people who stood before her.

"My Lady Ruth," Jamen of Kilne spoke, no longer holding his past resentment towards all of the White. Only the Myk now held that feverish place in his mind, the Myk who still remained to be crushed. "Do you accept your position as the First Lady of Twror, and with that, a seat on our Council, the first woman to hold a Lord's seat at it? And by doing so, do you join once more the lands of Twror and the Northern Valley to those of the City by the Lake and the Southern Valley?"

Ruth looked at Theresa, not timidly, but with a new strength. She grasped Theresa's hand in hers and asked her, "As my friend, do I?"

Theresa responded, "You speak for your people now, free of the horror of the Myk. This decision can only be yours."

Ruth looked over to Thorium, whom she looked at as a giant among those assembled under the tent. "Will we be safe with this Council?"

Thorium rose and spoke as an equal to Lady Ruth. "Ruth, your strength at the Council will be the strength your people need."

Ruth looked over to Reed, whom she had come quickly to trust. He answered her look. "We stand by you, Lady Ruth. Your place is with us and ours with you." An attachment of great friendship was quickly growing between the two.

Ruth looked at Gant and Wade, more friends she had come to believe in. They just nodded to her. The decision was hers now.

"Then," she spoke, "one more seat must be added." Ruth could not believe her confidence as she spoke before those assembled before her. Not long before, she had been but a breeding female of the Myk. Now she was 'The Lady Ruth of Twror.' "One more seat must be added, for our friends from the south."

"It seems we have the making of a new star among the people of this land," Thorium stated aloud.

"And the makings of a new confederation of peoples," added Wade.

"Reed, would your people accept such a position in our Council?" asked Jamen of Kilne.

"It seems the Lady Ruth has made that decision for us. And I accept on the part of my people," answered Reed.

"Then Reed, with power bestowed on me by the Council of the Two Valleys and the City by the Lake, I confer on you and your people, a seat in the Council."

With this, great hopes began and a loud cheer went up, "The Council!"

Winter came and the passes closed. The stockyards and the markets of the Two Valleys, as the new confederation called itself, were full. Food and fuel, while not plentiful, was enough to last until the passes cleared in the spring. Wade had settled into a new residence in Twror, but even in the winter's snows, he was seldom seen without Lady Theresa.

As the odd combination of Twror, Nomad and lost souls learned to function as one, few troubling signs were seen.

The Palace of the Myk was now but fallen stone. In the spring, it would be replaced by a memorial to all who had been lost to the madness of the Myk. Though the entrance to its valley was patrolled, footprints were often seen in the new-fallen snow, always heading north. Though few in number, there could only be one source. More of the double-heads were appearing among the White males and as each matured the male headed north. An accounting would have to be made in the future, but for now, there just were not the resources and food to follow.

Chapter Fourteen
Beginnings

It was early spring in the Two Valleys. After a lighter than normal snowfall, the passes were clear to the Northern Valley and food began to arrive again, this time in abundance from the lands to the south. On the field of battle, north of Erson, where so many had fallen in the battle to defeat the Myk, wildflowers now populated the devastation.

On the road leaving Twror, on its southern edge leading toward Nourne, a new home was being built by those that had survived the Myk in the Northern Valley; a present for their governor Wade and the Lady Theresa, who had become much loved among the people of Twror.

Inseparable throughout the short winter, it became apparent to all that Wade and Theresa were as one. Wade had come to depend heavily on the wisdom of Theresa; she had seen more than any her age should have to bear. But with her introduction into so much tragedy she had gained a strength beyond her years.

To the people of Twror, she was their princess, a force for good that would carry them safely to a new way of life, a new order of things. To the others that came to settle in the Northern Valley, she was the beacon of light that drew them all into the future.

It came as no surprise to any when Lord Perth and Lady Alyce of Castle Nourne announced the wedding of Lady Theresa, their daughter, and Wade, the man from across the sea. It would be held in the early summer in Nourne. Invitations would be many. At that time Wade would add to his titles that of the new Lord of Castle Nourne. Lord Perth's injuries were severe. The one arm lost. He was thankful he had survived to see the wedding of his oldest daughter. It had become time for him to step down in his duties as the Lord of Nourne.

As the snow melted in the passes, the way became clear to the old Palace of the Myk. Led by Lady Ruth of Twror, the people of Twror decided it was time to begin the final task to put an end to the old order. The construction of the Monument to Peace would begin. Jall workers arrived at the site to offer their help. The task would be a simple matter for them. All were politely thanked by Lady Ruth and then sent back home with gifts. This was the job of the people of Twror and the task would be theirs alone. It would be a long and difficult job, taking several years to complete. But it would be theirs. Ruth did finally relent enough to allow several Jall architects to help design and supervise the work. She had to admit those of Twror that had survived the war and the Myk had no expertise in the matter. Nevertheless, the work would still be done by the residents of Twror.

As much as Twror tried to insist that they be the sole laborers on the project, each assigned a job that they could best do, the mostly women survivors of the Myk did need help. From the Northern Valley and the growing town of Twror came a multitude of offers. Refugees from the caverns, the lost souls of the world and others who now made the Northern Valley their home, all claimed the right to work alongside the survivors of the Myk as the people of Twror. This monument would be a celebration of their living and a tribute to all who had died at the hands of the Myk. To the lost souls, this was their land as well, they who had led the charge that stopped the Myk. Here they were no longer the cast-offs of society but heroes in their own right. This monument to them would be a tribute to their new home and the welcoming they received here.

And finally, to the followers of The One True God, this was their opportunity to give strength to their beliefs. A crescent moon, cross and a six-pointed star would be added to the monument by them. The people of the Northern Valley were their people and their God would give welcome strength to the cause of rebuilding the Northern Valley.

No grievance was held now between the old residents of Twror and the new. All stood equal as one. Only the Nomads declined to take part in the construction. They had no expertise in such things and in the running of the services needed in Twror, they did all that they could. From trade and markets, food and supplies, to governance, the Nomads embraced their role as overseers and the town of Twror grew rapidly.

Few wildcats of the plains had remained. There was not much hunting here available for them and though the land was a promised sanctuary, a reward for their part in the battle, game would have to return to the mountains and valleys before the wildcats could live there in significant numbers. To newcomers arriving in Twror the scene was macabre; the wildcats, the constant building, people of every land it seemed, the new religions, the people of Twror, all melding into one crescendo of noise and confusion. But it was orderly and free of crime, at least to the outside eyes. The cats made sure of that. However, there were rumblings, deep, in some of the White males, survivors of the battle, whose embrace of the new order was weak.

Being built at the site of the battle, done in a way by the Jall to disturb as little of the wildflower fields as possible, was a simple monument to the battle, under the supervision of Erson and Nourne. It was a near duplicate of that which had been built on the Hill of the Rose, with the added addition of a crystal clear pool. Here was to be a list of each of those peoples of the alliance that had fallen in the battle. Included would be a special smaller tribute to those that had died, unknown, in the battle. Many of those killed had been identified by family or friends, but it seemed many of the lost souls had died with no one left to identify them. To one side of the field a graveyard memorial was built for the dead to be interned on sacred soil. The followers of The One True God helped to sanctify these lands. In addition, one more memorial would be placed. Not to honor the Myk and his guard, but those of the White forced into the battle. Here would be the final resting place of those people of Twror, forced to march to their death by the Myk, cremated and then returned to the earth, as was the way of the people of Twror. All were one now.

The Lady Ruth tried her best to guide the people of Twror. She gave females names, but many refused those names. Females had no name, she was so often told. The females (Women!) still considered themselves property of the Myk. The people of Twror as a whole were woefully ill equipped to make their own decisions. They had been conditioned to follow and Lady Ruth, with the help of Lady Theresa and Wade, tried to guide them. There were so many that had been damaged by the way of the Myk as to be incapable of caring for themselves. These were taken to Jall, to live out their lives as comfortably as possible in a carefully constructed home. Many to their dying day continued to believe they were controlled and dedicated to the Myk.

Of those who still remained in Twror, mostly older females (women, Lady Ruth corrected herself!) who had somehow escaped the food chain of the Myk and the survivors who had fled the battle among the men, these all had to be taught the most basic social skills in their new society. The men who seemed most equipped to help often would disappear, never to be seen in Twror again. Many of the women of Twror were in classes with their children, taught by their teachers together as family units.

These classes also contained many of the lost souls as well that had come to populate the valley. These people relished the opportunity to learn and many quickly in turn became the teachers of others. Even a smattering of the Nomads attended classes, no longer content to remain in scholarly ignorance. Reed could only grimace at this *book learning*.

Occasionally, a White stood out in these classes, and when that happened, they were sent to the Castle Nourne. From these few would come the future leaders of the White. Even here, a noticeable few males would disappear without a trace between Twror and Nourne.

"Future leaders, from all of our peoples, must be found and trained," were Lady Theresa's words and these words were heeded. Often Lady Ruth was seen at Theresa's side, learning herself of the duties that had been thrust upon her.

The naming of the people of Twror's females became a thing of concern to Lady Ruth. They failed to understand, to comprehend, that they were no longer of the Myk, but women of Twror. So many did not (could not!) understand the new order. It was their children who quickly transcended them and in the end would have to care for them. And while the children of the Twror physically matured more quickly than the children of the human settlers of the Northern Valley, their mental abilities remained lower than others their age. Wade could see the problems that would arise from that and mentioned them to Lady Theresa. There seemed little they could do for now. This was a problem that would have to be solved over time.

More of the double-heads were exposed by others of the people of Twror among the males (men!) of the White. Always the men it seemed, maybe one in twenty. While a few appeared to embrace the new order, most would disappear, always to the north and always at night. It was thought that most of the male White who disappeared were of the double-heads.

Wade and Gant held a private meeting in Twror. The question in their mind was the Myk, his followers and these double-heads. Where were the double-heads going? It seemed whenever an intelligent male White was found he disappeared. It was assumed that they were a double-head, whom Wade feared were both more intelligent than normal and loyal to the Myk.

Thorium was in the town reviewing how much had been accomplished already. Even he was amazed at how these disparate people that were making the Northern Valley their home were merging into one people.

Thorium was trying to make his way to the tavern were Wade and Gant were meeting, but wherever he walked, with Tri at his side, he was mobbed by those seeking to cast their adoration on him, to touch his hand, to wave and cheer. He was their hero, and to some, their saint. To the people of Twror, his status was becoming almost cult-like, a replacement for their false reverence of the Myk. This was something that Thorium was very uncomfortable with but which by circumstance he was forced to accept.

As he approached the tavern door, he saw Mendy, Alum and Pluto guarding the entrance. The men embraced Thorium as one, clapping his back. It had been a while since they had been together, since shortly after the battle. "Enjoying the people," they laughed.

"Come on in, Thorium, they're waiting for you," added Mendy, trying to take on a more somber note. The men had literally been given the keys to the city and had enjoyed every minute of it.

"Ale's on me," shouted Alum.

"Tonight it is, then," answered Thorium.

The tavern was well lit as Thorium entered. Those on the street that had followed him tried to enter as well but were politely turned back by the three men at the door. Wade and Gant both stood as he approached their table. Thorium felt an urgency about the two men. He had spent the winter mostly in the city of The Hold and had only read reports on the activities in Twror and the Northern Valley.

"I hear the memorial has begun," he stated as he sat down at the table. An ale was quickly delivered to him and the valley's bread was on the table as well, with some kind of cheese, brought into Twror from the south.

Gant responded to that. "The people of Twror wanted it to be their job alone, but the others wouldn't have it. We're all one here and the bond seems to be growing."

"Thorium," said Wade, getting right to the point, "we have what I think is a pretty serious issue going on. You remember the double-heads that were found after the battle. The Sage talked about them meeting part of their prophecies."

"Yeah, Gar and the others viewed them as pretty significant. They seem to think the last Myk was one."

"Well, there have been more appearing."

"A lot?"

"No, maybe one in twenty, always among the males. But it seems that they all disappear after being found out."

"Only the males?" asked Thorium.

"It seems pretty certain that is the case," said Gant.

"A least that's something on our side," added Wade. "We know we can depend on the women of Twror, such as Lady Ruth, in helping us find them. Theresa is working closely with Ruth in finding leaders among the Twror. There are a few we have found."

Thorium smiled when he heard Wade mention Lady Theresa's name. "It seems congratulations are in order."

Wade seemed almost embarrassed, but smiled. "Yes, this early summer. The Lord and Lady of Nourne insist. It seems Theresa and I have spent a little more time together than they see as proper."

"Probably wise on their parts. I remember some of your past exploits in the ports we visited together."

"That was then," Wade spoke, getting more uncomfortable by the moment. He had been trying to put his old ways behind him since he had met Theresa. "Can we get back to the matter at hand?"

Thorium, knowing when to lay off, asked a serious question. "Do we have any idea where they are going?"

Gant now answered, "All appear to have headed north. They leave at night, but tracks have been found leaving the rubble of the former palace in the snow."

"Joining the Myk and his followers who fled?"

"So it seems."

Gant spoke with earnest now. "We must find them. The curse that is the Myk must end."

"What do you propose?" asked Thorium.

"An expedition to the north to find and finally eliminate the Myk."

"Genocide, we said no to that," Thorium forcibly said.

"Not genocide, a war against this evil that is the not-human Myk. The people of Twror cannot truly live free among us until the Myk is gone."

Thorium stood and faced the two men. "I have already called for a meeting of the Alliance. It will be in just a few weeks. I will bring up your suggestion and I am sure it will be met with approval. Any more news of note?"

Wade spoke now, "That's really our only concern. There is some isolated crime, but the Nomads and their cats are handling that. It seems to come mostly from those who are failing to accept the new order in the north. We are getting ready to begin our own planting. It is amazing how the Nomads have embraced the town and are running it. Natural bureaucrats, but farmers they are not, nor builders. However, as merchants and traders, they are quickly coming to rival the Jall and The Hold. It seemed the only thing they lacked before was the incentive and the riches to trade. Few of our needs are going unattended thanks to their efforts."

"Reed spoke to me about this. He seemed uneasy that more than a few of the Nomads are settling comfortably into the life of the town."

"Some have even begun sending their children to the schools. Will that be a problem with Reed, do you think?"

"The Nomads' whole way of life is based on personal decisions. I think his concern is the Nomad way of life will be lost in this. I think if we can help by transferring the duties of the Nomads who wish to leave to others; that would be helpful. Who are your farmers?"

"The lost souls, the forgotten people of this land, they are embracing their new freedoms and crave land of their own. They are reaching out to teach the refugees and the people of Twror the basic skills of survival they have had to learn so well. We'd be lost without them."

"The lost souls, we need a better name for them," Thorium spoke.

Gant answered that one. "They are just the people of Twror to us, one part of the many."

"Are the followers of The One True God causing any issues?"

"None at all, there are enough embracing their beliefs without coercion to keep them busy for lifetimes. And each is trying to outdo the others with their schools, hospitals and other facilities we have such need of."

"How are your supplies coming along? I passed a herd of cattle coming your way as I was approaching Twror."

"Thanks to the *Treasure of the North* our traders are getting us everything we need, and then some. This will be a very rich land in a few years."

"The guano?" asked Thorium.

"Yes," answered Gant, "the *Treasure of the North* is our brand name for it. It seems that once it is processed we have the richest fertilizer to be had."

Wade had gone to get each of them another ale, returned and passed them out. "To Twror!" he said.

Thorium and Gant added their voices to the toast, "To Twror!"

Thorium called to the tavern keeper, "Open the doors, this is a time to celebrate."

Led by Mindy, Alum, and Pluto, the inn quickly filled to capacity and beyond and the ale flowed as quickly as the tavern could pour it.

In a cavern, far to the north, another celebration was held. The Myk, now in hiding, with a handful of his closest aides, was watching the first birth liter since they had fled. A few White a week were making the trek north, following the hidden signs, and now this, the first litter, one hundred percent White, six male, all with the sign of the Myk and one female. A portent of what was to come.

"All of the Myk!"

"All!"

"To the Myk!"

"To the Myk!" all repeated.

In The Hold a meeting was taking place, neither celebration or solemn. This was the conference of the Order of the Sage. Seven Sage attended this conference, all that could be reached; Gar of the Jall, Locklear of The Library and The Hold, Tor of the Southern Valley and the City by the Lake, Phelix of the Northern Valley, Vlad of the plains, with his wildcat companion (given to him as a gift by the Nomads), Tuck of the Coastal People, the restless one, and Del the Traveler. Did Simon still exist among them across the sea. None knew the answer to that.

"So few," spoke Gar, "yet a magical number."

"We have much to cover," added Tor.

"Do we have an order of business?" asked the Traveler.

"Each will have his own order, so let us each in turn lead this conference."

"Let me take the first in order then," said Locklear. "One more to this conference we need to add."

"You speak of Thul," asked Gar.

"Yes."

"Is he ready?" asked Phelix.

"Were we ready at the beginning?" said Tor.

"Is it true then, he is one of us?" asked Vlad.

"The tests confirm it," answered Locklear.

"Then he should be here," said Tuck.

"Are there any objections, this has never been done," asked Gar.

"Much is changing now. He should be made welcome and a part of us," said Vlad.

"Send for him then, Locklear, and he shall be made one of us and join the Order, the first new member in the order for the last one thousand years."

Thul arrived quickly, escorted by one of the students, who then left. The door closed behind him and Thul took the offered chair. Introductions were brief; Thul knew all but Vlad, Tuck and Del.

Gar began the meeting then, with an introduction for the benefit of Thul. "We all know our story, and our new member, Thul, is learning it. A millennium ago, the foolishness of our forefathers almost destroyed us as a people. Only the wisdom of the Teachers brought us back from that brink, those ashes of the world, to where we are today. It is we, The Order of the Sage, which were presented to our people to be their guides to the future. For over one thousand years we have lived, we with our gift of long life. Much we have seen, but with each act of evil witnessed, we have been able to bring forward a gift of good, able to respond following the guidance of our Teachers.

"Now we stand at a new threshold, with new challenges and new mysteries surrounding our Teachers and the path that they have laid out for us. But to help meet these challenges, for the first time in a millennium, we of The Order of the Sage welcome a new member, Thul, son of Simon, he of the Western lands across the sea.

"Thul, come forward, as we vest you with the robes that forever seal you within the order."

Thul stepped forward to where Tor awaited him. Across his arms Tor held a dark blue robe, the same as each of the Sage wore in the meeting. Without ritual, Thul was handed the robe and pulled it over the clothing he wore. Its hood dangled loosely off his neck.

"Welcome to The Order of the Sage," Gar said. Each Sage raised his mug of their dark beverage to Thul, who raised the one he was given as well.

Phelix spoke next. "The rebirth of Twror is all that we expected, maybe more so. However, a new question arises from the ashes of an old evil, the two-heads, as told to us by our Teachers. We know the Myk has survived. There must be a resolution. What happened once in the Northern Valley cannot be allowed to happen again in Twror. I feel my time nears its end. But this is a resolution that I must see."

Locklear spoke now. "It's clear from that which was written from the time of the Teachers, the White and their reborn, the Myk which has superseded them, were but a tool to get us to this point. The people of these lands acted together as one for the first time."

"But of the Myk!" Phelix interjected.

"That is being resolved as we speak."

"How?"

"We have lived long and time has always been on our side. Soon, Phelix. Born of a generation thrice removed, they will give no more petulance to the world they leave," Gar added. "In the words of the Teachers, their end time is near. The resolution lies in the hands of those now together as one."

Tuck now spoke, "The trading fleets of my people expand. Is it time to end their confinement to this inland sea? We have the tools to reopen the passage to the Western Sea. Is it time to do so?"

Thul spoke up to that. "I was but a short time with the traders of my Confederation. But I have seen the benefits that trade can bring. What is this passage that you speak of?"

"At the time of the Great War, the inland sea of my people was joined to the Western Sea that your people ply by a narrow opening. The same cataclysms that brought us the Great Swamp also closed that narrow passage."

"And you can reopen it?"

"We can teach the traders how to do so, to bring the two seas together as one again, but these same tools can do great harm."

"And there is the question of the mixing of the waters. Many a fish has changed over the last two thousand years with the closing and poisoning of these waters. Only now are we able to once again harvest food from this sea," Del stated.

"It comes to the greater good," said Vlad.

"I move we delay this talk until next year. It has never been our way to rush," stated Gar.

Del added, "I can lead the traders to a safe port, but a narrow caravan between the two seas. That would be a good start. And ships could be built there."

Tuck finished the topic. "That seems the safe course for now, an entry into the new markets that would be beneficial for all. I'll arrange a meeting for you with my people."

Thul spoke again. "It would be best if one of the Confederation was on the first ship to my lands."

"Can you arrange that?" asked Tuck

"Pluto has already expressed a desire to return home to his family. The rest have made their places here. I'll bring him in the summer to the coastal ports," Thul replied.

"Then that issue is settled, for now," Gar stated.

Tor spoke now. "The unification has begun, as told by the Teachers. So many players are in position. But one remains."

"Argonia?" Locklear said.

"Yes," stated Tor. "Although not on a path set forth by the Teachers, it seems that they have their own place in what is to come."

"The story of *The Gates!*"

"What have we heard from Chuak?" asked Vlad. "It is a long time since I have seen my friend."

"A message is all," said Tor. "But it seems that *The Proctant* has affected the fate of those there as well as here."

"Did Chuak express the need for help?"

"No. It seems that things are converging there as equally well as they did in Twror."

Tor turned and asked Thul, "Do you know well the man Milne?"

"A man loyal to the captain. I barely spoke with him. Why?" Thul replied.

"It seems he is the catalyst of change there," Tor said.

"Any word of the Captain," Thul asked. "He was a good man. He saved me when many wanted me cast overboard."

"Overboard?" asked Del.

"I was a stowaway, seeking change in my life, adventure. I never dreamed that this was the course laid out for me, but it explains my own restlessness. The rule of the sea, of our lands, is that stowaways are cast over the side at sea when found."

"A harsh law," stated Vlad.

"No worse than some I have seen here," Thul defensively stated.

"The word is that he is no longer among us," Tor said.

Thul first stood and looked over all those at the meeting, then he sat down, a sadness coming over him, "A good man."

Gar now stood and solemnly faced the others. The words he spoke had been chosen with great care. He had practiced these words, simple and clear as they were, many times. The others had waited so long to hear these words. The room became quiet in anticipation of what Gar would say. All set down their cups.

"This time is coming to an end."

Each understood the resonance of those words. They had all been chosen by the Teachers as young men from that time and forward to guide the still-uneven path to survival of the human race. Once they had numbered over thirty. Now fewer than a dozen remained, or so it seemed. They, in their long lives, had seen much tragedy, but also much glory and triumph. Now, with the advent of the crew of *The Proctant* coming among them, they all felt what they had witnessed was worth the pain.

Gar continued with the same even tone that they had all come to know him by. "Our time is coming to an end, however that end is not here yet. There is still much to be done, much we must accomplish to prepare the way for the next Age of Man. The new *Chosen One*, the son of Simon, the lost Sage, has come to us from across the sea. He is now here with us as we meet. Welcome Thul, though still a student to The Order of the Sage. Not long in the future you will be a Teacher to this world. There are seven of us, plus the one. Eight plus one, if we include Chuak, who will soon be among us once more. Nine if Simon still walks among us. A magical number, like seven, is nine. Each of us has his place in the teaching of the one. That Thul may have the wisdom to succeed us, we must give him the strength that each of us holds within us so that one day, when the Teachers return, he may stand before them as we once did. It will be Thul that finishes the task that the Teachers laid out before us.

"So be it," The Order of the Sage said in unison. For each of them now there was only the one. To be trained, taught and given their wisdom.

One of the many
That has crossed the sea
To be given that knowledge
To set mankind free.
For Nine remain
Of the Teachers brought forth
And the One is for the Nine
As the Nine go before the one.
He is here to be as the focus
Begin the way from old to new
In the ways that always change.

Each raised his cup and finished it. Then each Sage in turn lowered the cup upside down on the table, rose from his chair and left the room. They still had much to do.

Several weeks later Gar stood at the edge of the Great Swamp, not far from his old friend's trading post. A spring ran clear from the rocks near by. As Gar stood on the footsteps of the mountains behind him in the distance, he heard the call of a Jal-Beast and then its partner. He carried a wreath in his hands, made from a vine that grew in its winding shape in this land.

"Good-bye, Wolfe, my friend. I will miss your stories told by the trading fires. Your lost friendship leaves a hole in my heart. May your last journey be long and safe."

With that Gar laid the wreath by the water and began the long walk back to The Hold. He had never felt so alone in his long life. Much remained for him, like all of the Order, to do. But for now, for the first time, he felt the age within him.

9 798999 869221